3/20

RAGE

FEATHERS AND FIRE BOOK 2

SHAYNE SILVERS

ARGENTO PUBLISHING

CONTENTS

This is a work of fiction. Names, characters, businesses, places, events, and incidents are either the products of the author's imagination or used in a fictitious manner. Any resemblance to actual persons, living or dead, or actual events is purely coincidental.

Shayne Silvers

Rage

Feathers and Fire Book 2

ISBN: **978-1-947709-04-1**

© 2017, Shayne Silvers / Argento Publishing, LLC

info@shaynesilvers.com

ALL RIGHTS RESERVED. This book contains material protected under International and Federal Copyright Laws and Treaties. Any unauthorized reprint or use of this material is prohibited. No part of this book may be reproduced or transmitted in any form or by any means, electronic or mechanical, including photocopying, recording, or by any information storage and retrieval system without express written permission from the author / publisher.

HELL HATH NO FURY LIKE CALLIE PENROSE...

*E*ver since Callie – the Vatican's rookie monster hunter – killed a demon a few weeks ago, Kansas City's been eerily quiet.

But she soon learns it's just the calm before the storm.

Because werewolves begin abducting young women in Kansas City, and a new church opens its doors, pronouncing death to all idols, including these 'make-believe' monsters and wizards.

But when one of their congregation is disemboweled by a monster on the steps of the church with the phrase *God is dead* painted in blood, someone in the church decides to take a lesson from the Salem Witch Trials... And the police seem to be helping.

Callie must catch the killer before Kansas City erupts in civil war. A civil war she inadvertently started. Before everyone decides to kill each other. Or worse yet, her.

But she's being stalked. By something unseen. More than one something... And with so many new faces coming to Missouri – gods, legends, and nightmares – Callie begins to realize it's all someone's sick idea of a game.

And that Hell never really left Kansas City. Or Callie Penrose.

After all, they say Missouri loves company...

DON'T FORGET! VIP's get early access to all sorts of Temple-Verse goodies, including signed copies, private giveaways, and advance notice of future projects. AND A FREE NOVELLA! Click the image or join here:
www.shaynesilvers.com/l/219800

FOLLOW and LIKE:

Shayne's FACEBOOK PAGE

www.shaynesilvers.com/l/38602

I try my best to respond to all messages, so don't hesitate to drop me a line. Not interacting with readers is the biggest travesty that most authors can make. Let me fix that.

CHAPTER 1

*R*oland glared at me, actually grinding his teeth as he shook his head in the morning darkness. "No, Callie."

"What? I thought you might need it," I said in a sweet tone, casually sweeping the streets with my eyes, not paying particular attention to the lights in the bakery shop before us. Two young men sat at a table inside, but after a brief look at us through the window, they resumed their conversation. *Only two*, I thought to myself angrily, using my peripheral vision to keep tabs on them as I readjusted my light jacket absently.

We had just climbed out of my truck, prepared to take out the trio of werewolves I had tracked to this bakery. With the local wolves having fled town a few weeks ago, these three had decided they could make a name for themselves and start a new pack. But these frat-boy werewolves were rogues, feral, or just plain stupid, because I suspected them of abducting and murdering young women on their way home from the local bars.

And that didn't sit well with the local Shepherd – the supernatural sheriff for the Vatican.

Or me, the assistant extraordinaire to the Holy Hitman.

"Just because I was injured a few weeks ago doesn't mean I need a walker," he seethed, pointing at the contraption I had pulled out of the back of my pickup truck.

I shrugged, feigning surprised hurt. "I was just trying to be considerate. We *are* going after wolves again." I pointed at the walker. "It even has spurs. Maybe you can use them as a weapon or something." He grimaced at the bad duct tape job I had made of attaching the cowboy spurs. I had found the spurs in the same antique shop as the walker yesterday and had known they were meant to go together, for this exact purpose.

"There are dog toys in the basket," he growled even lower. "You're mocking both my injury and the task ahead."

I placed my hand against my chest. "I would *never*."

"We'll talk about this later," he muttered. His eyes flickered over the bakery, and then down the street, making sure we were alone. It was just before sunrise in the Westport district of Kansas City, and it was Saturday, so we didn't have to worry about commuters seeing us on their way to work. The only risk was the occasional walk-of-shame victim stumbling down the street in heels, clubbing clothes, and smudged makeup. But those majestic beasts were elusive, fickle creatures, and apparently hadn't finished sleeping off their bad decisions.

Leaving us all alone. Perfect.

Roland deftly sliced open his palm with a blade, letting his blood fall to the pavement. He pocketed the blade, grasped the walker in front of him, and then stumbled into direct view of the bakery, holding up his bleeding hand. I darted after him, a look of horror on my face. The two wolves inside glanced up, and then froze as they saw his crimson-stained hand.

The blood had the desired effect on the frat-wolves.

The two of them burst out the front door of the shop, eyes excited as they quickly realized the injured man and young woman before them were the only people in sight. They were true bros in every sense of the word, wearing polo shirts with popped collars, skinny jeans, and trendy boat shoes. The one in front was tall and scrawny with dark brown hair and a long, gaunt face. He looked starved, or as if he hadn't hit puberty yet, waiting for that pubescent shot of testosterone that made men, men – or as so many seemed to think.

But the other was short and pudgy, with short, light blonde hair. He looked like a wrestler – a scrapper. I bit back a grin as an idle thought crossed my mind. His choice of pants made his legs look like sausage links. I wondered where the supposed third wolf was – the handsome Hispanic kid, as he had been described. I had visited each bar where the victims had last been seen, and every bartender had remembered three men leaving shortly after each victim left the bar. One bartender had been the victim of Mr. Pudgy's unwelcome flirtations, and had remembered him mentioning they could pick up fresh croissants in the morning at a bakery right next to his place... but he knew just the way to make her burn off those extra calories ahead of time.

She had instantly thrown cold water at his face, and several of the patrons had rushed him out of the bar, lucky for her. He was a dead ringer for her description. As was the scarecrow. But not the third man. Did one of them own the bakery?

"Come inside, Sir," the tall one said, taking a step closer. "We'll get you taken care of in a jiffy." His eyes latched onto the walker, and he somehow managed not to lick his lips at his luck.

"You're always hurting yourself, Grandpa. Let them help you, and then we can go get your coffee."

The pudgy one smiled – to my eyes, a very wicked, hungry smile. "We have coffee inside."

Roland shot them a thankful smile, latched onto his walker, and began hobbling closer to the frat-wolves. "Such kind words, my boy. Thank you. At least *some* of today's youth gives a damn about their elders," he said, shooting an accusing look my way. "My granddaughter could learn a lot from you fine, young men." I averted my eyes sheepishly for the wolves, but it was really so that I didn't kick Roland in the ankle. Bastard. He continued shuffling closer to them with pained steps, playing his part perfectly.

Their faces smiled at me, but their eyes raped me.

There's a difference between a look of honest appreciation and one of dark fantasies, and most girls can sense the difference in an instant, no matter how discreet the boy thinks they are being. It's all in the eyes. These two self-proclaimed badasses looked hungry, and I could tell they considered themselves untouchable.

Whoopsies. Because little did they know, death had arrived this morning, and she fancied a fresh croissant.

I flashed them a shy smile, shifting from foot to foot uncertainly, as if appreciating their personal interest as well as their obvious concern for my grandfather.

The chubby one held the door open, and the taller one stepped through, encouraging Roland to follow. He did so at a glacial pace. The chubby one motioned me closer with a greasy smile that he no doubt thought made him appear handsome. I smiled back at him, forcing a blush to my cheeks as I let my fingers fidget nervously at my hips, unconsciously straightening my shirt at his attention. He sucked in his gut as I neared, puffing out his chest self-importantly.

I took one step inside the door to find Roland approaching the glass display case of pastries, which was illuminated from within by a fluorescent bulb. The room smelled like a new pot of coffee and freshly baked goods. I craned my neck while inhaling deeply for show, using the motion to scan the room. I spotted the light switch on the wall to my left, and managed not to smile. The display case provided more than enough light for this. As if reading my mind, Roland stumbled over his walker and the skinnier wolf darted forward to help him. I hit the light switch beside me, instantly dimming the room so that anyone outside would have a hard time seeing exactly what I was about to do.

Castrating two feral dogs.

I felt a brief pulse of magic, and the walker broke apart, revealing Roland clutching a spur-tipped aluminum baton in each hand. He spun them in his wrists, bringing them up high, and then down onto the taller man's collar-bone with a loud *crack*. The boy shrieked and dropped to the ground. I spun, ready to take out the pudgy puppy, but was suddenly yanked out of the way by a thin tendril of magic from behind. I skidded on my ass into the display case of pastries. I quickly climbed to my feet, staring at Roland in surprise as his first victim gasped and cried out on the floor. It wasn't that Roland wasn't a badass, but that he was usually much more reserved.

The metal batons were a blur in Roland's hands as he clocked the pudgy man in the forearms – which were outstretched from the wolf attempting to grab me from behind. The spurred tips scored across his forearms, and the boy howled in pain as he began to shift into wolf form. His clothes exploded into confetti, and Roland dropped the bent batons as he dove at him.

The Shepherd tackled him into the wooden door, causing the wolf to yelp before they crashed together to the ground. Roland grasped for the wolf's throat as they rolled into tables and chairs, each fighting for control of the other. Roland got the upper hand, seeming to wrap something around the snarling wolf's throat, and then he yanked back with all his strength, forearms corded with muscle, causing his veins to pop out under his skin. He was choking him out with...

The rope toy I had put in the basket on the walker.

The wolf whined, snapped his jaws, and scrabbled with his claws on the floor, but Roland scissor-locked his legs around the wolf's belly, pinning him as he hugged him tight. I spun at a sound behind me to find the scrawny guy coming to his feet, snarling as he continued his agonized grunts of pain at the broken collarbone. "We're taking over this city, bitch. No matter what you two think. God is dead, and many of us feel that the days of the wizards are over."

His words reeked of zealotry, as if repeating a mantra.

"Don't take this too personal or anything, but... fuck your feelings." He bared his teeth at me in outrage, and then burst into werewolf form. I grabbed something on the counter behind me as strips of clothing rained down around a tan-colored werewolf. His teeth were still bared as he shook his ruff, but he lifted his front paws gingerly, the broken collarbone still hurting him in his wolf form.

"Puppy want a treat?" I asked in a mocking voice. "Sit."

He didn't.

"Bad dog," I admonished, and I threw the glass pot of coffee at his face. He yelped outrageously loud as the steaming liquid burned his eyes, crashing to the ground as his paws clawed for purchase. I prepared to smash him with a bar of air just as I heard an unsettling *snap* behind me, followed by silence. Before I could turn to look, Roland was shoving me out of the way, and proceeded to stab the wolf through the heart with one spur, and then he swung the other across the screaming wolf's face, breaking his jaw or neck, I wasn't sure.

To put it simply, it was the most violent, heartless, and efficient execution I had ever seen Roland perform. No sympathy. No forgiveness. Just death.

He stared down at the wolf, panting lightly.

I began humming in a low tone. *"Dunna-dunna-dunna-dunna-dunna-dunna-dunna-dunna—"*

"Callie, don't you *dare* finish that stupid jingl—"

7

"*VAT-MAAAAAAN!*" I belted out, loud enough to be heard over his protests.

He rolled his eyes and let out a long, patient breath, ignoring my maniacal grin.

Then I heard a door slam in the back of the shop, and was running before I consciously chose to. The third wolf.

CHAPTER 2

I ran through a darkened storage room, a kitchen, and then a dingy hallway before shoving open a back door that led into an alley. I paused, waiting, completely still, listening.

But I heard nothing. He or she was long gone.

With a curse, I stormed back inside. As I entered the hallway, I peeked into a side room that appeared to be an office of some sort. I wasn't sure if the wolves actually owned the bakery or if they had simply taken it over. Before I could do more than open a desk drawer to find out, I heard a muffled whimper from one of the rooms I had just run through. I bolted out of the office to enter the storage room, following the sound of sobbing. I flicked on a light to find Roland standing before two forms tucked behind a stack of boxes.

Two brunette women sat chained to a wall, mascara running down their faces, their hair tangled and greasy. They squealed in unison, flinching at the sudden light. One wore only panties and broken heels, but the other was covered in what had once been a cocktail dress, now ripped and shredded, tossed over her like a dirty blanket. My vision flashed red with rage as I realized that the wolves had done much, much worse than simple murder.

They both had savage bite marks and bruises on their forearms and biceps, belying the fact that the werewolves had managed to infect them –

or at least had attempted to do so. Only time would tell if they were successful. Sometimes it didn't work, depending on the victim's antibodies.

I locked eyes with Roland, and gave him a brief, approving nod at his level of violence. It had been warranted, even though he hadn't known that ahead of time. He gave me a grim nod back.

Then we were kneeling over the women, speaking softly to them, but they only whimpered, keeping their eyes downcast and not answering us. Roland finally sighed and waved a hand before them, a tracery of magic settling over them like a silk blanket before disappearing. They passed out in an instant, going limp. Roland used a quick slash of air to slice the chains and then picked up the young woman with the cocktail dress without any noticeable effort.

"Check outside," he said, staring sadly at the sleeping victim in his arms.

I nodded, climbing to my feet ahead of him to look out the windows. I flipped the sign to *closed* as I scanned the streets. They were still clear. I walked up to Roland and tugged the hood of his light jacket up just in case. He grunted and exited the building, carefully laying the woman into the back of the pickup truck, and then waving a hand over her. She disappeared from view, hidden by an illusion spell. Good thinking, on his part. A few minutes later he had both women concealed in the bed of my truck.

He walked back inside and glanced down at the two dead werewolves, who were now naked in their human forms. Dozens of strips of clothing covered the floor from where they had shifted, destroying their clothes.

"A dog toy," I said conversationally.

"Anything can be a weapon," he muttered with a wry grin. "Like a pot of coffee."

I smirked. "A walker and a dog toy. You're like the Holy MacGyver. But way older."

He didn't even look at me as he rasped, "Get off my lawn."

I chuckled, staring down at the pieces of the walker. I could see where they had been magically sliced to break into batons. Light, fast, subtle magic. Then again, the wolves hadn't been that experienced. Or else we would have had a much harder fight on our hands.

Just a couple of punk rapists.

"You... took that kind of personal. Up close..." I said softly. I waited a beat, but he didn't respond. "All joking aside, you sure you're okay? I mean, if I would have seen what they did to the girls, first, I would have been there right with you, but…" I trailed off, careful not to sound judgmental, because I wasn't. But he had come down on them like a force of nature, *before* he knew the depths of their depravity.

He was silent for a few moments before he looked up at me meaningfully. "You could say I have a soft spot in my heart when it comes to missing girls."

And a very warm smile split my cheeks. I nodded back. It was how we had met, after all. "So, hypothetically," I began, "if there was a boy I liked, you'd want to meet him first…" I teased.

"Whether you like it or not, I'll be having a private talk with him about ground rules." An accusing look crossed his features, not so subtly asking if I had something to tell him – a boy in my life. I waved a hand at him dismissively, crouching down on my heels to assess the body, anger roaring back up as his nakedness reminded me of what he had done to his captives.

"Now what? Burn them?" I glanced back at the pudgy one. "Put them on display with some genital mutilation?" I asked, my voice shaking slightly. This was beyond a crime in my eyes. Taking advantage of another person was the worst thing you could do. Period. Especially when the captors had oh so bravely shackled up their victims, removing even the illusion of a chance at escape.

Roland smirked at my comment, but waved his hand without preamble. A Gateway appeared a foot away from the scrawny werewolf. It revealed a frozen wilderness, and the sudden chill air blasted my face like a grocery store's entrance. A heartbeat later, another slash opened in the air on the opposite side of the body, and I squawked, scrambling away as a wall of water burst into the room from the second Gateway, hammering into the body and splashing me with dark green water.

The water picked up the body, shoving it through the first Gateway and into the frozen woods, washing away the blood on the floor and sending the majority of the mess through the opening. Then the water stopped as he closed the second Gateway, and I saw him grinning at me. I stared at him in disbelief. That was actually… very clever.

I shivered at the frigid breeze, my partially wet shirt feeling like ice. "You're going to make me rip my shirt," I said, glancing down at my chest, and my very prominent biological temperature indicators.

Roland frowned, following my eyes, and then instantly blushed. "Not funny, Callie," he growled, instantly averting his eyes.

I rubbed my arms together, smiling lightly. "Boobs," I said, just to drive home the... point. His face almost purpled. "Payback for getting me wet," I said.

He cast a thread of bluish magic toward the second body, and I watched as the cord of power latched onto the werewolf's cankles and then whipped the body through the opening as if tossing out the trash. Roland brushed off his hands and scanned the floor appraisingly. He pointed a finger at a smear of blood the water had missed, ignoring the scraps of clothing here and there.

I spotted a roll of paper towels on the counter and scooped it up. I tore off a wad and crouched down to wipe up the small splash of blood. Seeing no more, I wadded up the evidence and tossed it at the bodies of the two naked rapists in the frozen tundra, but the Gateway winked out of existence right before contact. I glared at Roland as the wad of paper fell to the ground.

He folded his arms and shook his head. "We don't litter."

My eyes widened in disbelief. "But body-dumping is cool?"

He just watched me and then pointed at a trash can.

"Why the hell would I throw evidence of blood into the trashcan?" I argued in surprise.

"Because it's a very small amount of blood, as if a baker had cut himself. And there's already evidence of criminal activity here. Manacles and chains in the storage room. It would be strange if there *wasn't* sign of a struggle." He waved a hand at the strips of torn fabric in the room unconcernedly. "It will give the police something to do while we take care of the girls. And," he added with a dark look, "it will serve as a subtle message to the third wolf."

My face flashed with embarrassment, but not a flicker of accusation touched his face. "He was long gone."

He nodded. "I know, Callie. Or else you wouldn't be here right now," he said, shooting me a proud look. Inwardly, I smiled at that. It was a compliment.

I angrily picked up the paper towel, tossing it into an open trash can.

"Let's head back to the church. We need to figure out what to do with the girls. In case they change," he growled, sounding frustrated at the thought of them turning. But I knew he was also furious at the thought of a third rapist running free to potentially do more damage.

I cringed. Sure, we had saved the girls, but their lives were forever changed. Now, we needed to find them a pack. Because we couldn't turn them loose as they were, or else they might end up just like the two we had just killed. Feral.

"I've got something important to do first," I whispered, feeling guilty.

He blinked, rounding on me with his impressively wide shoulders. "Something more important than taking care of two rape victims?" he asked in a heated tone.

"No, it's… Claire," I said, turning pleading eyes on him. "She's been out of it since…" I waved a hand, and although I knew he understood, it wasn't a priority for him right now with two women lying in the bed of my truck.

A demon named Johnathan had attacked Kansas City a few weeks ago. Claire survived a mild tussle with some punks outside her house in the chaos, but two things had hit her very hard. One, I had come very close to death. Two, the guy she had been flirting back and forth with hadn't been so lucky. We hadn't known he was a Nephilim – the offspring of an Angel and a human – at the time, and the two of them had grown close. Whether Gabriel's interest in Claire had been authentic, or if he had used her affection as a way to keep tabs on me, we would never know. And Claire had been reclusive ever since. Probably for both reasons. He had died, and he hadn't told her the truth about him being a Nephilim sent to watch over me.

"Surely that can wait an hour," Roland said.

"No," I argued, shaking my head. "It really can't. I've tried meeting with her a dozen times and she always cancels. I've heard every excuse imaginable. I haven't seen her in well over a week." I'd spent about a week in the hotel room after I killed Johnathan. Claire had stuck around for a few days, checking up on me to make sure I was alright – and to take advantage of the swanky hotel – but I had seen the shadows in her eyes. Grief. I hadn't seen her since I left the hotel.

"Callie—"

I shook my head, holding up a hand to stop his argument. "I won't be long. This is very important, Roland. Thirty minutes, tops."

"At least help me see to the women first—"

I tossed him my keys, interrupting him. He caught them instinctively as I said, "Remember that time when—" And I was suddenly gone, Shadow Walking to a partially-enclosed parking lot behind a coffee shop near my apartment. I let out a deep, ashamed breath at my cowardly exit.

Roland was right about the victims. They would need help, supervision, and we would have to make some tough decisions concerning their future. But… Claire was my best friend, and she was hurting, whether she admitted it or not.

I felt terrible about ditching Roland, but I couldn't risk the chance of missing Claire for coffee. Something was bothering her, and as her best friend, I needed to be there for her.

Even if she said it was nothing and that she had gotten over it.

Roland would just have to eat my ass.

I had no doubt that he would make me pay and that I would deserve it, but sometimes you just needed to pay the piper.

CHAPTER 3

*A*fter checking that I wasn't covered in blood, I walked into the coffee shop. A ninety-pound pale-faced kid with ten-pound dreadlocks manned the counter, looking bored. Or stoned. Or both. But Ramsey was always nice to me.

Sometime in the last few months, he had developed an interest in spirituality and other mystical concepts: energy crystals, Tarot cards, and wands. At least, he had spent a lot of time telling me about them, as if trying to convert me to his newfound beliefs. He even had a *Dark Mark* tattoo on his forearm. Part of me wondered why the sudden switch, but then again, the dreads combined with his herbal aroma kind of gave me a good guess.

"Hey, Eve," he said, teasingly. He always flirted outrageously with me, but never actually did anything. More as if he was using me for practice, which was fun. I usually scored the effectiveness of his pickup lines on a scale of one to ten to help him on his so-called quest to decimate the female population of Kansas City.

I smirked back at him, rolling my eyes. "The usual, Ramsey. The hundred-proof."

He nodded somberly. "Black coffee brewed straight from Hell, with a dozen shots."

I smiled and gave him a twenty-dollar-bill. "I'll grab a turkey sandwich, too. And my friend will want something when she gets here. Smoking hot blonde. She loves dreadlocks," I added with a wink.

He looked suddenly petrified. "Oh," he stammered, discreetly sniffing his shirt as he readjusted it anxiously. *Lock up your daughters, lock up your wives.*

It looked like the women had a few more years of safety before his conquest began.

But I didn't let him see my amusement as I scooped up a sandwich from the display case and made my way down the line to the pickup counter. The purple-haired, ever-quiet, female barista manning the espresso machine had apparently started my drink the moment I walked in, because she was sliding it forward before I even got there. Not really a dozen shots in my coffee, but more than three. She never spoke to me, just moved mechanically as if she had never been given the ability to show emotion. But she was efficient, like a good little automaton.

I smiled warmly, scooping up my coffee. "Thanks, Emily."

She graced me with a polite nod, giving me her usual robotic smile. That was it. *Maybe next time I'll get her to speak*, I thought to myself, not for the first time. I found a private couch near a vacant corner of the room in front of the window. I set my sandwich down on the table and tossed my jacket on top of it, just in case I did have some blood spatter on my back or something. I had used my phone to check my ponytail, because blood stood out on white hair, let me tell you. I stared out through the glass as the morning sun began to illuminate the streets. It looked like it was going to rain, which wouldn't affect me since I would be Shadow Walking to the church after talking to Claire.

I let out a sigh and rolled my shoulders.

Things had been... hectic lately.

It had only been a few weeks since my encounter with Johnathan – a real bastard of a demon. He had been intent on sacrificing me in a ritual for some crime my biological parents had apparently committed. But I hadn't known my birth parents, because they had abandoned me on the steps of Abundant Angel Catholic Church as a baby. The only mom and dad I knew were Terry and Sarah Penrose, the ones who had adopted me.

In my eyes, family was earned, not granted through blood. My mom had died of cancer years back, but I was still incredibly close with my dad. He was currently in Chicago for some horror movie convention, of all things. Splatter-something or other.

Since my father had never expressed interest in such movies, I could only imagine that he was courting a new woman, which made me smile. Although thinking of him with another woman hurt me on some deep level, it hurt more to think about him growing old, all alone.

We only get one life, people, and I wouldn't dream of ever holding someone back from a chance at love. I was pretty sure my mother would agree with me, shouting him on from Heaven, encouraging him to go out and conquer – to vanquish new prey. Sure, she would be a judgmental cheerleader, critiquing the woman's clothing, career choices, and makeup, but in the end, we both wanted that stubborn man to be happy.

But finding out that my biological father had been a Nephilim, and that my birth mother had been a wizard named Constance, had been what many would call a *shocker*. Apparently, demons had been fruitlessly searching for me for a very long time, until Johnathan struck gold. A traitor at the Vatican had given me up, and paired with what Johnathan had already known about me, it was enough for him to find me. He had then used an elaborate scheme to draw me out of hiding by stealing the Spear of Longinus – the one that stabbed Jesus on the Cross – and setting me up as an enemy of almost every freak in Kansas City. Hell, the local werewolf pack had chosen to leave town rather than stand up to him, and they hadn't decided to return yet.

I had managed to kill Johnathan, but the Spear went missing.

But there were a lot of hazy parts about that night. A silver droplet of blood inside a feather had infused me with an alien power, and everyone seemed to agree that it belonged to an Angel.

But was that specific Angel dead? Or was he alive and looking for the punk wizard who had tapped into his blood? Was an army of Angels or Nephilim currently hunting me down to take that stolen power back? Because the word on the street was that the Nephilim were like the Navy Seal Team for the God Squad. And Shepherds – twelve holy hunters for the Vatican that wandered the earth slaying monsters, demons, and generally pissing off bad guys – were just the regular grunts.

Like Roland Haviar.

But I didn't want to be a Shepherd like Roland. *Or* a Nephilim. Firstly, because I didn't want my life to be dictated by others – a group of people with the authority to command me to kill, and then force me to obey. I was a fan of neither authority nor command.

Secondly, because ironically, I didn't want any strings tying me to the church. Especially not strings tied to something as all-encompassing as the *Vatican*. And *definitely* not after learning one of their employees had given me up. I had met Roland through sheer luck when he saved Claire and me from a gang of vampires as teens. He had seen me use magic for the first time, and had taken me under his wing to teach me how to control my powers.

He had chosen Abundant Angel Catholic Church as his home base while in Kansas City – the same church that had found me as a child, still run by the same man, Father David. I wasn't a fan of coincidences, but I had found no proof of any other explanation, and I had tried, being a naturally skeptic little shit.

So, the big question was what was I? A wizard, something else, or several somethings?

I still had no answers.

The demon situation had also introduced me to Nate Temple, who had helped me out with everything. I had done quite a bit of research on the billionaire wizard from St. Louis since that time, but hadn't spoken with him since his departure. I had seen another wizard – one without ties to the church – do some incredible things. An almost primal level of attraction had threatened to overpower me, but I had stoically kept that down, to both of our frustrations. I wasn't sure why I had done so, but he seemed to have serious baggage in the relationship department, and I definitely wasn't looking to get tied down.

Especially with someone as dangerous as Nate Temple.

Nate had brought a pal to my city to keep my friends safe during the chaos – Death. Thankfully, I hadn't seen the reaper since, but he had made quite an impression on my father, letting him see the spirit of my mother, Sarah, again. I had lost count of the number of times my dad had asked to see if I would arrange a dinner with Nate and Death. I had stalled him, even screening my calls until he finally got the hint. I didn't want to see my dad fangirling for Death, a Horseman of the Apocalypse.

Nate had left me with a parting gift – a book he had bought at the auction where we met – and he had paid his ritzy hotel room a week in advance, telling me to use it to recuperate, strategize, and recover from my wounds – both mental and physical. I had spent some of my recovery time reading through the book, but I had too much on my mind to really get into it. As far as I could tell, it was some ancient treatise on magic, with a whole lot of *thou* and *thee* statements.

Boring.

Roland had also been injured, but had recovered quickly. Much more quickly than anyone had thought possible. When asked, he had simply told me, "I'm a Shepherd. Health benefits are part of the job."

And if I wanted to know more, he was going to make me ask about it, which would lead to his recruitment speech. But like I said, I didn't want to be a Shepherd. I liked working with him off the books, so to speak – still helping him fight bad guys, but having a little bit more freedom.

The bell on the door tinkled and I looked up to see a hard-looking, bronze-skinned man walk in. He scanned the room casually, his messy brown hair contrasting with his light eyes as they marked the various exits out of habit. As I studied him, I realized he was just incredibly tanned, as if he spent all day outdoors. He wore light jeans, a pair of sneakers, and a long-sleeved tee that was pulled back to his mid-forearms. He assessed each table of patrons, lingering on a few older women sitting around a table near the door as they discussed something in soft tones, motioning to a stack of flyers before them. Each had a bible before her, and they looked to be on the same page. Bible study of some kind, which wasn't uncommon here.

The striking man went to the counter, grabbed a black coffee, and then sat at a table by himself, unfolding a newspaper before him as he took a sip of his steaming drink. I watched all of this through the reflection in the mirror, trying to be discreet. Ex-military, perhaps, to take note of the doors. He was young, but he had an air about him, a heavy gravitas that made him appear much older. He was soon engrossed in his newspaper, chuckling lightly as he flipped to the comics.

I dismissed him, thinking back on my most pressing concern as I waited for Claire.

Johnathan hadn't been working alone. He'd had a... *sister*, or so he'd called her. Amira. I had even met her. She'd been working as a grocery clerk – a young, pretty woman with an almost Asian look about her. I had since gone back to the grocery store to take her out once and for all, but the manager had informed me that she'd quit and hadn't come to pick up her check.

Not liking the sound of that, Roland and I had gone back to the house where it had all happened, hoping to find some trace of her, but we had come up with nothing. Almost as if she had fled town immediately after her brother's death. We had burned all evidence of that night, but had never found the feather, either. Perhaps it had disintegrated after the blood had been taken out. Or Amira had taken it before leaving. Like the Spear.

I was confident she had been there that night, hiding in the forest, because I had seen someone lurking. After killing Johnathan, though, I had woken to find her and the Spear gone.

No normal person could have seen the insanity and death that night and not called the cops, so my money was on Amira.

The Vatican had tried purchasing the home, but had been unable to verify the owner, or at least had been unable to track them down. I had also failed in that regard. All we knew was that the property was owned in trust by a group called Circle Holdings 7, LLC.

Right.

Which pissed me off, but we couldn't legally do anything about it.

So, Amira was still out there, and I doubted she had any warm fuzzies about the wizard who had killed her brother, or whatever the two's relationship had really been. But I had found nothing on her.

Since then, I had been stepping in for Roland while he recovered from his injuries. This morning had been his first day back in the field, so I had done all the legwork with tracking down the mutts. With that job mostly finished now, other than that third wolf, all I really wanted to do was find Amira and skin her alive. To find out why I had been so important to Johnathan.

I sighed, taking a sip of my coffee. But Kansas City had been pretty busy lately with what seemed like a spike in abductions and hate crimes. At least from my discussions with bartenders. They seemed to believe that the local news had the numbers wrong by half...

In the reflection on the glass window, I saw the church women from the table stand as one and approach the handsome man with the newspaper. I bit back a laugh as I watched the oncoming train wreck in slow motion.

I loved watching recruitment talks.

CHAPTER 4

*T*he man sighed, leaning back into his chair as he looked up at them, smiling politely. I couldn't hear what they said, but he nodded amicably and accepted a flyer.

"You don't say," I heard him say in a low tone, sarcasm clear to me, but it didn't look like they noticed. They beamed, nodding back at him as they spoke louder, clear enough for me to hear this time.

"It's just not right. All this talk of monsters and demons taking over the night. Even if it's all a hoax, we can't just sit by and condone such talk. The Lord will protect us from this hateful speech. He always has. And our church hopes to take a stand against this idolatry."

"I do hate idols," the man agreed, straight-faced.

Then his eyes flicked to mine in the glass reflection as he brushed his fingers through his messy hair in a familiar gesture. His gaze was piercing. I hid my blush by sipping my coffee and pretending I had actually been staring out the window. When I turned to casually look back, he was nodding to the women, who seemed to be closer to the table now, assessing him more intently as if they were realizing he might not be as young as they had initially thought, as if his voice had awoken their libidos. I didn't get the vampire sense from him, so wasn't concerned.

Having nothing better to do, I turned back to the glass, straining to hear them.

"All we want is to stop the violence," the lead woman continued, looking like the type to spend a lot of money on her upkeep, because I could tell that the skin on her face didn't match the age depicted by the back of her hands. She also didn't have a ring on her finger. Mr. Light Eyes needed to be careful here. "The murders, the kidnappings, the abuse – even though it has nothing to do with," she used air quotes, "*monsters*, of course. Merely the suggestion of them seems to have encouraged honest, hard-working people to embrace their sinful natures..."

As fun as it was, I suddenly lost interest as I spotted Claire shuffling down the street. She was shooting wary glances up at the sky as if expecting a storm at any moment, and not wanting to get her hair wet. She wore dark jeans, black flats, a jacket, and a colorful scarf – because she adored them, no matter the weather. I grinned, waving at her through the glass. She noticed, smiled, and crossed the street. I turned to face the door, excited to finally see her again.

Mr. Light Eyes suddenly tensed, turning to face the door as well.

Before Claire even touched the handle.

She pushed open the door, and they locked eyes. Claire stopped, frowned at him, and then shook her head as she broke contact and walked up to the counter.

The women roped him back into conversation, but he didn't seem to be paying as much attention as before, and I saw two of them shoot dark glances at Claire for ruining their chances.

Had he seen me wave and turned to look, expecting to see a man at the door? But... he hadn't looked upset *or* relieved to find out my date was a girl, just... aware. Maybe he knew Claire.

Claire strolled up to my table, clutching a steaming cup of coffee. I smiled at her, forgetting about everything else, simply glad to see my friend again as she set her coffee down and took the purse off her shoulder to set on the table.

"Claire—" I began.

She interrupted me by wordlessly wrapping me up in a bestie squeeze, enveloping me with the fragrance of strawberries and a wave of physical love. Her grip said *I'm sorry* better than words could have, and my heart swelled. My shoulders relaxed, and I squeezed back, feeling my eyes moisten.

She finally stepped back, still holding my shoulders. "You look beautiful," she said. Then her features slowly transformed into a scowl. "But you're in deep shit."

My smile faltered. "Um…"

"I know you put that hipster octopus up to flirting with me," she accused, tapping her foot. "All I caught were nervous stammers and random sentence fragments, but I *know* you, Callie."

I grinned guiltily. "You got me. Ramsey is harmless."

"Poor boy didn't know what to say first. Just jumped from topic to topic as if trying to hit every highlight that might catch my attention." She smiled regretfully. "I need someone with a bit more spunk than that." She glanced back at the counter to see Ramsey staring at us. Caught red-handed, he immediately began fumbling with items on the counter, rearranging them unnecessarily. "And a bit more meat," Claire added before turning back to me.

"It's so good to see you," I said, still feeling emotional. It wasn't that it had been so long since I had seen her, but that I'd had nightmares about what she must have been going through, and even though she had obviously wanted space, I had jealously hated giving it to her, for fear of that night breaking her. People had died, and I had almost been one of them.

"Oh, stop it, Callie. I'm fine." She avoided looking at me as she sipped her coffee. Her face was devoid of makeup, and although she was still beautiful, she looked very tired. As if she hadn't slept or eaten much lately. I arched an eyebrow at her and waited. "Fine. I'm not fine," she admitted with a sigh, squeezing my thigh with her palm. "It… was just a lot to process."

I nodded compassionately. "I know." Then I faltered, silence stretching as I struggled with what to say next. Now that I had her in front of me, I didn't know how to make her feel better. "Everything I want to say sounds so cliché," I finally said. She shrugged. "But I'm going to say it anyway. That night was… terrifying. And I'm sorry I got you involved with it—"

"Callie, stop. You went through way worse."

I shook my head. "That's my world. I've trained for it. You haven't."

She sipped her coffee for a few seconds. "I'm fine. I just needed some space. I wasn't going to waste your time with my pity party."

I squeezed her thigh this time, turning to face her directly. "It's not a pity party, Claire. That was a fucked-up night. Demons, Death, Nate…"

A wisp of a smile tugged at her gaunt cheeks. "Yes, Nate. Let's talk about that one," she said with a hungry purr.

I squeezed her thigh harder and she laughed. "Let's not. I didn't come here to talk about boys."

Her face grew somber as if I had flicked a switch, and I winced. "Yeah, you did. Gabriel. You're wondering if I'm okay. Because… he was killed. But I hardly knew him… I don't have a right to feel anything like that."

"Sure you do," I argued. "Just because you only knew him briefly doesn't mean you can't mourn. But I can tell you that he went into that night knowing full well what was going on, even though I sure as hell didn't," I admitted sadly. He had seemed like a cool guy, but I felt doubly guilty to learn that he had initially appeared to keep an eye out for me – a Nephilim guardian of some kind – but I never got the chance to talk to him about it.

"Are *you* okay, Callie? Any luck with…" she trailed off, not wanting to say the name.

I shook my head. "Nothing useful. I haven't found Amira. But I've been looking…" I decided to change topics. "You know those missing girls that have been in the news?" She leaned closer, interested. "We got the bastards. Well, two of them. A third asshole is still free, unfortunately. But that's not the best part." I felt a small twinge at my choice of words, but kept it from my face. Sure, we had saved the girls, but they had glimpsed Hell first. "We found two of the girls."

Claire smiled weakly, likely reading between the lines. "Were they… okay?" she asked guardedly. I idly glanced up to see the church women had left the man with the newspaper in peace, and he was back to reading, not looking our way at all. Weirdo.

I shrugged back at Claire. "They'll live. But we put two of the wolves on ice," I said, emphasizing the word. She frowned, so I dropped my voice and told her everything. She nodded mercilessly at hearing the gritty details of the wolves, but I could see her empathy for the girls.

She was silent for a few moments. "Were the girls… changed?"

I sighed sadly, staring down as I swirled my cup absently. I was surprised to see more than half of it was gone. The caffeine had no effect on me. I think my tolerance was too high. "I don't know," I admitted. "They were bitten, but we'll just have to wait and see. It takes time…"

Her eyes were distant as she leaned back over her coffee. "How long until you know?" she asked softly, swirling her coffee in a jerky motion. The still-steaming liquid splashed over onto her wrist, but she didn't flinch back in pain. She just frowned down at herself, making sure she hadn't gotten any on her clothes. She sucked it away with a quick motion, proving that it wasn't hot enough to burn her, because she was a baby about things like that, and definitely would have had a meltdown.

I shrugged. "A few weeks. A month to be sure. Lot of factors that could affect it," I answered honestly. Even though fledgling wolves typically changed at the first full moon, there had been cases where it had taken up to two months. Roland told me it depended when they were bitten. But if nothing happened after a few months, you could consider yourself lucky... as you sat in a padded room, telling your therapist that werewolves were real.

Claire nodded, staring out the window with a sad look for the victims.

"Did you know that guy over there?" I asked. "Don't look, but the one who stared you down."

Claire's face changed in an instant, an angry look slamming into place with the speed of a guillotine. She tried to take a sip of her drink to hide it, but she had been a heartbeat too slow. When she lowered her cup, the anger was gone as if I had only imagined it. "No," she said flatly.

I waited for more, obviously realizing that *something* had just happened, but not knowing what it could be. If it was an ex – even a casual one-night stand kind of thing – Claire would have told me, even laughed about it. But... she didn't. Just that angry look, and then a flat denial.

"Okay. Just... kind of a weird thing for him to do."

"Yeah," she said, eyes distracted as she glanced outside through the glass again – which was now slightly foggy, making me think another of the recent cold fronts had dropped the temperature outside. Or the humidity. Whatever. Something science-y had happened.

I opened my mouth to press her, but she interrupted me.

"What's that smell?" she asked, scrunching her nose.

I scowled at her, thinking she was subtly telling me to shower. But the look on her face was playful, as if she had smelled something delicious. She was staring at my jacket. I lifted the sleeve to reveal the sandwich, smiling as her eyes lit up eagerly.

She licked her lips and took off her jacket, folding it over the chair next to her. I slid the sandwich over, rolling my eyes, and she attacked the container with mock ferocity like it was a dessert dish she had been eyeing for some time. She did look like she hadn't eaten in a while. She moaned as she took her first bite. My eyes took in the mark on her arm and I froze, keeping my face studiously neutral as I suddenly connected a few dots.

"I'm going to make a call really quick. I kind of ditched Roland for girl time, and he wasn't happy about it," I explained in a rush.

She waved me off, not even looking up from her sandwich.

I plucked out my phone and took a few steps away to a quiet corner of the room, calling Roland. "Where in blazes are you?" he demanded as a way of greeting. Roland was all heart.

"We have a problem," I whispered, studying Claire from behind.

"We have two of them," he snapped. "They're currently in a cell where they can't hurt themselv—"

"No, Roland. I'm talking about *Claire*," I urged in a louder whisper, trying to get him to listen. I saw Claire stiffen, and then slowly turn to look at me, face pale as she met my eyes. My voice was shaking with both fear and fury as I continued. "I... think she was turned."

Claire's shoulders sagged ever so slowly, as if I had just confirmed her biggest fear.

Roland muttered a prayer, and then asked where I was. I told him. "Hurry. Because I've got somewhere to go," I said in a low growl, my throat dry. My hands were actually shaking.

"Where are you going?" he asked anxiously.

"I think it's time for Goldilocks to go meet the neighbors..." I said. Because the mark I had seen on her arm was exactly where she had been hurt that night a few weeks ago, when she had been jumped outside her house. Or so she had said.

And I suddenly remembered that the bears had promised to make me pay. They weren't going to be happy about my response. I was panting as I imagined it, and Roland knew me very well.

"I'll be right there," he said urgently, and then hung up.

CHAPTER 5

I took a deep breath, trying to calm myself. Then I moved. Claire was silent as I carefully walked back up to the table. She stared down at the unfinished sandwich, avoiding my eyes. "I wasn't sure..." she said in a very soft tone. "Can you tell what kind?"

My anger surged at seeing my best friend in pain. Not physical pain, but soul-deep pain. A look of guilt, as if she had done something wrong. I placed a palm on her shoulder – very gently, so as not to startle her. "Oh, Claire," I said sadly. "It's okay. You didn't need to hide anything from me. You big idiot," I added to ease the tension. "And I'm guessing it was a bear."

She frowned unhappily at that, staring at her hands as if expecting to see a sudden change. "But... what if I become a monster? You *hunt* monsters." She sounded disgusted with herself.

I wrapped her up in a bear hug, no longer caring about being cautious. "Becoming a shifter doesn't make you into something you're not."

She squeezed back. "Except sometimes it does," she argued, sobbing into my shoulder.

"No. We'll get through this together... Claire Bear." She laughed and cried at the same time, still clutching my shoulder tightly. Now that I knew what to look for, I realized she was squeezing much harder than usual. Stronger. "Is this why you've been calling in sick at work?" I asked, pulling away, but smiling at her as I remained close, wanting to reaffirm that I wasn't scared of her, for her, or for those around us. She wasn't dangerous.

She nodded back sadly. "I kept seeing them as *food*..." she said miserably. Then she grunted. "Well, except for the bears, I guess. But seeing them in cages did make me angry," she added thoughtfully.

Her entire demeanor was like gasoline to the fire of my rage. Someone had hurt my best friend... to get to me. The fucking bears had made good on their vague promise. It was the only thing that made sense. But I needed to be sure. "It was outside your house, wasn't it?" I asked sympathetically.

She nodded. "It was the strangest thing. This guy, hairy as I've ever seen—"

"Wait. You said it was a group of guys..." I argued. "You said you Maced them."

She sighed loudly, staring down at her lap, shaking her head. "I was embarrassed... I'm sorry, Callie. It was just one man. He cut my arm and told me he would *see me soon*. Then he just walked away. I tried running to my house, but it was like I ran into a brick wall. I think it knocked me out... Next thing I know, Nate was waking me up, asking if I was okay..." She glanced up at me sharply. "I almost told him the truth, but then he said he couldn't find you. That you were missing. He looked so scared. So, I lied to him, embarrassed by the truth. Then we *did* find you, and you were unconscious. Nate had to *carry* you to the car, Callie..." she said, sobbing softly. "And then I heard Gabriel was killed." She pounded a fist on the table angrily, spilling her coffee. "I wasn't about to complain about some random guy *scratching* me and then walking away. So, I stuck with the lie. The truth sounded too stupid."

I growled angrily. Not at her, but at what they had done. "It was one of the bears," I said, recognizing her description, although I didn't know his name. "That's why you couldn't walk through the ward we put around your house. Even though you weren't changed yet, you had the venom inside you. Or however it works. I'm not really sure, to be honest. I know bites do it, but sometimes claws can as well. Roland will know what to do."

"He's coming," she said in a soft tone, sounding scared. "To take me in, isn't he?"

I nodded. "Just to make sure you're safe. I'm going to have some... words with the bears, and then I'll come back to you. I promise. You're not alone,

Claire. I will not leave you behind just because you were attacked by Winnie the Shit."

She laughed miserably. Just then, the bell above the door jingled, and I looked up to see Roland enter the coffee shop. Mr. Light Eyes was gone, although I didn't remember hearing the bell. Maybe he had left when I was on the phone. The church women instantly approached him, handing him a flyer. He took it absently, responded politely, but detoured around them as he spotted us.

They carefully watched his ass as he passed by, and I couldn't help but smile.

Sin catches us all, folks.

Claire looked ready to bolt, so I placed a comforting hand on her thigh.

Roland stepped up to her with a sad smile, and then knelt before her. "It's okay, girl. You're safe with me. I hear all women turn to monsters a dozen times a year," he said with a rare, mischievous grin. Claire punched him in the shoulder, unable to stop the laugh that bubbled up at his comment. Roland toppled over and I squeezed Claire's thigh excitedly.

She whirled as if I was about to yell at her. I held out my hand for a high five.

She stared at me for a second, and then down at Roland. A slow smile spread across her tear-stained cheeks as she slapped my palm thoughtfully. Roland glared at our grins, muttering under his breath about women in general. The trio of church women perked up at that, saw him climbing to his feet, Claire and I laughing, and silently decided that he had gotten no less than he deserved. But they did very thoroughly verify that his ass was intact as he stood.

"I'll be back soon, Claire," I said. "I'm going to get to the bottom of this."

"I should go with you," Roland argued, sounding torn about which of us to protect.

I held up a hand. "No, you really shouldn't. I kind of feel like sinning."

"That's *exactly* why I should go with you," he pressed.

"You're going to make sure my friend is safe, comfortable, and happy as a baby after a bottle of warm milk. Or else I'll be coming to have a talk with you, too," I warned him with an arched brow. Claire folded her arms, backing me up as I snatched my jacket from the table.

He threw up his hands, frustrated. "You realize you're getting angry with me for trying to help you, right?"

"Even though we lesser creatures look dainty, I promise you..." I leaned forward, shoving him lightly. "We ain't." I stormed past him, imagining crushing bear testicles under each foot as I did.

The trio of churchwomen clapped as I walked past the table and out of the coffee shop.

Now free of distractions, my fury pulsed behind my ears, tainting my vision in a dark, slightly red hue, and I noticed that my knuckles were crackling with white arcs of electricity. One of the benefits of the Angel's blood, although I really didn't understand it, yet. I let my magic go with a calming breath.

Claire had been turned as a consequence for me beating the alpha bear in a one-on-one fight. And he had used one of his minions to get his revenge. I had met the man Claire described as her attacker – a wild, ridiculously hairy guy with a chip on his shoulder.

I decided it was time to put a very real chip on his shoulder. And on the alpha, too.

I entered an empty alley just as the clouds began to pour down with lukewarm rain, and I Shadow Walked to a familiar home that I had once invaded with Nate Temple. I wasn't concerned about hiding this time. I strolled right up to the front door.

And kicked the motherfucker down.

CHAPTER 6

*J*scanned the very wide hallway before me, not having seen it before since my last visit had been when I Shadow Walked into an upstairs bedroom with Nate – after which I summarily kicked the alpha bear's ass. We hadn't had time to exchange names, believe it or not.

The walls, floor, and ceiling were all wood, and varied hunting décor decorated the walls, like a luxurious hunter's lodge in the woods. Everything seemed spaced accordingly, in case they happened to be in their bear form, making me feel much smaller than I was. A subtle reminder that these creatures could be up to twelve-feet-tall and weigh over half a ton.

I stood in the entryway, trying to get my breathing under control, glancing over at the broken door I had just kicked in. I didn't hear any cries of alarm, but that didn't mean I was alone. After a few seconds, I was more or less level-headed, enough to listen clearly for sounds of movement.

I had come here to make a very decisive statement, and to make the bears pay for attacking a Regular as opposed to coming after me. But I wasn't going to do anything too stupid. If I found myself against overwhelming odds, I would heroically Shadow Walk my ass to safety.

And then plot my return. Rinse and repeat as necessary.

But there was something to be said about being bold and decisive. And if you did something *ridiculously* bold, it was often the case that your enemy would assume you had the cavalry waiting outside as backup, because surely, no one person would ever do anything *that* insane. Like one tiny woman kicking down the front door of a pack of shifter bears who were double her height with ten times the weight. I idly wondered if they called themselves a pack, or had some other name.

Regardless, it would hopefully give them pause. Essentially, it was a bluff.

And I hoped that bluff – coupled with my very real anger – would be enough.

No one came barreling down the stairs to demand what the hell I was doing, so I began to walk, listening acutely. Maybe they weren't home and were out hunting. Or collecting honey. Or whatever bears did. Hell, it was only just past sunrise, so they might be napping upstairs.

"Christina Robin requests your presence, you fat, hairy dingle-berries!" I called out, my voice reverberating off the wooden tunnel of the hallway. I waited for a shout of alarm, or a wave of padded feet pounding across the floor above me. But only silence answered me.

They should have heard me by now. With a calm breath, I used a whisper of magic to mask my scent. Then I used another spell to settle some magic around my body like a cloak. I lifted my hand and saw only a faint smear – like water-color – where my hand should be, blending in with my surroundings. An impromptu camouflage. Not that it would give me too much of an edge if their sense of smell was up to par, like the other shifter breeds.

I began to walk with stealthy steps, since the wooden tunnel of the hall was basically a megaphone, marking my position if the bears were simply being sneaky and pretending not to hear my shout, so as to coordinate an attack at their own time and location. I tried to step carefully, focusing on where the joints and nails appeared, trying to prevent a creaking sound that would give me away. But the bears were apparently master craftsmen, because the wood didn't make a single sound.

I walked down the hallway, peering around corners into darkened rooms, and although I smelled fresh coffee, I saw no one, heard no one, and smelled no one. I began to grow uneasy as I meandered the halls. Then I finally heard a sound, just as I was entertaining heading upstairs.

The sound was faint, but it came from a door just ahead of me. Peering underneath the crack, I saw faint light, and then a shadow moved. I froze, waiting, but the shadow remained still. Something was on the other side of the door, but I couldn't hear any voices.

I knocked.

There was a startled gasp and then the door flew open. My foot had already been drawn back, and I extended it with every fiber of strength I could muster, striking a surprised man right in the stomach.

What I hadn't known was that he was standing at the top of stairs that led down into a basement, so he tumbled and rolled, flipping head over heels before crashing into a shelving unit at the base of the stairs where he struck his head and fell into the *wet towel* yoga position.

"Well…" I said under my breath, watching to make sure he wasn't faking it. He didn't get up, so he must have knocked himself out. He wasn't as large as the other bears I had seen, looking almost like a teenager. I waited for another bear to burst into view, wondering what had caused all the noise, but again, I was disappointed.

"I should probably not go down the creepy stairs into the bears' basement," I murmured under my breath. "Because that would be really stupid."

I leaned out over the stairs, trying to get a view of the area below. All I saw were stone walls, like an unfinished basement. I took a step, waiting. Then another. And another. Then I lightly raced down the steps, my magic forming a black feathered fan that hovered before me.

A shield.

I stood in a vast open space devoid of any real furniture. Just a textured concrete floor with smooth concrete walls. Only one exit left the area, and it looked to have been designed by merely breaking down the concrete wall. Steel I-Beams surrounded the jagged opening, bolted into the concrete and above the doorway to connect with the open wooden support beams on the ceiling.

The opening was lit with Christmas lights attached to an extension cord plugged into a makeshift outlet hastily mounted on the ceiling. My black fan swayed before me, back and forth, feathers rippling at the gentle motion, obviously detecting nothing, even though I heard faint voices from deep within the tunnel.

With nowhere else to go, I entered the tunnel, which quickly began to feel more like a cave. Which figured, because you know, *bears*. I kept my magic up as I slipped between the rough rock walls, keeping my eyes down

– away from the string of lights – looking for openings in the walls that might hide a bear, or spider, or something equally sinister.

The hallway ran longer than I had thought, but finally opened up just ahead of me into a large open space, where I saw two bears sitting on their haunches on the opposite side, not in human form, but full-on bear. They were black with tan noses, and their fur looked so fluffy I could have died, wanting to wrap them up in a hug and take them home. Luckily, I was using magic to mask my scent, and the distortion spell kept my silhouette from attracting their attention.

The bears stood on either side of a large, ancient-looking wooden door with carvings etched into the surface. Nothing fancy, but heartfelt – almost as if taken from an old Viking's cabin. Lovingly made, but not by a particularly skilled hand. I slowly slipped closer, trying to get a wider view of the room before the door, not wanting to discover – too late – that half a dozen more bears stood in the room, maybe guarding either side of the tunnel I was currently in.

I got close enough to confirm they were the only guards, and took a deep breath.

I strode out of the hallway, forming crackling tomahawks in either fist, my body still a water-colored blur. The bears flinched in startled surprise, and then bounded up to meet me. I flung both tomahawks and hit them each in a thigh, sending them crashing to the ground as their bodies convulsed with the current of electricity I was now pouring into them. Then I was standing over them, casting twin bars of light against their throats to pin them down.

"Play dead or you die," I said softly, verifying the door was the only other exit than the tunnel I had used. "My quarrel isn't with you… yet."

One of them snarled back at me, straining to break my restraint and I made a small gesture with one hand, which they likely couldn't see since I was just an indistinct blur in their eyes. Chains of solidified air suddenly bound his ankles and neck, behind his back, so that as he continued to struggle, he only succeeded in choking himself out.

The other watched this with his lips curled back to reveal long, white teeth, and then he settled a very dark glare my way, but obviously not wanting the same chains as his pal. "What do you want, Callie?" he snarled. I was very surprised that he recognized me, but even more surprised that he could talk in bear form. It had long since been a general understanding that only the strongest of shifters could talk when in animal form, but more and more over recent years I had heard mention of all sorts of shifters talking without trouble. Maybe they had found a loophole.

Or it had been a lie from the very beginning. I would ask Roland about it.

I placed a hand over my chest and let my concealment spell drop. "You know me," I smiled at him. "Should I be flattered?"

"Armor has been expecting you. Go on in. We bears are known for our hospitality." He shot me a toothy sneer. I assumed Armor was the alpha bear's name. I nodded and bound him the same way I had bound his partner, who wasn't struggling as intensely anymore, but the murder shining in his eyes was still alive and well.

"Consider it a compliment."

"Doubting a bear's integrity is not a compliment. We would never attack your back," he spat.

I rolled my eyes. "Well, considering that I'm here because one of you shit-stains lacks honor, you really shouldn't be too surprised that I don't trust you."

He began to growl and rattle at his ephemeral chains, arguing that no bear would ever lack honor. I ignored him and approached the door. Still, his words struck a chord in me. He had sounded genuine. I had bested him, and that was that. He wouldn't have attacked me from behind, and was offended I had restrained him after my victory. I still didn't trust him, but it was something to consider. I honestly knew next to nothing about werebears.

I placed my hands on the handles – great iron rings – and shoved the door open, using a boost of magic to hopefully send them slamming into either wall with a loud *fuck you* factor.

CHAPTER 7

*I*nstead, the doors struck two very solid objects on the way before hammering into the wall with an odd sound. I strode into the room a few steps, deciding it was better to always be moving. I was in a gargantuan cavern, and two groups of bears massed about a hundred feet away from me before three very large, raised thrones. Spears of sunlight filtered down from natural holes in the ceiling, illuminating the space, and I heard a faint gurgling as if from a waterfall nearby.

Finally clear of the doors, I glanced back to see two polar bears moaning on the ground – briefly knocked senseless where the doors had struck them – and then slammed them into the stone walls of the cavern. Good thing I had used magic to help me with the heavy doors, or I would have just ended up giving them the equivalent of an ass slap in a dingy bar.

I brushed my hands together, and turned back to the silent bears before me, continuing on in a measured pace, looking confident and at ease, I hoped. Three bears sat on the thrones.

About a dozen bears sat in pockets on the ground before the thrones, turning to face my entrance. They didn't look surprised, but they did look angry. At realizing that one slip of a girl had just taken out five of their guards. *And the majority of them had been taken down with doors*, I thought to myself smugly.

Two of the bears on the thrones were familiar. One was Armor, the big, brown alpha that I had beaten the living hell out of during our last meeting. He sat in the center throne. Another slightly smaller bear with lighter, tan fur sat to his right, my left, and I recognized her because she had rushed to protect Armor during that same fight. I didn't see the third bear from that night, the one Claire had described as her attacker – the cowardly hairball.

The one I had come here to kill.

But this third bear was as black as midnight with a gray-flecked snout, and was much smaller than the other two. Like a little teddy bear. His head was cocked to the side, making him look curious and happy. He was also playing with a large stick, chewing on it at times.

"You must be Armor," I said, studying the alpha. He nodded, one ear flickering. "I'm here to kill someone," I said politely, dipping my head, "for being a cowardly bear."

This, of course, caused every bear to bristle. "What are you talking about?" Armor snarled, sitting up straighter in barely restrained anger, but not actually standing.

"One of you turned an innocent woman, Claire Stone, to get revenge on me." Surprised gasps filled the room, but I overrode them, raising my voice. "The third guy I saw that night a few weeks ago when I… hurt your feelings." Armor's eyes grew stony, and the bears quieted. "I can remind you of the details if you've forgotten," I offered, staring him down.

"Oh, I remember," he said gruffly, and I could have sworn I heard knuckles popping, followed by the scratching of claws on stone as he squeezed his armrest.

"Good. Saves me time," I said smugly. Then I spoke loud enough for everyone to clearly hear me, ignoring Armor's snarl. "Attacking a Regular is a crime. Even though I'm not a Shepherd, one of you is going to pay for that. Whether by me, the church, or the Academy. You know, the ruling body of wizards. Nasty bunch."

I pulled the Academy card for credibility, because what the bear had done *was* a crime. Also, I wasn't sure where the bears stood on the whole *God* thing, but everyone feared the Academy.

"We would never attack a Regular," Armor growled. "If we wanted revenge on you, we would have come for *you*. Mark my words," he said, brandishing a claw.

"You sure about that, Sweetheart?" I batted my eyelashes at him.

Stone crumbled between his other paw as he squeezed his armrest. The female bear slapped a restraining paw on that forearm and shook her head. Then she turned cool eyes my way.

"You were there too, honey," I winked.

"My name is Kona," she said in a clipped tone. "Not *honey*." She jerked her nose toward Armor. "And he isn't *sweetheart*. Use proper names or you will die. Disrespect isn't tolerated."

I laughed. "Disrespect? After my accusation?" I leaned closer. "Eat. My. Ass. *Honey*."

Her shoulders actually rippled in outrage, but the third bear suddenly pulled his chew stick away, and looked at her. Just a look. She stopped. Instantly. Then he spoke in a soothing, lullaby voice. "Everyone has hot blood right now. She accuses one of us of a crime. I don't think demanding her respect is fair. If what she says is true, her anger is quite justified."

After a long moment of stunned silence, Armor and Kona dipped their heads at him. I smiled back at him, somewhat surprised to find an ally. He held up his paws as if mimicking a scale. "I have questions because this is news to me. But please start from the beginning for all to hear. And before you decide to get cute with me, too, I am Starlight." He winked at me.

I let out a breath, reining in my thirst for blood. I could at least try to be civil, and if things still didn't go as planned, I would resume my first tactic. So, the beginning...

"A demon came to town a few weeks ago and pitted everyone against each other." They nodded stiffly, lips curling in anger at the memory. "You thought I was an enemy, a thief. And I heard you make promises to get revenge." They stared back at me, unyielding. I scowled. "I'm trying to be polite, here. Please nod or we may as well throw down right now."

Starlight glared at Armor, who finally growled. "Yes. We thought you had robbed us, so we discussed revenge. In conversation, *only*," he emphasized. "Then you broke into our home. We fought..." He seemed to have indigestion as he finally added, "And you won."

The rest of the bears fidgeted uncomfortably, and I knew how hard it was for everyone to accept that statement, let alone for him to say it himself.

"I killed the demon that same night, for all of us. For what he had done." The cavern grew silent, and I wondered if that was news to them or if they had already known. "But something else happened shortly after I left your home, and I only just discovered it." I met Armor's eyes, letting him see my pain and rage, but not directing it at him specifically. I directed it at the crime. "Someone who matches that third bear's description turned my best friend. Attacking her outside her home, and saying *see you soon*. Then he walked away. I would very much like to talk to him... Or the one who gave him the order." I met Armor's eyes again. "Then I'm going to kill them. Slowly."

That was about as polite as it was going to get. My words echoed in the silence.

Armor held up a giant claw as grumbles began to fill the room. Whether they were against me or for me, I couldn't tell, but they died down at his motion. His paw was shaking as he rotated it for all to see. And then he clenched his fist. "This is between Callie and me. Period. I am the Alpha. This is *my* Cave." They grumbled unhappily, but complied. I idly wondered who Starlight was in the hierarchy. When he spoke, everyone listened, even their alpha. Maybe he was their moral compass.

I saw that many of the eyes were thoughtful, likely realizing that I might have some truth to my words if Armor was denying them the chance to stand up for him. He finally turned back to me. "You invaded my home and stole something from us. Then you appeared again in stealth, with another who had disrespected us."

"Nate—"

"Do *not* speak his name here," he roared, and his voice had an odd tremor to it. Whether he was unbelievably angry, or trying to hide his fear, I couldn't quite tell. Either way, it was telling. I opened my mouth to argue, but he pressed on. "So, when we saw you the second time, you can understand how furious we were..."

"What with all the ass-kicking, I didn't really notice."

Starlight spoke up, interrupting Armor's snarl. "The young should sometimes use silence as a weapon, rather than blabbering on and on with sharp comments they mistake for wit."

I squinted at him, but he wasn't looking at me, almost as if making an idle observation.

Moral compass, indeed.

Armor continued. "We discussed revenge, but it had nothing to do with your friend. Yuri, the third man you speak of wanted revenge for what you wizards had done to us, and would not entertain the fact that we had all been played by this demon, who was just a rumor at the time. But we do *not* tolerate the idea of attacking an innocent. *Ever.*" His voice rang with moral outrage at the thought of even *speaking* the possibility of such a thing. "He was banished from our Cave, after repeatedly proposing and defending his idea to attack one of those close to you."

Well, shit on a unicorn. So close, yet so far. I had a name, but no bear.

CHAPTER 8

I stared at him, considering everything about him, reading him. I had a name, now. Yuri. But… Armor sounded like he was telling the truth. I had come here thinking he was behind it all, that he had ordered this Yuri to do it, but looking into his eyes, I began to wonder…

Here he was, admitting to being beaten by me, in front of all his people. Not one of them had done anything disrespectful to me this morning. And I had given them every reason to do so. In fact, it had been a tactic of mine. Get them to show their true colors by pressing their buttons.

But… at every turn they had shown me the opposite. I wasn't gullible enough to buy this completely, but if they were such vicious, conniving, soulless bastards as I had anticipated, surely one of them would have retaliated by now. Especially when they were all in bear form, which typically inhibited the rational side of their human nature. And I was outnumbered, not really a threat against so many. And they were still letting me speak. Even rudely.

Armor leaned forward. "Regarding your second accusation, let me put you at ease… He took a deep breath. "I did not attack your friend. Nor did I command, hint, or suggest it. If I lie, every bear has the right, duty, and obligation to tear out my throat without reprisal."

He leaned back in his throne. Then Kona repeated the words, staring straight at me. Then Starlight. Then, believe it or not, every other bear took turns stepping forward enough for me to clearly see them deny as well, until everyone but the unconscious or incapacitated guards had sworn their innocence, and their obligation to take down their Alpha if he was lying.

Armor leaned forward again, resting his elbows on his hairy thighs. "Let me fill you in on a little secret about bears. When we turn someone, they want it. We try to pick those who will be assets to us, and those who are fed up with their situation. Whether without family, facing fatal disease, or disgusted at the lack of honor they see in the world. We offer these individuals the opportunity for a second chance. A gift. Healing them in exchange for their obedience to our creed... Honor. But when one breaks this, they are cut away." I saw every bear nodding proudly.

Starlight spoke next. "If Yuri did this thing, he must face justice."

I nodded, feeling truth to their words. "Bring him to me and I will gladly take out the trash."

"To have a punishment, we must have proof of the crime. Right now, you have a suspect, but not a case. Suggestive evidence, but not a concrete fact." He held up a paw, seeing me open my mouth to argue. "Has your friend actually turned yet?"

And my mouth snapped shut. I had an eyewitness. But... her word against his wouldn't hold water in the traditional courts, either. Even though I knew Claire was telling the truth, it had yet to be officially proven. She hadn't yet turned.

I shook my head angrily. "But I'm not sure the Academy will require such evidence," I said, hoping to sway Starlight's words.

He tapped his lips thoughtfully. "You keep mentioning the Academy, and yet you have no ties to them. Neither does... Temple," he said, looking as if the word was distasteful to him. "In fact, I have it on good authority that the Academy doesn't hold anyone outside of their jurisdiction in high regard. Not the Vatican, and especially not Temple. So why would you not warn us of the Shepherds' wrath instead?"

I sighed. "I'm not a Shepherd."

"Neither are you Academy, so why the distinction?" He tapped his lips again, thinking. Then his eyes brightened. "Oh, my..." he said in a surprised tone. "That is unnerving..." The skin pebbled at the base of my neck as I wondered what conclusion he had come to. "You could have brought Roland with you today, but that would make things official, alerting the Vatican. I can only assume this means you lack trust in your Holy employ-

er," he said softly, not using it to bludgeon me, "that we both may have traitors in our midst." I let out a breath, and he sighed, not sounding the least
bit pleased at this revelation.

Stunned looks met mine, which basically meant the bears' eyes widened
and they seemed to stop breathing for a few moments.

"I'll take care of Yuri if you take care of our mole at the Vatican," I said
dryly.

Starlight's eyes twinkled with amusement. "No. Both are your problem.
You are the accuser."

Armor cleared his throat, which just sounded odd on a bear. "You must
find Yuri, prove his crime, and then bring him to us to face justice. Do this,
and we will owe you a favor…"

Starlight nodded at that, but the rest of the bears looked surprised, especially Kona.

"You'll have your evidence soon enough, when my friend turns. You find
Yuri, and I'll gladly kill him for you. Because I have no idea where to find a
bear, if he's even still in town," I said, growing angry.

"We cannot find him. The burden of proof is on the accused," Armor
grunted.

"And we will be busy," Kona added, sounding suddenly excited for some
reason.

"With what?" I growled.

"Taking care of your friend," she said. "She will die without our help."

"I don't like the way that sounds," I growled at her.

"Facts rarely give a flying fuck about one's feelings," Starlight offered in a
light tone.

Despite my anger, laughter bubbled up. "I really like that one…" I admitted. But they did have a point. Claire would need help, and I didn't like the
idea of keeping her locked up in a cell below the church. And sooner or
later, she would need to meet the bears.

"Bears are quite strong," Starlight said. "Especially during first shift. And
it would ease her transition to spend some time with us, getting to know us,
first. Learning more about our ways." I nodded slowly. I couldn't speak for
Claire, but their proposal did make sense. Starlight smiled at me with his
big, dark eyes. "We will keep her safe for you, Callie. Never fear. I swear it.
Now, regarding Yuri, Kona has some news that might interest you."

I turned to her, feeling eager. "I received word that Yuri is still in Kansas

City, and has been seen in the company of new... friends from other factions," she said carefully. I blinked. He was hanging out with other flavors of Freak? That didn't sound good. Had someone hired him as a goon? Extra muscle? She pressed on, not elaborating. "There are a lot of new faces in town these last few weeks. Several of these friends will be at a fundraiser tonight. One you are also attending, if my sources are correct." I kept my face neutral, but I'll admit, I was curious how the hell she knew that. Roland had only just told me about the fundraiser yesterday.

Then again, it wasn't much of a State Secret. The Vatican had lumped me into every single gala or auction event as their go-to attendee after the fiasco a few weeks ago. They wanted the world to see that the church had nothing to do with the chaos that went down that night. And seeing the same face at several more functions without the buildings erupting in flames or demons put people at ease.

I saw a giant claw rise into the air from the crowd of bears, a monster of a Grizzly. The three bears on the thrones studied him thoughtfully before nodding. He climbed to his feet in a lazy, rolling motion, letting out a snort of effort as he stood on all fours, turning to face me.

"I heard Yuri muttering something over and over in the days before he left. Not sure if it means anything, but figured it might mean something to you," he grumbled in a deep, deep baritone. I nodded eagerly. "God is dead." He paused, letting me know he was finished. Then he sat back down.

I kept my face blank, and nodded my appreciation. "Thank you. I'll look into it."

Starlight was squinting at me very intently, but I maintained my poker face. I'd heard that exact phrase just this morning. From the Scarecrow wolf. Had Yuri been working with them? Was the frat-wolf's claim of taking over the city more than I had initially thought? Some kind of code? The city had been crazy lately, with a noticeable uptick in crime. But since this was my task, I didn't want to voice it here. But I knew one thing. That third wolf had just become my priority. My only lead.

"We will watch over your friend in exchange for your service," Starlight finally said. "We are able to take a beating, so even if she doesn't shift into a bear, we can take a lot of her frustration without serious harm. But if she is a bear... even better. You will have your proof, and she will see familiarity as soon as she makes the first change. We can ease her fears."

I thought about it, considering all angles. I held up a finger. "She chooses her future. If she doesn't want to be a part of your club, she won't become a part of your club."

He chuckled at that. "Deal." He turned to the other two bears on the throne, who dipped their heads in agreement. Then Armor sliced his paw, held it up into the air, and made an oath.

"I swear to watch over Claire Stone, to keep her safe, to pledge my life in her defense, and to not influence her in any way whatsoever, other than to assist her in controlling her new abilities. And all present will do exactly the same. I forfeit my life if I fail. And any traitors forfeit their life if they act independently to counteract my oath and bring the..." he met my eyes, seeming to smirk, "*rage of Callie Penrose* down on us all. Do all present hear me?"

I scowled at him, but let it slide.

The cavern was silent as a tomb, and then, one by one, each bear independently voiced their acknowledgment, stepping forward so that there could be no hiding, and then stepping off into a new group, literally allowing no one to pretend or slip by the oath. They also sliced their palms, and held them up in the air. I felt the air in the cavern tighten, grow thicker, and begin to hum stronger with each promise. Starlight had his eyes closed, but not as if napping, more as if he was... using magic.

No way.

I hadn't felt him use magic, but something was binding their oaths.

When all were finished, Kona and Starlight took their turns, slicing their palms and trading grips with each other, getting blood all over the place.

I frowned, tapping my lips thoughtfully as the power seemed to pop, and then fizzle away, leaving filaments of energy to dance about the room like fireflies. Starlight winked at me.

"What about the sleepyheads over there," I said pointing at the Polar Bears who still hadn't regained their feet, although they were groaning. "And the three outside?"

"This oath bonds all present. Not just in this room, but in my Cave. My *pack*," he clarified, seeing me frown at the word *Cave*. "Which includes them. And they forfeit their lives, by my hand or any of those you just heard speak, if they try to act otherwise." He stared at me very intensely. "I hope you realize the significance of this, Miss Penrose. You could very literally ignite a civil war between my people. Now, go do this thing."

I nodded woodenly, not having thought about it like that before. "Right."

"What will you do next?" Starlight asked, leaning forward with a curious grin.

"I think I'm late for my AA meeting," I said absently. He frowned, looking suddenly concerned. I shook my head, smiling. "Abundant Angel Catholic Church," I elaborated. "A.A."

He blinked twice, and then burst out laughing. "Wow! I can't even *begin* to fix that level of broken," he finally said, wiping at his eyes.

I shrugged, smiling crookedly, because my mind was already elsewhere. And, because I had nothing else to say, I simply walked out the way I had come.

What the fuck was I going to do now? Give Claire to the bears?

I had the presence of mind to remember to remove the restraints from the bears in the outer room, but I didn't look at them or acknowledge their snarls as I walked past them. I heard them growling as they entered the cavern, likely wondering what the hell had just happened, and if they were about to be killed for letting me in.

The bear I had pushed down the stairs was sitting on the ground, leaning against the wall at the base of the steps, rubbing his head. Seeing me, he froze, blinked, and followed me with his eyes as I walked past him. Not afraid, but very, very alert. I nodded at him as I would a stranger on the street, and walked up the steps. He didn't follow me.

I needed to get to the church and talk to Roland and Claire.

Right fucking now. Because I needed to find Yuri, and also come up with a plan for this fundraiser. Because the Vatican really didn't want me to ruin any more of those.

But I never said I was a churchy kind of gal. And I'd never learned to turn the other cheek...

CHAPTER 9

I grabbed a water bottle from the fridge, and guzzled it. Father David blessed all the water bottles at Abundant Angel, but Roland took that water, and blessed it again before taking it down to our secret subbasement training area. Twice-blessed water bottles, for crying out loud.

Where others had to worry about lime, BPA, or fluoride in their water, I had trillions of angelically enhanced water molecules in mine.

It washed the sin out, and restored the soul.

All joking aside, it did seem to taste better than the water upstairs, and definitely better than the water from home. I'd asked Roland to bless the water filter in my fridge, and he had simply refused to talk to me for a day, thinking I had been making fun of him.

I passed through the training room, which appeared to be all concrete tiles and grates at the moment, but when activated would turn into a death trap to make a certain tomb raider weak in the knees. I had spoken to Othello, one of Nate's friends, about hacking into it to sync it to my music playlist, and she thought she had a way to do it, but I hadn't moved on the idea yet.

The next area was a bamboo-walled room full of punching bags, targets for projectile weapons, and various martial arts contraptions designed to improve hand eye coordination and speed, like the dreaded Wing Chun dummy in the corner where I hid it from Roland. One wall held wooden practice weapons, but the other side was the real deal – all the blades sharpened and blessed by Roland himself. Because, come to find out, Vatman was freaking ordained!

It made sense, really, but seeing him and Father David in the same room sometimes made me grin as I imagined what courses of study they had chosen in school. *Latin* or *Exsanguination of Vampires 101.*

The various blades gleamed in the dim lighting, but the cudgels seemed to absorb the light, a contrast of lethality. I knew how to use them all. Of course, with my stature, certain weapons weren't ideal for me, but I still knew enough to not be embarrassed if I had to use them. They were all very deadly, and carefully placed in positions of prominence like family heirlooms.

Because they were.

Long story short, each weapon had a history. It wasn't just an ornate set of nunchakus, but had been used by a famous master, or had been wielded in a historic battle and reengineered to make sure it was ready for modern day combat.

It was a very non-modern arsenal. Roland had told me that Shepherds didn't just rely on magic, because not all Shepherds were wizards. One or two were entirely Regular, as a matter of fact. A few others were different flavors of monster, because Catholicism was open-minded these days.

Or so I'd been told.

But my favorite weapons were the acrobatic ones. Roland had bought me a Dragon Chain – a chain with spear points attached to the ends – for Christmas. The links were made with titanium, so it was super light, but the blades were made of something he called Damascus Steel, that he swore was nearly indestructible.

It hung on a wall of its own, because I had pointed at the wall and shouted at Roland in a booming, Biblical voice, *Let that be mine!* And now it was so.

I walked through the training room, and deeper into our secret bunker under the old church.

I entered the utility room, glanced about to make sure I was alone, even though I had not seen a soul while walking through the rooms, and placed my hand on a loose brick that looked like a hundred others. It slid inwards with a scraping noise to reveal a keypad. I placed my thumb on it and the entire wall shifted back, and then to the side, revealing a rickety service elevator.

I stepped inside, and pressed the lowest button. Which was five levels below me.

As the elevator began to descend, I watched the stone wall change, showing old doors as I passed each level. I furrowed my eyebrows, glaring at the doors as they passed, even taking a second to share that anger with the buttons that marked the levels I passed.

Because I hadn't been allowed to enter them before. And I had been training with Roland for ten years. These levels were only for Shepherds. Judging by the levels I *had* seen – the training room and the dungeons on the floor I was currently heading towards – I had no idea what could be so secret that I wasn't allowed to see.

I was allowed to see and use a floor full of hundreds of weapons, and a floor where we could house almost any kind of monster – even a demon.

So, what was on those middle floors? Before I could begin to imagine them for the hundredth time, the elevator came to a jerky halt, and the door opened before me, revealing a medieval style passageway of large stone blocks and iron bars as thick as my wrist on either side of me – with twelve feet of solid stone, metal, wood, and whatever else between each cell.

Each iron bar was etched with runes, and had veins of silver and gold in the metal.

I wasn't a blacksmith, and didn't pretend to understand their sorcerous abilities, so simply assumed they had thrown gold and silver into their melting pot when making the bars. But I knew it had something to do with strengthening the bars from supernatural beings. Like a circle drawn on the floor.

Speaking of...

Each cell had a trio of metallic rings stretching from wall-to-wall, sitting underneath a sheet of perfectly-fitted bulletproof glass, so the prisoners couldn't tamper with them. Small openings in the hallway floor – out of prisoner reach – would allow the jailer to activate the metallic rings in a magical binding with their blood. For any high-risk inmates that we invited to a sleepover.

I'd seen occasional beasties stored here for short periods, but nothing to warrant the level of protection built into each cell.

Claire was in one of the back cells, designed for the strongest of the prisoners. Not magical strength, but physical strength. I wondered if there was any shifter stronger than a bear. As I approached, I noticed the two rape victims were also here, but they both seemed to be sleeping in their own cells, since they didn't stir as I walked by. I wondered what we were going to do about them, or which girls they were on the list of missing persons. The state we had found them in hadn't made positive identification possible.

Claire stared at me through the bars, tears streaming down her cheeks.

"Oh, sweetie," I said. "Why are you all alone? I'm going to kill him," I said, wondering why the hell Roland had left her alone.

She shook her head with a weak grin. "He just left. He's been here the entire time, but needed to speak with Father David about a trip, or something. I'm not crying because I'm alone, Callie. I'm crying because I'm scared, and I was worried about you." She placed her hands on the bars, trying to shake them with all ninety-eight pounds of her body. She laughed futilely – at the ridiculousness of it all.

I placed my palm on the pad outside the gate, and her cell whisked open. I rushed inside to give her a hug, leaving the door open. She squeezed back, and then pulled away, waving a hand at her room. It wasn't the typical cell, but had a luxurious bed, a private, closed-off toilet, and a sink replete with hygiene supplies. At least Roland hadn't let her feel like a criminal.

"He shouldn't have left you alone. Not even for a minute," I argued.

Claire sat down on the bed, motioning for me to join her. "It really has been only a few minutes. You must have just missed him on your way down here. He was sharing what he knew about bears, performing tests, checking my eyes..." she trailed off, smirking at me. "Honestly, I think he was getting payback for when I was taking care of him a few weeks ago," she said with a laugh. "I guess I deserve it."

"Yeah, he probably enjoyed that. Not the cell thing, but the vengeance," I said. I took a breath, not happy about this next part, doubly so since Roland wasn't here. "We need to talk."

She inhaled deeply, as if gathering her courage, too. "Okay."

"Was Roland able to confirm you're a bear? Or that you even caught the gene? Maybe we're overreacting," I said, having absolutely no doubt inside me, merely saying it for her benefit.

She met my eyes, brows arched in disapproval. "Callie, stop treating me like a child." I let my shoulders relax, and nodded back guiltily. "He confirmed I've been infected by a bear, but there is no way to tell if I will turn or not until it actually happens. But judging by my subtle changes already, I'm thinking it's pretty much a guarantee," she said calmly, accepting the situation.

I squeezed her hand in mine. "Claire, you're going to be the coolest, hottest, meanest, smartest bear in the world." I lifted her chin with my fingers. Her skin was fever hot, but she wasn't sweating. I caught a faint, wild spark in the depths of her eyes, and managed not to flinch.

She smiled back at me. "Thanks, Callie."

I managed to keep my anger in check, although I had imagined ripping each limb from Yuri's torso numerous times on the way here. Claire was a veterinarian at the zoo. The head-honcho, in fact. But what would happen now? Was that still an option? Not for a while. Not until she got control of her new... interests. Maybe not ever.

"This isn't the end. Just a very interesting plot twist," I encouraged. "You can now officially become a sidekick. You'll heal fast, be able to beat up every punk at the bar who hits on you..." I said, smiling at the thought. "It's actually kind of cool, as far as drastic life changes go."

She sighed. "Unless I can't control it."

"We won't let that happen," I promised. "Your brain is always in charge, and you've always placed intelligence and rationality ahead of feelings. I really don't think that part will be an issue. It will be the little things that frustrate you. You've always lived in this carefully controlled bubble, in charge of every detail. But that bubble just got bigger..."

She let out a long sigh, nodding slowly. "In a way, it's kind of an interesting situation. I sometimes feel like I understand animals better than humans, and now I'm going to partly become one. As a doctor, it's actually... well, scientifically amazing. I'll get to live what I've spent my life studying," she said, sounding more excited by the moment.

I lifted a hand. "But first, like with any experiment, we need to figure out the ground rules."

She nodded firmly. "Right." Then she met my eyes. "What are those, exactly?"

I leaned back on the mattress, thinking to myself. "Well, we need to control the change, at least the first one. The shock of it often makes the victim act feral, more wild and instinctual. We'll need to keep an eye on you at all times, to make sure you don't hurt yourself..."

"Or others," she added sadly.

I shrugged. "Not much different than I had to go through. I've spent a decade with Roland, learning how to control myself."

"I think it's fair to say that becoming a bloodthirsty beast is a little different than flinging fireballs around," she said with a teasing smile.

I kept my face very, very serious. "Be thankful you aren't going through this *and* experiencing puberty for the first time," I said in mock solemnity.

She burst out laughing. "Oh! I hadn't even *thought* of that!"

I nodded seriously. "I was already transitioning into a bloodthirsty beast – a woman – and I had to learn how to use magic at the same time."

"That means I need to be supervised. Will you stay with me, Callie?"

I grimaced, unable to lie to her. "I... can't. I have to find the guy responsible for this and make him pay. His name is Yuri, by the way." Her eyes flared momentarily, latching onto the name. "The demon is still out there, too. And the third werewolf," I added, pointing back at the other cells with the two girls. *God is dead*, I thought to myself, wondering at the possible connection between Yuri and the wolf, and if it was related to the increased violence in town, or the new faces the bears had mentioned.

Rather than worry Claire with that, I continued on.

"Roland has to travel to Italy to clean up some of the mess from a few weeks ago. And I have a few obligations for the Vatican myself. But don't worry," I pressed, seeing the look of anxiety on her face. "I have an idea other than the cell. You really do need to be supervised, just in case anything goes wrong during your first shift. So, the bears kind of offered—"

"Wait!" she snapped incredulously. "The same bears you just confronted and likely pissed off? *Those* bears?"

I nodded meekly. "But I made them swear to keep you safe, and they literally can't back up on their oath. If one of them breaks that promise, he dies. Even their alpha. Basically, if you are harmed, every single bear is duty-sworn to avenge and defend you, or they all forfeit their lives."

She considered this in silence for a few moments. "Which won't matter to me, because I would already be dead..." she whispered.

I sighed. This was exactly my first thought, as well. Sure, they had sworn a big old punishment on the guilty, but that wouldn't bring Claire back if one of them decided to become a martyr. I opened my mouth to agree, but she held out a hand, stalling me.

"What about Nate Temple? Can't you send me to him?"

I had actually considered that, but had quickly discarded it. He had a Beast Master friend, one who could very literally control shifters – all shifters. But I really didn't know Nate, or his friends, and didn't like the idea of handing her over to him. He also had quite a bit on his plate already, although I didn't have all the details on what exactly that was. And he was friends with some pretty dangerous people.

There were simply too many variables I didn't know. Who to trust, being predominant. I didn't know Nate all that well, but I did trust him. But his friends? I'd met a couple very briefly, but he had a lot of friends, and I couldn't vouch for them all.

"I don't think that's a good idea, Claire." I told her why, and she nodded after a few moments.

"You just don't want me swooping in for the kill," she teased me, using her hands to draw a male specimen in the air, focusing on her formation of his rear, and then giving it a figurative squeeze.

I rolled my eyes at her. "You got me." I wasn't really sure what to make of Nate in that regard. There was definitely something between us. There was no denying that. It was a raw feeling, as if we couldn't help it. But when rationality kicked in, I always got the immediate feeling that I needed to...

Back. The fuck. Up.

As if the universe was warning me, for some reason. And one should listen to the universe.

Claire was studying me curiously, likely realizing – or knowing ahead of time – that she had struck a chord. "If I can't be with you or Roland, I want to go to the bears. For multiple reasons. I want to understand this about myself. And if they wanted to kill me, they very easily could have that first night. I think they're telling the truth. A conspiracy just doesn't make sense. Plus, I think it will be fascinating to see a group of animal humans."

"I don't think they like to be called animal humans," I offered with a weak grin.

She laughed lightly. "I'll remember that. But in all seriousness, if I'm going to do it, I may as well go all in. If anyone can help me, they can. Sitting here alone in this cell will make me go nuts. I already feel violent," she said dryly, holding up mock claws with her fingers.

I let out a conflicted sigh. She had a good point. But I still didn't like her out of my sight. "Okay. Let's go tell Roland. You don't feel particularly feral right now, right?" I asked teasingly.

"The faster you get me out of here, the better I'll feel," she said, standing and brushing her hands together.

"Let's go see the old man, then," I said. "He's really not going to like this idea," I added with a smile as I led Claire out of the cell.

CHAPTER 10

*R*oland studied us, face serious. "I really like this idea," he said the moment I finished laying out our plan.

I blinked at him, and Claire burst out laughing. Roland frowned at us, not understanding. I sighed, then shot him a scowl. "At least pretend to be angry. I had my arguments ready."

"Oh, well, why would I be upset about this?"

I threw my hands up. "I don't know. Because you're always angry about everything! If it's not your idea, it must suck," I said, letting out an angry breath.

Roland frowned, but looked to be biting back a smile. "Claire's a bear. They're bears. Who better to help her prepare?" he asked very seriously. *Was he rhyming on purpose?*

Claire burst out laughing, and I slowly turned to face her. "You're not helping," I growled.

She was clutching her belly. "You were right, Roland. She really does love me to a fault."

I blinked back at her, and then slowly turned to Roland, my mind catching up with a dark suspicion. "Wait, you two already decided on this outcome, didn't you?"

Roland finally flashed his teeth at me. "Pretty much. As long as you didn't kill any of them, I told her it would be best if she spent some time

55

with the bears. I've spent some time around them. The only variable was what you would do when you ran into them. If, for example, you found one of them guilty and killed them. Well, then we probably wouldn't be open to sending our delicate Claire over there for at least a day or two. But this really is the only option, don't you think, Callie?" he asked in an overly sweet tone.

I threw a bible at Claire. She squawked and ducked, letting it fly over her shoulder to knock over a lamp on Father David's desk. He didn't even flinch, and I realized I had actually forgotten he was present.

Because he had been silently staring at us the entire time, shaking his head slowly as he repeated sections of our conversation with an open, but silent mouth, as if not believing any of this was really happening. He still had some cuts on his face from when Johnathan had put him in the hospital, and complained often about his ribs, but he was healing well.

"Well, pick it up, Davey!" I snapped.

He flinched, realized he had zoned out, and scrambled to pick up the lamp and the bible, finally finding his fire again as he glared at me for throwing the Holy Word at my friend.

"You okay?" Claire asked him.

"Bear..." he repeated dumbly.

Roland let out a tired sigh. "He didn't believe me when I tried to explain it to him," he admitted with an amused glance at Father David.

He sparked up at that. "It's not that I didn't believe it was possible, it was that I didn't believe the *situation* was true. You all look way too casual about this. Isn't it some sort of crime? In fact, the only one who seems upset is Callie," he finally grumbled.

I locked eyes with Roland, catching the fire hidden in those depths. And I knew. He was definitely furious, but he was purposely playing everything cool, even pranking me, to keep Claire at ease. He nodded slowly, and I turned to Father David, feeling much better about being the brunt of the joke after I realized it had all been for Claire. "Oh, it's most definitely a crime. I'll take care of that part." I shot a scowl at Claire. "Thanks for leading me on, asshole."

"Must be my baser instincts kicking in," she jibed. Although she seemed much better, I could still sense the undertone of anxiety in her posture. She was scared, but using humor as armor, which was really the only thing left to her. That was the thing about Claire, something that I had learned from her only recently. She could be terrified to the bone, but once she spent some time to compartmentalize that fear, she simply pressed onward. Still scared, but not letting it fuel her actions. She simply embraced that she had been thrown into the deep end of the pool, floundered in it for a moment, and then started to swim back to the shallows to get her feet back under her, and be scared there instead.

It was a pretty incredible feat, in my opinion.

Not an immediate, instinctive sense of self-preservation, but at least she got there eventually. The world typically consisted of those who flailed about in the pool, screaming about the world being unfair, and those who were so jaded that they weren't scared. I had never met someone who straddled the two ideologies.

Claire Stone was the only one.

This insight had actually helped me overcome some of my own fears recently, and since that time, I hadn't had a single nightmare about my past.

Roland interrupted. "My flight is tonight—"

He was interrupted by a polite knock on the door. As one, we all turned to face it as Father David called out, "Come in, please."

The door opened to reveal Sister Agatha. At least that was her birth name. I made it a goal to learn all the Sisters' birth names, using those over their newer, religious names. Agatha was one of the few who found it endearing.

She dipped her head at us politely, and then stepped to the side to reveal three figures waiting patiently behind her. They murmured gratefully to her as they walked into the room. I shot Roland a look, but he was busy studying the newcomers with a disarming smile.

An elderly man stepped in first, looking kind, wise, and weathered. He walked with a slight limp, and had a twinkle in his eyes that was full of cheer. Two middle-aged adults walked beside him, smiling politely, but seeming meek – a nondescript man and a woman. I reached out with my magic to sense them, gauging their danger, and relaxed. Total Regulars. Roland shot me a dark look, and I lowered my eyes guiltily.

I hadn't meant anything by it. Just trying to protect everyone from a secret demon or monster of the night. And I was being chastised? I lifted my head to shoot him a look of my own, but he wasn't looking, offering his chair to the older gentleman with a polite smile.

Father David spoke up. "Pastor Benjamin Flood, welcome. Make your-self comfortable, and introduce me to your friends."

Pastor Benjamin chuckled lightly at Roland as he walked in. He placed his liver-spotted hand over Roland's scarred knuckles, and then sat down into the chair with a pleased sigh. "Thank you, son," he said. Roland dipped his head, shrugging off the words as unnecessary.

I stood. "Claire, we probably need to get going," I began.

"What is your name, child?" Pastor Benjamin asked, smiling kindly at me, as if my answer would be the most interesting thing in the world, and that it would be the rudest thing imaginable to deny him such a simple request. There was nothing magical about it, he just exuded kindness.

I smiled back. "Callie Penrose."

He beamed. "Well, it is an absolute pleasure to meet you, Callie. Is that short for Caroline, by chance?"

That was a new guess. "It isn't, actually," I said back with a wink. "But good guess."

He snapped his fingers in defeat. "Drat. I guess I'll have to think on it," he grinned.

I nodded. "You do that."

"You don't have a tricky name, by chance, do you?" he asked, turning to Claire.

She beamed at him. "Claire Stone. And speaking of stones, this brutish lump of rock is named Roland Hav-tard."

Roland prickled at that, and I really had to force myself not to burst out laughing. "Roland *Haviar*," he corrected, scowling at Claire, who shrugged with a devilish grin.

Pastor Benjamin roared with laughter. "What spunk!" he chuckled, nodding to each of us. "I hope we didn't interrupt," he said, frowning to David. Then he remembered the other two behind him and looked suddenly mortified. "My apologies. That's what you get for letting old men ramble on. This is Brigitte Thompson and Desmond Kline. They're the ones doing all the real work for our new church down the street," he said, motioning them forward.

"Pleased to meet you," Brigitte said with a shy smile, as docile as a mouse. She wore a modest dress, thick glasses – which she had already adjusted twice – and had her dark hair was tied back in a bun, which made her look older than she probably was. I would have guessed her to be in her early forties.

Desmond rolled his eyes at Pastor Benjamin's attempt at being humble. He had buzzed hair, was as skinny as a twig, and tall enough to loom without trying. The crinkles at his eyes made me guess late thirties. "It's very nice to meet everyone, but I think we all know when we're standing knee-deep in—"

Pastor Benjamin shot him a very pointed look, and Desmond smirked back at him. Then he winked, and everyone laughed. I wasn't the only one who liked to press buttons.

"I remember when elders garnered respect," Pastor Benjamin complained, shooting a pleading look at Father David, who was nodding in agreement, but smiling all the same.

"Just be thankful the Lord didn't saddle you with these two," he said, indicating Claire and I.

I nodded back in complete agreement. "The Lord does not give a burden that cannot be managed," I replied in my most official tone.

Father David let out a sigh, motioning to me as if I had just proven his point.

Pastor Benjamin chuckled. "Well, I think they're delightful," he said, flashing us a grin. Claire and I accepted the compliment, and then simultaneously turned on Father David with expectant looks.

He slapped his table with the palm of his hand lightly. "See? You're only encouraging them!" he said, mock judgment on his face as he glared at Pastor Benjamin, who only shrugged good-naturedly.

"You're opening a new church?" I asked, switching gears. I wanted to get out, but at this point, I thought it may appear rude.

He nodded excitedly. "Technically, we're already open, but we wanted to reach out to our neighbors and say hello."

Desmond stepped forward, approaching me like a stork, extending a familiar-looking flyer my way. "I saw one of those at a coffee shop this morning. Three older women were handing them out," I said, accepting the flyer, and then taking a step back from him.

Desmond's smile looked crooked, likely wondering why I had stepped back. Rather than make an issue out of it, I read over the flyer as Desmond turned to hand one to Claire, Roland, and Father David.

"You met the *Abominable Three*," Pastor Benjamin chuckled, showing his teeth. I smirked automatically, finding his sense of humor contagious. I knew very well what he meant by that name, but I pretended not to. "If they spoke to you, there must not have been a man around."

I nodded. "There was, actually. They kind of attacked him like a pride of lions."

"He's lucky he's not already married off, then. To one... or all three!" he exclaimed, slapping his knee playfully. "They are very devout with their beliefs, but they are even more interested in finding their next husband."

I smiled politely, knowing the type. He was spot on about them. I flipped to the second page of the folded pamphlet, and blinked as I read some of the words. Then I looked up casually, waiting for Roland to read it. To anyone else, his face didn't change, but to me, it was a shout. He nodded absently, and continued reading.

Well, I wasn't one for political correctness. "You believe in monsters, Pastor Benjamin?" I asked lightly, pretending to continue reading, but in truth, I was finished reading this toilet paper disguised as a religious tract.

Pastor Benjamin leaned forward in my peripheral vision, and I could tell he was nodding. "Oh, yes. But monsters can take on any shape and size, so I'm not just hammering away at those conspiracy theories about wizards and whatnot." I looked up, acknowledging him politely, my face a polite mask. I ignored Roland's very discreet warning looks over his shoulder. "The Bible has many references to beings that obviously aren't human," Pastor Benjamin continued, "whether it's referring to demons, monsters, or those touched in the head," he admitted with a sad smile. "I put it in there because any kind of worship of such an ideal, whether real or not, only leads people further from God's Word. An era that idolizes demons and monsters, or really, anything, higher than God, needs to learn the error of their ways."

"If you aren't sure you believe in it, why put it on your flyer?"

"Oh, that is a long conversation, of which I would very much like to discuss at some point, but the short answer is that... well..." he faltered, as if not wanting to speak it out loud.

Desmond chimed in excitedly. "It's a conversation starter," he offered. I turned to look at him. "Everyone is talking about it with all the recent crimes, so we thought it best to have a stance on the issue, to help lead the conversation back to God."

I blinked at him. "This is pretty... ambiguous, though, isn't it? It seems that it could be taken as a call for violence," I said politely, managing not to grit my teeth. Roland and Father David looked genuinely alarmed, using their eyes to tell me to shut my mouth.

I ignored them, focusing on Pastor Benjamin. Desmond began to answer, but I held up a hand. "I'm sorry, Desmond. That question was for Pastor Benjamin," I said tightly.

I actually heard Desmond's teeth click shut.

Pastor Benjamin nodded thoughtfully, not noticing, but I could feel the bubbling energy from Desmond. He was ready to debate, not in a hostile way, but as anyone who was passionate on a topic would want to do. And practically fidgeting at not having the chance to speak his mind.

"Desmond is right. Everyone has an opinion on it, and we thought it best to include in the flyer. To give those seeking answers a path back to the light."

"Suffer not a witch to live..." I read aloud from the flyer. "Although *accurate*, that's kinda hardcore for a new church."

He nodded back. "But it is God's Word," he answered, sounding invested. "I'm not condoning violence, and although I know the words sound that way, I am simply shedding light on the topic with God's opinion on the matter." His eyes grew distant for a time. "I'm sure you can see it, everyone does," he said solemnly. I felt my skin beginning to crawl with the blood boiling in my veins. He was talking about people like me. "I should have been born during the Crusades. With a body like this?" he said, patting his mildly pronounced belly with a deep chuckle. "Lucky for the infidels, I wasn't," he winked. It was very obvious that he would have been a statistic during the Crusades, and he was trying to use humor to ease the tension in the room. He would be a good pastor. Looking at him, it was hard to remain angry.

But I was pretty good at keeping my anger stoked and ready to flame at any moment. Whether it was a girl thing or a wizard thing, I wasn't sure. Then again, Nate seemed pretty skilled in the anger department, so maybe it was just a wizard thing.

I nodded slowly, but before anyone could continue, I folded the pamphlet and placed it on the desk. "Well, it was a pleasure meeting you, Benjamin." I turned to the other two. "Desmond, Brigitte," I said, smiling with my face, but not my eyes. "We should probably leave, Claire. We have your appointment."

61

Claire slowly nodded, setting down her own pamphlet, a very thoughtful look on her face as she made her goodbyes. I ignored Roland as I walked from the room, barely keeping myself together.

Claire caught up with me in the hallway outside, and I heard the door close behind me. "Callie, where are you going?" she asked, her footsteps pattering to keep up with me.

"I need to go hit something. Let's head back downstairs for a few minutes. I just remembered this sword Roland had shipped here. I've been wanting to test it out."

Claire clasped my hand and let me tug her along. Her palms were sweaty, and she was silent for a few moments as we made our way back downstairs.

"Maybe I can try out that sword as well," she said under her breath, sounding distant and conflicted.

I nodded, realizing that this conversation must have been a severe wake-up call for the innocent Claire Bear. She was no longer a Regular. She was theoretically one of the monsters Pastor Benjamin was referring to, now.

I realized we were all very lucky that the fucking flyer hadn't sent her over the edge and caused her to shift in self-defense. And by we, I meant Pastor Benjamin and friends.

But there was always tomorrow…

CHAPTER 11

$\mathcal{C}$laire was napping in the corner of the training room, using a rolled yoga mat as a pillow as I sat in the center of the room, meditating. I'd spent about thirty minutes working on a heavy bag, deciding not to tempt myself with a sword in hand. At first, Claire had joined in, and I had shown her a few movements to practice. She had lasted about ten minutes before staring down at her knuckles, frowning, and then declaring she wanted to take a nap.

I had teased her about it as I continued working my bag, but it hadn't deterred her from curling up in the corner of the room to sleep. I worked until my muscles burned, and my breath panted, feeling much better.

Then I had plopped down in the center of the room to meditate.

I had a lot on my mind. I needed to get Claire to Armor and his bears, and I needed to track down the third wolf and Yuri. Knowing the two were tied together by the strange *God is dead* creed, I was nervous about these new friends he was supposedly spending time with.

Because it meant the fundraiser tonight could actually be a den of vipers. A creed meant a system. And if his new pals were going to a fundraiser, they had deep pockets. People with money typically had big agendas, and liked to use middle men to do their dirty work. If rich people had befriended Yuri, maybe there was a bigger game afoot.

Then again, maybe I was being irrationally angry after seeing the stupid flyer.

No wonder Mr. Light Eyes from the coffee shop had seemed so annoyed with the old women.

Religious tracts were typically written to elicit an emotional response. I knew that, but this one in particular had struck home to me. Maybe this was what it felt like when a gay person read one of those flyers that denounced their lifestyle. It sucked.

In that dark moment, a new thought hit me. What would happen when Pastor Benjamin's new church came face-to-face with the possible *God is dead* gang? I shivered at the thought.

Knowing I was angry, frustrated, and possibly too close to the situation, I had decided to vent my physical frustration out, and then to hopefully clear my head a little with meditation.

Because one thing had plagued my thoughts since a few weeks ago.

Something had… happened to me.

I had been helpless, tied to a cross with chains that blocked my magic, tortured, and forced to watch as a freaking Nephilim was murdered in front of me. But just when I had thought all hope was lost, something incredible had happened.

Johnathan had been on the verge of success, slicing open an Angel's feather for his ritual to open a Door to Hell. But something inside of me had connected with the single drop of silver, Angel's blood inside the feather, and I had been infused with strength like I had never imagined. That surge gave me the power to break free of my chains and kill Johnathan.

But in his dying eyes, I had seen something sinister. A shadowy figure with wings like shards of glass and shadows, sitting on a throne in a world of fire. And he had looked pissed.

The surge of Angelic power had faded somewhat since that time, but part of it had remained… like a whisper in the back of my mind. I no longer felt invincible, and my shoulder blades no longer ached, but I knew I had felt something back there, and the suspicious part of me had imagined wings.

My magic now had the potential to turn white when I was particularly emotional. And when that happened, whatever spell I was performing was… well, a hell of a lot more powerful than it should have been.

Had the Angel's blood reacted to me because my biological father had been a Nephilim?

But the stranger part was that Nate Temple also had this white-colored magic when he so chose. And that concerned me. Because he wasn't tied to the church at all. Not even remotely. He hadn't even heard about us before. And he definitely wasn't related to any Nephilim.

These thoughts had pestered me daily since that night, but I was no closer to finding the answers. My only option was to find Amira, the demon who had worked with Johnathan, and make her squeal. And to retrieve the Spear she had stolen, of course.

But I had struck only dead ends, there. I had retraced Johnathan's steps, and come up with nothing. I had even tried prayer, reaching out to Angels or Nephilim in hopes that my supposed bond with Heaven somehow gave me a direct line to the God Squad.

It hadn't.

So, I meditated. To stay sane.

I cleared my head of all distractions, all fear, all stress, all sensation, and imagined a single white feather rotating in the center of nothingness. As each sensation struggled against me, trying to catch my attention, I rolled it into the feather, and the feather responded with a light ruffle, as if catching a breath of air. Soon, all was still, and I let the sensation of peace roll over me as I focused on my breathing.

The feather began to darken in my vision, and then it ripped apart violently as dark whispers suddenly coalesced, screaming, shouting, and warning me to *move*.

Not knowing why, I listened. I rolled to the side and heard a heavy *thwack* strike the mat where I had been kneeling. I came to my feet fluidly, kamas of magic abruptly crackling in my fists as I slowly opened my eyes. Roland stood before me, grinning madly as he twirled a staff. Then he let out a laugh, seeing my kamas, and tossed it aside.

A dark purple, almost black staff appeared in his palms, seeming to make the very air groan as he slowly whirled it in a circle around his body before settling into an offensive stance.

I wanted to scream at him, to attack him, to ask *what the hell?* But I kept my face blank.

"I'm getting ready to go back to the Vatican," he said, watching me, "to meet my associate."

I began to nod until my brain registered how he had said it. "Your associate…" I repeated.

"The mole you've been searching for. The one who sold you out to Johnathan. He works for *me*. Did you really think the world was so complex? I worked for Johnathan, Callie. I let myself be harmed to give him a chance to get to you. After all, I couldn't very well get in his way, could I?" He chuckled. "I've always known you were special, that there was more to you. Not until Johnathan came did I realize just how special. But then you killed him," he said, frowning. "This made my job much more difficult. I had to seek out his partner, Amira. It took some time to persuade her, but I think my last task will finally earn her trust." He smiled savagely. "Bringing her your head will speak volumes."

CHAPTER 12

*H*is words hammered at me like a storm, but I dove back into my calm mental state, knowing if I focused on them for one more second, I would go insane. It just couldn't be possible.

And then he attacked with enough force to kill me, nothing like our usual sparring.

I met his staff with double strikes of my kamas, knowing his strength was way too intense for me to stop with only one blade. Sparks erupted, and I arched my back, guiding his spear over my chest as I played limbo to his staff, letting it sail over my head. I twisted my hips at the last second, and slashed out with my blades, slicing through the meat of his thigh.

He grunted at that, but it didn't slow him down. The smell of burnt meat filled the air as I stared him down with cold, dead eyes. He took a step back, studying me thoughtfully.

His confession whispered past my control, threatening to break me. I couldn't fathom it. That he had been behind it all, that he had sold me out to a demon…

But it made a hell of a lot of sense. Maybe it even explained why he'd been so cautious around Nate Temple, fearing that Nate would see through his ruse.

Roland swung his staff wide, the tip whistling as it sailed at my hips. I swiveled so that it struck only air, and flung one of my kamas at him. The blade screamed as it spun like a tomahawk, but he batted it aside with his staff, and was attacking me again, just as the Kama reappeared in my hand.

Rather than hooking my blade against his staff, I simply batted it to the side, using his momentum against him as I spun on the balls of my feet, leading with the tips of my kamas to stab into the side of his neck. Right before contact, my blades struck an unseen force, and I went flying backwards.

I instantly unleashed twin blasts of fiery light that resembled screaming crosses before I tucked my legs and flung out my hands to break the force of the fall onto my back.

Like Roland had taught me.

I slapped the mat with my palms, and kicked off with my feet, to turn my fall into a backwards roll, which I executed perfectly, landing in a crouch with my kamas out before me.

Roland's chest smoked where my crosses had struck him, obviously too fast for him to deflect, and he looked pissed. Then again, maybe they had hurt him because he was working with the demons.

When those events had started a few weeks ago, we had been fighting wolves, and they had behaved very oddly, even injuring Roland. And when he had retaliated, the wolf had been pinned to the tree in the shape of an upside down cross. Had even that been a sign I had been too thick to notice? How naive could I be?

Roland was chuckling as he approached. "You're beginning to see. To realize. To connect the—"

I threw both kamas, and then rapidly flung out a cord of power behind him, tugging it towards me so that it hit him in the back of the legs, sending him crashing to his knees as he focused on blocking or dodging the kamas, not even noticing the power behind him.

But I had started running before his knees touched the ground.

He lunged out with his staff in both hands, which suddenly had a horrific looking point at the tip. I jumped, almost horizontal to the ground as I batted it down with my left forearm – accepting the painful burn of its magic – and continuing my momentum to roll to safety over the staff. My feet touched down right where his knees met the ground, but I didn't stop moving. I pivoted on my left foot, spinning to my right again as I raised my right leg high up in the air. He dropped his spear, and grasped out to latch onto my base leg, but I was already too far into my movement, and my right leg came hammering down like an axe to strike the back of his neck. Rather than letting him take the full blow, I hooked my leg around his neck, the back of my knee pressing into the spine near his shoulders.

Then I let myself fall backwards, taking him with me. I grasped my right ankle with both hands as we fell, trapping his neck in a knee lock. One twist and his neck would break.

I stared into his eyes, panting, and watched as his face changed from disbelieving shock to…

Approval.

Then he tapped the mat.

I didn't let go, continuing to stare at him, not understanding.

"Callie, let him go," a nervous voice said from the corner of the room. I flinched, having forgotten Claire was here. She was staring at me nervously, as if fearing what I was about to do.

I turned back to Roland. "What the hell is going on?"

"This was a test," he rasped, throat still constricted by my knee lock. "To see if you could use your wits when everything that you stood for and knew as a solid foundation was shattered. You didn't cry, beg for an explanation, or yield. You acted. Defending yourself against your teacher, even though that betrayal should have broken your magic, rocking your trust. You over-came your emotions and reacted." He smiled at me. A light smile, but a very genuine, heartfelt smile.

"Swear it on your power as a Sheph—" I hesitated, changing my demand, "as a wizard."

He nodded slowly. "Very good, Callie. Even now, you prove your resolve."

"Fucking do it, Roland! Or so help me god, I'm about to sin all over this fucking place," I snarled, feeling my eyes burning, and my voice shaking.

But my knee didn't. Neither did my hand, ready to squeeze the life right out of my mentor.

"I swear on my power that I have never worked with the demons, never will, and have never done anything against your best interest, especially not the things I mentioned a few minutes ago. If I lie, may I go to hell and forfeit all knowledge to wander eternity blind, deaf, dumb, and powerless," he rasped, since I had subconsciously increased the pressure in my rage.

I let go, accidentally clocking him in the head with my heel as I released him. Then I accidentally stepped on his wrist as I climbed to my feet. Then, while tripping, I accidentally stomped on his crotch before regaining my balance.

Roland had twisted to protect his goods, but took the other blows with a grunt. Then he let out a low chuckle as he waited for me to get out of reach. His spear had crackled out of existence the moment I had solidified my victory over him. I stomped over to Claire, and accepted the blessed water bottle she handed me. I was shaking, and managed to spill a good chunk of the water down my chest as I tried to take a drink. Claire stared at me, sickened with pain at the look on my face. I ignored it, dumped some water over my head for good measure, and then slowly turned back to Roland.

He stared back at me, his arms folded over his knees as he sat on the ground. He looked both proud and sad as he nursed the fingers of the hand I had stomped on. I frowned over his shoulder, and he quickly turned to look. A Kama materialized in my fist and I threw it as hard as I could.

It stabbed into the mat all the way to the base of the haft, right between his legs – and microscopically close to his crotch. Then it began to burn the rubber mat, and he jerked back with a hiss. He finally looked up at me, an instinctive glare on his face, but then it faltered, and he let out a low sigh, nodding his head in understanding.

"I hate you, Roland," I whispered, trying not to cry. Then I turned to Claire. "Let's go take you to the bears." I began to walk away as Roland spoke.

"I've already spoken with Armor, and told them I will drop Claire off on my way to the airport," he said softly.

I slowed, breathing heavily as I kept my back to him. "Come on, Claire," I repeated.

Claire made a pained sound behind me. "I think it's best I go with him," she whispered meekly. "Especially if the bears are expecting me that way. And…" she hesitated, so I turned to look at her. She averted her eyes. "If you already had a rough morning with them, maybe it's best that you aren't the one to hand me off to them, reminding them of the embarrassment they faced this morning…"

I clenched my fists, and tried not to scream. Not at her. Not even at Roland. At the fact that she might have a point. I didn't want my introduction with them this morning to taint how they felt about Claire.

To be fair, my mind had literally just been fucked by the one person I thought I could always trust. But because of his twisted sense of honor and

70

dedication, he had used my trust as a blade to test my resolve, seeing if I would have the strength to stand up to my mentor if it felt justified.

Because he wanted to make sure I was safe while he was in Italy.

I slowly nodded and turned an arctic look on Roland. "Get to the Vatican, old man. Find my answers, and return with a full report. Better yet, call me with information as soon as you get it, because if they find out what you're really doing, you might end up dead before I get what I want. If I don't hear from you, we're going to have words. Short, sharp, burning words. And then I'll carve off your ears."

"Callie—"

"NO!" I shouted, suddenly gripping crackling white energy sticks in each fist. My hands were shaking as I glared at him, and he actually scooted a few inches back, face a grim mask at whatever he saw in my eyes. I let the sticks pop out of existence, but didn't lower my gaze. "I trusted you... And I don't think you ever realized what that means to me," I whispered.

And then I Shadow Walked back to my apartment.

I ran into my room, fell face-first onto my bed, and began pounding the mattress with my fists as I let the tears out, my jaws actually aching where I had managed to clench back the outburst until now. I don't know how long I did this, but at some point, I felt something fuzzy touching my face. I peeled open an eyelid to find my stuffed unicorn staring at me.

I latched onto it and squeezed it like a lifeline, inhaling the very faint smell of black licorice.

CHAPTER 13

$\mathcal{A}$fter a few failed attempts, I appeared before a giant wooden door with the Temple family crest emblazoned on the wood so that each of the doors held half of the symbol. I glanced behind me to see bonfires on the property, but since they all looked carefully controlled, and I could see several figures tending them, I dismissed them. I did take a moment to stare at a giant white tree on the property, easily hundreds of feet tall. But I didn't have time to gawk.

I pressed the doorbell, and a video feed sprang to life on a small screen – high and to the right of my head. An older gentleman in a suit looked at me, and then frowned. "Greetings, Miss…"

"Penrose. Can you take a message for Nate?"

The man looked perplexed, as if not exactly sure what to do. I heard shouting in the background on the screen, and spoke up as the confused man turned to acknowledge it.

"Tell Master Temple that the roof of the Ambassador is simply breath-taking this time of afternoon. Thank you," I said. I took two steps back, winked at the man's puzzled face, and then Shadow Walked to the roof of the Ambassador Hotel in Kansas City – the hotel where Nate had been staying when he had visited a few weeks ago.

I had never been to his house in St. Louis, but it really hadn't been that hard to find. Other than the odd resistance when I had tried to Shadow

Walk there, which I had never felt before, it had been a breeze. Maybe he had the place warded or something, and I had been able to break them somehow.

Probably a result of the Angel blood in me.

I sat in one of the two chairs before the table, and waited.

A circle of fire erupted a dozen paces away, and Nate Temple burst through with a whip of white electricity in one fist, a bulging satchel in the other, and a murderous scowl on his face. His tee wasn't all the way on, revealing chiseled abs.

His eyes darted about wildly as if searching for a threat until he saw me sitting at the table smiling at him. He blinked, lowered his satchel, and released his whip, letting out a heavy breath. The ring of fire extinguished behind him, and he fixed his shirt. Then he walked towards me on bare, tanned feet. He wore casual jeans, and his shaggy hair brushed his ears as he watched me.

He dropped the satchel beside the chair, sat down, and then rummaged inside without speaking to me. I waited, enjoying this.

He pulled out a dusty bottle, inspected it, and then blew on it. A patina of dust sailed into the wind, and he tore off the foil covering the top before twisting off the cork. The smell of heavy whisky suddenly permeated the air, and he took a drink straight from the bottle.

He silently handed it to me, still glancing about with a thoughtful frown.

I accepted it, took a drink, and instantly felt my eyes water. I pulled it away, coughed, and read the bottle. I didn't really understand much of it, but one thing I noticed was that it said 1937 on it. I looked up at him, and then tried again, this time ready for the smoky burn.

I took a big sip, pulled it away, and breathed what felt like fire for a moment. Then I settled the bottle on the center of the table, and nodded appreciatively. "I've never had anything like that. Do you always bring an ancient bottle of Scotch with you... to battle?"

He grunted, scooping up the bottle as if to use as a weapon. He scowled at it before taking a quick sip. "You damned well know how to cause an uproar, don't you?" he muttered. Then, he shook his head with a faint chuckle. He took another drink, stared off into the distance again, and began to laugh harder, until he was almost doubled over and panting.

I smiled at him curiously. "What's so funny?"

He sighed, finally turning to look up at me. "You. Just... you being you, I guess. We've got some nasty stuff going on back home, and my butler suddenly runs through the house like a Paul Revere impersonator, shouting about a white-haired wizard named Miss Penrose appearing at my front door," he flashed me a stern look from under his eyebrows, "past my wards, I might add... And something about the *Ambassador on the roof.*" His shoulders seemed to relax as he leaned back, resting the bottle on one knee. "Damn near caused a war. I had a line of people trying to come with me, thinking it was a trap related to our own problems. I had to bat them away with my satchel to come here alone."

I smiled back, and jerked my chin at his satchel. "Why did you bring the satchel and come here ready for a fight?"

He studied me for a long moment, eyes like green fire. "I thought you were in danger, but couldn't risk taking anyone from their rounds."

I laughed. But then held up my hands as I saw his face begin to darken. "No, no. I'm not laughing at *you.* It's just... I've had a really bad day, and the person I know the least is the most willing to throw down on my behalf. It's just..." I quested for the right words, but finally chose a shrug, "an unexpected gift," I admitted, smiling gratefully. "I didn't mean to cause a riot. I did mean to cause a *stir*, but I didn't know how nervous your crew was. I just thought it would be fun, and a phone call sounded lame."

He studied me for a long while before finally nodding, his shoulders seeming to relax. "Shitty days are my specialty, and you subtly hinted that all might not be well in paradise."

"I want to get an objective opinion. From another wizard," I said carefully. Because this wasn't my way of running for help. I genuinely wanted to talk to a colleague outside of the church. Someone untainted by their bureaucracy.

"Okay," he said, crossing his legs, waiting for me to continue.

I took a calming breath, and then told him about my situation. Not complaining, but as an academic discussion. I knew my emotions were raw, and that I might not be thinking objectively. My best friend had been attacked, and my trusted mentor had just thrown a huge curveball at me – for the sole sake of getting a reaction. I didn't want Nate's direct help, but I did want his mind. Someone with my knowledge of the world who was unaffected by the church.

He listened attentively, staring at me with his damning green eyes. I realized that I was babbling towards the end, more focused on his gaze than my story, so cut off abruptly.

He took another sip of whisky, turning to look out at the sky. "You were right," he said offhandedly.

I studied his profile – the sharp cut of his grizzled jawline, and the strong set of shoulders underneath his thin, plain white tee. I quickly looked away, refocusing. "About what?"

"The view," he said, gesturing outward. He slowly turned to face me, and then shrugged. "To be honest, Callie, it sounds like you're becoming a big girl." He didn't say it condescendingly. He actually sounded... sympathetic. "You went through some heavy shit with the demon thing, and in so doing, you showed Roland that you were one tough cookie. But he didn't see you in action like I did. He needed to really test you before he went off on his trip. It was a damned cruel way to do it, but most of the old guys I know are like that. They don't really think about feelings. Only the goal. The reward." He took another drink, and then set the bottle down carefully. "It sucks, but it is what it is. Even though he likely knew you would hate him for it, your safety was more important to him."

I was silent, considering his words. "I kind of suspected that. But... I felt too close to it to be objective. And in all fairness, his test could very likely be taken as truth and the shoe would fit."

Nate grinned wolfishly. "Ten bucks says he asks if you talked to another wizard about this the next time you two talk. That will be the second part of his test."

I frowned back at him. "No way..."

He grinned wider. "I guarantee it. The first step was to see if you could act in the moment. To keep your head. The second test will be to see if you sought out a form of objective proof to back up his claim, or if you simply took his word for it." He met my eyes, and his were ruthless, no longer smiling. "Like a good student would..."

"That's... no way. He would be *pissed* to hear that I blabbed about him to you," I argued.

Nate was shaking his head. Then he held up a finger. "Riddle me this. If Roland was in your shoes, would he have sought out proof? Tried to see if you were really lying or if you were telling the truth? Would he have simply taken your word for it?"

I opened my mouth to say *yes*, but hesitated. I leaned back into my chair, sighing in defeat. "He definitely would have sought independent verification..." I admitted begrudgingly.

Nate grinned proudly. "Looks like you passed both tests, then."

I found myself smiling faintly, still pissed, but proud, too. "Are old men always like this?"

Nate laughed. "You should meet some of *my* friends. Older than Roland by far, and they pull these kinds of stunts over a span of *years*. You don't even know about it until way later," he chuckled. "If it didn't sound like you had so much on your plate, I'd ask you to swing by for dinner," he said casually. "Everyone wants to meet you."

I nodded at him, smiling. "Soon. Once all this blows over. We have a lot to discuss."

"I don't think I can get away from my stuff in St. Louis or I would offer to help," he said.

I shook my head. "No, really. That wasn't why I called. I just wanted some hard truth."

He watched me intently. "Alright. Don't forget about that dinner, or lunch, even."

"I won't," I said, trying to hide the heat on my cheeks. It was just so hard to focus around Nate. I wasn't sure why. There was definitely an attraction between us, and it had almost gotten us in trouble when we first met. But we both had stuff to deal with, first. It would do neither of us any good to jump into bed together, as fun as that sounded.

At least... not yet.

This time, I did blush. He saw it, smiled a little wider, and then nodded, as if achieving a small victory. "Get out of here, rascal," I said, laughing.

"As you wish, Callie," he said, grinning like a schoolboy. He climbed to his feet, reaching down for his satchel. It was a tattered mess.

"Can't you afford a new one?" I asked, pointing down at it.

He glanced down, and then grinned. "I put them to hard use. And this one *is* fairly new."

I rolled my eyes. Boys. And they thought girls were hard on their purses.

"Just curious, but what's up with the claw marks on your stomach?" I said, pointing. "Baby werewolf?" I teased.

He cursed under his breath. "My cat's a freaking psychopath."

"You have a cat?" I asked, surprised.

He waved a hand. "I really don't want to talk about it," he said, blushing as he picked up his satchel, the bottle of whisky, and then hesitated. "I almost forgot. When this all blows over, I have someone you might want to talk to." His eyes twinkled in amusement.

"Okay," I said, mildly curious.

He flashed me a last grin, and then opened up a Gateway on the spot. He walked through it with much more arrogance than he had when he arrived. Or... a *different* kind of arrogance. Not ass-kicking arrogance, but a relaxed, calm arrogance, like a lion walking before his pride.

I leaned over, grabbed a piece of gravel from the roof, and threw it at his ass. He flinched slightly before glancing over his shoulder with a triumphant chuckle. "Later!" he shouted as he let the Gateway wink out of existence, leaving me alone.

I Shadow Walked back to my apartment, a big grin on my face.

My initial feeling of betrayal at spilling the story with Nate about Roland was now gone, replaced with a sense of satisfaction that I may have passed a second test from Roland. We would just have to see next time I talked to him.

I was still mad at him, but not as much as before.

Still, I would make his life hell for a few days once he got back to town. Just to keep him on his toes. I sat in a chair, glanced up at the clock, and nodded. Being around Nate made me feel restless, and with all the craziness after my training session, I felt as if I needed to let out a little more energy. I had time for a quick jog, which would limber me up in case things went to hell tonight.

I turned on some hardcore Kansas City rap as I changed, thinking furiously about what I wanted to accomplish, and how I could further impress Roland while he was away.

He wanted to test me, did he? Not without a price.

CHAPTER 14

The trees whipped past me as I pumped my legs harder, sucking in the cool breeze as it broke through the tall buildings around me. Whenever I found an alley, I would immediately dart through it, using it as a self-declared sprint zone. Firstly, I did this because if I was running for my life, I would be using alleys at every opportunity to help break line of sight with my pursuer.

Secondly, because it was amusing as all hell to watch people's reactions when they saw a young, petite girl suddenly sprinting for her life through dirty alleys, causing them to instantly search for my pursuers. The odd part about that was why these people were never around when I was *actually* being chased. Then again, it was most often at night, when people's sympathy and empathy for their fellow humans somehow faded away to nothing until sunlight once again reigned supreme.

But right now, I felt their eyes on me, even when I didn't catch them looking.

Upon exiting an alley, I would instantly slow back down to a steady, ground-eating pace, lengthening out my strides and keeping my motion fluid. It felt good, and I knew that this time the feeling wouldn't be ruined by Roland or Claire immediately after.

I had a few hours until the fundraiser this evening, plenty of time to finish a nice solid run, shower, change, and grab a bite to eat. I decided to swing by Pastor Benjamin's new church, since I knew it was close. I don't know why I cared, but knowing where it was seemed important, since their flyer had pissed me off so much.

I spotted another alley and ducked into it, exploding forward at top speed. The light extinguished as the tall buildings prevented any rays from touching the ground since it was late afternoon, and the sun wasn't at its zenith. Looking up, I noticed a chain-link fence barred my way, but I also saw a fire escape hanging down in front of a closed dumpster. Rather than turning around, I churned forward, leaping up to grasp the fire escape and swing before it could drop down. I landed atop the dumpster, took three steps, and then hurtled the chain link fence.

I sailed through the air, legs tucked and right arm extended. I absorbed the impact with my legs, squatting down into a shoulder roll, and quickly regaining my balance to continue my flat sprint. I looked up to gauge my direction, and saw a form slip out of sight just ahead. I almost skidded to a stop, because the way the form moved seemed way too fast. And one of the reasons it seemed too fast was because it had been entirely still before suddenly fleeing.

Not the slow measured pace of someone walking around a corner ahead of me, but someone peering around a corner and instantly taking off the moment I spotted them. All I noticed was a flash of brown skin, casually professional attire, and neatly pulled-back dreadlocks.

I decided to follow. Best case, I had startled someone and they had bolted. I would simply run past them, abolishing my paranoia. Worst case, someone was tailing me or at least doing something shady. I rounded the corner with my hands up defensively, and saw the same figure dart around another corner up ahead, which he couldn't have reached unless he was sprinting as fast – or faster – than I was. But he was doing it in a casual suit and loafers.

I poured on the speed, realizing we were now in a bizarre warren of interconnecting alleys wide enough to be loading areas. I dodged greasy puddles as best I could, trying to catch up to the running man.

Not sensing anyone else around, thus removing my fear of anyone noticing, I cast my concealment spell around me, transforming my motion into a water-colored blur that blended in with the brick walls around me. I listened intently as I reached the corner, and heard the patter of footsteps striking puddles ahead where the man could have either gone left or right.

I was panting as I skidded to a halt, glancing both ways at the intersection, but with all the echoes I couldn't be sure which way he had gone. Rather than wasting time debating, I chose right, knowing that it should lead back to the main streets faster. The alley ended in a forced left turn. I took it, running a dozen steps before I saw that it ended in a brick wall.

I gasped, shocked to find two sharply dressed people – a man and a woman – seated in oxblood chairs against the brick wall. The ground around them was perfectly cleared, not a puddle or piece of trash in sight, almost as if they had just swept it clean. But they didn't look the type to pick up a broom. No, they looked like they had a person for that kind of thing.

They stared back at me, sipping martinis, entirely unconcerned.

CHAPTER 15

The woman smiled sweetly at me. Sweet like poison. "This is no place for a lone wolf," she purred. Her face was pristinely smooth alabaster, and her wavy red hair glistened as if freshly styled and curled. Her eyes were wide and fearless in her long, narrow face, and she wore a red evening gown that displayed a nice swell of bosom. Her delicate neck was draped in fat pearls, and for the life of me, I couldn't place an age to her.

"Wolf?" the man murmured doubtfully, his voice clear and smooth. "I see a pup, dripping with desire, alcohol, and hot blood. My favorite," he said, licking his lips. But his tone wasn't threatening, more hyper-playful. He had long, sandy hair, slicked back to fit in with the professional crowd, and he wore a tailored charcoal suit with vibrant orange threads in a checkered pattern. He wore no socks, and bright orange loafers that looked ridiculously expensive. His pale-yellow shirt was open at the collar, and I caught a glittering golden necklace tucked into his wild swath of tan chest hair. His eyes were cunning, mischievous, and his double-cleft chin could have inspired a portrait or statue. Even with the unshaven cheeks.

"Darling, that should hardly impress you," the woman chided. "I always exude these flavors."

"True, Dear. Very true," he said, glancing at her hungrily as if seriously considering ravaging her right there in her seat.

I blinked back. "What the hell are you guys doing here?"

"Hell," the woman repeated, wiping a hand on her gown as if disgusted. "That crowd is too emotional if you ask me. Sulfur-scented millennials, complaining about the social injustice of their father abandoning them, and how it has held them back for *so* long." She flicked her hand, dismissing them from her mind.

"Well, Dear, their father did abandon them. Picked favorites and everything. Perhaps they just need a trophy to feel better. Then maybe they would get the…" his eyes sparkled for a moment, "hell out of our city."

"You can do better than that, Darling." She rolled her eyes. "Otherwise I'll have to move onto greener pastures. Like this fresh doe, here…" she said, eyeing me over the rim of her martini.

"Wolf," I reminded her, studying them openly. She made a soft sound of acknowledgment, smirking in amusement. "Are you Angels?" I asked politely.

"Hardly!" the man burst out laughing. "Much too stuffy for our taste."

"Honestly, Darling, the double connotations are getting quite thick, and none of them are altogether clever. Please stop or try harder."

"That's what she said," he said, obviously trying to rile her feathers. She sighed heavily in reply, but her eyes did smile faintly.

I interrupted their banter, realizing that if I didn't, they would jibe back and forth all day, an obvious hobby of theirs. "Did you two see anyone running this way before I came by?" I asked, not really sure why I was still standing here. Two finely-dressed strangers sitting on antique chairs in a dead-end alley, talking with a jogger. But they were definitely aware of the supernatural, which could be helpful.

"*The man in black fled, and the gunslinger followed…*" the man said, grinning excitedly. "Are you a gunslinger, child?"

I patted my empty hips. "Apparently not."

The woman spoke up, sounding clearly annoyed. "I don't care how uncouth it is for me to speak this openly, but you force my hand," the woman said, standing up to glare at me. I tensed, preparing for a fight. "Remove the spell. It's quite nauseating to see through it."

"Like a drop of blood in fresh milk," the man agreed, studying me as he took a sip of his martini. "It is a little jarring, child."

I blinked, and then realized what they were talking about. I still held up my illusion spell. But… it obviously wasn't hindering them much, just annoying them. Which pretty blatantly told me they were from my side of the railroad tracks. Not just aware of the supernatural, but they were some flavor of Freak. I dropped the spell, and shrugged my shoulders apologetically. "My apologies. It slipped my mind." I waited for the woman to sit and straighten her dress. "Do you mind if I ask your names?"

"Quite emphatically, I would imagine," the man said.

"One doth protest," the woman agreed. The man held up a palm without looking, and the woman slapped it with her own, also without looking.

Seeing my blank look, the man sighed. "I'm Darling, and this is Dear. We have many names, especially for each other," he said sensually, and I felt something as the woman shifted slightly, cheeks flushing.

"You are such a tush-man," she murmured coquettishly.

I stared openly. Had he just used magic to pinch her ass? If so, why hadn't it felt like a wizard? I had noticed *something*, but it wasn't anything like my magic or anything else I recognized. Alarm bells instantly began ringing in my head, but my curiosity was piqued, and since I had obviously lost the man in black I decided to question them, dig a little deeper.

"Oh, no you don't, Wizard," Dear warned me. "We'll have none of *that* nonsense."

I tried to make my posture unimposing. "What nonsense is that?" I asked, because I hadn't done anything.

"Colors. Colors swirling round and round, round and round," she said, motioning toward my head with her glass. "Makes me wish you knew half as much as you think. That would be fun."

Darling was nodding, sniffing the air. "Elderberry, sunshine, sawdust, and cut grass. It is rather confusing," he agreed.

"Right..." I said slowly, glancing at our surroundings openly. "Is this spot significant to you?" I asked, motioning at the emptiness around them.

"Why else would we sit here? These chairs are absolutely *orgasmic*," Darling said.

I couldn't hide my grin. "You sat here because you found nice chairs?"

"What chairs?" Darling replied, smirking.

The woman sighed unhappily, shifting on an antique wooden bench, the leather seats gone.

My jaw almost dropped to the ground. I had sensed nothing. The chairs were just... different all of a sudden. I waited for an explanation, but it became clear that Darling was just trying to get a rise out of me. I let it go, even though I wanted nothing more than to demand answers. "Have you two murdered anyone recently?"

Dear turned a questioning look at Darling, her pearl necklace clicking softly.

Darling leaned forward, swirling his martini absently. "That's rather relative. Define recently," he said. He sounded genuinely unsure, not mocking me this time.

"I don't know, this week?" I replied, getting frustrated. They turned to each other in silence.

Dear shook her head at him. "I don't believe so, Darling. I'm confident that was at least two weeks ago..."

He snapped his fingers in agreement. "I'm quite sure you're right. That was two weeks ago. And it was in Italy, or some such place. Somewhere with statues, anyway."

"Wasn't it Miami?" Dear asked, frowning as she tried to recall.

"How would I know, my Dear? I don't pay attention to every fly I swat or spider I crush."

She shrugged in agreement, turning back to me.

"I'm not talking about spiders and flies..." I clarified in a low tone.

Dear leaned forward suddenly, smiling as her eyes seemed to glow with intensity – swirling like different-colored paint mixing together. "Oh, but aren't you? These questions of Heaven and Hell. Your colors. Your scents. Do you know what you *should* be asking, Wizard?"

I studied her thoughtfully. "Please enlighten me."

She shook her head adamantly, leaning back as if I had said something distasteful. "Thank you, no. That is beneath me."

"Helping someone is beneath you?" I asked.

"No, the enlightening thing." She grimaced, taking another sip of her drink. "Or answering a question with a question."

I bit my tongue. "Well, if you haven't murdered anyone... *recently*," I added sarcastically, "can you point me to that new church around here?"

"The bloody one?" Darling asked eagerly, leaning forward in his now leather chair again.

"Ummm... maybe?" I answered, frowning at his description.

Dear chimed back in. "An aromatic pool of blood just painted her steps. Sadly, we don't have the time to enjoy it." She jerked her chin in a specific direction, looking regretful.

My skin pebbled. *"What?"* I practically shouted.

The woman dropped her glass, clutching at her ears. Then she shot me a dark scowl. "Learn your manners, and mute the trumpets and choir, Miss Penrose," she warned. Then, before I could ask what the hell she was talking about, she continued. "The new church on the block just recently received a shower of blood. A christening if you will," she said, chuckling.

"Baptism?" Darling offered as a polite correction.

She shook her head. "I don't believe they're Baptists, Darling."

"Ah. I see." He turned to me. "Regardless, while you have been quite entertaining, the blood is getting cold. It is only fresh for a few minutes, and it only happened fifty-seven seconds ago, by your bizarre measure of time."

"Oh, we must be off," Dear said urgently. "This part of town has truly gone to the Plebes if we can't even enjoy a drink in peace," the woman said. "And we do have a calendar to keep up with. Work to do. Orders to fill."

Darling turned to her. "I'll fill *your* orders," he said playfully.

She blushed. "Have at me, you rogue," she challenged with a sultry smile.

"That's my cue," Darling grinned at me. "Good afternoon, Miss Penrose. All that blood has reminded me of my appetite," he admitted, waving a hand towards the church.

"Are you two vampires?" I asked, suddenly nervous. It was dark in the alley. No sunlight.

They glared at me in unison, no longer playful. Then they let out a disdainful sniff, and shifted into smoky apparitions that abruptly dispersed on their own. As did the chairs.

CHAPTER 16

*W*ith nothing else to do in the dead-end alley, I turned and jogged back past the intersection where I had last seen the man. I soon found myself on the main road. A lamppost was littered with flyers, but the one on top was for the new church and pointed down the street to my right. I jogged that way, rounded the corner and saw the church less than a block away.

It was nothing special, just a modern building they had repurposed to their needs.

But a noticeable number of people were running away from the church entrance, and others were using their phones to take pictures of something.

Shit.

I pushed through the gathering crowd to find blood pouring down the steps in thick rivulets. A body lay in a contorted position, the stomach entirely missing, resembling a carcass in the wild. *God is dead* was written on the steps in fresh blood. I felt as if someone was suddenly watching me and spun reflexively, scanning the faces around me. After a second, I spotted the same black man fade into a crowd across the street. I took a step to pursue my stalker, but a cop car suddenly skidded to a halt on the street between us.

A young man jumped out of the car staring over my shoulder at the dead body. He was tall, dark, and handsome, as my mother would have said.

Strong build, but nothing obscene, and his longish hair brushed his cold blue eyes. He brushed his hair back with one hand, his face hardening – not with fear, but with fiery outrage and determination. Then he met my eyes, and I almost took a step back. His partner was already putting up crime scene tape around the perimeter, and I was within that perimeter.

The man nodded at me, motioning me closer. I let out a breath and retied my ponytail before approaching him.

I leaned against the back of the police car, eager to leave. Detective Beckett Killian was competent and thorough, but had only made me tell my account twice, where most cops liked to force out half a dozen repetitions – hoping to annoy you to the point that you might contradict your story, or remember an unrealized detail as you grew frustrated. It was a good tactic, but he didn't seem to ascribe to it.

"Could you help us with a sketch of this man from the alley?" His voice was like a low hum.

I shook my head. "Not enough to be helpful. He was African American, had dreadlocks, and was dressed in a casual suit with loafers. That's all I can confidently tell you."

He nodded absently, glancing back over my shoulder at the scene, eyes calculating. He had spent a considerable amount of time staring at the words painted on the steps.

God is dead.

"Alright. You're free to go. Keep your phone on in case I have more questions." He grew quiet, as if debating his next words. Then he leveled his blue eyes on me, face very serious. "Some sick bastard has a real hatred for the church, and with you working at Abundant Angel... Just be careful. Running through alleys might not be wise until we wrap this up."

I smiled, nodding obediently. "Good idea." I could see the frustration in his eyes, and it didn't look like it was just from this murder. "Shitty day?" I asked.

He turned, blinking at me, as if forgetting I was still standing here. Then he sighed. "You have no idea. Spent all morning at a bakery in Westport. And although it's obvious a big fight went down, we didn't find any bodies. Just a few wallets in the back room." He met my eyes. "Neither belonged to the missing owner."

I frowned, doing my best to look vaguely curious. "Weird..."

"But we posted their pictures on the news, and a few bar owners called in to say those two men had been there recently, causing trouble. Guess which bars?" he asked me. I shrugged back, my face a mask. "The same ones that last saw some of those missing girls…"

I shivered, not having to pretend. "Are you saying the bar owners are behind it?" I asked.

He grunted, shaking his head. "No. Just a strange connection. Then this shit," he said, eyes roving back to the body, which would soon be carted away by the coroner. "The bites are authentic. An animal did this. Last I checked, we didn't have anti-church bears wandering the streets. And it was done right here, not dumped after the fact," he spoke as if reciting the facts to himself, putting a puzzle together on a rainy day.

"Bears?" I asked, trying to look nervous.

He shrugged. "A big carnivorous animal. We don't know what kind yet," he admitted.

I nodded. "An animal eviscerates a woman on the steps of a church in broad daylight and no one sees anything?" I repeated, mind racing with implications. Was it Yuri and the wolf?

He grew silent, and I realized he was studying me curiously. "You don't sound scared."

I snapped out of it, grimacing. "Are you kidding me? Of course I'm concerned. But how would no one notice that?"

"That's the question," he replied, still watching me.

"Well, I'm at your disposal."

"Disposal…" he repeated, eyes flicking back over my shoulder. "I never liked that term."

I smiled warmly. "Just a phrase," I said.

"I don't like that answer either." A faint grin was tugging at the corner of his mouth.

"Well, hopefully I can be both helpful and useful, then," I laughed.

"One can hope," he chuckled. "Go finish your jog. But no more alleys," he warned. I nodded, saluted him, and began to turn away. "Callie?"

I slowed, glancing over my shoulder. "Yes?"

"You don't seem like a church girl."

I laughed, nodding. "You're a pretty good judge of character," I winked, and then began to jog, calling over my shoulder. "Just the wrong place at the wrong time."

"I wouldn't say that," he said loudly.

I grinned as I jogged across the street, hoping to catch evidence of the man I had seen, because I still felt his eyes watching me from somewhere nearby. I waited until Detective Killian wasn't looking to slip into the alleys. After ten minutes of fruitless search, I decided to head home. With cops crawling all over the place, I wasn't going to be able to get anything useful out of the scene. Maybe I would return after nightfall.

One thing was obvious. A Freak had murdered someone on the steps of the new church that was loudly standing up against monsters, and they had left behind a slogan that made my blood run cold. *God is dead.* Were Yuri and the third wolf behind this, or maybe their new friends? Was the black man one of them? Were Dear and Darling involved?

I needed to get cleaned up for the fundraiser. I could return to the scene later.

I did call Roland to give him a heads up, since I knew his plane would be taking off soon and that I wouldn't be able to reach him until tomorrow. I kept the conversation short, not opening it up for small talk, just letting him know I could handle it. He didn't sound excited about that, but he also didn't sound doubtful. Which, in an odd way, was comforting. But I still wasn't happy with what he had done.

He had dropped off Claire, and the bears had been as opening and inviting as Roland had ever seen. He casually mentioned that maybe I needed to work on my social skills, because he found them quite pleasant, as did Claire.

He surprised the hell out of me to tell me that the two rape victims were joining him on his trip to Italy. When he told them of his travel plans, they had suddenly remembered how to talk, screaming as they begged to stay with him. Apparently, the rapists hadn't been shy about showing them their wolf forms, and the girls were terrified to be away from the one man who had saved them from their captivity. Since he was taking the Vatican's jet, he had agreed to drug them, restrain them, and take them with him.

The son of a bitch did tell me that he hoped my talk with Nate had been enlightening. I hung up on him, cursing angrily.

Bastard men. Now I owed the billionaire from St. Louis ten dollars. That fueled my run home.

CHAPTER 17

I stood in the center of the room, my dark blue gown just brushing the marble floor behind me. My hair was pulled into an up do – held in place with silver chopsticks that sported a dozen tiny diamonds on the ends, a carat in total for each chopstick. Roland had given them to me – on behalf of the Vatican – after the demon ordeal a few weeks ago.

Some would call them a gift.

I saw them as a bribe. A flashy piece of bling to trick me into toeing the line for the Vatican and its interests here in Kansas City. It was also an employee uniform, since they had basically assigned me to every high society social event in town for the indeterminable future.

I did like pretty things, but I didn't like chains.

But... they were silver, and since I had reason to believe I might encounter some shifters here, practicality won out over my emotions. They were weapons on loan from the church. That soothed my disgust a little.

I held a flute of champagne in my hand, idly sipping as I kept the fake smile plastered on my face, scanning the crowd of tuxedos, old money and new money. This was basically recess for the elites, time to step out of the classroom and pretend to play nicely with each other – when in actuality they were mostly ruthless bullies, at least to each other. Some things never changed. The only way to beat the system was to change the rules.

I had received several pointed sniffs and numerous condescending looks over the course of the evening while listening to the mayor speak about the benefits of being charitable. Since I was on a job, I made the cross with my empty hand, and smiled sadly at each one.

This both offended them and forced them to not act offended. It was actually quite fun.

The men, on the other hand, glanced at me like they wanted to confess some sins in private – both past, present, and future. These were somewhat harder to deflect, but I did my best. The most fun way was to walk up to his spouse, compliment her outrageously, and subtly mention salvation or something else churchy and pious. Or about my wholehearted devotion to missions and God, basically a Sister in training.

Most left me alone after that. And the women seemed particularly grateful to see I wasn't on a serving tray for their husbands to nibble.

Still, it wasn't why I was here. Sure, it was why the Vatican wanted me here – to make a good impression, and to ease concerns over the auction that had turned into a warzone a few weeks back. My job was to be seen, look pretty, be nice, be sweet, mention the church, the Vatican, and then move on without ruffling any feathers.

But my personal reason was to sniff out Yuri and his pals. And as I assumed, I didn't see any other bears present. After telling me that I might find Yuri here, it wouldn't have made sense for one of their group to show up and possibly scare Yuri back into hiding.

I watched the crowd, but saw no familiar faces. No recognizable monsters.

The vampires hadn't received a warm welcome in my city over recent months. Apparently, Nate Temple had come to town and killed the entire coven, or Kiss, as they sometimes called themselves. Then, Master Simon had stepped in to take over, but he'd gotten involved with the Spear debacle, and Nate and I had killed him and a pile of his followers in self-defense.

I wasn't sure if any of his vampires had survived, but if they had, I wasn't expecting a Christmas card any time soon. The wolves were still out of town, too, which made me slightly nervous. They had fled because of Johnathan, so maybe they hadn't returned because they knew Amira was still here. A demon was keeping them out.

And in that vacuum, the bears believed new neighbors were moving in. Like Yuri's pals.

I was beginning to realize that it may be beneficial to become acquainted with the various factions in town, because it was hard to get a pulse on the city without knowing the players. For example, Darling and Dear. They were obviously Freaks of some flavor, but I had no idea what kind. Then, a predator had eaten that woman at the church. Wolf or Bear? Or something else? The stalker from the alley, too. He'd been too fast to be human. I needed to learn more about my city.

I spotted a tall, pale man slipping through the crowd, surrounded by beefy bodyguards in suits. I made my way closer, hoping to intercept him. To be fair, I was profiling him as a vampire, when he could have just been a rich, computer nerd, allergic to sunlight. But my magic told me that Freaks were present. I just needed to put names to faces. Or simply get a face. Or a name. Or at least get a grasp on what kinds of Freaks mingled with high society.

Before I could intercept him, two of the beefy guards stepped directly in front of me, barring my way. They didn't smile, and didn't apologize. I tried to sidestep around them as the pale man walked past, but they stepped with me, blocking my advance. I scowled up at them. "Is there a problem?" I asked icily.

"Not yet, Miss Penrose."

I frowned up at him. He was at least two-hundred-fifty pounds of solid muscle. His partner looked softer, less sculpted, but larger. They both had meticulous crew cuts and ear pieces. "Then let me pass," I said in a low, warning tone, since they obviously knew who I was.

"That isn't an option. Especially after today," the same guard said, staring down at me. Not kindly, but not unkindly either.

"Don't tell me he's scared of me," I said, holding up my arms with a disarming grin.

"Listen, you're beautiful, doll. And dangerous. You aren't meeting Haven. He's very well versed on Simon's brief tenure in Kansas City. It seems like you Missouri Wizards like to get directly involved. I'm sure he'll request an audience with you in the future. At a time and place of his choosing." He leaned closer, as if to tell me a secret. "But that is not tonight."

The new Master Vampire was named Haven. At least that was something.

The guard turned to leave, but I placed a hand on his shoulder.

His friend's hand darted out to smack mine away, but I dropped it just in time. Everything happened so fast that no one around us noticed. The three of us stared at each other in silence.

"Don't touch me again, Miss Penrose. You won't like it."

The doughier one leaned closer, murmuring in a very low, jovial tone. "But I might," he said with a dark wink. "I like playing with shiny things."

"Be careful, Igor. Shiny things can be sharp."

He chuckled, nodding. "I hope so. But I have cushion, if you haven't noticed," he said, patting his belly.

I couldn't help it. I smiled back, nodding. "This isn't over. I expect a meeting. I don't have a problem with Haven. I didn't even know his name. But I'm thinking we should all be a little more aware of each other. To avoid further misunderstandings."

The first man nodded. "I'll let Haven know your desire."

I rolled my eyes. "Please don't phrase it like that. Just because you work for a creep, doesn't mean you need to pick up the corny lines. Otherwise, I'll be forced to speak in Latin to really drive home the stereotypes," I added dryly.

He burst out laughing. "I think Haven will like you, Miss Penrose." He held up a finger. "But not tonight," he reminded me. "Go have fun. This has been a pleasant introduction. We should savor it like a fine appetizer to the future meal."

"Jesus. You really can't help yourself, can you?" I asked incredulously. I knew neither of the guards were bloodsuckers, which meant the macabre jokes were transmitted via osmosis.

He shrugged, eyes twinkling with silent laughter. "Comes with the job, I guess."

"Fine. I don't think they're serving protein shakes here, but I did see a trio of pretty girls looking for important men over there," I said, pointing discreetly. "Maybe you should say hello."

The bigger one looked suddenly interested, but the muscle-head smacked his arm. "We're working," he scolded. Doughboy sighed regretfully, and then they both left.

I watched them, sipping my champagne absently. I had no hope of getting past them, because in their eyes I had seen competence. These weren't blood-bags for their Master's traveling food truck. These were hired muscle, and they had experience. They weren't infected by a vampire's kiss – that addictive venom that turned their living victims into junkies.

These were clean, strong, able men. And there were at least three more still circling Haven.

And they had known me.

Maybe I was the only one who didn't know all the players.

Frustrated, I headed over to the bar, where I could see more of the younger crowd hanging out, talking to each other politely. Like the kiddie table at a big family dinner – secretly wanting to join the adults' table, but pretending not to care.

I had drifted through the crowd three times, but hadn't seen Yuri or a Hispanic man that smelled like a werewolf. I definitely hadn't seen anyone suspiciously exchanging envelopes in private corners. I guessed Haven could be involved with whatever was going on. He was new in town, so maybe he had hired Yuri to solidify his rule. Local help was always smart when entering a new city. They knew the players and underbelly already.

And a local bear as a bodyguard to a new vampire was a conversation starter, giving the other factions pause as they debated the significance behind it. Two Master vampires had died in town in a span of months, so it made sense that Haven was less than interested in meeting the resident vampire killer.

I sat at an empty stool, staring down at my champagne. It wasn't a favorite of mine. Quite the opposite, in fact. Remembering Dear and Darling drinking martinis, I ordered one.

Because the night was young.

CHAPTER 18

I felt eyes watching me and turned to see a handsome college student down the bar eyeing me. He didn't look pleased to be here, but I didn't recognize him. I smiled back, and he returned the gesture with a very hollow smile before turning back to the pretty girl next to him. Maybe he felt guilty about staring at another woman when he was obviously here with someone else.

I didn't get any dangerous vibes off him, so dismissed him.

"You may call me Prince Charming," a voice to my right said. I turned to find a thirty-something man staring directly at me, facing me fully as he swiveled on his chair. He wore a black pinstripe suit over a white silk shirt, and the buttons were undone to almost the top of his abs, displaying an expanse of golden jewelry that would make any mobster jealous.

He was leaning back with his legs wide open as if his jewelry was a neon sign pointing down to his love stick – like a Vegas slot machine whispering for me to try my luck. His pants were tight, emphasizing the jackpot potential.

I took a sip of the martini the bartender must have dropped off, glancing at his face. He had flowing, light brown hair that brushed his shoulders, professionally styled for maximum volume. His eyes were steel gray, and he had a very European look to his facial structure. Chiseled, but angular. He wore a tight lip ring in the center of his lower lip like a painted silver line, and his teeth were perfectly white.

All-in-all, he was stunningly... pretty. Handsome and manly, for sure, but also pretty. Flawless. Like those photo-shopped underwear models. Too pretty, really. Too much maintenance. I tried sensing him with my magic to get a read on him, but all I felt was a low humming sensation, like I was standing beside a purring generator. Nothing dangerous that I knew of, but definitely not a Regular.

I gathered my wits, and realized I hadn't actually answered him yet. "Call me Snow White."

"Truly?" he asked, eyes dancing merrily.

I blushed at that smile. Good freaking god. He wasn't a vampire, I could tell that much, but I definitely felt weak in the knees at that look. "No, I'm not Snow White," I said, rolling my eyes.

He blinked, then waved a hand. "Oh, I knew that. I meant about calling you. Does that offer stand?" He placed his forearms on his knees, leaning closer, allowing me a glimpse down his shirt to feast on the slabs of muscle perfectly situated on his chest. I just wanted to reach out and let my finger-tips trail over them to see if it was real.

I took a hasty drink, and then placed my elbows on the back of my chair, emphasizing my chest openly as I studied him. Trying to get a read on him by seeing his response. His gaze never left my eyes, and I realized that this entire time, they had never left the area below my nose.

Not once.

"Alright, not Prince Charming. You really need to work on your pickup lines. Why would you want to call me?"

He leaned back, mimicking my posture with a grin. "For fun, of course. And I guess you can call me Vane. James Vane. But that wasn't a pickup line. I tell everyone to call me Prince Charming." He leaned closer, whispering conspiratorially. "Even the boys..." He pointedly glanced over my shoulder at the young college student I had seen eyeing me earlier. I turned to see the kid blushing back. Until he saw me. Then his face grew cloudy again. I sighed, turning back to the entertaining Mr. Vane. The name was too easy to tease, so I let it slide.

I found myself smiling. "You go from a children's story to James Bond?" I glanced down, noticing his martini. "Shaken or stirred?" I asked in a fake British accent, rolling my eyes.

He whirled his glass in lazy circles, smiling. Then he slid it my way. "Neither," he said, motioning for me to take a sip.

Not being an idiot, I did no such thing, but I did sniff it. I blinked up at him, surprised. "Rumple Minze?" I asked. The peppermint schnapps smelled like a nuclear breath mint.

He nodded. "I like the stronger stuff. More fun." He finally studied me in full form. Not in a creepy way, but in an assessing way, as I would expect a girlfriend like Claire to do when I was trying on a dress. Then he met my eyes again. "I doubt you'll find what you're looking for, here," he said softly. "No sulfur. In fact, it seems everyone is disgustingly shy and polite. Blech," he said, sticking out his tongue.

I blinked, suddenly very interested. "What am I looking for?"

He squinted. "You don't know? Well, that *is* my specialty."

I leaned closer, trying to keep our conversation quiet and private. "You mentioned sulfur. Where would I find someone with that particular perfume?" I asked carefully, not even caring that he seemed to know quite a bit about me. Maybe he knew where I could find Amira.

"Not here, like I said."

"Well, what about a bear?"

He shrugged offhandedly. "I think one was here earlier, but he wasn't very good looking, so I didn't pay much attention," he replied honestly, as if speaking of the weather.

I wanted to grab him by the shoulders and shake the answers out of him. He was maddeningly playful, but now that I knew he had useful information, it was no longer cute. "Tell me something!" I whispered urgently.

He studied me thoughtfully, toying with his lip ring. "The Freaks are going crazy in this town. Two Master vampires killed, a demon killed, wolves killed, a Shepherd, and his woman in white," he said, winking at me. "Then you have a church denouncing us, and a retaliation murder on her steps. It's all shaping up to be quite fun, really."

I really couldn't tell if he was flirting with me or the boy down the bar, so wasn't sure how to best manipulate him. He seemed to like fun. Chaos. Drama. "I do know how to have a good time," I said softly, staring straight into his eyes as I took a sip of my martini.

He smiled back, not necessarily falling head over heels or anything, but very aware of me all of a sudden. "You and that Temple fellow," he said, eyes growing distant. "So intriguing…" he snapped out of his reverie, looking disappointed. "But I hear engaged life suits him. Pity. I hear he almost has no fun anymore."

I coughed into my drink. "I think you'd be surprised. And from what I hear, I don't think the engagement is going as planned," I admitted, wondering if I could use Nate to get him to open up. It was pretty obvious that James Vane was open to dudes. Maybe even both women and men. It sounded like it fit him.

He surprised me by clapping his hands. "Delightful! Perhaps you can introduce us…" He turned a quizzical eye my way at a sudden realization. "Which means I must enamor you, first. A lavish evening. Or two. I fear I must dazzle you, Callie. It really is the only way." He sighed dramatically, as if exhausted at the prospect, and I couldn't help but smile. James seemed very knowledgeable, and might be just the one I needed to learn from. It was becoming obvious that my name was known around town and that I was the only ignorant one in the city. I needed to mingle with the monsters. "The things I do to get my foot in the door." He sounded pained, but didn't bother to hide his mischievous smile at the prospect of seducing me to get to Nate.

"You want to seduce me to get an introduction with Nate Temple?" I asked, making sure I wasn't mishearing him entirely.

"Oh, don't worry about your honor. You're exceptionally stunning, but you stink," he said.

"I beg your pardon?" I spluttered.

"Of morality," he said, waving a dismissive hand. "Not my thing."

"I'll have you know I don't stink of any such thing," I argued, feeling my face growing hot.

"Please. You work for the church. I can smell the feathers from here. You hunt monsters who are just trying to have a little fun. You even wrecked what could have been a very enjoyable auction a few weeks ago," he added as an afterthought.

I almost dropped my glass. "You were there?" I asked incredulously.

"Damn and bother, no," he growled. "I was otherwise… engaged." He laughed at that, slapping his knees. "But I will take you out for a night you won't forget."

I sighed. "No thanks. I came here for answers."

He frowned. "Most of the people you're really looking for will be at my soiree tomorrow night. Bring a friend. No one will dare harm you in my care. Have a good enough time, prove to me you're not a Puritan, and I may even have some answers for you."

I nodded, hiding my excitement. "Answers to what? You don't even know my questions."

"Oh, honey. It's all over your face. I know the answers you seek, trust me. Even if you don't know the real questions yet." A tall, lithe man leaned in close to whisper into Vane's ear. He sighed regretfully. "I must go." He reached into his coat pocket and pulled out a card. He handed it to me and I glanced down at it, frowning. All it had was an address on the front, and a phone number on the back.

"More details would be great… Like a time." I said.

"Eight." Then he leaned in and pressed his lips against my cheek – his silver ring like an ice cube between his hot lips. I almost gasped, but before I could pull away, he was already gone, walking away without a glance.

I scanned the room, noticing that quite a few people had already left. I spotted Haven, still surrounded by his wall of man meat, but I knew I'd have better luck propositioning my stool for a quickie than I would at getting the chance to talk to him.

I turned back to the bar, tapping the card against the counter as I stared ahead, thinking about James Vane. I felt a presence sit next to me, and glanced over. The college kid met my eyes, and then began tapping a similar card against the counter, mimicking me. He looked pissed off.

I rolled my eyes with an impatient sigh. "I'm bringing a date. He's all yours."

He grunted. "Everyone brings a date, obviously. Three is more fun than two." Then he stormed away, leaving me baffled.

I was beginning to realize Kansas City was one fucked-up place.

With no sign of my suspects, I decided I had better things to do with my time.

CHAPTER 19

The night enveloped my city like a warm blanket. I wore black spandex workout pants, black cross-trainers with the familiar white stripes, and a black jacket over my sports-bra – which had won by lack of competition since all my workout shirts were dirty. It was warm outside, but I wanted to cover up as much flesh as possible. I had brushed out my hair and tied it back into a ponytail again before hitting the streets to visit the church. I wanted to return to the crime scene in hopes that the cops had left, and that I might be able to find evidence they had missed.

Something Freaky.

My walk had turned into a jog halfway there, impatient to see if this was another waste of time. Because all I had to show for tonight's fundraiser was an invitation to a party tomorrow with a sexually fluid, stunningly pretty man. If I wanted answers, I needed to prove that I wasn't a saint. Or use Nate as a bargaining chip, since Vane seemed so interested in him.

I hadn't found Yuri, the third wolf, or Amira. I decided to revisit the mansion in the morning – where I had killed Johnathan. I felt a slight rise of bile in my throat, remembering how he had tricked me into thinking we were dating potential. Before I discovered he was a demon.

You could understand why I was a little slow in the dating department. I either swooned for a troublesome billionaire who was already engaged, a demon, or a man who played both sides.

Roland and I had visited the house a few times already, but perhaps searching by myself would be more productive. Rather than following Roland around like an obedient puppy, maybe being there would trigger something in my memory. At least it couldn't hurt. Because I was sick and tired of Amira haunting my thoughts. I wanted answers, and the Spear back. Because I secretly felt like a big failure. I had relinquished a holy item to demons.

I had been jogging more often, trying to use myself as bait to lure Amira out into the open. Basically, tempting fate by placing myself in perfect ambush spots with no one around to hear me scream. But she hadn't revealed herself. Maybe she really had fled, deciding to use the stolen Spear in a different city. Maybe I wasn't as important as Johnathan led me to believe.

I let out an angry sigh, putting thoughts of Amira and demons off until tomorrow.

As I scanned the quiet streets around me, I remembered the strange man who had been stalking me earlier. Was he the murderer? He was in the right place at the right time. Perhaps he had purposely led me away from the crime scene so I wouldn't interfere. Carefully guiding me into the hands of Dear and Darling – the strangest couple I had ever met. Were they in on it? Were they friends with Yuri? Had I stumbled onto something and just didn't know it yet?

The problem was that everyone seemed to know about me, where I was ignorant to the other players in the game. I guess being notorious might prevent one of them killing me in my sleep.

I pounded the pavement harder, stretching out my legs as I heard loud voices nearby.

As I rounded the last corner, I stumbled to a jerky stop, staring. A small crowd – maybe a dozen people – filled the sidewalk in front of the church. They held candles or signs that read varying renditions of what the church's marketing flyer had said. A whole lot of scripture about idols, monsters, demons, and *suffer not a witch to live* type stuff. I even saw one that said *Kansas City Witch Trials* with a crude, stick-figure drawing of a woman burning on a cross.

Several of them were shouting their message, which was what I had initially heard.

Good lord. This was getting way out of hand. There was no way I was getting anywhere near the scene. I very consciously thought about my hair. Although it wasn't red, it was startlingly different from most people, and I suddenly thought about an angry mob seeing something that stood out, and deciding *we don't need that kind of thing in this god-fearing town.*

Fear. Hate. A ticking bomb.

Whoever had killed the woman was laughing their ass off right now.

Two policemen stood beside the crime scene tape, looking very uncomfortable at the growing crowd, who were beginning to chant things that made my skin pebble after only a few words.

I was still out of immediate eyesight, and had a sudden idea. Mob mentality was easy to manipulate if you knew the hot buttons. I turned my back and rounded the corner, out of sight entirely. I tried something new to me, not seeing any reason why it wouldn't be possible.

I opened a tiny Gateway in midair, the size of my shoulders. With a nervous gulp, I leaned forward so that my upper body was entirely through the opening – which would startle the living hell out of anyone who saw my legs, so I made it quick. My head was in a narrow alley on the other side of the crowd, about a block away from them. It was empty, thankfully. Or else I would have been able to add *scaring the actual shit out of a homeless person* to my resume.

Considering one of the chants I had just heard, I belted out a loud, mournful howl, impersonating a wolf. The sound reverberated off the narrow alley walls, echoing and amplifying. I did it one more time, in a slightly different pitch, and then quickly pulled my head back out of the alley, letting the Gateway vanish. I walked back around the corner, staring ahead as if I had heard the wolf howling as well, and was nervous about continuing forward.

But no one in the crowd noticed me, because they were suddenly shouting, screaming, and running towards the sound, brandishing their candles and several bludgeoning weapons I hadn't noticed before: tire irons, sticks, and baseball bats. Since we were in Missouri, I knew there would be a handful of guns as well, and instantly felt bad, hoping that no one accidentally stumbled into the alley.

The cops followed the crowd, hands on their pistols, and obviously unsure whether they should be halting the crowd or supporting them, because my howl hadn't been the type of sound a dog would make. It had been more feral, wild, and dangerous.

Which left me a minute or two to observe the crime scene undetected.

I ducked under the tape and extended my magical senses, holding out my hands. The steps had been scrubbed clean. I felt nothing immediately alarming, but I did feel a presence that was definitely magical. I sniffed the air, not just with my nose, but enhancing my senses with magic to pick up on any supernatural scents.

And then I caught it.

A familiar stench. Werewolf.

But something else was present, too. I tried to focus on it, but it slipped away elusively. I realized my emotions were running hot with the wolf angle, focusing on the third wolf I had let get away earlier this morning. The local wolf pack was gone, so it seemed likely he was my guy.

I took a deep breath, closed my eyes, and focused on my mental feather, discarding all personal thoughts, and focusing on the scene before me. Something was... wrong. Like a flicker of motion out of the corner of my eye, but when I turned to look it was gone.

I pulled deep, trying to force the scene to talk to me. Force the world to obey. I struggled, strained, reached, clawed, stretched...

And I felt a small flush of heat deep within my stomach. I gasped as something astonishing seemed to open up inside me. Not *entirely* open, but as if I had cracked open a door.

I slowly lifted my head, frowning as my fingertips began to tingle. I stared at the scene.

That's when I saw it. Something entirely different than the wolf. A cloaking spell. And it was much more recent. I followed the trail, relying solely on this strange power inside me, turning as the world seemed to whisper to me, pointing me away from the church. It almost felt like my senses were heightened – much more so than with my usual magic – and that it was an extension of this strange feeling inside me from within that cracked door. Not really that I was more aware of the world around me, but as if...

The world around me was talking *back*.

The street before me abruptly flushed silver, as if everything had just been splashed with chrome. And I saw a wavering ribbon hovering in the air, leading across the street. A hooded figure abruptly materialized at the end of the ribbon, and he flinched looking startled as his hood locked onto me.

I heard a throat clear politely, and flinched as I realized someone was standing only a few feet away, staring at me.

Detective Killian studied me with a frown, dressed in colorful workout clothes. I blinked back at him in confusion at the sudden colors, then glanced over his shoulder where I had seen the apparition in my mind. The chrome world was no more. Had that chrome power showed the present, or some replay of earlier in the day? I saw a faint shift against the bricks, almost like a heat wave, and I was suddenly running.

CHAPTER 20

I barreled past Detective Killian and across the street, ignoring his shouts as I pursued the hazy blur that was suddenly tearing down the sidewalk. I heard Killian racing after me, but I ignored him, trying to bring back the chrome world I had briefly glimpsed, whatever the hell it had been. Because trying to keep my eyes on an almost invisible heat wave couldn't last.

My fingers tingled abruptly, and the chrome world flickered back into view. I gasped at what I saw, reacting instantly as the silver world flickered away, revealing a clear sidewalk. But I had already leapt, extending my foot forward and tucking up my back foot like I was running a hurdle race. The trash can that had been leaning against the building abruptly slid underneath me. Without my jump, I would have slammed into it. And I hadn't sensed even a whisper of the magic that had shoved it into my path at the perfect second.

But in the silver world, I had seen the trash can skidding sideways in slow motion, directly into my path.

I strained for that silver world again, pulling through the cracked door inside me as I ran. It began flashing intermittently over the real world, like I was running in a strobe light that wasn't bright enough to hurt my eyes. I heard the cop trip and stumble behind me, but I didn't turn to look, stretching out my strides to catch… whatever this hooded guy was.

The figure darted into a dark alley right before the silvery world flashed into view for a moment – revealing a silver comet slowly shooting out from the depths of the alley. The world flickered back to normal, but I trusted the silver world and ran up the alley wall directly ahead of me rather than darting down the alley in immediate pursuit. I managed three steps up the wall before turning it into a backflip.

As I spun upside down, I saw an icy flash of power brush the tip of my ponytail, singeing the hair slightly. My feet struck the ground a heartbeat later, and I continued to run.

I heard the policeman shout in alarm as the blast shot past him and into the street, but I didn't hear any major damage – like I would if it had struck him or a vehicle or a window or something.

Briefly seeing another silver warning, I dropped to my knees, skidding as I leaned all the way back – parallel to the damp ground, feeling my hair sliding through a greasy puddle.

A nearby dumpster exploded outwards, the contents flying laterally across the alley, directly over my head and chest to splatter into the opposite wall. I heard a muttered curse ahead of me as I scrambled to my feet, following the trail that kept flashing into and out of existence. The darkness of the alley made it so that the only time I knew I was on the right trail was with the silver world wrapped tightly around me, so I grasped it like a lifeline, feeding my power into the strange world, feeding it. If it disappeared, I would lose my lead. But I knew the power was fading, because I felt it slipping.

I lashed out with a blast of power that was not magic – simply a duplication of what I had seen the figure ahead do – and three golden ribbons of light launched from my hands like a braid of golden rope, hammering into the figure and blasting away his concealment spell, leaving him visible to the naked eye for the first time.

He stared back in surprise, but the dark alley didn't let me get a clear look at his face. It was more his body that looked familiar to me. Strong, stacked proportionately, and very athletic.

But that didn't help me. Every single guy I had seen lately had exhibited a banging body.

I didn't slow down, but actually increased my speed. He abruptly did the same. He made a sharp left a few steps ahead of me, and I held up my hands as I rounded the corner, shielding myself from whatever might be coming my way. The silvery world almost flickered into view one last time, but instead vanished like a cloud of smoke, and I almost collapsed with a groan.

I stared at a dead end, and I was entirely alone.

I heard panting behind me accompanied by pounding feet.

I let him approach, folding my hands on my hips, breathing heavily as I glared at the wall, making sure I didn't appear threatening. The exhaustion seemed to fade quickly now that I wasn't trying to tap into my strange new power, but I knew that if I tried again, I would likely pass out in a heartbeat.

"Good fucking god, woman! What the *hell* is going on?" Detective Killian wheezed, stopping a few paces behind me.

I slowly turned to face him, and found him clutching his knees, staring up at me. He didn't look threatening, especially not doubled over like that. But he also looked like he was trying not to *appear* threatening. As if he hadn't suspected me of doing anything wrong, and had simply been pursuing me to make sure I was okay.

"I saw someone. He looked shady."

He blinked up at me, sucking in air. "I didn't see a damned thing. Other than some kind of fireball shooting out of an alley and things exploding."

I nodded absently, not answering his unasked question.

He finally straightened, leaning back against the wall and peering over my shoulder curiously. Seeing nothing, he assessed me. "Does this have anything to do with your hocus pocus stuff back at the crime scene?" he asked.

I blinked at him, suddenly very nervous. My eyes shot to his hip, looking for a gun, but he slowly lifted his hands, showing he was unarmed. He even spun in a very slow, dramatic circle. I remained silent.

He took another deep breath, seeming to regain his control. "You could literally push me out of the way right now, and I wouldn't be able to stop you. You can fucking *run*," he said, shaking his head as he laughed, complimenting my speed.

"Yeah," I said numbly, not sure what else to say. "You saw me at the crime scene?" I asked. I had been standing in the center of it when I noticed him for the first time, but my question was more *what* he had seen me doing.

He nodded, and then let out a casual shrug. "You weren't hurting anything," he said.

My eyes might have widened at that. "That really doesn't matter, though, does it?"

"No," he said, shaking his head. "Most would cuff you and bring you in."

I let the silence stretch, cocking my head at him, at a loss for words. He was definitely a Regular. No power at all radiated from him. I realized I was using my magic without effort, proving that the new power had nothing to do with me as a wizard. I studied him, not understanding. He didn't seem terribly concerned about me tainting his crime scene. "Well… I take it you aren't going to cuff me?"

"I'm not really into bondage," he said, smiling teasingly.

Against all odds, I found myself smiling in relief. Because if he found it necessary to arrest me, I was pretty sure I would have to comply. He already had my information and knew where to find me. So even if I escaped, he would just be back in the morning to arrest me, probably with a contingent of fellow officers.

"Neither am I," I admitted, referring to cuffs.

He nodded, folding his arms. "What I do want to know is exactly what you found out and why you took off like a bat out of hell."

He must have seen the confusion on my face, my inner debate on how to answer him.

He held up a placating finger. "How about we walk and talk," he offered.

I nodded, and he turned to lead the way, a subtle gesture that this was entirely voluntary and that he wasn't escorting me out under guard.

Then again, maybe it was a whisper of chivalry – to walk ahead of a lady in a dark alley.

I wanted to laugh and say that monsters rarely struck from the front. Like animals, they struck from the side or behind, from the shadows, from stealth. And if they did come head on, they intended to simply rip him in half to get to me.

A coffee cup rolled on the ground loudly and he instantly brandished twin daggers.

Big long ones. Definitely not standard issue. They were butterfly knives. I hadn't even spotted them on him. Seeing it was only a cup, he glanced over his shoulder sheepishly, sheathing the blades at the base of his spine. He met my eyes and shrugged. Then continued on, hands at his sides.

I followed in silence until we reached the street. Then he sat on the bench, patting the seat next to him as he glanced over to the church. "I don't want to be over there when the crowd returns," he said casually. "I'm assuming you don't either…"

I shivered. "No thanks."

"So, I take it you're not a pyro technician in disguise as a beautiful woman..."

I smiled sadly, shaking my head. "No. I'm not," I admitted.

"Okay. Well, I'll be honest with you in hopes that you'll return the favor. But I want to make one thing clear." He met my eyes, and I nodded. "You're not obligated to answer me. But... I really hope you do, because I feel like I'm going crazy."

My breath caught. Who the hell was this guy? He could legally force me to talk. Badge on him or not. And... he had seen magic, that much was obvious.

"The tooth marks on the body belonged to a very large animal, resembling a wolf, but different. For example, the saliva didn't match anything in our database. We were planning to run more tests..." he hesitated, sounding angry. "Until the paperwork on the evidence got mixed up. The body and evidence were incinerated. All of it."

I blinked at him, mouth opening wordlessly. Shit. That meant the killer wolf had friends in the force... He nodded, reading the look in my eyes.

"I just watched you make a ring of fire out of thin air, and then half of you disappeared. I saw you howl, since I was close enough to you to actually hear *you*. But at the same time, I heard the howl two blocks *away*." He met my eyes meaningfully, and I began to fidget. "Then, you twirl around in the center of a crime scene with your eyes closed, smiling. After finally noticing me, you bolt past me as if you saw your mother's murderer." I flinched as if struck at his choice of words. He winced, not knowing the reason why, but sensing he had misspoken.

"It's... fine," I whispered.

He cleared his throat. "You run down the street, dodging things *before* they were in your way, as if looking into the future, not once, but three times. And then I see a flash of golden light and find you standing alone in a deserted alley."

I swallowed nervously as he waited. "I'm..." I let out a quick breath, seeing no other option. "I'm a wizard. And I was chasing something dangerous. I just don't know what it was," I said in a rush.

He mouthed my confession silently, as if it would help him suddenly make sense of it. He did look startled, but not horrified. More like a teacher had just taught him something he hadn't known. I pressed on. "A werewolf killed that woman."

"Well, I did ask," he finally said with a tired sigh.

I watched him warily, gauging his reaction. Was he in shock? I decided to bring us back to his reality. "Why don't you have your badge? Or your uniform?"

He glanced down, tugging at his shirt. "I find it more helpful to return to a crime scene in plain clothes. Witnesses are more likely to speak freely with a compatriot than a uniform."

I nodded. "That's... actually very clever."

"I know," he said, smiling.

"You okay? With all of this? Or do you think I'm crazy?"

He let out a tired sigh, leaning back. "If I hadn't seen it, maybe I would think you were crazy. Or that I was crazy. But... I *did* see it. I can't deny what I saw with my own eyes. This actually makes more sense than anything else I came up with."

I frowned at him. "Have you already suspected things like this before? Because most people who hear about this for the first time aren't so calm."

He shrugged. "I'm not most people," he said unabashedly. "Now, tell me how to keep myself safe. Is it pretty much like the stories?"

I rounded on him. "That's it?" I asked, almost shouting.

He looked tense and uncertain, but... there was a fire in his eyes as he nodded. "What do you want me to do? Freak out? Cry? Shout? Denounce what I saw with my own eyes?" he said, shaking his head angrily. "Fear will get me nowhere. I just found out something horrifying, but rather than focusing on that, I'd rather know what will keep me alive. What to look out for."

I just stared at him. "That's not rational," I said, "you should be scared..."

He chuckled, and shrugged. "Maybe it's *hyper* rational," he argued. Seeing my doubt, he pressed on. "If I was hunting in the woods and saw a dangerous animal I'd never heard of, I wouldn't run around screaming that it was a monster. I would just... figure out what to do next," he said, shrugging. "I've never really been scared. Not for more than a few seconds, anyway. My mind just kind of rolls with the chaos, I guess. Then I just... *adapt*. Fear gets you nowhere..." he trailed off, eyes distant for a minute. I scanned him for magic again, delving deep to see if this was all some ruse. But he was clean. "Fear got my partner killed," he finally said in a whisper.

I finally opened my mouth to respond when I heard a collective scream from nearby. We both jerked to our feet, staring at the alley where I had mimicked the wolf howling, and where a sudden crowd of protestors were suddenly crashing back into the street, screaming, shouting, and crying.

Killian and I shared a look, and then took off toward the chaos.

Maybe he had a point. You could get used to fear...

If you learned how to adapt to the crazy.

CHAPTER 21

*W*e reached the opening just as the last of the crowd raced past us, practically invisible to them in their terror. We slipped into the alley, Killian just behind me this time. "I thought the alley was empty!"

"It was!" I snapped, preparing myself for whatever might be lurking in the shadows. Maybe it was the hooded figure I had just been chasing across the street. The one who had mysteriously disappeared. I grimaced as I saw the two police officers on the ground, still breathing, but unconscious. Killian cursed, checking on them, but I pressed on.

I rounded a corner and skidded to a halt. A large werewolf was pinned to a dumpster. I felt eyes watching me and growled under my breath. One of the stalkers was peeping again. Was it the silver hood or the other one? I scanned the rooftops and fire escapes, but found nothing.

I turned back to the wolf, realizing it didn't matter.

As I stared, I heard Killian catch up, and then grunt from over my shoulder. He held both daggers in his shaking fists, but I wasn't concerned about that. Not after seeing this.

"Watch and learn, Killian. And welcome to the dark side..." I warned him.

The fur began to fade away, revealing a male humanoid torso. Killian sucked in a breath loudly. Then the wolf's claws and jaws slowly made the change back to human. I studied the face in disbelief, clenching my fists. The Hispanic kid, the third werewolf. Motherfucker.

I took a breath and studied the body clinically. He was riddled with railroad stakes, but they must have been made of silver – because the blood around the wounds was cracked and dry, where it had burned on contact with the metal.

A giant cross painted the ground beneath the body, white paint still wet, and a Bible lay open at his feet, bookmarked with a crust-stained silver spike.

I took a few steps closer, eyes alert to any sign that the killer was still here, and I felt Beckett doing the same behind me, checking the area like a military veteran. I glanced down to see that a section in the book of *Matthew* had been highlighted. I grimaced, recognizing it after a few lines.

"So, every healthy tree bears good fruit, but the diseased tree bears bad fruit..." Beckett read.

This was most definitely a hate crime. Against my suspect for the church murder.

And judging by what we had seen, the crowd of protestors had definitely seen the werewolf pinned to the dumpster, and they had heard howling from this very alley. Of course, when the police showed, they would find a naked human, but they would still connect the two murders, what with all the religious paraphernalia around the body. Lucky for them, the other murder scene was just around the corner, and their flyers were encouraging this very act.

So... had someone in the crowd done this? Taken out the cops? Or the man I had just been chasing? Or the black stalker from the previous murder? Whoever it was, the killer had time to set up the scene, paint the ground, and then leave without attracting attention. And it had been quick, because the werewolf had only just changed back as we arrived. The killer knew his stuff.

I almost gasped at a new thought.

Maybe the killer was one of the other eleven Shepherds, deciding to head to town after hearing about the uptick in crime lately. Or learning that Roland had left town. But... Shepherds kept their kills low key. That was the point. I knew one other thing, though. If the third wolf had been killed, I was betting his pal, Yuri, was next on the list. If he wasn't the killer.

I reached out with my magic, scanning the area, but after a few seconds,

I let it go. I couldn't sense anything other than the victim. Definitely no bear scent. And I didn't have the strength to try the new power. My fingers began to tingle painfully even thinking of it.

I glanced at Killian, who was silently watching the body. He met my eyes, swallowed, and then spoke in a rasping voice. "That's… a werewolf."

Even though it wasn't a question, I nodded. "Technically, it's also my number one suspect for the first murder."

Beckett stared at me, mouth working silently. He likely just realized the worst part about straddling both worlds. What you learned in my world didn't typically hold up in the courts of the Regular world. In the cop world, he had nothing to link this body to the first murder. His eyebrows began to bunch up with frustration. "What's going to happen?" I asked him. "If word – official word – gets out that monsters are real…" I waved a hand at the scene before us. "This will only be the beginning…"

He nodded thoughtfully. "I see a dead man. Although murdered with religious motives, still, just a man," he said carefully. "People heard a wolf howling, and then they entered a dark alley to chase it. They saw this, and mistook it for a wolf. Not surprising, with their zealotry."

I closed my eyes, and almost whispered a prayer. "Thank you," I said.

"What are those?" he asked carefully, pointing at my hands.

I glanced down to see a crackling energy Kama in each quivering fist, popping like a cattle prod, but brilliantly white. The black feathered fan hovered before me, feathers ruffling lightly in an unseen breeze, but otherwise motionless.

My face colored, and I released them, grimacing guiltily. "That wasn't for you," I said, realizing how it might have looked. That if I hadn't liked his answer I would have killed him.

He smiled weakly. "You've had them out since we rounded the corner, otherwise I might have considered them a… form of persuasion," he said. He stared at the empty space where they had been. "Magic?"

I nodded. "Yeah."

"Okay," he said distantly. Then he straightened his shoulders, regaining some confidence. "Looks like I have a night ahead of me. And you should probably leave. I won't be able to hide that you were here, but I can put you in the report as a witness that I previously interrogated, and that you had returned to the scene of your own volition, hearing about the crowd outside. No different than the other protestors, really."

"I think the other protestors might need to be questioned, because they kind of read the same book, and their signs share the same love for... people like me."

He nodded. "I'll call it in." He met my eyes, a very determined look on his face. "If you want this kept quiet, you need to tell me everything. I can't be lying to my people and still be unaware of the truth. Or I might say something I shouldn't." My eyes must have flashed with heat, because he instantly held up hands in an innocent gesture. "That isn't a threat. It's simply the truth. I don't know what's real and what's not anymore. If you want me to keep your secrets, I need to know what those secrets are... I already have two men down," he added, glancing back.

I let out a nervous sigh. Shit was piling up, and I was only getting more confused. "Okay. Let's talk tomorrow, Detective Killian."

He nodded. "Call me Beckett. And you should probably leave." I noticed the sound of sirens approaching, and sighed.

With a roguish smile, I opened up a Gateway right there in the alley and stepped through into another nondescript alley a few blocks away. I wanted to jog home, clear my head.

I saw his eyes widen with wonder as I glanced back through the Gateway. Then he smiled, shook his head, and waved goodbye. I did the same before letting it wink out.

This had just become a freaking nightmare.

But maybe I had a Regular on my side, now.

Still, Roland needed to know about this. As did Father David. So he could talk to Pastor Benjamin. And maybe get the psychopath to calm his congregation down.

CHAPTER 22

I stared at Beckett across the table of the diner. Everything about him looked tired, except his deep blue eyes. They danced with an almost feverish excitement. Caution, as well, but mostly excitement. I took a sip of my coffee, letting him digest the supernatural crash course I'd just given him. Next would be the dozen questions.

After leaving Beckett at the crime scene last night, I had jogged home to get some shut-eye. I had three missed calls at five in the morning when I woke up. Two had been from Roland, and one from Beckett, asking to join me for breakfast.

Guess who won first callback?

I had met Beckett and his partner, Detective Sanchez, at a local diner to give them an official account of the previous night. They told me the two cops had suffered blows to the head, but with so many fleeing in terror, they had no idea when it had happened. Detective Sanchez dutifully took down my statement while Beckett asked questions. We had all left the diner at the same time, Detective Sanchez taking his own car, and then parted ways. Five minutes later, Beckett and I had met back up a block away to enter a different diner for a more clandestine discussion. That way his partner didn't grow curious as to why Beckett was privately meeting with a witness. Or a suspect, depending on their analysis of my story. But I didn't really fear that, because Beckett had included in his report that he had been with me the entire time, watching the protestors enter the alley.

Which was true.

"That's it?" he asked, almost sounding disappointed.

I laughed behind my steaming coffee. "That's just the tip," I winked at him.

His eyes widened in disbelief, and then he burst out laughing. "Wow. You had to put that in there."

"That's what she said," I muttered dryly.

"Alright, you're officially a member of the boys' club. That was an easy one, but I had to be sure you were willing to go there," he winked.

I nodded. "Politically correct, I am not."

He took a bite of his toast. "And a nerd, to boot," he said, between chews. "I think we're going to get along fine." I nodded back, studying him discreetly as he glanced out the window, assessing the pedestrians with an efficient glance.

He was handsome. Very handsome. And although I wasn't looking for a slap and tickle, I found that I might be persuaded into changing my mind. Not today, but maybe later.

Which made me think of Nate. I quickly buried both thoughts as Beckett turned back to me.

"Basically, every supernatural movie, show, or book I've read is really a documentary of sorts, right?"

I thought about it, and finally shrugged. "In a way, I guess."

"Okay. We can get to specifics as they come up. Silver for shifters. Stakes or decapitation for vampires. Holy stuff for our downstairs neighbors…" I nodded with each point. He studied his coffee thoughtfully. "Is Nate Temple like you?" he asked softly.

I almost choked on my coffee, and his eyes latched onto me like a bird of prey. "How—" I cleared my throat, ignoring the flash of triumph in his eyes. "Why would you think that?"

He rolled his eyes. "You already ruined it. You should probably work on that." His face grew pensive. "There are so many strange stories about him. And when he came to town during a concert a few months ago, there were a bunch of weird stories going around the watercooler. Eye witness testimony telling an entirely different, crazier story." He leaned back in his chair, shaking his head as he laced his palms behind his head. "So many cold cases could suddenly be solved…" he murmured regretfully. He must have noticed the look in my eyes, because he sighed. "Don't worry. I'm not an idiot. They would think I'd snapped under the pressure. But still, it sucks. Like that fucking bakery case. It just doesn't make any—" He paused, seeing me squirming. "Spill."

I let out an uneasy breath. I didn't want to tell him, but maybe his resources as a Detective could help lead me to Yuri. "Fine. You know the missing girls?" He nodded, face blank. "The two wallets you found belonged to werewolves. They had been abducting the missing women. We tracked them down to the bakery and killed them. Even saved two of the girls…"

His eyes widened. "What?" he asked in a low whisper. "You *saved* two of the girls? That's fantastic! Where are they? Which girls—"

I held up a finger. "They were kidnapped, raped, and turned," I said with a low growl, killing his cheer. "An associate of mine is keeping them safe. Out of town."

He studied me, face crestfallen, but finally seemed to understand. "Turned… into werewolves. After surviving all of that…" he said angrily, shaking his head. "Those sick fucks."

I nodded. "A third wolf got away, but he conveniently decided to get staked in an alley last night," I said. "No way to know for sure, now, but I suspected him for the church murder. I think he has another friend, Yuri, who I would really like to meet," I said with a hungry look.

Beckett scratched his chin, thinking. "How are you connecting them together?"

"Before my associate killed the two wolves at the bakery, one of them used that catchy slogan, *God is dead*. Yuri was heard saying the same thing several times. I think they might have been part of an organization."

"An anti-church organization," he muttered, frowning in disgust. "Or… Yuri is the last member of their tiny club, and there is no big conspiracy," he offered, gauging my reaction.

I smiled mirthlessly. "Glass-half-full kind of guy?" I asked.

He shrugged. "Just throwing it out there," he said, leaning back. "I like to consider all possibilities." He looked frustrated. "Everyone would be better off if we could work together on this. Your information, combined with mine, could solve a lot of crimes, put a lot of people at ease." He trailed off, then shook his head. "But it's more likely that everyone will go crazy with terror and join ranks with the church mob instead."

I met his eyes, very serious. "Another point is that you don't know which of your fellow officers might not be pleased with your sudden... revelations."

He nodded slowly, as if the thought had never occurred to him. "Fair point..."

I shrugged. "Just something to consider."

"Okay, so you think this wolf killed the woman at the church. But who killed *him?*"

I leaned closer, making sure our conversation was private. "I have no idea. Nothing concrete, anyway. But," I held up a finger sensing his doubt, "it was definitely something aware of my side. Because they used silver, and the victim was in wolf form. Not many could stand up to a werewolf. Unless they had foreknowledge or were a Freak themselves. Wolves are no joke."

"A godly person who hates Freaks. Gee, I wonder which church they go to..." he said dryly.

I sighed. "Maybe. But that seems too easy, doesn't it? Like a setup."

He shrugged. "Or a response to the first murder. Occam's Razor."

I nodded at his point, but I wasn't convinced. "Well, go do some police stuff. See if you can find anything out about Yuri. He might be the key to unraveling this whole thing, or he might be the next victim, since his pal was just taken out. But keep it low key. You don't want your officers trying to take out..." I realized I hadn't told him what Yuri was. "A werebear."

He stared at me incredulously. "Are you shitting me?" he whispered. I shook my head.

He nodded uneasily. "Okay. But don't go dark on me. I think I'm going to have questions in the future as I try to wrap my head around everything. What to say, what not to say. What to kill, what to arrest." He ran a hand through his hair, frustrated. "And with the message at the last crime scene, I'm pretty sure you're right. This killer is just getting started. It's like watching the beginning of a war..."

I nodded, disgusted at the thought of it. "I could very likely be a target," I said softly.

He leaned forward, a very dark look in his eyes. "Looks like I'll have to keep you safe, then," he promised, his eyes as hard as a marble pillar. "Both within the law, and possibly without," he added in a severe tone.

I smiled, placing a palm over my chest. "How touching..."

He scoffed. "I'm just looking after my C.I."

I arched a questioning brow at him.

"Confidential Informant," he explained.

"Ah, got it. I'm an investment, now."

"Hell yeah, you are," he said with a playful grin, a beam of sunlight striking his blue eyes through the blinds beside him.

"Well, I need to get going."

"I'll stick around for a while so we aren't seen leaving together," he said, leaning back into the booth.

I smiled at him, probably a bit longer than I should have, and then left in a rush, feeling slightly embarrassed. "Rein it in, horn-ball," I muttered to myself as I pushed open the door, walking towards my car in the parking lot. I needed to get to Abundant Angel to do some damage control. Warn Father David, and see if he could talk some sense into Pastor Benjamin. He needed to calm his people down.

Unless one of his people was the killer.

I sighed, remembering Roland's missed calls. I needed to call him back before he had a panic attack.

CHAPTER 23

I parked in back and headed towards the door, talking urgently and succinctly into my phone.

"I'm fine, Roland, but I really need to know if any of our people are in town. This thing is going to blow up, and I'd rather not accidentally kill or get a Shepherd arrested by accident."

"I'll check, but I find it doubtful. Since Kansas City is *mine*," he said with a territorial growl, "I should have received notice ahead of time if they were even considering it. And with me digging into other things here, I don't want to attract attention."

"On that front, have you found anything?" I asked anxiously.

"No, but I'm working on it. Something is definitely wrong here, but I don't want to push too hard and send them fleeing before I can catch the mole." He paused. "Callie, keep your eyes open. Even if a Shepherd was in town, you mentioned two stalkers…"

I nodded angrily as I entered the waiting room for Father David's office. Roland was right. The stalkers were a problem. I pushed the door open, trying not to slam it with anger as my thoughts drifted back to the mole, hiding in the fucking Vatican, working with demons. "Listen, Roland. I don't care if you have to personally strangle the pope in person! You have to—"

I stopped short to find Father David wasn't alone. Pastor Benjamin and Desmond sat before his desk, all turning to face me, eyes wide at my words.

I frowned guiltily. "I'll talk to you later," I said into my phone, hanging up hastily as I shot an apologetic look at Father David. "Just kidding?" I asked sheepishly.

His eyes were tight with displeasure. At my comment *and* my rude entrance in front of guests. Seeing Pastor Benjamin here, I was pretty sure I knew why he looked frustrated. Murder at a church, and then another murder near an angry mob that followed the same church. Even if it wasn't his church, that struck close to home. God was being slandered. Mocked. Degraded.

"Callie," Father David said in a tired voice. "We were just speaking of the horror last night. Please, take a seat in the lobby. We can speak once I'm finished."

I nodded, beginning to turn away when Pastor Benjamin spoke up. "Actually, would you mind staying? Perhaps you have some input that may help," he said as if struck by a new idea. I arched an eyebrow at him as Desmond nodded his agreement. "Much of the community is of your age, as were most of the protestors last night. Perhaps your input could be invaluable here."

I shrugged, and walked over to a nearby chair. "I can try to help however possible, but I'm not very good at social events," I lied.

Father David shot me a discreet look, but didn't speak. And the other two were too busy looking at me to notice.

"You were at the Fundraiser last night, though," Desmond said with a frown. "For the Vatican, right?"

"I told them of your other duties," Father David said, sensing my anger.

I bit back my scowl, wanting to slap him. I turned to Desmond. "Yes, but that's just as a figure piece. I'm not there trying to convert anyone or to make a case for our views. Just to show we are a presence."

Pastor Benjamin nodded. "Simply being seen at an event lends credibility, oftentimes."

"Look, what happened last night was terrible," I began, my anger at his congregation getting the best of me. "I'll be the first to say it. But I won't be paraded into the spotlight to make people feel better. We don't even know what happened. For all I know, some of your crazy followers tried to get extra credit last night," I snapped.

Benjamin and Desmond both reeled at that, eyes widening in shock. I realized I was breathing heavily, and leaned forward with a sigh. "I'm sorry. I just… I was jogging last night and got wrapped up into it. I saw the crowd. They were not peaceful. Trust me. I had to answer questions last night and this morning. All because I wanted to take a jog. My fuse is very short right now."

Pastor Benjamin nodded, not looking pleased, but at least conciliatory. "And you aren't pleased about the message we preach…" he said softly.

"I'm not a fan of any kind of hate speech."

"It is not hate speech to repeat God's word," Desmond said politely, but defensively.

I locked eyes with him. "Tell me how spreading fear leads people to God. Oh, wait. That's not a new tactic, is it?" I asked with a low snarl.

Father David cleared his throat. "Callie, perhaps you need to go take a walk," he said softly.

I leaned back into my chair, closing my eyes as I took a few deep breaths. "No, I'm fine. He's right. I don't like the message. But I'm not being stubborn just to be a jerk. That crowd was full of hate, not peace. During times of fear, pouring gasoline on the fire is the worst solution."

Benjamin leaned forward, studying me. "Perhaps you are right. What would you think of a luncheon of some kind? Where we provide food and drink to the community. An open house of sorts. No hate speech. No messages of fear. Just love." He turned to Desmond. "I believe Callie has already been invaluable in this conversation," he said with a faint smile.

Desmond looked doubtful, but he finally nodded.

"That could work," I said carefully.

He clapped his hands excitedly, rounding on Father David. "What do you think? A joint effort between us to promote the message of peace. We don't condone the actions of a few zealots," he said in a stern voice. "Let's make sure our flock knows this."

Father David thought about it for a long moment, and then finally nodded. "At worst, we help those hurting and afraid."

Benjamin nodded, steepling his hands. "And earn their trust in the process."

I grunted. "Is this just a marketing stunt to you? I know your church is new, but that's just low."

"Callie…" Father David began.

Pastor Benjamin held up a hand to Father David. "She has a fair point." He turned to me, eyes apologetic and kind. "It is really no different than attending social functions like fundraisers, galas, and auctions," he said softly. "We all do what we must to guide those less fortunate to the truth. You see it as a sales tactic, I see it as an opportunity to save souls."

I grunted again, my patience gone after my long night, my talk with Roland, and my priority of finding Yuri. "Don't try to make us look the same. I do it because it is requested of me, not because I want to scare people into joining the church."

Father David settled his head in his hands, seeing a train wreck in slow motion.

"I don't accuse you of anything. I'm merely pointing out that – although it might not be your choice – the Vatican is doing the same thing as I'm proposing. Making sure the citizens are aware of their presence." He shrugged innocently. "We aren't selling steak knives, Callie, we are investing in souls…"

Desmond nodded matter-of-factly.

I sighed. "I'm sorry," I finally muttered. But I wasn't entirely convinced. Even though he hadn't given me any personal reason to hate him, I didn't like him. His congregation was out of control thanks to his flyers, and he hadn't accepted responsibility for that. Sure, he was kind, nice, rational-sounding, and sweet. But he looked like a shark in a clerical collar. Like one of those mega-church pastors. This man had goals.

Or I was a broken soul and saw the worst in everything.

I didn't know anymore.

But something was off about him. Choosing those types of messages for his flyers didn't sit well with me. Father David was solid, and although he knew about the supernatural, I was pretty sure that he had never spewed hatred at us before learning of us.

Either Pastor Benjamin secretly knew of us and hated us, or he was simply using fear tactics to grow his fledgling church. There was always the possibility that he genuinely believed these things, but to me, that was almost worse. Like one of those fabled snake-oil salesmen. Find a reason to make people buy, and then pounce on it.

"I think we've strayed far from the point. Death is death. It is not something to capitalize on, but something to comfort. For those left behind. That is my goal. To establish a safe perimeter for those who are scared. I think we can agree on that, right?" Father David asked gently.

I nodded. "Yes."

"Good. We hope you can join us, Callie, but understand if you can't make it," he said in an accepting tone, but his eyes let me know the truth. He had heard the tail-end of my conversation with Roland, and understood that these killings likely involved me, and that I hadn't simply been out for a jog last night.

I dipped my head and stood. "I wish you luck." I left before I screamed or did something to convince them I was possessed. I felt their eyes follow me from the room. I closed the door behind me and leaned against it, letting out a breath.

Was I overreacting or was I the only sane person in the building? I could imagine Roland's stern glare if he had heard the conversation. Well, I wasn't some dainty flower to go with the flow, and Benjamin had been right. Me debating them had been beneficial. A theory without argument and adequate defense was weak. Ideas needed to be challenged and defended.

But maybe I would leave the challenging to others next time.

I began to realize that this angry wizard needed a nap.

CHAPTER 24

I woke from a dead sleep, feeling as if I had only just closed my eyes, but also as if I was being born for the first time. This might sound odd to some people, but my naps were like that. An instant unconsciousness, where either ten minutes or ten hours could go by, and I wouldn't know without looking at a clock.

I glanced over at my phone, which was blaring at me from within the pages of the book tucked into the pillow beside me. The book Nate had bought at an auction and given to me. It still smelled like him, as did the stuffed unicorn next to it. The one he had named Grimm.

I wiped my eyes and mouth, chuckling. Those commercials with beautiful women waking up glorious, limned in rainbows and lingerie, hair perfectly styled, and make up unmarred…

Were a big fucking lie.

The Nyquil commercials were more honest.

At least when it came to me, and how I felt when I woke up.

I snatched up the phone, answering it without looking. "We have another one," Beckett grumbled. "This one knew his way around a dentist's office."

"What *year* is it?" I rasped. "I just woke up."

"It's after two in the afternoon!" he said incredulously. "But I have *coffee*," he said, changing his tone to sound like he was offering a complimentary full body massage.

"Mmmmm…" I purred, and too late, realized that it probably wasn't appropriate for coffee.

But I hadn't been thinking just about the coffee. A skilled masseuse might be nice…

"Get your ass down here," he pressed. "I think we might be on borrowed time."

"Where are you?" I asked, snapping out of it, registering the time.

"Near the coffee shop by your place. In one of the alleys on the East side of it. Use your hocus pocus to get here—"

I hung up, jumping to my feet. Luckily, I had slept in my clothes. I snatched up a mint toothpick – one that was labeled as *impregnated with tea tree oil* – before whipping my hair into a tight ponytail. Then I opened myself to my magic and Shadow Walked.

I appeared in an alley behind the coffee shop, knowing it was typically deserted, and heard a startled gasp behind me as a faint *cracking* sound echoed off the walls around me. I thought I had muffled it better, but I turned to see a homeless man rubbing his eyes and staring at me.

I waved at him. "Sorry. I threw a stick at the wall and didn't think of the echo," I said grinning impishly, hoping to use my looks to abolish his concern. "I didn't mean to wake you. Go ask the coffee shop for a drink on me. Tell them to add it to Callie's tab."

And then I was running, glancing down alleys as I searched for Beckett. I could hear sirens in the distance, racing closer, so tried to determine where they were heading by where they were, avoiding that direction. I stumbled into an alley and saw Beckett staring at a brick wall, shooting nervous glances over his shoulder where the sirens were closest. He held two cups of coffee.

He saw me and sagged in relief, motioning me closer. "Hurry!"

I ran his way and saw a man kneeling before us, as if praying to the golden cross in front of him. His chest was a fan of wet blood, and ivory reflections decorated his head in a ring like a garland. Upon closer inspection, I saw it really was a garland of string.

Adorned with teeth. Vampire teeth.

I shot Beckett a questioning look. He grimaced, but finally nodded at me to do whatever necessary. I heard car doors slamming in the distance. I snatched up the garland, inspected the scene one last time, and then ran back the way I had come, not bothering to grab the extra coffee he held. I heard Beckett walking towards the oncoming police, shouting them his way like a game of Marco Polo before I rounded a corner, out of sight. I felt eyes on me. I looked both ways, but saw no one. I held up my middle finger for good measure, deciding it was one of my stalkers, and that I couldn't do anything about it with police nearby. I pocketed the string of teeth, and then I shuffled off to the coffee shop I had told the bum about. The same one where I had met Claire yesterday.

I saw no one on my way, and even better, no police outside the coffee shop. I pushed open the door, eager for some caffeine. The homeless man stood just inside, fidgeting uncomfortably under the scrutiny of several regular patrons. Mr. Light Eyes sat in the same chair as yesterday, studying the homeless man thoughtfully. The dreaded Three, Benjamin's church-women, were also present, and they didn't look pleased. The homeless man winced upon seeing me, but I strode right up to him, placed an arm around his shoulder, and gave him my winningest smile.

"Let's get something to eat, shall we?" I said. "What's your name?"

He tried to shy away from me, but I pulled him closer, staring into his eyes. Surprisingly, he didn't smell, although his face was dirty. His clothes were obviously filthy and threadbare, but he didn't have body odor. Maybe he had found a fountain to bathe in. Kansas City was nicknamed the City of Fountains. The man finally blushed, averting his eyes. "Arthur," he answered.

He had thick, shaggy, brown hair, an equally thick, unkempt beard, and bright blue eyes, much lighter than Beckett. He had faint crinkles near his eyes, but didn't look very old. Maybe late forties. His posture was bowed and slack, as if exhausted and broken from life on the streets.

"Where are you from, Arthur?" I asked, leading him towards the counter where Ramsey was shooting me a very uncertain look.

"I... don't remember anymore. It seems like I've always lived on the streets..." he whispered. His voice was deep and soothing, like a documentary commentator. Some voices were just like that – compelling. Like Morgan Freeman and Anthony Hopkins. "But I don't need any help. I don't think they want me here," he said, casting furtive looks at the other patrons, who were openly holding their noses.

I accidentally bumped into one such table on my way by, spilling three cups of coffee over the *Abominable Three*, as Benjamin had called them. The three very well-coiffed churchwomen.

So, you could say I was defending Arthur from their judgment. But you could also say I was being petty towards their hypocritical churchiness. Both would be correct. One would be truer.

They squawked and spluttered, but I had made it very obvious that the stumble and fault belonged to me, not Arthur. "Whoops. Did I get your novels wet?" I asked, pulling Arthur closer to me companionably while motioning at their wet bibles. Their faces purpled at my comment, but they were too angry to reply. They quickly mopped off their books and clothes, then stormed out with disdainful sniffs.

I made sure to remain beside the table, not helping them, until they were gone.

Mr. Light Eyes began a slow clap, staring straight at me with an approving nod. I smirked back, dipping my head. Everyone else was suddenly very interested in their coffees, no longer displaying an opinion on Arthur's presence. We made our way to the counter.

I ordered more than we needed, asking Arthur's input occasionally, but otherwise splurging on anything his eyes rested on for longer than a second – which was almost everything in the display case. Then I asked for a bag, and had Ramsey set everything inside.

Ramsey was smiling the entire time, loving the drama. I glanced over his shoulder to see the manager poking his head out of the kitchen in back. I smiled at him politely. He looked somewhat mollified by the fact that at least I was getting everything to go.

I lifted a finger dramatically. "Actually, Ramsey, we'll take a plate for the muffins," I said glancing at the last two items. Ramsey almost choked, grinning wide enough to show teeth. The manager's face instantly tightened at realizing we would be sticking around for a while.

Arthur spoke up. "It really isn't necessary. I don't mind eating outside—"

I placed a finger on his lips. "Well, Arthur. I'm not as polite as you. I'm actually rather delicate, and would rather eat inside, like the other paying customers," I said, loud enough for the manager to hear.

He looked like he had swallowed something rancid, but plastered on a fake smile as the door jingled behind us. I turned to see a pair of cops enter the shop. I smiled, and turned back to the manager. His teeth now sparkled with compassion.

Arthur looked extremely uncomfortable, but Ramsey winked at him, smiling brightly as he handed the bag to the homeless man, not me. "Have a wonderful day, Arthur," he said. "And thank you for your business."

Emily, the normally gothic, emo barista, was openly smiling, staring at me as if she had never seen me before. The cops watched us thoughtfully as we turned to face them. I smiled pleasantly and guided Arthur past them. I picked up one of the sodden religious pamphlets on my way by, wiped it off with a napkin, and then dropped it off on Mr. Light Eyes' table. "Thought you might want some reading material," I said casually as I continued on.

He burst out laughing, but I didn't turn to look as Arthur and I sat down at a table.

Arthur clutched the bag like a miser, eyes darting from the patrons, to me, to the manager, and finally to the police, looking ready to bolt. I was sure to sit between him and the door, to prevent his escape. Fuck the police and the snooty patrons. Arthur seemed like a cool guy.

And he was an excellent alibi.

"So, Arty. We met in the alley, you were nice to me, and I walked you back here. Because an ex-boyfriend made me angry enough to throw a fit, which rudely woke you from a nap. Then you chased him away, defending my honor." I grinned at him.

He studied me thoughtfully, and finally smiled. "That's about how I recall it."

"Good. Tell me the story of your life, old one. I have a wish to hear an adventure."

Arthur's eyes twinkled with tears and a very sad smile. Then he dropped his head, staring down at the table. In a whisper I almost couldn't decipher, he spoke. "No one... has ever asked me that before. At least, not that I remember..." When he lifted his eyes, I saw trails down his weathered cheeks, washing away some of the grime.

And what I saw underneath was a face of justice. A face that had seen more, lived more, and stood for more than anyone I had ever met. Kind of like Roland. But it looked like it had been so long ago that he had forgotten it. A shadow of his former self.

My compassion had woken something inside Arthur, and I could tell it had been years since he had experienced even the most accidental form of kindness. He probably hadn't been looked on as another human being in years. Simply another piece of trash in the streets.

I reached out, squeezed his calloused hands, and smiled. "Dazzle me."

It didn't cost anything to show kindness. Sure, some homeless were junkies or terrible people, but like most humans, you could never know that at first look. You had to brush off some dirt to find some treasure.

"Okay…" he said, studying me with a silent question.

"Callie," I said, smiling.

"Callie…" he repeated with a distant look. "Is that short for…" he mouthed the last word.

I leaned back in surprise. "You're the first person to ever guess correctly, Arthur…" And I waited for him to tell me a tale.

CHAPTER 25

J had sat with Arthur for an hour, and even wandered down the
street with him to buy him a disposable cell phone, strictly to
contact me. I wanted to make sure he was taken care of, but I had other
things to do that couldn't wait. One of those things was a party, but the
other was a short trip.

We left with a hug, and I was sure to tell him to swing by Abundant
Angel for a change of clothes and a makeover. It wasn't far away from here,
or I would have called him a cab. I did call Father David to let him know
ahead of time, but I was sure that he would've been entertained as a king if
he had walked into the church on his own. Still, I felt protective of the
old man.

And his story—

My phone rang, and I glanced down at it. I didn't recognize the number.
"Hello?"

Beckett sighed on the other end of the line. "Burner phone."

I lowered my voice, stepping into an alcove in case someone walked by
and decided to listen in. "Everything okay?" I asked.

"As well as, considering," he said tiredly. "Although a couple officers
couldn't stop babbling about a *smoking hot white-haired chick hanging out with
a homeless guy at a coffee shop nearby*," he said, trying to mimic the tone of his
fellow officers.

I laughed. "Yeah. He was a good alibi, and one hell of an interesting guy, actually."

"Well, you convinced them of the virtues of charity," he said, laughing. "They offered to live on the streets if you would consider continuing your good deeds."

I laughed. "The Lord works in mysterious ways," I said cryptically, smiling to myself. "Now, tell me what happened. And how did you hear about it?"

His tone grew more formal. "Anonymous tip. I might have been lurking around your apartment, keeping an eye out for you, so I was closest when the call came in."

I was silent on the other end of the line, surprised. "Oh... Thank you."

He grunted, sounding embarrassed. Then he cleared his throat. "Anyway. You might not have noticed, but he had a wooden stake in his chest. And all of his teeth were ripped out." He paused, speaking quieter after a few seconds. "Vampire?"

"Yeah," I said, withdrawing the garland from my pocket and studying the abnormally long canines. "Definitely. Did anyone suspect anything?"

"No, but theories abound about where his teeth are. Other than the religious angle, no one thinks it's the same killer, thank god. Or else we would be creeping up on serial status."

"Any leads?"

"Nothing," he growled. "The call was anonymous. Probably the killer. We tracked it to a nearby payphone. It has the same motivations as the wolf. Do you think it's the same guy?"

I sighed, thinking about the caller. If a Regular had seen it, they would have been running into the precinct for protection, so I agreed it was the killer. Which meant he was bold. And that he had no fear of using a payphone right after. Just strolling around my neighborhood, killing a vampire in broad daylight while I was asleep. It made me shiver.

"You still there?" Beckett asked.

"Yeah, sorry. I would think it's the same killer. I mean, not many could take on a Freak, especially two different kinds of Freak. But I didn't have time to get a feel for the area. And there wasn't any sign of struggle, right?"

"None."

"Which means the victim was easily overpowered and tortured. While alive, judging by the blood. Right?" I asked, not extremely familiar with things like that. But knowing my side of the fence, it made sense.

"We'll have to wait for the official report from the medical examiner, but it looks like the dental work happened while alive. Real sicko," he muttered angrily.

Which made me feel very good about Beckett. Most might decide to side with the killer, since he had only killed monsters. But to Beckett, a killer was a killer. And anyone who tortured another was below evil. Now, if the victims had simply been found murdered, he might have leaned closer to agreeing with the killer, but in a way, the torture had swayed Beckett to think like I did. That although monsters, we could also be victims. And we were being targeted merely for that reason.

"Do you know who it is? Either of them?"

"The werewolf's name was Horatio Gomez. He worked in human resources at one of the insurance companies nearby, but I don't know about the vampire. I don't know if I was being paranoid or not, but I was sure to keep the body out of sunlight."

I almost slapped my forehead. "I'm glad one of us is thinking clearly!" I hissed. "The body would have likely disintegrated into a pile of ashes," I gasped.

"Yeah, well, glad I considered that, then," Beckett said, sounding relieved he wasn't crazy. "I guess the killer wanted us to see the body. If it was simply murder, he could have left him in the daylight and we wouldn't have ever even found a body…"

I nodded. "Yeah, that's likely why he chose the alley. For the shade. No reason making a display if the body disappears. Although, he was likely hoping you would transport him during the day and see his body disappear," I said, thinking furiously.

The other line was quiet for a few seconds. "He's trying to show us the truth. That's why he left the teeth… He's probably not very happy right now."

I felt a sick feeling in my stomach. "Which means he's probably going to strike again, soon. And worse than the other two. To make the facts impossible to refute."

Beckett sounded about to throw up. "Could you imagine if he recorded one of these? Brought a vampire into the daylight so everyone could see him disintegrating?" he asked with a shaken breath. I grimaced in agreement. "There would be no hiding that."

"We need to find this guy. Now," I said angrily. "But how? We don't have anything to go on, but…"

And a sickening feeling hit me.

"That new church…" Beckett said softly. "You think they are behind it?"

"I… maybe." Sure, I had considered someone in their congregation. They had the same motives. But the leadership? Pastor Benjamin? Desmond? Brigitte? I hadn't sensed an iota of magic on the three, so it was more likely that one of their sycophantic followers was a die-hard.

"Well, how do we find our way into their fold to sniff out the killer?" Beckett asked.

I groaned inwardly. "They're having a luncheon tomorrow. To stand up against the violence."

Beckett was silent on the other end. "I haven't heard about that. How did you?"

"Well, I work for the Catholic Church. Abundant Angel."

"Yeah, I remember… But you said you were an assistant. What would your church have to do with this new one?"

"I'm not really an assistant," I admitted.

He was quiet for a minute, likely scowling. "Wait. Are you a… magic *Sister*?" he asked incredulously. "The fucking church *knows* about this stuff?" He began to babble. "No, wait. If the church knows, why would the new church actively take a stand on witches and stuff? Unless… only the Catholics know this stuff is real, and aren't happy about the new church pointing it out?" He let out a long sigh. "I don't get it," he admitted.

"Listen, we probably need to meet up. I have an errand to run. Want to join me? Can you get out for a few hours?"

"Sure," he said, but he sounded wary.

"Okay, meet me in twenty minutes."

"We need to meet somewhere out of sight. No coffee shop, church, home, or police station. You're technically a witness, so we can't just meet up in public. How about the Sprint Center?"

"Good idea. I'll be there soon. Second level parking lot. Be ready to drive. And arm for bear."

"Okay. Hold on," he said, his tone growing urgent. "You're not being literal, right? We're not going to go fight freaking care bears, are we? Because that sounds monumentally stupid."

I smiled to myself. "No, it was a figure of speech. But speaking of, have you found anything out on Yuri?" I asked.

"No. Nothing."

"Worth a shot," I sighed. We were back to square one. "Gear up for a fight, Beckett. I'll see you in twenty."

"Look forward to it. I think…" he admitted, sounding resigned.

I let him. It was a healthy feeling. Roland always sounded that way around me.

CHAPTER 26

I got to the parking garage early, and called Claire, just to make sure she was okay. We spoke very briefly, but she confirmed everything was fine, and that everyone was incredibly kind. "I think we misjudged them entirely," she had said before we hung up.

I was simply relieved that she was okay. She hadn't changed yet, but she had been learning a lot about their past, their hierarchy, and about shifters in general. Bears were solitary shifters, and didn't typically form packs or anything, like wolves. Sometimes one or two would partner up, but it typically didn't last more than a few years before they grew apart and wandered their own way.

Which made the Kansas City Cave kind of an anomaly.

Claire had found a family of sorts, which meant more protection. With a killer hunting Freaks, this made me unbelievably happy.

With one of my concerns appeased, I focused on my upcoming tasks. I had the party with James Vane tonight, but I wanted to first check out the house where I had fought Johnathan. And since Beckett was getting a crash course in my world, I decided he could tag along. We could talk and work at the same time.

Also, he was a cop, so his skills in searching the house for clues might prove useful. I had Shadow Walked to the Sprint Center, not wanting to leave my truck behind in case any of his pals on the force decided to follow him here. I realized that I really knew nothing about Beckett.

Was he married? Single? Kids? How old was he? Was he from here?

He pulled up, as if merely thinking of him had summoned him. He was staring into his rearview mirror as he drove, and seeing nothing, parked his car. He drove a new Jaguar, of all things. Not one of the low-end models, either. Had I stumbled upon another rich guy?

Another thought hit me. Was he more than he seemed? Every rich person so far had been. Nate Temple was some kind of deadly more-than-just-a-wizard, and Johnathan had been a demon. What was a cop doing with such a nice car? And... he had been lurking around my place this morning. Before the murder.

But at the same time, I factually knew he wasn't either of my stalkers. He'd helped me chase down silver hood – making him innocent of the wolf murder – and I had seen the black stalker outside the murder on the church steps – while Beckett was standing right in front of me.

Still, I felt suddenly wary of my decision to share my world with him. But he had seen me do magic. All I had done was confirm it for him. But he had been so... accepting of magic.

I needed to keep my guard up.

I approached his car, and was surprised to find him already outside of it, locking it with a *beep* of his alarm. He studied me thoughtfully, and then glanced back behind him.

"Is everything okay?"

He nodded absently. "A few of the guys were ribbing me. They connected that the white-haired girl from the coffee shop was the same witness from the murder outside of the church. And that I had questioned her."

I frowned nervously. "And?"

"They found your homeless friend. Questioned him, too." He saw the territorial fire in my eyes and held up a hand. "I was present. They were as kind as I've ever seen them. Trust me. He backed up your story that you were there the entire time with him. Still, they've grown mighty interested in you, and were very curious about me leaving work a few hours early."

I nodded slowly. "You think they would follow you?"

He shrugged. "Ever since the evidence with the... werewolf disappeared, I've been edgy," he admitted. "I don't think anyone would follow me out of suspicion of what's *really* going on, but I know a few who would follow me for more nefarious reasons…" His face was serious, and then it split into a faint grin. "Trying to catch me out on a date, since I'm suffering such a long *dry spell*," he said with air quotes.

I smiled, the tension in my shoulders fading, somewhat. "Dry spell, huh?"

He nodded, but his smile was gone. "Yeah. Ever since my partner died."

I frowned. "You were married to your partner?" He closed his eyes for a moment, and I had a sudden thought. "Wait, you're gay? I didn't even think of that. I thought you meant *police* partner," I said, blushing with embarrassment.

He laughed loudly. "No, definitely not gay," he said, holding up his hands. "But I've found it's easier to say that my partner died, and let people assume I meant a cop." He took a deep breath, then let it out in a rush. "I'm a widower. My wife was… taken from me. A long time ago, but still. I've found it's less of a buzzkill if I say *partner*, rather than *wife*. Less pity. Like you're showing right now…" he added with a frown.

"Well, of course I pity that. You should be upset if I *didn't* pity that," I said forcefully. He met my eyes for a long second, unblinking, and then nodded.

"I don't want pity, Callie. But… I do appreciate it."

I studied him curiously. "You said she was taken from you… and you weren't surprised about magic and monsters. Do you think…" I trailed off, watching him.

His shoulders stiffened and he nodded. "It actually makes more sense than any other theory…"

I swallowed tightly. "Okay. Maybe I can help you look into that. Later. If you want."

He turned away. "Thanks. Are you ready?" he asked in a rough voice, changing the topic.

"Yes. But why did you lock your car up?" I asked. While his back was turned, I took a step closer, reaching out with my magic to see if I could sense anything supernatural about him. I hadn't attempted to replicate that odd chrome sight I had used to chase down silver hood, slightly afraid to try.

But I realized I had slept… a lot, recently.

Sure, I had been up late, and gotten up early, but I had still managed to get a solid five hours of sleep. And I had napped hard. Harder than I usually did, and that was saying something.

I began to consider the fact that I had been so short tempered with Roland, David, and Benjamin – before my nap – but had been so kind to Arthur – after my nap.

Like I was bipolar. None of my actions were out of character, but they were two very different swings of mood in a short span of time. And I began to wonder if that new power – being able to follow that man in the alley with the silver hue to my surroundings – had somehow affected me.

So, like an idiot, I tried it again. I dove deep within myself, and found the cracked door, tugging at the faint sliver of light.

And stared at Beckett.

He stood before me, outlined in shining silver between one second and the next, startling me enough that I almost dropped the sight, the real-world flickering into existence as if trying to force it away. I gritted my teeth and grasped on, surprised that it had come so much easier this time. Maybe my rest had helped more than I thought.

The vision solidified, and I realized that Beckett was standing in the center of a silver ring of light on the pavement, and that unknown runes were circling the interior of the circle, like I was staring at a cell under a microscope, the runes the individual parts of the cell. The mitochondria or DNA, or whatever those squiggly things were. Claire would know what they were called.

Regardless, Beckett stood in the center of that ring of light, and the runes circled around him. I wondered what it meant, and then remembered that the last time I had used this, it had almost felt like I was seeing into the future by a small portion of time.

Without realizing it, I lifted my hand, and a glowing orb of light appeared in my fist. Beckett spun, eyes wide, especially as the orb began to drift closer to him.

"Callie, what the hell is—"

"Shhh…" I said. "I won't hurt you, but I need to check something before we go anywhere," I said in a very cool voice, more like I was hearing someone else speak, because it didn't sound like my voice.

Beckett gasped, staring at me as if he had never seen me before. "What…" he began, eyes dancing around the parking garage, as if searching for something. His eyes finally shot back to me. "What is that? It sounds like… singing," he said in a very soft tone.

I didn't know what he was talking about, and couldn't have cared less in that moment. Whatever was going on, I wanted it done fast, in case the power faded away again. I forced the orb closer to him. He tensed as if expecting a bolt of electricity to the sphincter. But instead, the orb touched him and he shivered in ecstasy, eyes almost rolling back into his skull. Then I pressed the orb deeper into him. Whispers filled my ears as Beckett froze completely still.

Whispers of pain, anguish, and outrage drifted into the parking garage – softer than whispers, but clearer than a bell. Screaming, shouting, cries of outrage, despair, hopelessness…

Then… silence.

And a faint grumbling roar grew from the pain, as if eating the previous sounds, gaining strength from them, devouring them, and wrapping that pain around it like armor.

And I saw a superimposed face over Beckett – that of a warrior, a chrome face of such clarity and resolve that I almost shied away from it. But I couldn't. His mouth was closed, but that roar grew louder, and I realized I was experiencing his transformation – a transformation of his life, from the moment his wife had been taken… to now.

He had used that pain to strengthen, to grow, and to gird himself.

He had re-forged himself around one single motivation.

That what he had experienced would never…

Ever…

Happen to anyone again. Not if Beckett was nearby.

Like a pricked bubble, the vision washed away, and the sudden blast of color physically hurt my eyes. Beckett collapsed to his knees, crying without sound, tears staining his cheeks.

I realized I was kneeling in front of him, holding his hands.

And I was crying as well. With sorrow, adoration, and relief.

He wasn't a bad guy.

The furthest thing from it, in fact.

He stared back in wonder, not bothering to hide his tears. "What… *was* that?" he whispered.

I smiled back apologetically. "I wanted to make sure that you were who you said you were. You could say I have… trust issues," I admitted guiltily.

"Nothing against you, Beckett. But I've been lied to by pretty packages before. Because their magic was hidden deep inside of them, where I couldn't see. I tried something different this time..." I said, feeling breathless.

"You could have warned..." then he realized what he was saying. "Well, I guess you couldn't, could you?" he admitted. He looked hurt by my lack of trust, but also understanding. "Well? Did you see what you needed to see? I sure hope so, because I don't know if I could handle another of whatever that was. I feel scrubbed raw." Then he cocked his head, frowning at me. "What did you see?" he asked very softly, almost guardedly.

I opened my mouth a few times, wondering exactly what I had seen. "Your heart?" I guessed out loud. "Maybe your soul? Whatever you want to call it," I said, realizing we were still holding hands. I withdrew them carefully, hiding my blush. "It was beautiful."

He watched me for a few moments, and then climbed to his feet. He held out a hand, and I smiled up at it. Then I took it, and let him pull me to my feet. My fingers tingled against his, whether imagined, or some aftershock of my new magic touching his soul, I didn't know.

"I want to travel your way," he said in a rush, pocketing his keys as if that act would eliminate the possibility of taking his car.

I frowned at him. "You sure?"

He nodded stiffly. "Yes."

I thought about it. I remembered how Roland had once Shadow Walked Claire and I – when we first met him – so knew that a Regular could easily survive it without any ill effect, but it was still a big thing to ask. He was testing himself. His bravery. His resolve. And I couldn't take that from him.

"Okay. Hold my hand, Beckett."

He did, his jaw tightening. And then I Shadow Walked us to the mansion where I had fought Johnathan. And where I had teamed up with an Angel after watching a Nephilim tortured in front of me. Where I had seen that dark, sinister, horrible reflection of a demonic king in Johnathan's eyes before he died by my hand.

Where the Spear of Longinus had last been seen.

Where I had last seen Amira.

And where I had first kissed Nate Temple. Kind of.

And where a drop of Angel's blood had struck me in the forehead, filling me with power.

The wind whipped at us, almost chilly, snapping me out of my thoughts as I released Beckett's hands. He was too stunned to notice, staring around us in awe.

Then he hooted with laughter, hoisting a fist into the air triumphantly.

"Boys," I chided, heading towards the mansion. "Get your cop glasses on, and be ready for anything. This place isn't safe."

I heard the mechanical sound of him checking his pistol behind me, but I didn't turn to look. The gun likely wouldn't stop Amira, but maybe it would be enough of a distraction for me to send her screaming, sobbing, and pissing herself back to hell with her dearly departed brother, courtesy of Kansas City's resident bitch and demon-hunter.

Callie Fucking Penrose.

CHAPTER 27

*W*e paused before the house, staring up at the looming façade of marble pillars and widow's walks. The house was a not-so-silent display of wealth, like a giant middle finger from the one-percenters to the rabble.

Beckett grunted in approval, and I wondered again where he stood on the financial totem pole. "What exactly are we doing again?" he asked me, eyes alert and wary.

"Demon hunting. Or demon tracking, I guess."

The place hadn't changed. As I quested out with my wizard's magic, I sensed no other presence had been here. But the air did feel... thick. Almost humid, despite the cool wind.

But my magic had failed me in the past. Specifically, when dealing with demons. It hadn't shown me Johnathan's true colors. That he was very literally from Hell. In fact, none of the wizards who met Johnathan had known he was a demon.

Which meant that I couldn't rely on my wizard's magic to find a demon trail. Because the two I'd met seemed to know a way to thwart that. But what about my new power? This cracked door. It had pierced the illusion of the fleeing stalker in the alley, and had shown me things when looking at Beckett, almost as if letting me see into the future – and also his past.

The Angel's blood had also been silver...

And since then, my wizard's magic would sometimes be white, and significantly stronger. But it was still my wizard's magic, operating exactly the same way. If that white boost to my magic was a result of the Angel's blood, then what was this silver vision... thing. This cracked door. Were the two changes related? If so, why did they operate so differently?

And could one help me here?

I was a little nervous to try, since I didn't truly understand what it was, exactly. Was it something to do with my birth, or the Angel's blood? Johnathan had mentioned a ward placed on me at birth, but I didn't know anything about that. Was that ward unraveling? Was I some kind of hybrid Nephilim wizard?

Heaven was in for a bit of a disappointment if they had secretly decided to recruit me. And if they had recruited me, why hadn't I been able to track any of them down? Shouldn't they have held a *coming out* party for me?

"Are you doing something magical? Because it looks like you're just standing there."

I scowled at him pointedly. "Always assume I'm doing something magical. It's safer." He chuckled as I took a deep breath and walked up to the doors.

I muttered a word under my breath, and pulled open the doors, checking the wards we had placed here. We hadn't had keys for the place, after all, but needing to search the place, we had decided it was acceptable to add a crime to our resume – breaking and entering. Not wanting anyone else to enter the property, Roland had added a few different wards to the place. One was a shock that would strike any Regular who tried to break in. The other was a magical lock of a sort. If you didn't know the counter spell, the door wouldn't open.

I obviously did, so the door opened with ease.

No one had disturbed the home.

But it felt different, and I began to realize that with the demon's ability to hide their presence, maybe our spells were too juvenile to prevent Hell from taking back what was theirs. Or, since they owned the home, that our wards didn't apply to them. Which would actually make sense.

"Be alert for anything strange. Trust your gut. Shoot first and think later," I said in a cool, distant tone.

"Okay," Beckett said from behind me.

We entered the home and stepped into a giant marble foyer, complete with a round center table that stood before a giant marble staircase. The table had three vases, all with synthetic black roses. Like Halloween decorations. Black and white tiles – like a giant checkerboard – covered the floors throughout the house, revealing a giant dining room and a massive living area. The open concept was made all the more impressive by the thirty-foot ceiling, which was painted with Angelic artwork of sorts. Like a rendition of the Sistine Chapel.

But different, somehow.

The pressure was stronger here, more noticeable, almost like I needed a breeze to make it breathable. I pointed in one direction. "Keep your weapon out, and check everywhere."

He nodded, checking the slide of his pistol – a great big chrome-looking piece. "What am I looking for?"

I felt distracted, drawn to something in the living area, like a whisper of a whisper. "I don't know. A secret entrance of some kind, maybe…" I began walking away, leaving him to his own search. I was soon in the kitchen, running my hands along the walls, opening every cabinet, door, and drawer, but other than the typical ware, I found nothing. No library cards, ID's, or utility bills. The place had been cleaned. Wiped of anything personal, but leaving behind the other typical things in a lived-in home. Rubber bands, paperclips, pens, note pads.

I even checked those in the light, hoping to find an indentation of an address or phone number – any kind of lead. I cursed as I tossed them back into the drawer, and continued on.

I picked up a large kitchen knife absently, spinning it around my knuckles as I moved onto a bookshelf. I checked every book with my other hand, hoping against hope to find one was actually a lever of some kind. But no dice.

I heard a sound, and spun, hurtling the knife through the air on instinct.

The knife slammed into a painting on the wall. The painting showed a man in a Victorian Era suit sitting on a velvet chair with a woman in petticoats on his lap. His smile seemed evil, and the woman was crying. The knife quivered in the center of his throat.

But as I looked closer, ignoring the quivering blade, I saw no such thing. Both were smiling. But… I spotted blood slowly dripping down the painting from the edge of the knife. I gasped, staring down at my hand, wondering if

I had cut myself on the blade before throwing it. But my hand was whole and unharmed. Which meant… the painting was bleeding.

I jogged closer, staring up at it. Definitely blood. I climbed the shelf and tugged the painting off the wall. The knife surprisingly stayed with the painting, rather than tearing through it. The painting was ridiculously heavy, but I kept my hand on it as I set it on the ground and climbed back down. I spun the painting around, staring at the back. A still-beating heart thumped, oozing blood down the back of the painting where my knife had pierced it. I hissed in both disgust and fear to find a living heart behind a painting.

That meant someone had been here. Placed it behind the painting. But…

How had I sensed it? Behind a painting? And why hadn't the wards gone off.

I spun at a new sound, ready to unleash a blast of magic, but let out a gasp of relief to find Beckett staring at me and then the heart with a disgusted frown.

"What the hell is that?" he asked, pointing with his gun.

"A living heart," I said, turning back to study the painting.

CHAPTER 28

*B*eckett sucked in a breath. "That's... ominous." I nodded absently, inspecting it. The fact that it was still beating pretty much told me that Amira was behind it. This was some dark shit. "I checked the entire floor but found nothing," Beckett continued. "And architecturally, I don't know how anything on the upper floor could lead to a secret room. Is there a basement?"

I shook my head. "Not that we've found, but that doesn't mean one isn't here." The silence stretched as he waited for my next command. But I didn't have anything else, still staring at the heart.

"Are we just going to chalk up the heart as normal and continue on, or..."

I felt that faint power again, and frowned. The thick air, the heart. The whisper of sound I had heard in the first place. I was missing something.

I reached out a hand behind me, not knowing why, and was comforted when Beckett placed his free palm in mine, squeezing tightly. Rather than accepting the comfort, I led him towards the center of the living area, stopping when I felt I was in the thickest of the sensation.

Beckett was silent, and his eyes continued to scan the house.

I closed my eyes, and reached out to the cracked door in my mind, hoping it might have something to show me. The door immediately began to rattle and shake as if standing against a storm that was trying to force it closed, and a chorus of dark whispers abruptly surrounded us.

Drink the blood, gobble the kidneys...

Come play with us, Heaven Walkers...

We're all mad here. Everything's all topsy-turvy...

I pushed the voices away, trusting in Beckett to see any immediate threat since my eyes were closed. But his grip tightened, letting me know he heard them, too. As those voices fought to slam the door closed...

I strained to yank that motherfucker open.

Because if they wanted it closed, I definitely wanted it open, no matter what was behind it. The door squeaked open another inch, and I figuratively fell on my ass, eyes opening.

The world flashed silver, as if splashed with chrome paint.

And my stomach dropped out of me as if I was on a rollercoaster.

Beckett gasped, and his grip was suddenly painful.

Because we were standing on the ceiling – the painting at our feet – and staring up at the checkered floor on the ceiling. Nothing else had changed. The furniture, the fireplace, everything was where it had been – on the checkered marble floor. But Beckett and I were standing on the ceiling, like some giant optical illusion.

My silver vision winked out, and my shoulders sagged with sudden exhaustion, my eyes burning slightly. Nothing changed, though, thank god. We still stood on the painted ceiling. And my hair wasn't pointing straight up, telling me that we weren't actually upside down.

I nervously pulled a quarter from my pocket and dropped it from my shaking hand. It struck the painted ceiling at my feet.

"Callie?" Beckett asked, staring down at the quarter. "Tell me this isn't normal to you..."

"I think the house is spelled..." I said in a faint whisper, scanning the ceiling around us.

"You think?" he asked nervously, a hint of sarcasm plain in his voice. "Why?"

I very carefully let go of his hand, ready to grasp him if he began to fall, not sure if it was my new ability that kept us up here or if it was now our new reality. Beckett stood without issue, not falling, but his eyes were wide at the anticipated fear that he might – at any moment – plunge to his death on the marble floor above us.

I laughed mirthlessly, and followed Beckett's now curious gaze. His eyes riveted on something to our right. I turned to look and found the painting sitting on the ceiling with us, the heart still beating where my knife pierced it.

But if this was the natural way of the house, why hadn't the items from the drawers shot up to the ceiling? Or the furniture? Not really wanting to understand it, in fear that it would make me insane, I approached the painting. It felt disrespectful to walk across such a beautifully painted floor, but knowing the house belonged to a demon, the feeling quickly vanished. Also, some of the figures in the painting seemed to be watching me. I ignored them entirely, and stared down at the framed painting with the knife and still-beating heart. I nudged the frame with a boot, and it moved like a normal painting would if kicked. It didn't suddenly fall back to the marbled floor above us.

"This is fucking trippy, Callie. Are you doing this or is the house doing this?"

"The house," I confirmed, scanning all around us, wondering why we were up here, and why the painting had followed us. I scanned our surroundings, and noticed a slight discrepancy in part of the painted floor, where it met the crown molding against the corner wall. I approached it, motioning for Beckett to follow. I knelt down closer, wondering what exactly had caught my attention. As I reached out a hand to touch a goblet in the painting, I almost gasped when my hand seemed to sink into the painting to grasp a very literal goblet. I crouched down, leaning to the side, and realized that the goblet had been included into the painting like an optical illusion, but that it was very real. It had a faint hole in the bottom, making it useless as a cup.

I tugged at it, wondering if it was the lever I had been searching for – something that would open a door to a secret room. It didn't budge.

Beckett crouched down, inspecting it. "Does that say *communion?*" he asked, pointing at a cursive word carved into the base of the goblet.

I looked closer, nodding slowly, my stomach wanting to revolt. I turned back to him with a disgusted look, and then pointedly glanced at the still-beating heart on the back of the painting. His face paled, but he finally stood and walked over to the painting. He hesitated before gripping the heart in one hand and tugging it free.

He jumped back a step as the framed painting and knife flew straight up into the air, crashing and shattering on the marble floor above us. He crouched warily, as if fearing he was about to fall at any moment. But I couldn't stop staring at the blood dripping from the still beating heart. It pattered to the painted floor at his feet.

He followed my gaze, frowning as he saw the blood at his feet. Then he shivered, and forced himself my way, looking sickened by the pulsing hunk of flesh in his fist. The painting and knife had fallen, but the blood had dripped onto the ceiling, confirming my disgusted assumption. The heart was a key, the goblet a lock.

What did it say about me that I kind of understood what was required next? Or that some part of me had been able to recognize the heart in the first place, even though hidden from view? Was it some instinctual part of me to see through hell's trickery?

Or was I just as twisted as the demons?

I took the heart from him, my stomach twisting as it throbbed in my fist, and quickly set it inside the goblet. The blood began to form a small pool inside the goblet, and I jerked my hand back as rows of teeth suddenly erupted around the interior rim of the goblet, chomping down the heart like a Venus flytrap.

Beckett retched slightly, turning it into a cough. "That is not communion," he whispered disgustedly. For hell, it probably made a sort of sick sense. An unholy communion.

I froze as the goblet finished devouring the heart and blood, seeming to swallow it through the small hole at the base of the chalice. Then a line of purple fire raced up the wall in front of us, outlining a door.

Once fully outlined, it began to open away from us with a long, sinister groan, revealing a void of complete and utter darkness.

I shivered, sharing a look with Beckett. He smiled nervously. "Ladies first?" he asked.

Despite everything, I smiled, and stood. Then, just to be safe, I grasped his hand and led him through the doorway. Darkness swallowed us, so complete that I couldn't even see what we were standing on, but it crunched and shifted underfoot like piles of bones.

The psychotic voices from earlier returned with a vengeance – louder and more insistent – but beneath them all was a deep, dark laughter, as if I had just done the stupidest thing in the world.

I gritted my teeth and led Beckett onward into blackness.

Because there was no longer a doorway behind us…

CHAPTER 29

*a*fter only a dozen seconds of walking across the unseen bones – because I had been counting out loud in my head to distract myself from the voices – we were suddenly standing in a large stone room. The walls were massive gray blocks adorned with torches that flickered with purple flames. Every piece of furniture was ancient and simple, as if we were in some hellish version of an old European castle.

Beckett was muttering under his breath, sounding as if he was praying – or at least thanking god for getting him out of that darkness and the voices.

I gasped, falling to my knees and clutching my head.

My vision rippled violently, shaking, distorting, and jerking like I was seeing through the lens of a falling camera as it crashed down a flight of stairs. The whispers and laughter from the darkness returned with a vengeance, loud enough to physically hurt my ears. Then they were gone, the abrupt silence making my ears pop.

My vision suddenly steadied, but I was no longer seeing the room.

I saw a vision of Kansas City. And then St. Louis. They alternated back and forth, a few seconds at a time in one continuous stream. Both cities blazed – flames as far as the eye could see – and chain gangs of humans shambled in the streets, eyes downcast, chains dragging across broken pavement, and their backs bleeding.

Massive demons – scaled, slimy, fiery, or with skin like stone – whipped and bloodied the humans, laughing at their torment as they forced them to walk in circles for no reason.

The fear from the humans was palpable, but so was their hopelessness. They were broken.

I fell to my knees and did something I couldn't remember doing in years.

I prayed.

I closed my eyes and began to beg. Not for myself. But for those below me in the cities – those bleeding, crying out, living a life of despair... Those forgotten, broken souls.

I begged, sobbed, and pleaded for someone, anyone to give their strength, confidence, and hope back to them – to remind them what they *were*...

Beautiful Miracles.

Warriors.

Mankind.

I don't even know what I asked for after that. It was just an unconscious stream of words and emotion given sound – fueled by my outrage and protected by my heart.

My back began to burn in twin straight lines, my muscles aching and on fire as if I had been whipped across my shoulder blades, or as if someone had poured salt into an open wound. I ignored it, using the pain to shout louder, beg harder, love more.

And as I lifted my eyes, crying, screaming, and grasping the earth with my fingernails, every single demon below looked up with a unified snarl, glaring at me with undying hatred. And the humans woke up, shaking their heads from a daze.

Beyond the skylines of the flickering cities – still alternating back and forth repeatedly – I suddenly saw a giant mountain that didn't exist in the real world. The impossibly tall peak was ringed in white flame and black clouds.

And like an arrow from a bow, five black lances suddenly flashed down the mountain like racing snakes. Faster than possible, they were at the base of the mountain, and hurtling towards the cities, and the demons spun away from me, screaming in outrage at the oncoming lines of darkness as they formed a flying V formation. With a bell that seemed to shake the world, the two forces met, and existence exploded.

I cried out, gasping as I lay in someone's lap, back in the stone room, no longer seeing the terrifying vision.

Beckett was stroking my hair, murmuring prayers of his own and rubbing my shoulders urgently, as if trying to calm me. I let out a shaky breath, staring at the room.

"What..." I whispered, unable to sit up straight.

"I have no fucking idea. You fell to your knees and began to pray like the world was ending. You looked like you were being attacked, and that you were fighting."

"How could I look like I'm fighting while on my knees?" I asked, frowning.

He was silent for a long second. "I... have no idea, but I don't know how else to describe it. You looked like you were being beaten... But your back was straightening, defying the pain, and your voice kept getting louder and louder, until you were screaming and laughing at the end."

I relaxed, lying back into his lap. My abdominal muscles ached, as if I had just performed a thousand crunches, and my back was on fire. I looked up at him to find crusted blood around his ears. I flinched, rolling off of him awkwardly and clumsily to grip his cheeks, staring at his ears.

He shrugged, smiling weakly. "You were really loud..." he repeated. "I'm fine, though."

"I... made your *ears* bleed?" I asked incredulously. "What was I shouting?"

He shrugged, frowning at me. "I don't speak Latin, so I have no idea. But at the end you were repeating one word over and over and over." He met my eyes curiously. "Caballarii," he said, furrowing his brows.

I blinked at him, keeping my face studiously blank. "Must have been something I heard a Sister say or something," I said absently.

He studied me thoughtfully, but finally climbed to his feet, helping me to mine. I could read his eyes. He didn't buy my answer. But he also knew he was out of his depths, and I was his mentor in this brave new world.

I sure didn't feel like it.

I shoved the word from my mind, wanting to get the hell out of here. I felt like I needed a shower. Because for the second time now, I felt like someone had used me for a mouthpiece, speaking through me.

I shivered, and turned back to the room.

It looked like a terrorist cell. Books, news clippings, religious artifacts, and printouts from random websites were pinned to the wall, strewn about a desk, or lying on the floor.

Several pictures were also pinned to the wall, and I recognized one of them.

Nate Temple.

I shied away from that, but mentally took snapshots of some of the other pictures. Then I heard Beckett taking pictures with his phone. I wondered why I hadn't thought of that.

He shrugged. "Habit," he admitted, and then continued clicking away.

I met him with a stern stare. "This isn't a police case. Swear not to share this information with anyone but me or someone I tell you to share it with." His forehead creased – not in retaliation – but in thought, as if wondering why I would want to keep it secret. "Or I will burn your phone to ashes right now."

He finally nodded. "I didn't plan on sharing it. The layout is important, and can show you things later after you review the items individually. This is a workspace, so the positioning of the items is vitally important to... whoever the hell owns this place." His face paled. "Also, I don't fancy returning here. Ever."

I didn't look away. "Anyone who sees those images will likely be a target."

He nodded. "It's my burner phone, anyway. I wouldn't use my personal phone for something like this." And then he continued taking pictures.

I watched him. That was smart. To think to use the burner over his personal phone, and yet I hadn't seen him consciously give it any thought. I was beginning to believe that having Beckett around would be incredibly beneficial. He was more competent than most Freaks I knew.

I turned back to the walls, studying them, trying to get a feel for them, imagining Johnathan sitting here, working on... whatever this was.

After Beckett had taken a few pictures, I shuffled through some of the papers and found a large glossy picture of me standing at the steps of Abundant Angel Catholic Church, talking to Roland. But it was clear from the focus that I was the centerpiece of the picture. Roland was simply in the picture with me. The demon photographer had even caught me fully facing him, looking at the camera, which made me shiver.

I couldn't tell when the picture had been taken, but it had to be fairly recent.

I prowled the room, approaching another wall that was full of maps. I recognized one as Kansas City. Lines broke the city into five separate areas, almost like territories. A picture of Abundant Angel was pinned in place with an ancient bone blade, but seemed to be outside of the five territories.

I turned to another map to realize it was St. Louis. A large picture of Nate with the word *DIE!!* written with red sharpie under his name, and a bunch of clippings about his companies hung above the map His city was divided into many more territories than Kansas City – several of them had an angry *X* marked through them, and some lines had been scribbled out as if combining two territories together.

A sharpie between the two maps had been used to write directly on the wall.

WHY MISSOURI???

It was written in a very angry looking script, and in very big letters.

Beckett took a picture of it, and then several of the maps. He placed his hands on his hips, frowning at a desecrated bible on the ground. "I don't think God—"

As if the word was a catalyst, the table erupted in flames. Black, hungry flames.

I grabbed onto Beckett's shirt, shoving him ahead of me towards the door...

That was no longer there. In fact, there were *no* doors in the room. Why hadn't I noticed that earlier?

Feeling the flames at my back roar as they trebled in size, I stared at our shadows on the empty stone wall, desperately scanning for a crack that would mark the door. I noticed Beckett's eyes widen as he stared over my shoulders, but judging by the heat, I didn't need to turn to look. The fire had grown in size, and was about to engulf us. I stared at the wall one last time, and was surprised to find an altogether new shadow on the wall – great big wings, as if a demon was standing right behind us.

Amira.

With no other ideas, and not wanting the demon to slice off my head, I Shadow Walked us out of the room, fearing that it might not work as I planned, judging by how we had gotten here in the first place.

CHAPTER 30

I stood in the center of a worn, wide, stone bridge. The night sky was a smothering blanket of black, but tiny, faint pinpricks of stars struggled to pierce that veil. The bridge stretched before me and ended in a circle of stone.

Where a throne of smoke wavered.

A shadowed figure sat on the throne, but through the shadows I saw flashes of yellow fire, and great big black wings tucked behind it.

A familiar, feminine voice chuckled with amusement.

I realized, for the first time, that Beckett was gone. I spun to look for him behind me and saw that the bridge extended the same distance back to another circular ring of stone, but the sky was blue, blinding, and full of life. In the center of the stone ring sat a throne of glass, almost transparent enough to miss, as if made of air.

I turned back and forth, from night to day, blinking in disbelief. The line of demarcation was right where I stood on the bridge.

Nothing existed beneath the bridge, just more open sky – night or day.

When I turned back to the demon, she was standing. And she was very, very big. More so than the last time I had seen her. Amira. The first time I had seen her had been in an alley outside the church. She had been shrouded in yellow fog with white hot claws. But it seemed to have been a less vibrant version of her true self.

She was now swathed in yellow flame, her hair fanning out from her head as if she was underwater. Despite the flickering, dancing flames, it was pretty clear to recognize her very feminine form by contours and emphasis – like one could see a burning coal through the flames of a bonfire. From the hips up, she was a hauntingly beautiful woman, but from the hips down she was a goat, the flames actually flickering downward as if mimicking fur. Her cloven hooves were huge, easily the circumference of my head.

"Your toy is safe. For now…" she purred as if talking to a startled puppy.

I squared my shoulders and faced her. Finally, I had my proof that she was still in town. She'd been hiding from me like a little bitch. "You'll pay for what you've done. Stealing the Spear—"

Amira simply cleared her throat, and then grinned with lips of brighter fire than the rest of her face. Her eyes seemed to be focused on my hip. I glanced down to see that I was holding a blinding white spear in my fist, as if made of freshly bleached bone.

I blinked down at it, almost gasping and releasing it in shock.

And I also realized I wasn't wearing my clothes from earlier. I wore a fashionably short coat designed from straps and patches of leather. The garment was liberally laced with straps and buckles, making me look vaguely dystopian. It also looked like armor. At least thick enough to be armor. I wore similar leather pants and worn, distressed leather boots.

I looked back at the spear, considering. As I looked closer, I saw that the white was infected with veins of black, like tiny fractures across two sections…

As if the weapon was about to break… or had been broken…

Into three separate pieces.

Although somehow re-forged, it still looked weak, as if about to break, or struggling to hold itself together.

I slowly lifted my head to stare at Amira, who was nodding hungrily. "The Spear of Longinus…" she whispered adoringly. "I can still smell Johnathan's blood on you…" her eyes seemed to roll back into her head and she let out a moan of satisfaction.

"Let's finish this," I said in a low tone. "Wouldn't want you to spend too much time away from your Master, Johnathan."

The demon blinked at me, and then began to laugh. "Master? Ha! I have only one Master, girl. And He is not *Johnathan*," she spat reproachfully.

Literally spat, sending a glob of acidic phlegm onto the stone at her feet where it sizzled and crackled, eating through the rock.

"I don't give two shits who your master is, Amira. But I still want to send you back to that naughty place. Like I did with Johnathan," I said, stepping closer. As I did, the spear vibrated in my fist, the black veins – like black rings around the wood – began to grow more severe. I took a hasty step back, and the spear stopped vibrating. But the black veins did not recede. Taking even a single step closer to Amira had hurt the weapon. The Holy Spear that had stabbed Jesus on the Cross. Which was somehow in my hands. Was this another vision, or was this real? If so, *how*?

I took another step back, and this time, the spear began to grow slightly brighter around the black veins, as if healing. I smiled, trying to take another step back, but a sudden presence prevented me, like a wall at my spine. I glared up at Amira, and she nodded slowly.

"My house, my rules," she said. I simply glared back. She had a point. I had no idea where we were, but I could guess a general location. "Now, as fun as it would be to watch you destroy the Spear by trying to attack me – and I won't be letting you step backwards to heal it – we are at an impasse. You were fun, at first, distracting my competition, Johnathan. But now, you are merely a nuisance. I think I will kill a few more of your church mice, first. But a quick death won't do for you. No, you need a grander farewell."

"What are you talking about, bitch?" I seethed.

Instead of answering my question, she continued on as if I hadn't spoken. "How does tomorrow evening sound? Midnight." She leaned forward conspiratorially. "Well, technically, that's Noon for me," she said with an amused laugh. "Meet me at the old Kansas City Bread Factory." I knew the place. It was now a blighted area of town, having shut down a long time ago. The perfect place for a scrap. "I'll have a present for you. You should bring one for me, too. Maybe that policeman. He looks positively *delicious*." Her fiery eyes grew thoughtful. "As a matter of fact, maybe I'll bring the policeman…"

I began panting, gathering my power to unleash on the demon, reaching for that cracked door.

The next thing I knew, I was falling, and other than the wind whipping my ears, all I heard was laughter echoing around me like I was in a cavern.

Down, down, down…

I struck something hard and muscular, which grunted at the impact, sending us both down to the ground in an awkward tangle of limbs. I blinked, wondering why it was so hot since the sun was so low in the sky.

A firm hand grabbed me by the shirt and lifted me up. I stared into Beckett's panicked eyes, and behind him, the entire mansion was in flames.

"What happened?" I rasped, my throat dry. I glanced down at my hand, but saw no spear, which made me very, very uneasy. Had it been my imagination? Amira tricking me?

"I landed here as soon as you did your teleporting—"

"Shadow Walking," I corrected absently, staring up at the burning mansion, watching as timbers cracked and fell, sending sparks and flame up into the air to join the columns of thick, black smoke in the sky. I heard sirens in the distance, and almost flinched in terror. Then I realized we had at least a few minutes, maybe more before they arrived.

"Fine. Shadow Walking," Beckett said. "I appeared here, but you were gone. The house went up in flames. You've been gone at least an *hour*! It's almost seven o'clock. I've been yelling your name over and over. I could hear you talking, but I couldn't find you. What the hell were you doing hiding from me?"

I turned back to him, frowning, both at his comment and the time. It meant I had a party to get ready for. "You heard me talking? What was I saying?"

He stared at me, dumbfounded. "I probably need to make one thing clear. I can take all this craziness pretty well, but after this trip, I need to know something." He folded his arms. "Are you a crazy person? Is there something I need to know about you? This is the second time you haven't remembered what happened, and haven't given me an explanation. Tell me the truth. I don't mind being in the dark, but I do expect honesty."

I sighed. "I'm not crazy, and I'm not lying, Beckett. I swear. It's just… something beyond me is going down, and I don't understand it myself. Both times you just mentioned, I felt like I was in another place. The first time, I don't remember saying anything. But just now…" I met his eyes, allowing my fear to show for the first time. "I met Amira, a demon. And we talked…"

He swallowed, glancing about nervously, as if expecting the demon to show up. "I think I saw her. For just a second. In that room… What did she want? What happened?"

I shivered, not sure how to respond. "It's not good. She wants to meet tomorrow night at the old Kansas City Bread Factory. She said she's going to kill more people in the meantime, but that we would finally have our confrontation tomorrow at midnight."

He nodded slowly. "I know the place. It's a wasteland," he said, frowning. Then he remembered he hadn't answered my question yet. "You were speaking Latin again. I couldn't make out anything this time. It was too fast." He cocked his head at the sirens. "I think we both need to get the hell out of here. Do you have a safe place we can go to discuss our next move?"

I glanced up at the sun. "Yes, and I can tell you about our next move as soon as we get there. Do you have a suit?"

He nodded with a frown. "Sure. Why?"

"We're going to a party," I told him.

It was time I pushed James Vane into giving me information, whether he liked it or not. Because I was running out of time, and Amira had sounded very aware of current events. As if she was behind everything, pitting the church against the Freaks – maybe even riling *both* sides up. Maybe she was behind this *God is dead* group, and maybe she also had a hand in the church.

I had been so busy chasing the pieces that I hadn't realized we were playing a game.

That was about to change.

"Just a question, but what are Freak parties like?"

I smiled at him, grasping his hand. "Oh, they're a real fucking blast, Beckett…"

He swallowed nervously, and then I Shadow Walked us back to the parking garage.

I let go and met his eyes. "Get ready and meet me at my place as fast as you can. The party starts at eight, but I'm sure we can be fashionably late. Arm—"

"For bear," he sighed, cutting me off. "I got it." Then I left, Shadow Walking to my apartment. I needed to find a way to outsmart this bitch, to turn the table on her. And probably let Roland know what was going on.

And tell him… that I might have had the Spear all along, and that it was much different than we had seen, and possibly in more danger than it had been before?

I sighed, and tried to call the Spear into existence. Nothing happened.

"Fine. I don't need a shiny Spear to kick ass, just a killer dress," I mumbled. Because if James Vane needed to be impressed to give me what I wanted, I would impress the hell out of him. Or burn the place down trying...

But first, a shower.

CHAPTER 31

*W*e climbed a set of wide steps leading to the entrance of a mansion. The door was easily twice as tall as we were, and four times as wide. The valet had taken Beckett's car after assisting us out of the vehicle, and the detective was shooting thoughtful glances at my dress when he thought I wasn't looking. I smiled inwardly, but didn't let my appreciation show on my face. Because I was more concerned about the fact that as soon as we had entered the property, my magic had disappeared.

Inaccessible.

I tried reaching for the cracked door inside me, and let out a sigh of relief as my fingers tingled pleasantly in welcome. I felt anticipation building inside me. The block on my wizard's magic meant I was around *my* people, and that Vane's information would likely be actionable. A pink tuxe-doed butler opened the door, much too young and pretty to be a simple servant. More like a toy. He pinched Beckett's ass on the way by, which almost made him draw down until I stepped between them.

The butler had the audacity to look offended, but quickly turned to the next couple behind us, who were outrageously drunk already, and seemed more than open to light petting. Beckett leaned close. "I'm being literal here, not homophobic," he began. "But is he some kind of fairy? He was way too pretty to be real."

I chuckled, shaking my head. "Nothing from my side." Beckett frowned as if wondering if I was teasing him. "And who wouldn't want to pinch that ass?" I asked, smirking as I turned away.

"Damn right," he said without missing a beat. We entered a heavily wooded room that almost resembled the demon's mansion by sheer audacity standards. I was immediately assaulted by a flute of champagne, as another pink tuxedo whisked past me, already pouncing on the couple behind us. I gawked up at two sets of silk streamers hanging from the ceiling a few dozen feet overhead. Two stunningly beautiful girls were doing the most interesting acrobatics – climbing, spinning, twisting, falling, and overall, looking sensual and inviting. They did this naked.

And they nailed the naked thing, judging by the blank stares from almost every male present.

I shoved Beckett with my shoulder and he grunted, not averting his eyes. Not an ounce of shame. He finally turned to look at me, still not showing any embarrassment. He leaned closer, and whispered, "Imagine the chafing!" before looking back up at them and clapping.

I burst out laughing, surprised by his reaction. He wasn't as hard-boiled as I had initially assumed, but exhibited a playful side. I wondered if that had to do with his world changing around him, a world of magic. Most men would have feigned embarrassment, especially while standing beside their *date*. But Beckett openly acknowledged the beauty before him, and then made an utterly ridiculous joke about it all. Like we had known each other for years. He saw me studying him and winked back playfully. "I know you want to try." He jerked his chin up at the streamers. "I'll hold your drink."

I turned away, ignoring his laughter. A grand marble staircase led from the center of the room to an upper floor railed walkway. At the top of the stairs was a massive painting – at least six-feet-tall – depicting James Vane in Renaissance attire.

I'd heard of this before. Using photo manipulation software to insert your face onto that of an actual painting. A bunch of assholes thought it made them look cool. I just considered it a passing fad. But... perhaps if I found a cool painting of a strong woman, I might like to at least see what I looked like. For fun.

"Arrogant bastard, eh?" Beckett said.

"We all are. In one form or another." I hid my guilty flush. But I almost laughed out loud when I momentarily imagined getting one done with Roland's face on a Vatican Cardinal or something. Maybe a Christmas present. He would hate it. Perfect. I'd have to ask Vane about it, because this one looked very well done. His artist was good.

Beckett followed me through a set of open doors to the left where I could hear a wave of human sounds and light stringed instruments playing. We stared at the mass of lounge chairs, couches, divans, and areas on the floor that were literally covered in pillows. Two fireplaces were lit on either side of the massive ballroom.

Upon closer inspection, I realized it was a library of sorts. Not just books, but art. From all over the world. The room was also designed with wood in mind – great mahogany and oak timbers decorated the ceiling, and wall-to-wall cabinets were built flush with the walls themselves, and covered in glass so one couldn't simply grab the items illuminated within by built in lighting. I saw everything from figurines to jewelry, books and manuscripts to small pieces of art, luxurious pipes, flasks, horns, mugs, jewelry boxes, and much, much more. Like a high-end antique shop.

Giant chandeliers hung from the two-story ceiling, bathing the room in a romantic glow, and a second-tier balcony lined three walls of the room, lined with priceless paintings – each with their own individual lighting. But… I gasped in horror as I realized that each of the paintings had been defaced with spray paint – as if we were in an underground subway. From beneath the paint, I could tell that the paintings were legitimately priceless, and not simple renditions. The gilding on the frames alone would bankrupt me.

With absolutely everything so beautiful and elegant, it was a jarring contrast to see such horror painted over such historic pieces. I was no art snob, and couldn't tell one virtuoso from the next, but I had a feeling that if Nate saw this place, he would burn it to the ground on principle alone.

I hid my instinctive abhorrence to study the people in the room for the first time, my eyes catching onto the jewelry and coiffed hair, and…

Pale, sweaty skin.

I won't say that everyone was naked and enjoying carnal activities, but I suddenly felt like I was witnessing an after-dark special. Dozens of groups – of all combinations – were draped over furniture, pillows, or even pretending to dance while they… consorted.

Somehow, the stringed instruments seemed to balance out the cries of pleasure so well that I hadn't noticed it at first.

And no one seemed the least bit concerned. It was evident that the majority of guests had started off fully clothed, judging by the amount of furs, suit coats, jewelry, shoes, and everything else in various piles here and there. Sensing new guests accumulating up behind us, I grabbed Beckett's hand and led him around the various orgies. He looked highly interested – scientifically, as was I – in several of the groupings, not unlike one would look at a contortionist with fascination. Not that they wanted to try it, but that they needed a closer inspection to understand just how complicated it really was.

We stayed near the edges, not wanting to accidentally find ourselves tag-teamed into the action, and came to a halt near a giant bank vault door built into a wall between two cabinets. Directly across from us was a floor-to-ceiling window that almost stretched from wall-to-wall. About a mile of thick velvet drapes concealed the party from those outside, but I guessed it was also to keep the chill out, because the temperature had dropped significantly. A cold front was moving in, and we had heard distant thunder on our drive over here.

I studied the room from our relative safety, the very definition of a wallflower, looking for Vane. Something about all of this was bothering me, but I couldn't place a finger on it.

A bald man with a giant tattoo that seemed to cover the top of his head stood a dozen feet to our right, and a thick, fragrant cloud of smoke drifted into the air above him as he puffed on a canister. *Vaping*, I thought, shaking my head. He was large and shirtless, wearing only an elaborate kilt. "I had no idea who he was at the time," the man said loudly. "We were at a Johnson Beaver concert, for crying out loud. But here's the best part. I tried to take out this centaur, and accidentally punched that St. Louis wizard straight in the nu—"

The crowd around him burst out laughing, shaking their heads in disbelief, cutting off the end of his story. Many of them were completely naked, just standing around the kilted vaper without a care in the world.

Was he talking about Nate? I let my eyes scan the room, deciding that without Vane, I may as well go talk to this guy to get some dirt on Nate. But my gaze locked onto a familiar face across the room, and I instantly frowned, forgetting all about the kilted vaper.

Before I knew it, I was storming across the room. Beckett followed, batting away grabby hands for the both of us, and stopped behind me as I stared down at the man sprawled out on the red velvet couch who was smoking a cigar with one hand over his head. He was shirtless, his tan skin heavily layered with muscle, and his messy brown hair was sweaty. He smiled up at me, puffing away on his cigar. Thankfully, he still wore suit pants – even if his belt was undone – and expensive-looking dress shoes. Everything about him told me this was a celebratory cigar after a vigorous conquest.

"You," I said in a low tone, recognizing Mr. Light Eyes from the coffee shop these last few days – the one who had been pestered by the religious women.

"I," he replied, taking another lazy puff of his cigar.

"Who are you, and what are you doing here?"

He smirked. "Why, I *was* having a good time. You?"

"You know what I mean."

"Just a traveler. A vagabond."

"Why Kansas City?" I pressed.

"Oh, I spent some time in St. Louis, too. Not as fun, though."

That struck me deeply after what I had seen at the demon's house. "Why Missouri?"

He finally sat up, studying me thoughtfully. "Why indeed?" he replied, as if hoping that I had the answer. Seeing I didn't, he shrugged. "Missouri loves company?" he offered.

I scowled at him, ignoring Beckett's stifled cough. "Who are you?" I repeated.

"Some call me Cain," he said offhandedly.

Now, in any other place, that name might not have made my skin crawl. But here? With a bunch of Freaks having sex all around me? Yeah. It did. He wasn't really saying he was... His eyes twinkled as if reading my thoughts. And he gave me a slow nod, puffing his cigar happily.

"Why are you following me?" I asked instead, suddenly wary.

He chuckled, and then leaned in closer, speaking low. "I ain't the only one following you, honey. Maybe I was following the one following you..." he said meaningfully.

I took a step back, suddenly recognizing his frame. "You... you're the one from the alley. Just before the wolf..." Silver hood.

Cain nodded slowly, eyes very alert all of a sudden. Not afraid, but ready to react. I studied him thoughtfully. "That was a neat trick," he said cautiously.

I ignored that. "You're a murderer," I whispered, feeling Beckett stiffen behind me.

"Sure. But sometimes a thing just needs to be done. Even if it makes you a pariah." He shrugged. "But it's only Freaks." I leveled him with a flat stare, and he finally laughed. "Okay, you got me. Not just Freaks."

"You can't just go around killing people," I hissed.

"Of course, I can. I do it all the time. Just not *lately*," he said, eyes suddenly hard.

Beckett lunged for him and Cain simply disappeared as if he had never sat before us. His cigar rested on the ashtray beside the couch.

Beckett grumbled unhappily. "He's the murderer?"

I met his eyes, speaking in a low voice. "I'm not sure about the current murders. I was referring to him being the world's first murderer, and I think I was right."

Beckett blinked at me. "What?"

"Cain and Abel," I said. Beckett stiffened. "The sons of Adam and Eve."

"You've got to be *shitting* me..." he said under his breath. "God is really *real?*" he asked, staring at me oddly, likely remembering that I worked for the church and hunted a demon.

"God is dead," a new voice spoke from behind us. We both flinched at the phrase, recognizing it from the murders. But we kept our cool, turning to find James Vane smiling at us politely. "God remains dead. And we have killed him. How shall we comfort ourselves, the murderers of all murderers..."

I blinked at him, but Beckett spoke up. "Nietzsche..." he said, frowning in thought.

Vane nodded delightedly, then held out his hands at the assorted vices, as if connecting the quote to his guests. Then he turned back to us. "Welcome to my party. I see you scared off the... *First*," he said in a cryptic tone, watching my reaction. I nodded, letting him know I understood. "He's first in a lot of things, as a matter of fact. First to come, first to leave..." he winked darkly, and I felt my face heating.

If that wasn't a double entendre, I didn't know what was. But I suddenly had a lot more questions than I had when I arrived. I opened my mouth, but he silenced me with a look.

"Let me show you around my home," he said in a polite tone. "We can talk elsewhere."

"I don't think the local police would be pleased to find a brothel here," Beckett said.

Vane blinked at him. "No one is buying sex here, Detective Killian, I can assure you. Let's keep the government out of the bedroom tonight, shall we?" He glanced around. "Well, out of the living room, at least." If Beckett was surprised that Vane knew him, he hid it very well.

Vane extended an elbow. Since he was still fully dressed, and obviously not walking off a sex marathon, I accepted the risk of touching him. I wanted to keep things as peaceful as possible, for as long as possible, in order to get my answers. But if he was involved with the murders, he would die. And he currently thought I didn't have access to magic. The perfect fool.

He met my eyes. "I thought you were going to show me how fun you could be tonight…"

"I'm trying," I said, forcing my features to a semblance of normalcy. "Cain threw me off. I've run into him a few times lately, but didn't realize who he was."

Vane clucked knowingly. "Yes, he told me about that. I only just discovered he was in town. From St. Louis, no less." He glanced back at Beckett, and looked suddenly abashed. "I'm terribly sorry. Would you please take my other elbow?"

Beckett shook his head stiffly. "No, thanks."

Vane pursed his lips. "If I wanted to pinch your ass, I would pinch your ass. Touching me will protect you from the overzealous," he said, glancing pointedly out at the crowd. It was true. Anyone who walked too near to another group already in coitus was likely to be roped into the party, judging by what we saw happen twice in a span of seconds. "Our stimulating walk and conversation will go much smoother if you aren't batting away affections every two steps. I assure you, you'd be quite the catch," he said with an amused wink.

Which was how we found ourselves linked elbow to elbow on either side of James Vane as he led us from the room and back into the main lobby.

Beckett shot me a look over Vane's shoulder, but I merely glared back. Something was still bothering me about the whole experience, and it wasn't the sex, vape smoke, or Cain.

CHAPTER 32

*W*e stared down at the swarming mass of bodies from the second tier, which was much more instructive than the closer view we had seen earlier, answering a few of my unasked questions. Several guests spotted Vane and gave him dark, hungry looks that promised all sorts of things. Male, female, young, old – it didn't matter. He returned the looks with a devilish grin of his own, and then continued on. It looked practiced, rehearsed, and... positively bored.

Many in the crowd had already sated their bodily desires, and were now seated on couches or pillows, still in various stages of undress, conversing casually, drinking, and smoking clove cigarettes. Faint whiffs of marijuana drifted up to us, and I saw Beckett scowl.

Vane didn't even turn, sensing it. "I would ask Callie how best to proceed before you level charges, Detective," he said absently, not seeming to care one way or another.

Beckett turned to me, frowning. "Please let it go, Beckett. Vane has information he's willing to share. Then again, if that information isn't forthcoming..." I said in a warning tone.

Vane chuckled, patting the banister with a palm. He really was ridiculously good-looking. Fresh-shaven, and hair perfectly styled. I could sense that this seemed to bother Beckett, seeing a criminal so handsome, professional, and polite. Also, Vane was very handsy with me. Not inappropriate, but very… familiar. Which made me smile, sensing Beckett's displeasure at that.

"What do you think of my art?" Vane asked, turning around to lean against the banister, draping his elbows over the edge. One casual shove and he would fly over the railing, slice his head open on a chandelier, and most likely land on his neck.

I shivered at that thought – the smooth, heartless concept of murdering him.

I turned to the art he was indicating – a giant, expensive looking piece that was covered with a layer of glass flush against the painting. Underneath, the painting had been disgustingly vandalized with neon paints. So why cover it up with protective glass?

Without asking permission, I began to meander down the walkway, noticing the same with each piece of destroyed art. Defaced, yet covered in protective glass, and illuminated to highlight each piece. The art itself was varied, judging from many different artists, styles, and time periods, but all looked expensive.

I reached the end and then turned around to walk the other side. Vane smirked as I walked by him, and Beckett looked curious, wondering what game I was playing. I took time to study each painting, glancing back now and then at Beckett and Vane who were watching me with different types of interest. One piece in particular caught my attention as an oddity – a portrait of a man standing in a hallway. Of course, with all the spray paint it was hard to make out much, but sections of the picture looked extremely detailed. I gave it no more attention than the rest, thinking wildly as I continued on, sure to inspect all of them. Ever the polite guest, if it got me what I wanted. I reached the end, and made my way back to the men.

I paused in front of the oddity, reaching into my purse to pull out my breath freshener, but I dropped it clumsily. I bent down to pick it up, spraying a few bursts into the air to test that it hadn't broken in the tumble. In this small act, what I saw made everything click into place in my mind. I plastered a smile on my face, shot two bursts onto my tongue and then tucked it away. I walked back to the men, a disgusted frown on my face as I considered Vane.

"You buy ridiculously expensive art pieces and then destroy them."

"Everyone has a different perception of what constitutes art."

I nodded absently, leaning over the rail to stare down at the debauchery. "Why didn't you tell me your real name?"

He chuckled. "I wanted you to meet me before labeling me with your preconceived notions."

I turned to look at him, arching a doubtful brow. "And was this," I waved a hand at the party below, "supposed to make me think any differently than the story?"

He shrugged. "I hoped my charm would help. And it's easier to deal in information when you're acting as everyone expects. Inviting you in private to give you secret information would definitely piss off quite a few people in town."

Beckett piped up, frowning. "James Vane... I *knew* that name sounded familiar."

Our host turned to him, face curious. Hell, I was curious. Beckett had recognized that obscure quote by Nietzsche – which I hadn't – and I sure didn't know who the real James Vane was.

"James Vane was the brother to Sibyl Vane. He swore to kill..." Beckett trailed off, shaking his head uncertainly. Our host merely smirked, nodding slowly. Not proud or arrogant, but impressed at Beckett's knowledge. Hell, I was impressed. I didn't know squat about James Vane. I had come to a dark conclusion via good old sleuthing and from reading old stories.

"Dorian Gray," Beckett finally said, a look of disbelief on his face as he appraised the man before us.

Dorian held out his hands. "It truly is a pleasure to finally meet you."

CHAPTER 33

*D*orian leaned back over the balcony, not overly concerned with our discovery as he winked at a young man on a couch. The same college kid I had seen from the bar. He grinned back, but frowned when he saw me. He promptly stomped away in search of greener pastures.

I shook my head in disbelief. Dorian Gray, in Kansas City. I tried to remember things about him from my cursory knowledge on the book, but I didn't have a memory like Beckett. I just knew the basics. Wild parties. A painting. And a ridiculously handsome man up for anything.

But I didn't let on what I had discovered...

Dorian turned to me. "What's his story?" he asked, jerking his chin at Beckett.

Beckett's shoulders stiffened. "My story is that my knuckles have been aching all day," he said, rubbing his knuckles pointedly. "To pound some teeth into the back of someone's throat. Just been looking for the right set." He smiled darkly.

Dorian rolled his eyes. "Well, go right ahead," he said disinterestedly. Then he turned to me, looking bored. "He's cute. So ignorant he doesn't even know how stupid he is."

"Dorian Gray. A cursed painting makes you immoral. I mean, *immortal.* Loves excess everything – gluttony, sex, drugs, any kind of thrill. The consequences of your actions transfer to your painting, leaving you healthy and whole. But… destroy the painting, destroy the man," Beckett finished with a casual shrug. Dorian turned to him thoughtfully. Beckett was staring down at the vault door below us. "That door looks familiar. Has five tumblers. Only one person has successfully cracked it. I wonder what's valuable enough to warrant it?"

Dorian stilled for a moment, a flicker of anger crossing his features. "Astute. But still defenseless."

Beckett shrugged. "If defenseless means I know how to crack your vault, then I guess so." He finally lifted his gaze, a playful twinkle dancing behind them. "Want me to show you? If you're looking for some fun. Some risk. Some thrill. Maybe turn the heat up. Party's dying, anyway," he said absently, glancing down at the crowd, who did appear to be slowly dispersing, sated.

I laughed, clapping my hands delightedly. Dorian scowled at me. "I told you I was fun."

"He is more interesting than I thought. Not your average detective," he said, studying Beckett before turning back to me. "You may keep him. Now, I've got people to do and things to try."

I shook my head. "You want to meet Temple, you'll give me some answers."

Dorian sighed. "You want to meet monsters?" He held out a hand to the party. "I've invited you to a horde of them. Kansas City's finest. But none would dare talk to the woman in white," he said with a grin.

"Woman in white? Is that a church joke of some kind?" I asked, frowning.

Dorian stared at me intently, neither confirming nor denying, and I had the sudden feeling that my usage of white magic was maybe not so secret after all. "God is dead…" I said flatly.

He frowned, turning to me. "You probably shouldn't say that."

"But a lot of people are saying it these days."

He… blinked. "Pardon?" I stared into his gray eyes, and felt myself frowning. He was telling the truth. "Did I miss something?" he asked, turning to Beckett. "The Nietzsche quote?"

Beckett was very still, watching me nervously. "It was painted in blood at the church murder," I said, still watching him. But his eyes didn't even flicker. Not like the other times we had caught him in a lie. I wanted to scream.

"Churches can be nasty places," he murmured, finally turning away. "Full of such vitriol. You wouldn't catch me dead inside one." Then he grinned wolfishly. "Speaking of, did you hear the news?"

I blinked at him, ignoring his lame joke. "No." Had there been another murder?

He pulled out his phone, tapped a few times on the screen, and then handed it over. It was a news article... my breath stopped, and I almost dropped the phone, forgetting everything.

There had been a bombing at the Vatican. Today.

"Churches," Dorian agreed. "What has the world come to when you can't find safety in a church. *The* church, as a matter of fact... Maybe God *is* dead," he mused, more to himself.

I handed Beckett the phone, and he grimaced in disgust, but missed the significance.

Roland was at the Vatican, digging out a mole, and trying to find answers to my past.

"I'm just here to make friends, so that whoever comes out on top remembers me showing them a good time. I'm not into the murder business. I'm a concierge to monsters. But churches can be nasty places," he finally said, and when I looked up, he was simply gone.

Beckett flinched, eyes darting around us, but not finding him. "We need to go. Right now," I whispered. He nodded slowly, not understanding my reaction, but sensing that something was horribly wrong.

He gripped my elbow, supporting me as my legs threatened to give way. He led me down the stairs and outside, slapping away another ass grab by the butler in the pink tuxedo outside.

We climbed into our car, which was oddly waiting for us already – as if Dorian had told them we were ready to leave. Beckett helped me inside the passenger seat, and I had to force myself to sit still rather than simply Shadow Walking away. I growled under my breath. Well, I *couldn't* Shadow Walk anyway, because my power was inaccessible here.

I focused intently using my anger and fear for something useful, embracing that new power inside me, through the cracked door – the mercurial, quicksilver world. Although I didn't fully understand it, I was beginning to get a better grasp at sensing it. I reached out, sensing a rippling mirror before me that showed a chrome reflection of myself. My reflection smiled at me.

It was different than my wizard magic's version, but it had still worked.

A Gateway. A *Silver* Gateway.

I was smiling as Beckett climbed into the car. I could still use *this* magic, here. I just needed to figure out what to do with it. As Beckett pulled away, I glanced back at the house. One room in the corner revealed a man staring through a window, watching us leave.

Dorian Gray.

We were far from finished. Even though he didn't know about the *God is dead* slogan, he definitely knew something that could help me. And I was going to get it.

I had things to learn from him, because I hadn't gotten to my other questions. And I had a lot of them, but first I needed to check on Roland.

I dialed him as Beckett drove in silence. It didn't even ring, just went straight to voicemail. I cursed under my breath.

"We're no closer to catching this killer, unless you think it was Cain or Gray," Beckett said thoughtfully. I grunted noncommittally. I didn't think it was either, although I knew both were dubious men to say the least. "I still can't believe that was Dorian Gray. Are all the stories real?" I nodded distantly. "That was an asshole thing for him to do, making fun of the church."

I frowned at that, my worry over Roland making my thoughts cloudy with concern.

Then it hit me. "No..." I whispered to myself. Could it be that Dorian had given me an answer, and not just a parting jab? But as I thought about it, the pieces seemed to fit together all too well.

"What's wrong, Callie?" Beckett asked, exiting the property. My wizard's magic washed back into my reach like an incoming tide. I touched it for a moment, thinking furiously.

"I think Dorian gave us what we needed."

"What? When? Because I'm pretty sure he's just an asshole."

"How do you feel about kidnapping a priest?" I asked with an angry grin.

He blinked at me, so I told him my plan, giving him the chance to poke holes in it.

He nodded after a time, eyes growing darker.

It made sense. The church was at the center of it all, and their message was one of hate. And with Dorian mentioning the church, it all made sense. I thought Pastor Benjamin was an asshole, but hadn't considered him to be a killer. He did have Brigitte, but she seemed scared of her own shadow. But he also had Desmond – a younger man, a disciple – to do his dirty work. Because those two had heard me talking to Roland on the phone while he was at the Vatican. About strangling the Pope in person.

I couldn't do anything about Roland. Except get a little vengeance.

And quench my rage in those sweet screams.

I didn't feel like I understood the entire picture, but enough to move ahead, and maybe lance a few of Amira's little helpers – whether they knew they were being manipulated by her or not.

Because one thing I was sure of was that the demon had caused a handful of disturbances in my life, just to keep me busy, or to torment me. Before she set up whatever she was planning for tomorrow night.

Only one way to find out, though.

And I needed to keep my eye out for Cain. The silver hood I had surprised in the alley. He was either working for one of the bad guys, or he was genuinely watching my back – the way he had made it sound. Following those following me.

But I still had the black stalker to look out for. Because if Cain wasn't bad, he was following that guy. Maybe there really was a Shepherd in town, and he had just picked a hell of a time to stir things up.

Sensing I would need all the power I could muster, I told Beckett to drive me home.

Tomorrow would be interesting.

CHAPTER 34

I lurked at the edge of the steps, trying to keep attention from myself. It was cold enough that I was justified in wearing a hoodie, so was using that to somewhat disguise my distinct white hair. The cold weather had lessened the crowd somewhat, but not entirely, and for the most part, everything had been very peaceful.

A few of the church members had tried to start up hateful chants, but Desmond, Benjamin, and Brigitte had quickly pounced on them, handing them plates of food, and deftly breaking them up to introduce the loudest to random people from the community. I even spotted a familiar werewolf from a few years ago – who was actually a member of Abundant Angel Catholic Church – forced to politely talk with the protester. Father David nodded gratefully over his shoulder, before stepping up to a pair of loners in the crowd and striking up a conversation.

All in all, it was exactly what they had told me it would be. A peaceful gathering, complete with food, friendly faces, and sodas. They had initially given a brief sermon to the crowd, and then divested of the religious aspects and simply mingled. Father David had seen me, given me a brief nod, but hadn't pointed me out to anyone, as if sensing that I didn't want to be recognized.

Thank god.

I waited until the right time to strike, when I could catch Desmond or Benjamin off guard.

I swooped in for the kill, slipping past a gathering of faces that were conversing lightly, and caught Pastor Benjamin at the burger table.

"Hello, Callie," he said without looking up. "I'm glad you could make it."

I hesitated, thinking I had been sneaky. He turned to face me, and must have seen the conflict on my face. He smiled kindly, and my rage exploded in an instant, imagining this man smiling after what he had potentially done. Or what he had encouraged his followers to do. I kept my face blank, cautious, pleading. Seeking counsel. "We need to talk. In private. I think I discovered the killer, and you're not going to like hearing who it is."

He stilled, face entirely serious all of a sudden. "Shouldn't you be going to the police?"

I nodded. "Yes, but I thought you might want to talk to the person first. Maybe convince them to turn themselves in. Which would be better for everyone."

At these words, Pastor Benjamin grew very thoughtful. If he was innocent, this was good news, giving him a vision of all the press and attention he might get for his new church. If he was guilty, my words would make him think I had found someone else to pin the blame on, and that he could get away scot free. Either way, I was giving him favorable news. Because he didn't think I was dangerous enough to lure him away. I would have called the cops if I suspected him.

He nodded. "I see. Should we bring Father David into this?"

I shook my head. "Not yet. I wanted you to know first. It's... unsettling."

"Very well," he sighed. I let him lead the way around the side of the church. I glanced over my shoulder warily to find Father David watching us from far away, his lips tight with concern.

Then we were in private, and he turned to face me as if bracing for bad news. I slowly lifted my hand, allowing a ball of flame to coalesce before me. I watched his eyes, and didn't miss the pure hatred that suddenly replaced the gasp of shock.

"I disgust you," I growled, "because I can do this."

"It's an abomination!" he snapped. "Only god should have the power to do such things. Demons stole this and gave it to the worst of your ancestors. How *dare* you! If Father David knew," he spluttered in outrage.

I blinked in disbelief. "Let's say that incoherent string of words is true. That makes me guilty without choice."

"No," he snapped. "You could choose not to use it, or to turn yourself in!"

"Or... I could choose to use it for good, just like everyone in the world does with any of their gifts," I snapped.

"I see the devil already has your ear, blinding you with temptation. It's disgusting. I don't even want to be *seen* with you. I *knew* there was something wrong with you. Ever since you saw my flyer. You've used your serpent tongue to infect Father David and Roland, haven't you?" he seethed, spittle flying from his mouth, his eyes wild.

I took a maddening step closer, watching his shoulders tighten, and his face contort in rage. "You hate us. Want to kill us. Don't you? On God's behalf."

He was actually shaking as I took another step closer. He tried to step back, but a bench was in his way. "I..."

"Exactly. The game's up, Benji. No more murder. No more inciting riots. It ends. Now."

"I—"

I slapped him across the face, my vision pulsing red. How dare he? To preach to crowds, and incite hatred with subliminal messages. Hate was hate. It didn't matter who the target was. Either he had killed, or he had convinced some of his followers to do it. Because of this deeply ingrained hatred that was so apparent on his face.

"How dare you?" he roared. "You are vile, disgusting, a temptress—"

I slapped him again, breaking the thin skin of his lip this time. A drop of blood splashed onto his chin. I grabbed him by the shirt, shaking him, and heard a crash from behind me. I let go and spun, hands up to defend myself.

Desmond stared, horrified. Brigitte stood behind him, a mask of absolute terror covering her face. I smiled at Desmond, waiting to see his honest personality erupt to defend his mentor.

Instead, he dropped like a sack of wheat, falling boneless to the ground. Brigitte darted down to Desmond, patting his cheeks, and shooting terrified glances to Benjamin, sobbing openly, her hands shaking. She finally glanced at me, face a mess of tears, pleading with me. "Please... Please, just let him go. He'll give you whatever you want. Just let him go," she begged, holding her hands together in prayer.

I blinked. "What the hell?"

181

I rounded on Benjamin, who was staring with concern at Desmond's form, all his anger and disgust with me snuffed out. "Blood sickens him. Never has been able to stomach it. Let me go to him. Make sure he didn't hurt himself in the fall," Benjamin pleaded, not meeting my eyes.

I shook my head, bewildered as I stepped aside. Brigitte latched onto him, clutching his face, and seeing only the split lip, she squeezed him in a hug, as if he had been on the verge of death.

Father David's voice called out. "Is everything alright back here?"

Then he was standing before Desmond, staring down at Benjamin and Brigitte who were both now checking on Desmond together, brushing back his hair and speaking soothingly to him.

Father David slowly lifted his eyes to meet mine. "I think you need to leave. Now."

"This is Shepherd business."

"And you're not a Shepherd!" he snapped.

"Maybe I should call Roland," I argued. "I hear bombings are wonderful for cellphone reception." I clenched my fists as I glared at him.

"Leave. Now, Callie," he warned, fire in his eyes.

With nothing else to do, I turned and ran, heading away from the celebration. I wanted to scream, to shout, to kill. Roland could be dead. The killer was still out there. Amira was still laughing as I chased pawns on the board.

I growled as I ran, thinking furiously.

Cain was doing whatever the fuck the world's first murderer did in his spare time. Dorian Gray had led me on a wild goose chase. And I still had the black stalker to worry about. Or, the man in black, as Dear and Darling had called him... Maybe I needed to seek them out and ask them a few more questions.

But what the hell did I do now? Had I let my emotions get the best of me? Had the Vatican bombing been entirely unrelated to my investigation? Because after that clusterfuck at the church, I was confident that none of them were involved. Benjamin hated me on a level I couldn't fathom, but he wasn't a killer. And his disciples were sheep, in every sense of the word.

I had picked up Benjamin, sensing only a frail old man beneath. Desmond couldn't even stomach a bloody lip. And the look of horror on Brigitte's face hadn't been feigned. If I had ever seen fear for the first time in someone's eyes, it had been right then. Her world had literally crumbled to the foundations at seeing me holding Benjamin by the shirt, blood on his lips.

To be honest, I felt a little sick to my stomach myself. What in the world had made me think that a single one of them had a backbone. Had I seriously read too far into Dorian's comment? Had it just been a jab about the church? My phone chirped at my hip and I answered it as I ran.

"We have another one," Beckett said regretfully into the phone.

"*Motherfucker!*" I shouted.

"Hurry," he said. "Head to the Sprint Center as quickly as possible. I already removed the most incriminating evidence, but this one's not going to be as easy to cover up." He told me which level, and I groaned. The same level we had parked at yesterday. I was getting sick and tired of my stalkers.

I hung up, glanced around me, and then Shadow Walked to the lowest level of a staircase in the same parking garage, not wanting to risk scaring the hell out of everyone.

Especially when showing off magical talents was getting people killed.

CHAPTER 35

I appeared in the stairwell, glanced around to make sure there were no cameras – even though it was technically too late to worry about something like that since I'd appeared out of thin air already – and took off up the stairs, counting the levels.

I opened the door cautiously, not sure which side of the parking garage the chaos would be on. And found myself staring right into Beckett's face through the crack, who was pointing a pistol at me. Seeing it was me, he hissed, but didn't lower his pistol. His face looked torn as his eyes darted to my feet and then back to my face. He mouthed two words. *Bear. Run.*

Then he shouted loud, but his eyes begged me to get the hell out of here. "Freeze!" I heard radios squawking, and then shouting as several voices suddenly demanded to know who was fucking with the crime scene. Then they were shouting into radios, calling for backup.

I released the door, turned around, and pounded down the stairs. What the fuck? Of all the stairwells, I had chosen the one where the murder was?

"Freeze! This is a crime scene!" A voice shouted from a few levels below. I heard the shouting on the other side of the door near Beckett, and the pounding steps of more police racing my way from below. I Shadow Walked, just as I heard the door above me opening.

I appeared in the alley where I had first met Dear and Darling, not having consciously chosen to go here, but it had apparently been the first place on my mind in my panic.

"Well, this just won't do," Dear chided from behind me with a sigh. I whirled to find the two of them sitting in the exact same chairs, almost in the exact same position, frowning at me.

"No, it really won't. Now she knows our secret spot," Darling agreed.

"Well, we may as well let her inside. Feed a stray once," Dear trailed off, smiling at me.

Darling nodded. "Come with us, Callie," he said, climbing to his feet.

"I'd rather stay out here if it's all the same," I said, voice quivering from the adrenaline rush.

Dear blinked at me, and then turned to Darling, face questioning. Then they both turned back to me. "Well, of course it's not all the same," they said in unison. "Nothing is the same. Not ever."

I frowned. Were we talking about something specific, or were they being weird again?

"Regardless, you really should take off those shoes. Bear blood smells so vile." Dear pinched her nose dramatically.

I flinched as if struck, glancing down at my boots, lifting them up to inspect the bottom. And a very nervous chill shot down the base of my spine. My right sole was covered in blood – almost the entire length of the shoe.

Which meant... I had left footprints in the stairwell. Which meant evidence. Now I knew why Beckett had glanced down at my feet so pointedly. And why he had wanted me to run. And I was already connected to a few of the other murders, at least as a witness. Still, having evidence of me at the fourth crime was not good. It was actually quite terrible.

"Ah, I see the blood is a surprise," Dear said, brushing at her dress absently. "Which means you've been poking your nose into things again. Come. We have just the solution. Freely given, mind you. Unlike those damned politicians, promising the moon and stars, lying their ass—"

"Easy, now, Dear. Don't get worked up. It makes you poor company. Are you coming?" Darling asked, turning back to me.

I stared at him, then the brick wall behind the chairs. They were both just standing there, talking to me over their shoulders.

"I... guess. Where exactly are we going again?" I asked, walking up to them nervously.

Darling sniffed pointedly. "You are not going anywhere *again*, you are going *somewhere* for the *first time*. But Dear and I are going there *again*." He shook his head, annoyed. "Honestly, it's like none of you think before you speak."

I was too focused on his words to realize they were both reaching for me, but before I could react, they briefly touched me with their fingertips on either shoulder, and I was suddenly in...

A swanky, old world shop of some kind. Oxblood leather couches decorated the place in artful positioning, and antique artwork, paintings, advertisements, and all sorts of newspaper clippings adorned the walls. Etched glass walls created tiny enclosures in the massive room.

And the walls were covered with shelves of shoes.

Of all sorts. And I'm not talking sneakers.

I'm talking quality, hand-stitched leather. Pirate boots, flats, loafers, and a dozen others. Nate would have been in heaven in this place, wherever we were.

I cleared my throat uncertainly. "Those are very nice dress shoes," I said, surprised to find that I was sitting in a very comfortable leather chair.

Darling slowly turned to me, as if I'd just insulted his mother. "They are not called *dress shoes*," he said, voice dripping with ire. Then he was pointing, firing off names like a gun as his finger flew. "Oxford, Brogue, Derby, Chelsea Boot, Loafer, Chukka, and Monk Strap," he added finally, pointing down at his own... dress shoes. He was breathing heavily. My head spun.

"Oh, okay. I like the... Monk Strap best," I said uncertainly, pointing down at his footwear.

He scowled doubtfully before Dear shushed him away. I could have kissed her.

Dim lighting suffused the place with a soothing, relaxing, and peaceful glow. Like a home. My eyes drank it in, wishing I had someone to share it with. Like Claire.

I realized Dear and Darling were now staring down at me from rolling ladders on the walls. They glanced from me to their shelves, then slid down a few feet before glancing back. They would climb up or down a few rungs, slide some more, shoot me another look, and then continue on. I watched them, speechless, for what felt like five minutes. I realized my boots were gone, and jolted in surprise.

"Easy, child," Dear cooed. "They're in the incinerator. No muss, no fuss.

We'll get you stitched up proper." Then she was back to searching, reaching back into the shelves to reveal even more shoes behind those in front, as if the shelves went back for eternity. Like the Mary Poppins rack of shoes.

"What... *is* this place?" I whispered, stunned.

"Darling and Dear. Finest leather goods in all the worlds," Dear said, her voice muffled as her head was buried into her shelf.

"I've never heard of you," I said thoughtfully, wondering why she had made that plural.

"Those who know of us don't talk of us," she called out, still buried.

"And if they haven't heard of us, they likely can't afford us," Darling added with a mirthless chuckle. "Ah, here they are," he said reverently, pulling out a pair of exquisite, calf-high boots that looked designed for my exact musculature. They looked about as comfortable as a fur stocking molded directly from my legs.

Dear sighed. "Well played. I was thinking the slippers, but you have the right of it."

"I always do," Darling chided confidently.

"Except when you don't, of course," Dear replied with a sweet, cunning grin. Then she winked at him in a manner that was more befitting a bedroom.

"Well, we do have guests, Dear. Perhaps later," he said, laughing loudly.

"If you ever learn to finish a job on time," she muttered, pointing at the boots he still held in his hands. Then, hearing how that sounded, she chuckled throatily. "Well, perhaps not on *all* occasions." And this time, she winked at *me*. But I wanted no part of this verbal swordplay.

"Okay," I interrupted quickly. "So, you guys make shoes?"

They frowned in unison, looking offended. "There are shoes, and then there are *shoes*," they said hotly. "But we don't *just* make shoes. Holsters, weapons belts, bags, satchels, saddles..." Darling hopped down from his ladder. "Anything, really. As long as there is great need. And if we're interested in the terms."

They approached me like snakes, stalking up on either side as if planning to eat me.

Then they were before me, kneeling at my feet, and sliding the shoes over my...

"Ohhhhhhhhhmygaaaaaaaawd," I moaned in disbelief, wriggling my toes. It might have been the best sensation I'd ever experienced outside of sex. I don't say that to be a drama queen about shoes, filling the obvious stereotype of girls and footwear. I mean it quite literally. It felt akin to a lover trailing a feather up my calves in the middle of foreplay.

The.

Shoes.

Fit.

Perfectly.

Like a second skin. Despite their perfect fit, if I wanted to wiggle my toes, it was as if the leather momentarily stretched to accommodate my desire, and then shifted back to the snugger fit immediately after.

"*These* are *shoes*," Darling said proudly, beaming at my ear-to-ear grin.

CHAPTER 36

*J*almost felt like crying. "I've never been alive before this moment," I said, face entirely serious. Dear clapped her hands excitedly. I laid it on thick, hoping to god that their price wasn't going to turn me into a bank robber. Because, for these shoes? I might just do it. "It's like I'm seeing color for the first time after thinking the world was black and white."

Darling's shoulders straightened like a peacock's tail. "That is very kind of you," he said, dipping his head in a slight bow. "Now, we must discuss price."

I prepared to Shadow Walk out of here without realizing it. I wanted the shoes that badly. I caught myself at the last second, knowing I couldn't resort to theft. The guilt would eat me alive.

"For showing me life for the very first time in my existence, I fear to hear the cost…" I said.

Darling's mouth clicked closed, and Dear shot him a very considering look. For a full minute, they didn't blink. I wondered if I was actually open to selling my soul for these shoes, and had decided that I might be, when they finally turned back to me as one, unified in whatever decision they had come to.

Dear cleared her throat. "Two things," she began. I nodded hesitantly. "One, that you show us mercy in the days to come, remembering this kindness between us." I nodded, waiting for her second request. "Two, that you end this nonsense going on outside."

I blinked at her. "Nonsense?"

Darling clasped his hands behind his back. "The murders, Callie. They really are bad for business, and our kind have more often than not been associated with such atrocities."

I opened my mouth, a dozen questions going through my mind. "It was always my intent to end this *nonsense*, as you call it. But I'm having trouble finding the killer, and I keep finding myself coming back to square one." I decided not to pounce on the obvious question. What were they, and why were they typically suspected of such heinous crimes?

They considered me thoughtfully. "And if we can assist you in this matter?" Dear asked.

I tapped my knees with a finger, considering. "Please don't take offense by this, and understand I have a point." They nodded, waiting. "I don't know what *your kind* means." I held up a finger as they clamored to answer. "And I wouldn't normally care, but I seek the truth. If *your kind* is typically accused of such things, and since I don't know what you are, how do I know you aren't simply guiding me towards a personal target, bribing me with *shoes?*"

They considered that in silence, not taking offense, and turning back to each other for another private conversation. After recent events, I wouldn't have been surprised to hear they were Isis and Osiris, or something crazy. Which briefly brought back memories of the demon's house, and how Johnathan had been obsessed with how many supernaturals that seemed to gravitate towards Missouri. What was I stumbling into, and why? Did Roland perhaps have another reason to make Kansas City a permanent home? Because it was in Missouri?

I realized they were staring at me, and met their eyes. "We appreciate your question," Darling said. "You have given this thought, and not accused us of anything at the same time, even though you called to question our intent. This is wise."

I wanted to guffaw at that, but kept my face neutral. I was simply haggling for information, distracting them from the boots and making them think that I could offer them protection in exchange for information. Turning them from sellers into buyers. A subtle psychological ploy. But I did realize they hadn't answered my question. Sneaky versus sneaky.

"What if we found independent information that aided you? Would this prove our motive?"

I nodded after a brief pause to consider it, which was really just for show. Making slow decisions kept people on edge. Answer too quickly and they wondered what they had unnecessarily given up. "That might suffice for our bargain," I said slowly. "Do you have any useful information for me right now?"

Dear nodded happily. "Oh, yes. Cain has been keeping you safe from… something."

I wanted to curse out loud, realizing another suspect was clean. "Cain… Son of Eve, Cain?"

Darling nodded vehemently. "Quite unlike him, really. Especially for a stranger."

I let my vexation show slightly. "He was a second suspect," I said softly.

"Well, that's great. We've saved you time," Darling said, clapping his hands together.

"Unless you are lying. With all due respect, I place high integrity on my tasks, and never want to wrongly accuse… or *excuse* anyone."

As one, they sighed in defeat. Then they sliced open their palms, drawing a bloody circle on the ground with acute skill, as if it was a regular occurrence to work with one's blood. From inside the complete circle, they stated their names, bound their words to their blood, and then began. "We vow to always speak the truth to you, Callie Penrose, lest our enemies immediately and swiftly come for us, only to find us powerless."

I nodded as they climbed to their feet. Although it was different than any oath I had heard given, I could feel the magical thrum in their promise, and the important part was that they mentioned my name, their names, their promise, and that the result of breaking the promise included some form of them being powerless. Even if the names they had given me were false, those names had been bound to their blood, so in essence, whether those names had been false or sincere, they were now a very literal part of them. And those names now had power.

"Okay. I need you to keep digging. I need to know what's going on. There is a third or fourth player in town. One is a demon named Amira, but I don't know exactly who she's working with. Needless to say, whatever she is doing is against me. And it's happening tonight at midnight."

They nodded, shivering at mention of the demon. Not that it was in town, but that it was hunting me.

"Right, child. You better be off. It's been a few hours. And we need to move quickly if we're to be of any use. Return to us in the evening. You can leave through the front door. No one will notice. Trust us," they said, giggling to each other playfully.

I tried not to cringe to hear that a few hours had magically disappeared, but after everything else I had just seen, I wasn't entirely surprised. I climbed to my feet and took a few steps. If possible, the shoes were even more comfortable than they had been sitting down. It was almost as if the earth gave way a little more than normal, just for my comfort.

I walked through the store, noticing that different goods were broken down by section.

One section was all satchels, and I found a grin splitting my cheeks. Maybe I would get Nate a new man purse. Not now, though. I didn't want to press my luck on my bargaining skills.

We reached the glass windowed door that neatly said *Darling & Dear, We Do it in Leather!* on the front. I wondered if we were still nearby or on the opposite end of town.

Darling placed a gentle hand on my shoulder. I turned to face him. "You're a good bargainer," he said winking. "Don't think we didn't notice your tricks. We just decided they were worth it."

Dear rolled her eyes. "Men! Always trying to save face. I can assure you he isn't aware of anything unless it hits him in the forehead and talks to him," she said, smiling teasingly at him.

I grinned back, dipped my head, and stepped outside.

I glanced around curiously, staring up and down the street. I was pretty sure I was right around the corner from the alley where I had met them. Maybe even opposite the brick wall.

I looked up at the sun, and decided that I needed to call Claire. A bear had been murdered, and I hoped to god it hadn't been a new friend of hers.

She answered on the first ring. "Callie!" she shouted excitedly. "This is so freaking amazing! It's a veterinarian's dream! Maybe I should start a union or something," she said. I heard a low growl in the background, and my back instantly stiffened protectively. "Back off, Kenai. You're not a vet, so you don't know what you're talking about," Claire snapped at the sound in her best no-nonsense tone. I heard him grumbling something else, and

Claire laughed lightly. "Wait until my first shift, and we'll come back to that comment." The phone rustled in my ear, as if she was walking or getting up. "Callie, have you had any luck? Anything exciting going on?"

I let out a breath. "Things are okay. I just… heard about a murder today. A bear…"

Claire growled at that. "We heard." She hesitated for a moment, then spoke in a low tone. "He was a friend of Yuri's. He was never part of the Cave. A drifter. His name was Ragmussen. We didn't even realize he was still in town."

I sighed, closing my eyes for a moment. Yuri again. "I really, really want to find this asshole."

"No luck?" she asked, voice tinged with concern.

"Not yet. But I'm narrowing down a lot of options."

She paused. "That wasn't code for your killing a bunch of people, was it?"

Despite it all, I laughed. "No, Claire. But… well, I did slap a priest. Twice."

She gasped. "Oh, no, Callie. Not that sweet one we met!"

"Yeah. Not one of my finer moments. But in all truth, I was pretty confident he was my guy. Now, I'm back to the chalkboard. But I have help. How about you? You haven't shifted yet?"

Claire sighed. "No, but they say it will happen any time now. Likely in the next few days. They keep talking about a trigger. Most experience some emotional trauma that sets them off. If not, it can take some time. Not like the damned mutts that get a recruitment call during the full moon, whether they want it or not. The bears seem much more… passionate about it all. Almost spiritual. Call me crazy, but they remind me of Buddhists. Sure, there's plenty of tough talk and wrestling, but for the most part, bears take a pretty mellow view of the world. Just kind of hang out and do their thing. Eat. Play. Sleep. Defend their territory when threatened, but otherwise pretty even-keeled."

I nodded thoughtfully, glad to hear she wasn't surrounded by a bunch of alphaholes. "Keep me posted if anything changes, or have one of them call me if you shift. I want to see you turn into a tiny Panda or whatever silly flavor you turn into. Unless you're going to turn into the same kind as the one who cut you. Is that how it works?" I asked, frowning to myself.

She took on a lecturing tone. "Yes, and no. Sometimes you take after your, well, the person who changed you. But most times your genetics take effect. So, if you're bloodline is American, you're likely to turn into a Grizzly, black, or brown bear. Something native to that geography. Then again, we're all mutts in the DNA pool, sharing a dozen races and nationalities. Maybe I'll be something new and fresh. Because I am unique," she said adamantly.

"Entirely," I agreed, smiling. I reached the corner ahead of Pastor Benjamin's church and hesitated. That probably wasn't a good idea. For all I knew, they were begging Father David to bring me in for assault. I leaned against the wall, glancing up at the sky. The sun would set soon.

I blinked in surprise. "Claire. I need to go. Stay in touch, okay?"

"Is everything alright?" she asked nervously, sensing my tone.

"Yeah, I just didn't see what time it was."

"Oh, okay. Stay safe, Callie, and don't slap anymore priests. They're as gentle as lambs."

I groaned. "Later, Claire Bear."

"You have no idea how many times I've heard that already."

"I can imagine. Later!" I hung up, staring up at the sky again. Darling and Dear had been right. Time had flown in their shop. But… why? I definitely hadn't been in there as long as they said. Was it some kind of safe house? A spell? Seemed like they would want it the other way around, where you spend an hour inside and only five minutes had gone by in the real world, letting them produce more shoes faster, and making shopping uber-convenient.

Maybe I would trade them my business analysis for another pair of shoes.

CHAPTER 37

I needed to get a hold of Beckett, but I didn't want to call him in case he was in front of others. They would think it odd to see him answering a burner phone, wouldn't they? Or maybe that was a typical thing with cops. I just didn't know, and with me not wanting to get too close to the investigation, I didn't dare risk it.

As I kept my eyes on the church, making sure there wasn't a mob gathering, I tried to focus on the facts.

Cain was keeping someone off my back. The black stalker?

Amira was playing games, baiting me. Was this all to get the Spear of Longinus from me?

Shifters were dying all over, and they all had ties to Yuri. His friends. *God is dead.* And I still needed to find the hairy bastard and deliver him to the bears, proving he had turned Claire.

Roland had showed up in Rome to find the mole who betrayed us to Johnathan. And suddenly the Vatican gets bombed. Since I hadn't heard from him, I had to assume he was dead.

But… only a very small handful of people had known about Roland's trip to the Vatican. Father David, Pastor Benjamin, and Disciple Desmond.

But Dorian Gray – the big fat liar – had done me wrong, there. Sending me on a mission where I concluded it was entirely acceptable to slap a priest, and almost give mild heart attacks to his disciples. None of them were strong enough to kill a Freak, and I hadn't sensed a whisper of power from any of them.

Which left Father David, and I highly doubted him. Johnathan had tried to kill him a few months ago, so I didn't see him teaming up with Amira. Not even considering that he was the head of the Catholic Church in town.

Darling and Dear were magical shoemakers who wanted my protection from what they saw as a new Salem Witch Trial bubbling up in town.

The church was up in arms about a murder of one of their own, and someone was going around killing Freaks in retaliation.

My guess was this mysterious stalker.

Or... Dorian Gray.

Or Yuri.

Or... my phone rang, and I jumped, so absorbed in my thoughts.

I glanced down at it and almost dropped it in my excitement. "Roland!"

He answered with a tired sigh. "I'm okay, girl. But if I ever felt like cursing, now would be the time."

I realized I had tears in my eyes, and that I was shouting at him incoherently.

He let me finish, and gave me his soft, comforting chuckle. "I deserve all that and more... Listen, Callie. What I did before I left is... unacceptable. I was raised in a different time. A... harsher time—"

"Oh, don't worry, old man. We'll talk about that. In person," I promised, sniffling.

"Any luck on your... quest?" he asked, grunting as he did. Likely trying to get out of a hospital bed early, if I had to guess. The stubborn bastard.

I hesitated, feeling guilty. "I should probably be the first to tell you. I slapped Benjamin."

Roland was silent for a few seconds, and then burst out laughing. "Good for you!"

"Wait, did you hear me?" I asked, confused.

He laughed harder. "Callie, you have a fist like a brick, and I only wish you would have used that instead. Any man of God who actively condones hatred of another group, especially blanket hate for any people different from himself, has lost his way. Truly. We don't have to personally accept a different way of life, and can even disagree with it, but to use hatred as a tool for promoting your agenda? The church foundations are sacred, and building one with a cornerstone of hatred is wrong. He should have begun with love. Hate should have never entered the equation, but especially not as the first stone." He chuckled, then. "I imagine Father David was none too pleased. You probably have a confessional booth in your future."

I straightened slightly, feeling significantly better. Sure, I hadn't succeeded yet, but at least I didn't need to carry the guilt of slapping a priest on my shoulders tonight. "Listen, Roland. I actually suspected his involvement in this. And I've met a few new people in town. We have a lot to discuss..."

And I told him. Pretty much everything. Because I wanted to know what was new and what was old news to him. Maybe I was just being introduced to people that he was already familiar with. But if not... the problem was exactly as bad as I now thought it was. You could say I was telling Roland because I was a good student, and that would be partially right. More accurately, I was trying to prioritize.

And hoping he would reassure me that he was already aware of most of it...

"Are you sure?" he asked in a gravelly tone once I had finished.

I swallowed audibly, not liking his response. Not one bit. "Yes. As well as I can be."

"Well, I confirmed that none of the other Shepherds are in Kansas City," he said helpfully. Not great news, but at least it removed a suspect. "I'm in no shape to travel at this moment. Even if I were, it would take me too long to get back in time to help you tonight. And I'm too weak to Shadow Walk. Can you get any other help?" He paused, as if debating saying the next part out loud. "Nate, maybe?"

I shook my head. "He seemed preoccupied with a war. Or a bad ex's visit. Maybe both. He didn't give me details, but he had freaking camps of people on his property."

Roland cursed. Actually cursed. Now, judging by my advanced skills in this area, it was pretty mild. But still, Father Roland cursed.

Which pretty much told me how much shit I was in.

Surviving a bombing at the Vatican hadn't made him curse.

But my current situation in the City of Fountains had.

I sagged against the wall. "Have you figured out anything about the bombing? Maybe it's related to my stuff. It would make sense. Or at least might help me connect a few dots."

Roland hesitated, not wanting to talk about his own problems. But then he seemed to see the truth to my words. "Nothing concrete. I've been digging through records, trying to trace who gave Johnathan his intel. In fact, I can't even find a trace of the knowledge Johnathan got. As if it was destroyed immediately after the traitor gave it to him."

I kicked a pebble on the street, pleased to find that I didn't even feel the impact through my fancy new boots. "How are the girls? The victims we rescued." I asked, curious.

"They're... better than I expected, actually. But don't worry about them, Callie. I need to tell you something." He paused, as if searching for the right words. "I think it's time you take off the training wheels. If you're dealing with all this, you might need to thank God that you aren't an official Shepherd. That you can't be held accountable for what happens." He sighed. "You have permission from the local Shepherd to do as needed, and any mistakes will be forgiven once I return." He said this very fast, as if wanting to get it all out before he changed his mind.

"Are you... giving me permission to go full vigilante?"

"Don't make me regret it," he said with a sigh. "But in all seriousness, none of these things are for... well, what I'm saying is that this is way above your paygrade. But for all of them to happen at the same time? I think you're right. Someone – likely Amira – is playing you. Personally. Everything else is just a sleight of hand. The murders, everything. And to win, you might have to play by your own rules. Cut loose, if you will."

I nodded slowly, not wanting to say anything that might change his mind. To be honest, I had pretty much come to the same conclusion on my own, but to hear that Roland backed me was pretty hardcore. "Okay."

"You don't have time to play nice. You need to do whatever it takes to get rid of her. If she's done all of this in only a few weeks, I can only imagine what she would do after a month, a year... And something seems off about the Spear. I can do some digging over here, but I'll have to be discreet. My concern is why she told you about it in the first place. She could have taken it from you without you knowing. Her motives sound directly contradictory to Johnathan. You need to find out *why*."

"Alright. I've got a few ideas," I said, mind racing. "Just know that whatever happens, I'm trying to do the right thing. There will be fallout, and I'm trying to minimize it, but there are too many players for me to be sure what's really going on, and I'm betting she set it up that way on purpose."

"I trust you, Callie. I'll keep working on my end. But I'll be praying for you, and will have my phone on me at all times. I will not rest until—"

There was an argument in the background, interrupting Roland.

"Woman! I will get out of this bed when the Lord grants me the strength to do so, and if that moment is now, you will pipe down and weep as you witness your first miracle!" he roared.

Silence answered him, and then I heard the phone drop, clattering to the floor, followed by a muffled female laugh. Roland came back on. "I'll be out of this bed soon, Callie. Speak a word of this to anyone and I will rescind my support of your activities tonight," he warned.

I tried not to laugh, but couldn't help it. "Oh, Roland. When will you learn?"

He grumbled unhappily, but I could almost imagine the humbled smile on his face. "She is a very strong woman. Perhaps I should have listened to her..." he mused, sounding like every lecher of a man that had studied a woman out of her view.

"Alright, Father Creep. Go do your thing. But remember your vows."

"Callie—"

"Bye!" I said, interrupting him. Then I hung up, chuckling to myself.

Well, carte blanche to do what I needed to do. That could be fun...

CHAPTER 38

I headed to Abundant Angel Catholic Church to gear up and clear my head. I had an idea, and coupled with Dear and Darling – if they came through on information – it might just give me enough knowledge to figure out how to lay a trap.

I was strong, capable, and dangerous in direct confrontations, but judging from my interactions with this demon, she was more of a thinker, a planner, a schemer. Sure, she would be strong as hell, but she valued strength *behind* her mind. Like me.

Which meant she likely had redundancies in place, so that even if I managed to beat her in a fight – if that was what she meant by meeting at midnight – that some hidden card would be ready to appear in the game, poisoning my victory, or perhaps preventing me from victory.

My first thought was hostages. That was the easiest way to get to anyone.

Luckily, the only ones close to me were either in Italy or guarded by a mob of shifter bears. My dad was still in Chicago with his mysterious lady friend.

Bottom line, my people were about as safe as they could get. Unless another bomber was lurking at the Vatican, or if one of the bears was planning on betraying me.

But I doubted the latter, because that would basically be a death warrant for any and all of them. It would start a civil war. I thought about that, hesitating as I entered the training room below the church.

Well, that would certainly be sneaky. Perhaps that was Amira's plan. Get the bears to annihilate each other. With Claire in the middle, which would hurt me at the perfect time.

But I couldn't really do anything about that, other than warn Claire. I shot her a text, not speaking outright, but telling her to be aware of conflict, my meeting with Amira, and to run at the first sign of trouble. I didn't want to make her paranoid of her new friends, especially when she needed their help to not experience her first shift alone and afraid, potentially becoming a murderer if no one was there to restrain her. But she was in the big girls club now, and she needed to be a little cynical.

I reread my text, and nodded. It would have to do.

My phone rang as I was kneeling to begin meditating.

I answered it, recognizing Beckett's burner phone number. "Hey—"

"An eye witness says they saw you at the murder," he hissed urgently, interrupting me. "But another witness vouches you were at a social function at the church. Regardless, the police are en route to your apartment. They have a warrant to search your place. Is there anything you might want to hide?" he asked with a tight voice.

I thought about it, pushing down my outrage, and shook my head. "No. My place is clean. A lot of martial arts weapons, but that's fine, right?"

He hesitated. "Could any of them match the wounds on the victims?"

I tensed, not even having considered it. "Well, I guess if they broke a handle of something and stabbed someone with it..."

"Well, have any of your weapons been broken or are suddenly missing?"

I broke out in a cold sweat at the ridiculousness of it. "I'll have to check."

"Now. Hurry."

I dropped everything and made a Gateway right there, stepping into my apartment.

Fists immediately pounded on the door, startling me, and I heard the police outside calling for me to open the door.

I frantically darted into the guestroom, scanning my wall of weapons, and my heart froze. Some were missing. Well, *pieces* of some were missing. Wooden pieces.

More fists pounding on the door made me jump into action. I snatched up the broken weapons, gave the wall one last look, and darted into my room as I heard the door rattling, and a set of keys falling to the floor as I heard the landlord babbling on the other side, trying to find the right one. I snatched up the book Nate had given me, not wanting the police to find a book on magic, which would only add another link from me to the killings. I ran back to my Gateway and jumped through, releasing it behind me just as I heard the door lock click open.

I crashed to the floor with a grunt back in the training room, a pile of weapons surrounding me. I was panting heavily.

I immediately dialed Beckett on the number he had just called me from. "You were right. Someone tried to frame me. I could bet that if you checked some of these weapons, one or two of them would be a perfect match for a piece used in one or all of the murders. The two pieces would fit together perfectly."

He sighed. "Shoes. You're still wearing them, right?"

"As a matter of fact, they were destroyed. Gone." I wanted to kill someone. Anyone. Trying to frame me for the murders when I was the only one fighting against them? But it only served to solidify my deep burning rage. Amira was going to pay for this. "Beckett, it is literally impossible that anyone saw me at the last crime scene. You're the only one I saw."

He let out a relieved sigh. "Thank God," he said. "But that means someone is setting you up. Any idea who yet?"

"No, but if you're free, I need a locksmith."

Beckett was silent on the other end, and then let out an amused chuckle. "Oddly enough, my determinable future is free. They took me off the case. Incompetence was the underlying cause. The misplaced evidence, my ties to a suspect, and digging too deep."

I growled. "You're being set up, too."

"Seems like it. That's why I saw them coming for you. It made sense." He sounded very calm, and I could tell he didn't want to talk about it, focusing on the problem instead, as was his way.

"Thanks. For the support and the heads up," I said gratefully.

He was silent on the other end. "Callie, I need to hear you say it. Not that I don't trust you, but I just need to hear you say it."

My anger flickered to a white-hot heat for a moment, and I struggled to get a hold of myself. Was he really asking if I was involved? After everything? How dare he ask me to prove—

Then it hit me. Ah, double standards...

I had made him do the exact same thing in the parking garage. Needing to know that I could trust him. I cleared my throat, trying to hide my initial anger. "I swear I haven't killed any of these people, and that I have not been a knowing accomplice in any of it. I would never do a thing like this. When a monster goes bad, my job is to hunt and kill them. Not torture them to death in a public place. Even if they were bad, and I wanted to, I would not do this. I swear."

"Thanks, Callie. And I'm sorry for asking. I just… all of this is insane, and I'm still coming to grips with it. If magic is real, anything can be real. And I'm not going to lie, the evidence isn't looking great. You've been seen near every location. Whether directly or indirectly. And they say the killer usually returns to the scene of the crime. This kind of bad luck screams guilt to cops."

"Don't sweat it. But I need you to be ready to meet me somewhere we won't be seen together. Soon. I have a date at midnight."

"I know. I was planning on playing third wheel. I have stakes in this, now," he growled.

"No, that's a terrible idea," I argued. "No offense, but you're way too green to go up against a demon, and she would only find a way to use you against me. She already told me so."

"Callie, I'm going to be pretty blunt here. Is there anything I could do to stop Amira from simply kidnapping me and taking me to the meeting on her own?"

I opened my mouth to argue, and realized that the only argument would be if he stayed by my side. Which meant he would be there anyway. I sighed. "Shit. Get any kind of weapon you can think of. I'll give you some stuff, too. But wear dark clothes. We have a stockpile here that will balance out whatever you bring."

He grunted affirmatively. "I take it we won't be driving?"

"No," I said, smiling.

"Okay, I'll find a place with an alley or something for you to get to out of sight. We don't want both of our cars conveniently found next to each other. Especially after the set-ups."

I nodded. "Good thinking. Let me know. I'll be ready." He hung up, and I stared down at the weapons on the floor, kicking them with my feet. "You're going to pay, bitch…"

CHAPTER 39

I had showered and changed, not wanting to look like Arthur. I sat on the floor of the training room, now, and I focused on absolutely everything – every single problem – allowing in my fears, my concerns, and spicing it all with an unhealthy dash of fury. I did this for a solid ten minutes, my eyes closed, and breathing steadily.

Then, as stressed out as I could possibly get, I discarded my feelings. My rage, primarily.

Next, was each obstacle and objective. Each priority. I had given them all a chance to voice their concerns in my head, had acknowledged them, and now it was time for them to leave.

I considered each person in my life, both old and new, imagining their faces for a moment, their motivations, their machinations, their desires and fears, and then I booted them from my headspace.

A few minutes later I was one with a single white feather in my mind, centered on a sea of black, at peace. Occasional thoughts, arguments, fears, and concerns tried to invade, but I dumped them into the feather, watching as it grew brighter, ruffling slightly in the unseen wind of my mind.

Confident I was as peaceful as I could get, I focused on the feather. I imagined it coated in silver, and felt an instant resistance. Trying to force a change into my habitual meditation totem was not simple. It was almost like starting from scratch, but I wanted to attach the silver color from the cracked door in my mind to something old, something me.

I hadn't wanted to change everything and imagine a single drop of silver bloo—

As quickly as that, a quivering droplet of silver floated in the sea of blackness, even easier to maintain than the feather. But that wasn't what I wanted. The silver was alien to me. It would take time to get used to it, and that was a distraction.

I felt sweat popping out on my forehead as I tried to merge the feather and the droplet of silver together, breathing faster as the two fought against each other.

But I was determined.

The feather was a symbol for me as a wizard. It had helped shape the woman I was.

The silver drop was new, and although I wanted to understand it, I didn't want to blindly adopt it without fully considering what it was, what it entailed, and what it might make me become. That mysterious cracked door in my mind. After all, I was confident that the door was a result of the Angel's blood, that single, silver drop that had merged with me. The blood from a literal Agent of Heaven. And although I believed in this stuff, I wasn't a fan of blind faith. But knowing Angels existed kind of made it abundantly obvious. Irrefutable, even.

But my problem was that the beings supposedly created by God had become known to me.

But... not God. I had never seen, heard, nor spoken with Him.

I know that's a pretty ignorant way to look at things, and that I was supposed to take it on faith, but I had a real problem with that. I just wasn't wired that way. I was too curious. Too inquisitive. I was confident that at some point in my life I might find a healthy way to marry the two, but I wasn't there yet.

So, I wasn't about to adopt a standard that went against my core beliefs. Something that would leave doubt in my meditations, distracting me from my goals.

I forced the two totems together, closer, closer, closer, until a single push would make the two edges touch. But I simply had no more willpower. I was actually panting with exhaustion, even though my body was entirely still, sitting in the middle of an empty training room.

The feather quivered slightly in the unseen wind, and touched the silver droplet.

And I felt a tingling sensation shoot from my toes to my head, almost making me gasp in surprise. The feather was instantly coated in chrome, spinning slowly in the field of black, and the silver droplet was no more.

I simply remained that way for ten minutes, acknowledging and accepting the transformation.

The strange power I had felt hadn't been all that strange, really. Just different. I pondered that, wanting answers. But questions weren't welcome right now. This stage was for introspection. Mostly idle, but sometimes I could directly focus on topics when in this state. Trying to do this typically snapped me out of focus, forcing me to start all over again, so I considered this abstractly, merely whispering a thought, and letting my subconscious mind run with it.

Almost like... working out. I could do a pull up and position my hands so that my biceps were targeted as I lifted my chin above the bar. Or, I could rotate my hands so that my triceps carried the majority of the weight. Either way, I was doing a pullup. I was just doing it differently. Same result, different path.

I considered the feather directly, studying it, thinking. Yes. This made sense to me.

The feather continued to spin, and I slowly opened my eyes, a smile on my face.

I stared at the space ahead of me, and imagined a small Gateway. I considered it as a wizard, as Nate had shown me. I studied each aspect of the process in making a Gateway. And then, I took a figurative step back, and considered how else I might make a Gateway, using my new muscles. Like I had done in Beckett's car.

The thought process slowly began to make sense to me, not just the action.

When I made a Gateway, I always focused on where I wanted to be, or where I wanted to get away from.

But...

What if I focused on where I *needed* to be...

A crackling ring of white and silver sparks erupted before me, startling me with its intensity. I stared at it, considering. But all I could see was a silvery reflection of myself, as if I had just made a mirror. Just like in Beckett's car. I frowned at it. But my reflection smiled back.

Which sent my hair to standing on end. Was it a reflection or not? Why had it smiled when I frowned? And why couldn't I see a destination like I was used to seeing.

I slowly extended my hand, watching as my reflection did the same.

Our hands touched across an icy plane of smooth power, and I shivered at the touch. But push as I might, my hand didn't pierce the surface.

"What's the point of a Gateway that doesn't go anywhere?" I mumbled to myself.

"This Gateway has taken you to what you *needed*," my reflection replied, grinning at me. I stumbled back, almost shouting out in alarm. My reflection giggled. "You are afraid," she said.

"Um, yeah. My reflection is talking to me. Or I'm talking to myself."

She shrugged. "You asked to see where you needed to go. Here I am." She smiled at me again. She was much prettier than me, even though she was supposed to be a reflection. "This really is how you look, you know…" the reflection chided.

I shivered, but finally scooted closer, wondering if Roland would need to lock me up after this. "What do you mean this is where I needed to go?" I asked.

She studied me thoughtfully, almost sadly. "You are afraid of yourself. Of what you may find out about yourself. It's why you've always been so aware of others. How they think. How they act. Why they do."

I blinked. "Why they do?"

She nodded. "Why they do what they do. It's why you are really quite exceptional at reading people. Most times, anyway." I nodded awkwardly. What was this? Was this a higher form of meditation or something?

"No, silly. It's you *seeing*. It's what one with our blood does. Sees. Witnesses. Whatever you feel comfortable calling it." She leaned closer. "We don't have much time, but you need to know this."

I nodded dumbly, simply accepting that I was crazy, and that I might just be crazy enough to teach myself something. "Okay."

"He loves you. All of you. No matter what you choose."

I stared openly. "He?" I finally asked. She nodded. That was the extent of her answer. "Okay. What do you mean, *no matter what I choose?*"

Her face looked troubled for a moment, but she still managed to make it look cute. I knew for a fact that I didn't look cute when I was troubled, so she was a big fat liar. "We can't really go into that without you making a choice, but you can reach me anytime. Just know that you are not obligated to do anything. To be anything. Although there are pros and cons to either choice." She grinned. "But your parents love you, too. No matter what path you choose. Just because you might be uncomfortable with their story, does not mean you have to follow their path. They chose as they did based on the consequences of their previous choices. As do we all. You do not need to fill their shoes, or live up to their expectations. You are you. I am I. The only one who is more than that is *He*," she said meaningfully. "The Alpha and the Omega."

My head was whirling. "Wait, you're not speaking very clearly."

"The Lord works in mysterious ways, right?"

"God is aware that I'm down here making a mess of things?" I asked, suddenly terrified. Both at the idea of God being very literal and the fact that he was watching my reality show on the God Network.

"He is aware of all His creations, no matter how small or how large."

This really wasn't going how I had expected.

My reflection grew very serious, almost sporting a disappointed look. "This is hard enough without you challenging your subconscious. I know you. I *am* you. I know your trepidations on religion. Just know that you have free will for a reason, and that it is a gift freely given. Of course, what you do with it is entirely up to you, and there are consequences. But there is not only one path to God. There are infinite paths. Even some that are not detailed in the Bible or spoken by the church."

I stared at her, hard. "You mean... good people that don't necessarily subscribe to God. Different religions."

She shrugged maddeningly. "Just to be clear, this isn't God talking. This is you talking to yourself. But yes, you believe this to be the case, and also that God would understand such positions."

I frowned. That didn't mean I was right about it. "Basically, you're here to help me see that I can be a good person no matter where I am Sunday mornings..." She nodded back happily. "But I could still be wrong with that assumption."

She shrugged. "It wouldn't require much to get to Heaven if the path had road signs, would it?" I scowled at that. "You'll like this one even less, then. The path to Heaven is not an escalator."

This time I actually growled back at her. "So helpful. It's remarkable, really."

"Long story short," she said, sighing, "is that you do not need to fear the future. Deep down, you believe that God listens to those who do good by others. Especially at great cost to themselves. Stay true to yourself, and know that whatever you learn in the future, you are not required to make a life change. Your parents are not judging you. *You* are judging you. That's what really matters, isn't it?"

I nodded slowly.

"Right. Well, you have some things to do tonight. Put your big girl pants on to match those fetching kinky boots." I grinned from ear-to-ear. "You were right. Need is the key to the Silvers. You just needed to heed this public service announcement first. In the future, if you want to gossip about boys or something, simply say your name into a Gateway…" She winked at me. "Good luck, and… Godspeed."

The reflection vanished, and I was staring at a Gateway leading to Dorian Gray's second balcony, where I had spent time talking with him and Beckett. I smiled to myself as I let it go. It was taxing, using muscles that had never been exercised. Not difficult, but definitely more draining than a typical Gateway. I wondered how much juice I had in the batteries, and not wanting to waste it, I decided I would only use it in case of emergencies. I knew with the wards around Dorian Gray's house that I would have to use it there, but it wasn't time for that yet.

I glanced down at my phone impatiently, and was surprised to find a text from ten minutes ago. I thought about it for a moment, realizing I knew the area well enough to wing it. I climbed to my feet, glanced around the room, and then used my magic to make a Gateway to a nearby alley where Beckett had asked me to meet him.

"Game on," I muttered, stepping through.

CHAPTER 40

I sat in the shadows of the upper balcony overlooking the living-slash-orgy room below. The couches, furniture, and woodwork glistened in the dim lighting below, and everything smelled of cleaning solution and fresh cut flowers. I would have just lit the room on fire to be on the safe side, but I didn't have a painting keeping me safe from things like that.

I was here for answers. No more playing nice. I was on a deadline. Literally. I had given Dorian the chance to help me, and he had instead led me astray. Perhaps I should have expected this from someone like him, but something he had said kept nagging at me. He was a concierge, and didn't want to get involved in any infighting between supernatural factions. Which led me to believe that he hadn't picked the side against me, but that he had very carefully tried to tell me something while appearing neutral. Just because it had fallen on deaf ears, wasn't his fault.

Still, I was leaving with clear answers tonight. One way or another.

Because with Dorian's connections in my community, I was betting he knew more than he had told, and not wanting to get involved, had tried to dodge the drama. But he had to know something about Johnathan's focus on Missouri, and why so many beings seemed to be popping into the state around the same time, like some silent dog whistle had been blown, and everyone was simply answering the call – whether they realized it or not.

This time I would try throwing a Temple Tantrum.

Another factor bothering me was that both Johnathan and Dorian were interested in Nate.

And then there were the five territories on Johnathan's map of Kansas City. But who ran which? I assumed that the vampires, bears, and wolves each ran one, but what about the other two? Other than as victims, the wolves and vampires hadn't popped their heads out of their respective kennels and coffins in quite some time. Neither had the bears, but at least I knew why they were absent. They were busy looking after Claire while I did their dirty work. Finding Yuri. But I hadn't heard a whisper of him, even though I knew his paw was deep in this honey pot.

But *no one* had retaliated to the murders. Not Master Haven and his vampires, not Armor and his bears, and not the wolves, who were still out of town. Really, Pastor Benjamin's new church was the only voice crying foul.

Almost like everyone sensed an impending storm and had chosen to batten down the hatches rather than scream at the sky. But was that storm Amira or one of these two unknown territories? Johnathan had made a mockery of the bears, wolves, and vampires only a few weeks ago, and perhaps everyone was still reeling, licking their wounds, or not wanting to fuck with the second demon that had come to town so soon after the first.

Maybe the territories were like the mafia. Different families entering town and trying to take power over the existing families. That seemed to make more sense. Because those lines had looked like gang lines. Freaks of all kinds lived in my city, but didn't have enough of a presence to own a territory. That didn't mean they couldn't live here, just that they likely had to pay dues to whatever family ruled their turf. *Keep your head down and you can live in my neighborhood.*

Regardless, I needed answers, because even if everyone wanted to fold, I had to go all in. I was being targeted, personally. Roland was right. Even the police were in on it somehow. Again. I wondered if all demons operated like this, more intelligent than I had anticipated.

I glanced down at the phone in my hand, and seeing the text, I typed off a quick reply.

Send it.

I waited, glancing down at the open vault door below, smiling.

It didn't take Dorian long. He entered the room on silent slippers, wearing a silk robe and looking angry, wary, and murderous. A dark... miasma seemed to follow him like a shadow, but whenever I tried to look directly at it, it wasn't there. More like a sensation I was feeling rather than a literal visible power. Since I had never looked upon him with my new power, this caught me off guard a bit.

But it told me something about him. Dorian had picked up a few things in his long life. Maybe despite his flamboyant persona, he wasn't as peaceful as he led others to believe, hiding a scrapper of sorts beneath his sinful façade.

He studied the room anxiously, glancing behind any potential hiding place, up at the balcony above, and then finally, to the open vault door. He hesitated upon seeing that, the darkness around him seeming to ripple in agitation, but he kept his face a cold mask. He walked over to a tray of liquor bottles and poured himself a splash of amber liquid.

He sipped his drink for a few seconds in silence, as if waiting for an attack.

When nothing happened, he downed his drink and pulled out his phone. My phone began to ring, and his eyes triangulated the sound like a wolf, locking onto the open vault.

I bit back a laugh as I watched him from my hiding spot above, clutching Beckett's phone in my fist. Because I hadn't sent Dorian the text. Beckett had, using my phone.

No one answered, and I heard Dorian growl instinctively. "Bravo, Callie. You can come out, now," he said in a resigned voice, carefully concocted to sound anxious, nervous, and fearful.

"I like the view better from up here," I called out, standing and then stepping into the open.

He tensed like a startled deer, staring up at me with a shocked look. I waved. "Observe the cowardly lion in his natural habitat," I said officiously, like those animal show narrators.

His lips tightened as he studied me. "Okay. I'm confused. You had me dead to rights with the vault. Why not stay there to threaten my painting? Or to destroy it, ending this farce of an existence once and for all. I almost regret that you didn't."

I shrugged. "I like the paintings up here better." I pointed at the open vault, which led into a small hallway with an alcove around a slight bend. "That one is much too vile." And that was the truth. The painting we had seen in there was downright horrifying. "But this one," I said, turning to face the painting that had caught my eye last night. "This one speaks to me for some reason."

His shoulders were tight, and he looked ready to use his super speed to stop me if necessary, but his voice was entirely calm. "You can have it. Or I can put you in touch with the artist."

I placed a hand over my chest. "Heavens, no. It's worse than the one in the vault. I wouldn't want anything else drawn by this artist, either." I made a point to glance at the adjacent paintings, clucking my tongue. "Yep. I'm sure of it. One of these things is not like the other."

"Since when did you become an art aficionado?" he asked harshly. "They're all defaced. As they deserve to be."

"Well, the other paintings are defaced, true. But this one," I said stepping back to tap the glass with a fingernail behind my back, keeping my eyes on him. "The *glass* is defaced, and you cleverly used laser lights to make it seem like the others. But the painting itself?" I glanced over a shoulder and shivered. "Although hideous, it's not actually defaced. Just made to look like it."

His lips thinned, but he tried to splash on a grin. "Why the interest in a painting left out in the open over the one keeping me alive? As far as threats go, your tactics are quite… obscure."

"I bet it would burn pretty easily," I said, as if not hearing him.

He took a step forward. "Your magic won't work here," he snapped, shoulders almost quivering.

I lifted my hand to reveal a butane torch – one of the disposable ones. "That's why girls always accessorize." I clicked it on, filling the room with the hissing sound of live fire. I waited, but when he didn't move, I moved the flame right up to the glass without looking.

"FINE!" he shouted desperately. "What do you want, you insolent child?" He was panting.

I clicked it off, smiling back at him. "Truce, and I won't incinerate your portrait."

"Yes. Granted," he snapped eagerly.

"Oh, for him, too," I added.

Dorian spun to see Beckett directly behind him, holding one of his gleaming butterfly knives in each hand. He wore a long dark coat, hanging below his knees, and was smirking. He dipped his head. "I really wish you would have come into the vault. I had something to show you."

Dorian grimaced. "Truce," he muttered darkly.

"Play nice, boys. I'll be right down," I called out cheerfully, not wanting to use my newfound powers in front of Dorian. I strode across the balcony to the stairs in the main foyer, calmly walking down them as I ran over my plan.

Dorian had to assume I had some ace up my sleeve to make it inside his home without setting off an alarm or using magic, but I wanted him to remain uncomfortable. Off balance.

Because I was beginning to realize that although dangerous, Dorian really wasn't a fan of confrontation. Sure, he might be deadly, but he didn't give off the vibe that he enjoyed it very much. Which seemed odd to me, seeing as how he was immortal as long as his portrait survived.

Then again, maybe it was because he owned a constant reminder of his impending death, and after living so long with it, it was pushing him further away from an immortal mindset. Forcing him to consider his weakness every day. To have to worry about keeping it safe at all times.

And little old me had just scared the shit out of him. Not only breaking into his vault, but noticing the subterfuge in his plan to hide the real portrait out in the open.

Which was exactly where I wanted him.

I entered the room to find them in the same position, glaring at each other.

CHAPTER 41

I stepped up to them, smiling brightly. "Let's try this again. Know any demons in town?"

He grimaced. "Johnathan, or whatever name he gave you. But you killed him. I already told you, I don't get involved in this kind of shit. I'm just here to have a good time."

I nodded. "What about his sister, Amira? Or his pet project at the house on the hill?"

He stiffened, blinking at me. "You know about..." he whispered in disbelief.

I gave him a level stare. "I know quite a bit. Enough to know when you're feeding me lies—"

As quickly as that, Dorian tried to escape, but Beckett had been expecting it. He instantly slashed out with his knife, scouring across Dorian's back. Dorian groaned, but didn't slow down, and I felt the unseen darkness suddenly growing thicker. Before I could do anything, there was a thunderous *boom*, followed by a splattering sound and a stunned, pained gasp.

I stared from the smoking barrel of the sawed-off shotgun in Beckett's hands to the groaning form of Dorian Gray on the ground. I could actually see through the hole in his stomach. He grimaced, staring up at us in disbelief. Beckett's coat had concealed the weapon.

I glanced back at Beckett, nodding approval. "That was really fast," I complimented him.

He shrugged back, not a quiver of fear on his face. "If Mr. Fancy-pants hadn't shown me his speed yesterday, I might not have been as trigger-happy."

"You *shot* me!" Dorian hissed angrily.

"Just a minute, Dorian, my dear," I said as if I was speaking to a toddler. I turned back to Beckett. "Still, impressive," I said, watching his eyes for any sign of delayed shock. But not a glimmer of empathy lived in those baby blues.

He finally let a smile touch his cheeks, chuckling as he lowered his gun to continue aiming at Dorian, ignoring the man's continued complaints about being shot.

"You... *lunatic!*" he screeched.

Beckett didn't even look, just thumbed back the hammer on his shotgun as he continued to give me his full attention. Dorian ceased complaining. "I tried to tell you, Callie," Beckett began. "When something doesn't work, I just move onto the next tool in my belt. Then the next. Then the next." He shrugged as if it wasn't a big deal. "The hard part was believing in this stuff. But once you accept that bit..." he smiled down at Dorian. "The rest is easy as pie."

There was definitely fire in this man. He didn't have an ounce of protection against Freaks, not inherently anyway. But... that just meant he needed a few more accessories than most. Simple as that. Have problem? Find solution. Beckett Killian's motto.

I found myself considering him in a much different matter, and quickly schooled my features.

Dorian began to grunt and gasp on the ground as I heard a rattling from the tier above us. I turned from one to the other to see Dorian's wound healing before our eyes, and the painting above rattling behind the glass.

"Huh. I wondered why the glass wasn't flush with that particular painting. It's to give it room to move and breathe, I guess. Makes sense. In a disgusting way." Glancing back down at Dorian, I found him panting, his wound now a smooth expanse of healed flesh. He glared at the two of us at the same time, somehow. I let him.

"If you're done pissing yourself, I believe the young lady asked you a question," Beckett said with a faint grin. "And just to clarify, you tried to run away, so I shot you. Nothing personal. Nothing to cry about later. You really wouldn't want to go crying to anyone about this. Wouldn't be good for your health. Just give her what she came for, since you wasted her time earlier." His eyes were ice. Emotionless. As was his tone.

Dorian glared daggers back, but finally climbed to his feet, moving slowly enough to not appear threatening. "I don't know any more than you about that cursed mansion. I know he had a secret room there, and was interested with the politics in town – which was actually more Amira's obsession – but I never saw the room. I swear it." I believed him, judging by the look in his eyes. He was terrified of us. More so than he was of the demons. The immortal Dorian Gray had been slapped down twice. By a young wizard and a Regular, of all people. After hundreds of years of safety, he had been put in his place twice in the space of ten minutes. He cleared his throat. "If you saw the room, I'm betting it's gone, now, right?"

"How would you know that?" I demanded in a low tone.

He held up his hands. "It's the way Johnathan worked. Redundancies and privacy."

"Again, how would you know that?"

He sighed disgustedly. "He tried to convert me. A few times. Until he finally found out my legend. That I was already more depraved than any of his roommate's downstairs. That he literally had nothing to offer me. Immortality? Nope. Sin? Nope. Money? Nope. And since I'm already pretty much guaranteed to wander the lowest pits of Hell when I do finally kick the bucket, he really had nothing to bargain with. It bothered him, but he kept in contact on occasion. The occasional brunch."

I stared incredulously. "Brunch…"

He shrugged, smirking subconsciously at the absurdity. "Yeah."

"And did Amira ever join you on these brunches?"

He shook his head. "If Johnathan was secretive, Amira was full-blown paranoid." His eyes grew distant, as if thinking. "He called her his right hand, but I always got a bad feeling about her. That she had her own game." He finally shrugged. "But I'm betting all of those bastards do."

I nodded thoughtfully. Nothing new, but at least it was confirming my assessment of her. "Rather than confronting me directly, she fled the scene after I killed him. She plays the long game. I have reason to believe she's the one behind all this chaos lately. To what end, I'm not completely sure. But the common denominator is that she doesn't like me very much, and is using others to get to me. At least I know the priest isn't involved," I added with a glare.

He blinked back at me. "You went after a priest?"

"After your warning, yes."

Again, he reminded me of a deer in headlights. "I simply made an observation about churches in general. I never trust them. I didn't mention a specific church. And definitely not a specific person. Hell, I could have been talking about *your* church. The Vatican and whatnot. Because this looks a hell of a lot like retaliation to me. You dig into the murders, and the Vatican gets bombed." He shrugged. "Seems like something Amira would do. To cover her bases, at least. It's why I've been reluctant to talk to you. She's fucking psychotic."

I decided to go for my original plan. Parts of it would still work, but I had hoped for more help from Dorian. "What about Yuri? A local bear."

Dorian grunted. "What about him? He was kicked out of his Cave for something, and spent a few days telling everyone he met that he would soon be the new Kansas City Alpha. But he's not been seen for a while, now."

I was doubly glad that I had warned Claire. Because if Yuri wanted to be the new alpha, things were going to get worse.

"Can you contact him?" I asked. I had the outlines of a plan, and the more I focused on it, the more it began to take shape. Beckett was studying me thoughtfully.

"Sure." Dorian shrugged. I slowly turned to face him, a terrible smile stretching my cheeks.

I let a slow, menacing grin creep over my face. "You want to get even?"

He nodded cautiously. "Depending on the next words out of your mouth…"

As I told him, the look of shock and disbelief began to fade, and he began to look very intense, as if he were planning every detail of a party. In a way, he was.

"That's… positively devious," Dorian said wonderingly.

I leaned in closer. "But know this, Mr. Gray. If one single hair on Beckett's head is harmed. If he trips over a sidewalk into oncoming traffic. I'm coming for you. And I will keep you in agony until the end of my days…"

He grimaced, a sickly expression on his face. "Understood."

"You've got work to do, and so do we. We'll see ourselves out."

CHAPTER 42

I took Beckett to Darling and Dear. Instead of just walking in unannounced, I knocked.

They answered almost immediately, smiling excitedly at me, and dipping their heads politely at Beckett. He returned the gesture, not sure what we were doing here. I felt these two needed to be experienced first-hand, not explained secondhand. They were an enigma, to put it mildly.

They locked up behind them and then led us deeper into the store, talking over their shoulders. "We were just going to visit you, but you were in a despicable place, uninvited," Dear said over her shoulder. "We didn't want to bother you. Then you were suddenly outside, so we just waited. We have someone we would like you to meet."

I tensed uncertainly, and Beckett must have noticed it. I felt his posture grow more alert beside me, but to anyone else it might have gone unnoticed.

They were just going to visit me? What did that mean? And who was waiting for me here?

We passed an area full of coats, and I found myself staring at one curiously, but Dear and Darling quickly moved past it, motioning for us to follow. I sighed, realizing that I could spend hours in this place thumbing through the racks. I shook my head, focusing. Dorian was in play, but I needed one more wildcard. Something to muddy the water... Darling and

Dear rounded a corner ahead of me, and I realized I had been dragging my feet, lost in my thoughts. I quickened my pace and saw them turn into what looked like a side room. How big was this place?

I stepped through the doorway behind them to find a large, cozy room with two leather-backed couches and a fireplace. A man was sprawled lazily on one of the couches, smoking a cigar. He wore custom Darling and Dear boots, judging by the looks of them. I wondered if they were as comfortable as mine.

"Cain..." I growled.

Dear and Darling cleared their throats. "You two got off on the wrong foot. Although a mercenary, killer, and all around terrible person, one thing is pretty sacrosanct to him. His word."

Cain grunted dismissively. "Except when it ain't," he grinned.

I studied him thoughtfully. "You remind me of an asshole I once met."

"That's probably because we've met before, Callie," he chuckled.

I shook my head, not rising to the bait. "No, a guy named Nate Temple."

Cain stiffened, boots thumping to the floor and eyes dancing with fire. "Oh, I met that smug bastard once. I wanted to have a chat with him. But he went and got all juiced up on me."

I smirked. "Scared?"

"Smart," he corrected, visibly relaxing. "I'm not saying we won't meet in a dark alley one day... But I will say I'm no longer actively searching for that alley," he said carefully.

I decided to try a different tact, aware of Dear and Darling watching us. "He is... a handful. Quite infuriating at times, to be honest. But I think he means well."

Cain guffawed. "Don't we all..."

I nodded. "So..."

He tapped out his cigar, studying the cherry for a few seconds. "You're being followed. Daily. I caught onto it by accident and decided to go to that coffee shop you frequent. Been hanging around ever since. It didn't seem right to be stalking a young girl such as yourself, but then I saw you take care of a problem or two, and decided you probably didn't need my help." He tapped some ash into the ashtray. "Then folks started dying. Using my detective skills, I thought they might be connected. I was keeping a lookout when you stumbled onto me." He met my eyes, as if trying to stare into my soul. "Someday I would very much like to know how you did that..."

I shrugged innocently. "Woman's intuition."

He grunted. "My ass."

I thought about his story, putting it in the back of my mind as I considered how to best use it to my advantage. "You're really Cain? The Cain?"

He nodded with a resigned sigh. "Yes. First killer, blah, blah, blah."

I held up a hand. "No, I wasn't judging you. I was actually curious. Maybe we can trade stories sometime…"

He squinted at me, assessing me. Then gave a brief nod. "That might be fun."

I nodded back, thinking on what I needed to set this house of cards on fire. I tapped my lips thoughtfully. "I need to draw everyone out of the dark. Bring them together."

"I know you're a nun and everything, but I don't think a prayer circle is going to fix this."

I laughed, replaying my words in my head. I turned, flashing him a delighted smile. "I like you, Cain. You're fun."

He hesitated, staring back at me curiously.

"I want to bring everyone together… for a bloodbath. With a demon. You interested?"

He sputtered on his cigar, coughing violently. Then he just stared at me for a time, his eyes ageless and calculating. Then a deep, rolling laugh bubbled up from his belly, and I saw that his eyes were actually moist with tears. "I think I like you, too, Callie…" He slapped his knees, hooting uproariously as he thanked Dear and Darling for the meeting. They positively beamed, but had looked concerned at my words. Cain fidgeted excitedly, waiting.

"So, what's next?" Beckett asked.

I played along with Beckett's act. Cain had never been part of the plan, but his help could push the needle just enough to make a difference, and with Darling and Dear vouching for him, I decided to extend some trust. Beckett had already volunteered, knowing that either way he was going to be in danger, and wanting to make the most of his aid. But we had to play to the crowd, let them see what we wanted them to see. I finally found a part for Cain to play.

"I think I want to go for a jog. Get warmed up for the wrestling match tonight."

Cain watched me, eyes calculating. "You want to lure out the stalker. You want me to kill him or something? I've been trying. This son of a bitch is savvy. And I think there might be more than one of them..."

I shrugged. "I doubt you could stop them. Nothing against you. I think they're more aware of what's going on in this city than anyone thinks, and more aware of the residents, too..."

Cain leaned forward. "You already know who they are?" he asked in disbelief.

I shook my head and smiled. "I have no idea."

Beckett cleared his throat. "I'm going to let them catch me."

Cain leaned back with a grunt. Speechless.

Dear spoke up. "That... doesn't sound beneficial."

But Cain looked very thoughtful all of a sudden. "That... holy shit. That's bloody certifiable." Then he turned to Beckett. "And you officially have the biggest balls God ever created."

Beckett shrugged unconcernedly. "I'm going to be used as a hostage anyway. Why not let them think they've won the first hand?" And a mischievous grin split his cheeks.

Cain grunted. "You realize that this can all go tits up at any moment, and that you're sacrificing early in hopes for the right layout at the end..."

I shrugged. "Sometimes you have to sacrifice some pawns to take the Queen..."

Cain nodded. "Mind if I have a few words with Mr. Big Stones?" he asked. I glanced at Beckett who shrugged. I motioned them away, watching thoughtfully as they walked closer to the fire, Cain speaking in low tones, likely giving him tips on what to do with various monsters.

If anyone knew how to keep Beckett alive, it was Cain. He had killed things for centuries. Millennia. I felt eyes on me and turned to see Darling and Dear studying me.

"It really is the only way..." I offered in a soft tone. "Pretending to play by her rules is the only way to enter the game. This is my ante."

They nodded sadly, and then motioned for me to sit on the empty couch. I did, preparing to defend my plan. "You need to learn how to use your boots, honey," Dear said.

I blinked at her. "What do you mean?"

"Those are Darling and Dears," Darling growled. Then he wiggled his fingers in the air dramatically. "They *do* things." At my blank look, he sat down beside me and tapped me on the temple. "Think about heels."

The sudden jab to my temple startled me into obeying.

And I gasped as my shoes quivered, leather whipping about wildly as if eating my foot. Before I could shout, it stopped, and I stared down to see that I was wearing a sexy pair of black heels. A pair I had seen in a magazine a few days ago.

Dear clapped delightedly. "We could do this all day, but we know you're in a rush. The shoes can change from boots, to heels, to moccasins, to sandals. As long as you have an idea in mind, the shoes will do the rest." She leaned forward as if preparing to nibble my ear. "In any color, fashion, or style…"

I shook my head in wonder, imagining them back into the brown boots from earlier. In a blink, they were back. I felt like crying. And shopping the rest of the store, Amira be damned.

As if sensing my thoughts, Darling cleared his throat. "They also sense demons. You'll feel a slight pinch in the toes of the shoe, indicating what direction they are in relation to you."

I felt like crying. I didn't really think that part was necessary, seeing as how I was confronting Amira soon, and would be staring right at her, but if I survived the night? That ability could prove very useful.

"I don't know what to say…" I whispered.

"Your face already said it, sweetie," Dear said, grinning.

Cain finally returned with Beckett under his massive arm. I cleared my throat and wiped my eyes, which instantly made the men uncomfortable, realizing they had walked into an estrogen zone. Once composed, he spoke uncertainly. "You want me to watch, and let him be kidnapped… Anyone could do that. Why do you need me?"

I flashed him a wicked grin. "Oh, no. That's what I want the stalker to see. To see the mighty Cain, lose. But here's what you'll do *right after that…*"

Beckett was very calm, not an ounce of fear on his face. I hoped he wasn't lying to appease me, and that he really was open to this. After all, this part had been his idea.

CHAPTER 43

I stared down at the asphalt, focusing on my feet. They instantly shifted from kinky boots to authentic moccasins – the kind that could take a long hike in the woods without issue, not the slipper kind. I stared at them in wonder, shaking my head. Darling and Dear were leather Gods.

Beckett stared down at his own shoes, looking disappointed.

"Remember the plan," I said under my breath, pretending to stretch out my hamstrings.

Cain grunted in response, and although we couldn't see him, I felt him leave – a vacant space remaining where I had sensed him only a second ago.

I locked eyes with Beckett. "You sure you're okay with this?" I asked, beginning to walk.

He nodded. "Cain gave me some pointers. And like I said, it really is inevitable. It's what I would do if I was her. So why not capitalize on it?"

I sighed. My plan wasn't foolproof. None ever were. In fact, it was about the wildest, most unpredictable plan I could think of. Enough to make *me* doubt it, but Cain seemed to see a sliver of a chance in it, and Beckett was confident enough to nominate himself as the bait. So at least two people believed in it. As did Dorian, if that counted for anything. But since he had lived a life avoiding confrontation, I wasn't sure if that was a plus or a minus in my favor. But the addition of Cain to our plan would make his job more palatable.

We rounded the corner and saw the church in the center of the block, the opposite direction from where we were going. But we both paused to openly stare at the crowd of rioters outside. Bigger, louder, and more explosive than last time. As I stared at them, shaking my head, I felt a dark presence looming unseen, followed by a pinch in my toes. I jumped instinctively, staring down. Then I remembered.

The shoes could sense demons.

I shook off the feeling and looked back to the church. Now was the scary part. I took a deep breath, and reached through the cracked door in my mind – which was slightly wider after my visit to Chateau Demon. Silver instantly washed over the streets like a tide, bathing everything in chrome, but the church remained dark. Chrome struggled to gain purchase there, as if something was blocking my vision, but it wasn't impenetrable, because flickers of silver would appear, be consumed, and then reappear in several places across the structure.

Which made me feel that the church wasn't entirely corrupt, but that some dark presence was pumping the bellows, encouraging the hate – Amira. And I wanted her to see me pressing against her stronghold, out in the open. Poke the bear.

I studied the crowd more intently and saw a lot of people that hadn't been there before. Rougher, wilder, more passionate men and women – the type who were usually drawn to violence disguised by the name of *peaceful protest*. I saw the Abominable Three – the churchwomen from the coffee shop, faces red with passion as they punched their fists into the air. *"Death to the idols! Kill the Freaks. God is coming!"*

They were shouting the loudest.

Maybe they were the problem – actively working with Amira, but disguised as peaceful old ladies. Regardless, all that mattered to my plan was that someone in the church was not who they said they were. I'd already tried the top of the food chain, and they were mouth-breathing, limp cucumbers. But as long as I knew someone in the church was dirty, my plan was still a go.

I glanced over at Beckett, directing us away from the church, confident we had spent enough time in view. "You better keep your ass safe, Beckett."

"That's always my top priority," he said, smiling crookedly. Then he began to jog, eyes scanning the streets warily, as if searching for something. I followed, catching up to him and also scanning the streets, muttering incoherently under my breath as if passing on information to Beckett. He jabbered back, maintaining the ruse.

Then he glanced down at his watch sharply, a smart device, and suddenly poured on the speed. "This way!" he snapped urgently, having seen something on his screen that prompted him to enter a dark alley.

I missed the alley, cursing loudly as I spun around to follow him, now a dozen paces behind him. "Wait, Beckett!" I hissed.

"We don't have time to wait, Callie!" he snapped, racing faster.

"We don't even know if—" but he had rounded a corner, out of sight.

I pounded asphalt, trying to catch up to him, panting loudly as I stumbled. "These shoes aren't made for this shit!" I cursed.

I rounded the corner to find him now at least two dozen paces away. Between one moment and the next, a hazy figure was suddenly there. I felt no pinch in the toe of my shoes.

I gasped, flung out my hand, and sent one of my energy sticks hurtling through the air to defend Beckett. I stumbled, and skidded to the ground loudly, landing in a greasy puddle. I groaned, clutching my ankle, and slowly made my way to my feet, limping after Beckett.

My trip had caused my magic projectile to fly wide, missing the stalker by a wide margin.

I heard a shout, and then a blur flew down from a rooftop and tackled the hazy stalker, but the stalker had anticipated it somewhat, because he spun, and the blur hit him, bounced off, and slammed into a trio of trashcans.

Cain appeared in full view, cursing angrily as he climbed to his feet. He glanced from the stalker, to Beckett, to me, and slowly stepped between me and the stalker, leaving Beckett all alone.

"Get him! He has—"

"No way, Callie. We can't let him have you!" Cain growled.

Beckett slashed out with his butterfly knives, and the stalker was suddenly moving. The vague form slapped the knives free and grappled with Beckett. He struggled, landing a few good blows, but was ultimately outmatched. The stalker held him in a rear choke, and then disappeared right as Cain threw a freaking hatchet at him.

I screamed.

The weapon sailed through empty air, hitting a dumpster behind where the two men had been.

I walked up to Cain, and slapped him with the full strength of my arm across the face. He flew into the dumpster, and I stared down at him panting. He stared at me and whispered under his breath. "That wasn't the one I've seen following you."

I pretended not to have heard anything. "You're as worthless as everyone says," I snarled loudly. "I can't believe I thought you could handle such a simple job as keeping an eye out on us. Leave Kansas City, or the next time I see you, I'll make Abel proud."

Then I Shadow Walked from the alley back to the parking lot of Abundant Angel Catholic Church. I let out a shaky breath, and although concerned about Cain's whisper, ultimately it didn't matter. I just hoped bringing up his brother hadn't gone too far, but I'd wanted to make it look authentic. It was paramount to my plan.

Despite everything, a slow grin split my cheeks. It was time for Act Two.

"Callie!" A new voice shouted, and I spun in surprise, ready to defend myself.

CHAPTER 44

I blinked at the handsome man before me, frowning. I lowered the crackling white kamas in my hands – since they had popped into existence instinctively – upon seeing his shocked face.

He approached slowly, a smile creeping back onto his face, but a hesitant one. "Callie. It's me, Arthur."

I blinked at him. "From the coffee shop?" I asked in disbelief.

He nodded, shifting from foot to foot uncomfortably as I took a few seconds to assess him. None of his clothes were new, but they were all clean and fit well. He had bathed, trimmed his hair, shaved, and...

He looked like an entirely different person.

A handsome, forty-something I would have expected to see browsing the philosophy section in a bookstore. Or toting kids on his shoulders. Maybe even sitting in a board meeting for a large corporation, addressing his executives after taking time off from his yacht to pop back into the office.

I whistled appreciatively. "Don't let the Sisters see you, or we'll have a mass confession on our hands," I said, laughing as I gripped him by the shoulders.

He grinned unashamedly. "I wanted to thank you. In person. Father David was so kind, and I have the feeling he would have helped anyway, but you should have seen his face when I mentioned your name. It was as if he had never smiled before."

I frowned at that, but hid it well. What the hell? Father David had been surprised? Like it was so surprising that I had offered help on behalf of the church? We would have words.

"I'm just picking up a few things, and then I need to head out."

He held up his hands. "Don't let me keep you. I just…" he stared at me, fully facing me as if preparing for a speech. "That was the kindest thing I remember anyone ever doing for me. And I truly appreciate it. The cops brought me in for questions, but I was sure to tell them our story," he said, winking. "Please let me know if you ever need anything else. I'm in your debt."

I shook my head. "Treating a stranger like a human isn't an act of a saint, Arthur."

His eyes seemed to twinkle. "Maybe these days it is…" Then he laughed at himself. "Listen to me babble on. Just know that I'm here if you need anything. Father David gave me a job. I watch over the courtyard to keep out ruffians!" he said grandiosely.

I laughed. "Well, we'll be seeing a lot of each other, then. I work here, too."

His smile stretched from ear-to-ear, making his kind eyes crinkle at the edges. "Perfect." He looked as if he wanted to say something else, but was debating it in his mind. I waited patiently, letting him decide for himself. He finally did, and opened his mouth. "I feel better around you, Callie. Please don't take that the wrong way, but I feel young again when I see you. Maybe it's just the kindness you showed me, but I feel as if I've been given a second chance. I won't let you down." He crossed his heart awkwardly. "Like that, right?"

I laughed. "Sure, Arthur. I'm not too good at that stuff either. Watch the Sisters. You'll pick it up easily enough."

He bowed formally. "Well, this courtyard isn't going to watch itself. Go about your business, my lady. I'll keep your castle safe." He winked at me playfully, and then turned away, striding up and down the parking lot like a soldier on his rounds.

I opened the door to find Father David standing there, as if ready to step outside. We blinked at each other, and I placed my fists on my hips. He smirked, but it wasn't heartfelt. "Callie."

"Davey," I replied coolly.

He grimaced at that. "Slap any more pastors lately?" he asked deadpan.

"Ask me again in a few minutes," I said, smiling.

He stared down at me, as if debating how best to chastise me, and then his face cracked into a grin. "Alright, fine. Although horribly inappropriate, childish, terrible, and basically every negative description we could come up with, it was also…" he trailed off, thinking.

"Hilarious?" I offered.

He snapped his fingers. "That." He leaned back against the wall, letting me come all the way in, but not before glancing over my shoulder to check on Arthur. He held something behind his back, because I heard it thump into the wall.

"It was misguided," I admitted softly, once the door had closed. He didn't reply, only watched me. "But in my defense, I genuinely believed he had done something horrible. Regarding the murders."

"And yet you think you were wrong, now?"

I nodded after a long pause. "I can't be sure, but I think everyone is a pawn in this. Whether they know it or not."

"We're all pawns, Callie. That doesn't excuse actions. We are still accountable for those."

I nodded. "I don't think any of them have it in them, but I know for a fact someone in that church is dirty. But none of that matters now. I have a plan to smoke them out, and that's where you come in."

He didn't reply to that. "Do you know what made me change my mind? I was so angry with you. Disappointed, horrified," he waved a hand, as if implying the list could go on for a while. "But I got off the phone with Roland shortly afterwards. I don't think I have ever heard him laugh like that. Never." He met my eyes meaningfully. "Whether you buy it or not, Callie, you have a gift." I began to argue that I had only done what we had all secretly thought about at one point in our minds after seeing that stupid flyer, but he held up a hand to stall me. "Then, wonder of wonders, a disheveled man shows up on my steps, belaboring the virtues of a mysterious white-haired young woman named Callie. How she had treated him like a king, while he was living as a beggar. Then, not only did you offer him kindness, but he will tell anyone about how you blatantly defended him, and attacked those showing disrespect. And *then* you told him to come to the church. That we would clothe, bathe, and offer him temporary shelter..." he shook his head, romanticizing the entire thing.

"Listen, Artie has a flare for the dramatic—" I began.

He again, stopped me. "No. Callie, you're an uncut diamond. You can be rough, callous, and covered in grit, but every now and then the diamond shines through. You, who repeatedly mock us, show us with your actions that you live closer to our faith than any of us. It's... inspiring."

"I just made an old bear laugh and offered respect to a vagrant."

He watched me thoughtfully, as if trying to understand a stranger. "Yet we now have a loyal employee. Even though temporary, I can pretty much guarantee that we'll have to arrest him to get him out of here, and that he will do the job better than any ten men."

I smiled at that. Then I suddenly remembered the time. "What are you doing awake?"

His face tensed, as if he had forgotten something important. "It seems like tonight is a night for visitors," he said, handing me an intricately carved wooden box. I stared at it, my heart dropping as I saw *Darling & Dear* carved across the top. "They spent more time arguing with each other than they did talking to me, but they told me you had ordered it."

I didn't open it, wondering if it was something that David shouldn't see. He sighed regretfully, no doubt intrigued to learn what such an odd couple would hand deliver to me. He cleared his throat. "I had another odd visitor appear not long ago. He asked me for... an odd favor." He searched my face curiously, but I kept mine blank.

"I hope you helped him."

He waved a hand. "Of course. It wasn't any trouble."

"Since you're in the favor business, would you mind doing one for me?" I asked with a smile.

"It's nothing illegal, is it?"

I shook my head. "Nope. I just need you to make a phone call or two, and then let me know how it goes. Immediately. I'll text you the details."

He finally nodded, but still looked suspicious. "I don't like the sound of this."

"I have Roland's blessing," I argued softly.

He sighed. "Oh, you don't think Roland told me that bit. I'm pretty sure it was the entire point of his call. Not to let me know he was okay and alive, but that I needed to stand behind you as I would him." He tapped his lips thoughtfully. "You know, for someone who claims not to be a Shepherd, you're doing a pretty good job of it."

I shrugged. "Don't get your hopes up. The night is still young." I shifted the box in my hands, trying not to dance on my toes in anticipation.

He chuckled, and then waved me off. After a few steps, he paused, glancing over his shoulder. "Will you be safe, Callie?"

I glanced at his back, wanting to lie. "None of us are ever safe, Davey. But I'll say this. The thing that sent you to the hospital a few weeks ago?" I saw his shoulders tighten. He was still recovering from that. Both physically and mentally. Johnathan had attacked him. He slowly turned to face me, cheeks pale. "I'm finishing the job. His sister is in town."

Father David shivered, and finally nodded. "I'll pray for you."

"I'd rather you keep an eye on your phone for that text," I said, winking. "But I'll take prayer as well."

"Keep your eyes on your feet, Callie. They haven't steered you wrong yet. But the path to hell is paved with good intentions," he quoted.

"Don't worry," I laughed. "I've got new boots." I wiggled one foot at him, which only seemed to confuse him further. "The Path to Heaven is not an escalator," I said, smirking at the baffled look on his face. He blinked at me, repeating the words with his lips as if reciting it to memory.

"That is going in my sermon next week." And then he was chuckling, walking down the halls.

I didn't wait, tearing open the box right there in the hall. The thick smell of leather assaulted me, but it smelled muskier than usual. Not stinky, but more pungent. A card rested neatly atop a folded pile of leather, a message written in elegant cursive.

Knew this piece was on your mind. Strong choice. Buckle up, it's going to be a cold one...

I squealed loudly enough to send a Sister running my way as I took out my gift. She found me clutching the piece of leather, laughing to myself, and with complete understanding, left me alone...

CHAPTER 45

*W*ith everything in place, I had chosen to walk to my meeting. One, to loosen up my muscles. Two, because I wanted to conserve my magic. Three, I wanted everyone to see me casually walking through the streets in my swanky new jacket.

I wore my Darling and Dear boots that climbed up to mid-calf, a pair of black jeans, and a black *Wu-Tang Style* tee. I wore my Darling and Dear hip-length leather jacket over it all... almost identical to the one I had worn in that other place when I first saw Amira at Chateau Demon. It was complete with straps, buckles, and enough patches of leather to make it look like a quilt, although it wasn't heavy. I didn't quite understand how Darling and Dear knew about it, or whether it was the same one I had briefly seen in their shop, but I loved it unconditionally.

I pondered their note as I walked, but didn't really understand it. I wondered what innate abilities it had, and why they hadn't openly told me in their note. Maybe in case someone else opened it before me? I knew it was strong, because the message had emphasized that, and I had tested this by dragging a blade across the back. It hadn't left a mark.

I hoped I wouldn't get a bill in the mail. Then I would have to flee the country or something.

With each step, I fed my anger, forming it, adding to it, feeding it...

Until it was a living, white-hot rage. Even if my plan went to hell, I wanted to make a splash tonight, and to do that, I needed to turn into an estrogen bomb – as my mother had always said. *The best defense against the ignorance of man.* It wasn't hard for me to do this, because I already felt like a ticking time bomb. All I really did was let down my guard. Where Roland usually cautioned me to be calm and rational, tonight I was doing things my way.

Calm and rational was what the demon was expecting. How she had gotten this far. Because she had fought the church for a long time, and knew their tactics.

But she was still standing, which meant that a new tactic was in order.

A good old-fashioned girl fight. With Hellish hair extensions and Heavenly manicures fighting for the end-all-be-all, no-holds-barred fight of the year. I was going to make this fun. It was a show, and the audience was hushed, waiting with bated breath for the next act.

Spotting the long-since abandoned bread factory ahead of me, I scanned my surroundings. I didn't see anyone walking, because it was cold out and almost midnight. It wasn't a typical party night, either, so the car traffic was nonexistent, even for this almost forgotten part of town.

I pulled out my phone, and clicked *send* on the pre-typed text for Father David. Then, holding it in my fist, I approached the meeting point – a large parking lot in the center of the old Kansas City Bread Factory. The building wrapped around the parking lot in a *U* shape, protecting us from prying eyes. A large crane with a wrecking ball, a dump truck, and a bulldozer were parked on the street near the parking lot, ready for the day they could pound the factory to ashes and replace it with some luxurious coffee joint or apartment complex.

But all was quiet.

No slowly-driving cars, no one walking the street, and no lights on in the nearby buildings.

I focused on my breathing, knowing I was being watched, and not wanting to show my slowly growing anxiety. To be fair, I was also anxious to cut loose. To see how it all played out. This was the best I had been able to come up with, and although not perfect, it definitely had some strong points, and I was hoping to make a small bit of notoriety tonight.

Whether that was as an epic failure or as an underdog win, was yet to be determined.

Several abandoned, totaled cars sat in the lot, less than a dozen in all, and most of them sitting on blocks where the local gangs had stolen the rims for a quick turnaround. The windows were bashed in, and a few of the cars had been tagged with graffiti.

All in all, a charming, middle-American neighborhood.

I reached the center of the parking lot and waited, glancing down at my phone.

Midnight. I quickly read the text, and then frowned thoughtfully before pocketing the phone. I focused on my boots, and casually repositioned myself to face a shadowy corner at the junction of two of the buildings ahead. I felt the telltale pinch, and almost laughed.

"Alright, Amira. I'd hate to die of boredom."

Laughter replied from the shadows I was facing. "I thought we were bringing dates," the familiar voice called out.

I let anger show on my face, not bothering to hide it. "Something came up," I growled. Amira laughed delightedly. "But I had a backup ready," I said coldly. Then, I waited. The silence stretched, but no one stepped forward. *Well, that part of the plan just died an agonizing death.*

"Maybe they're shy…" Amira offered, sounding amused.

"I don't need them to take care of Johnathan's sloppy seconds," I said, forcing a smile on my face. Oh, she didn't like that, judging by the hiss from her corner of the ring.

"Step forward," she spat, and I readied myself for an all-out war.

A dark laugh echoed off the walls, but opposite Amira's location. I spun, hands out, ready for an attack, but simply saw a great big man stepping out from behind a car. Yuri. And he looked positively delighted. His long, greasy hair hung loose, and his wild beard fanned across his chest, punctuated by the two parallel scars that ran from his temple to beneath his beard.

"I wasn't sure you would actually show. Imagine my surprise to find out that I'd get an open shot at you after all these games. But no tricks will save you tonight, girl," Yuri bellowed, shooting glances over my shoulder as if verifying I was alone. "Armor's Cave is weak. You thought you were so clever bringing them to your side, but that only proves their time is at an end. I'll burn their Cave to ashes and rebuild the bears into a respectable force." He stopped a dozen paces away, flexing his fingers in a groping motion. "The best part is that I'm actually getting *paid* to do this," he chuckled. "But I would have done it for free. Hell, I was coming here anyway, thanks to her," he said, pointing towards Amira.

Well, that confirmed one thing to me. Yuri had been *actively* working with Amira, promised to be the next alpha bear in exchange for his dutiful work.

"Horatio? You killed your friend to become an alpha?" I asked. He shrugged his shoulders, a smug look on his face. "I'm sure the other bears will be lining up to join you. Like Ragmussen. He's a friend of yours, right?" I lifted a hand to my mouth in embarrassment, seeing the flash of anger in his steel-gray eyes. "Oops. *Was.* Unless you killed him, too?"

Yuri's anger changed. Barely. But I saw it. He hadn't killed Ragmussen. And he wasn't happy about it, either. "Have to break a few eggs," he said, full of false bravado.

"God is dead," I said. "Was that your idea or the hell-twat's over there?"

He tensed, eyes flicking over to where Amira suddenly snarled from the shadows. I heard a faint clinking sound, but dismissed it. "Catchy, right?" he asked me. "Kept you busy. Which was the plan. Can we get a move on? I'd like to collect my payday tonight."

I settled my boots into the asphalt, as if ready to fight, but Amira finally stepped out of the shadows, in human form. "That's quite enough, Yuri," she warned, glaring at him.

I gasped as I realized she wasn't alone. "Beckett!" He groaned in reply, the chains around his ankles and wrists clinking as Amira shoved him forward. His face was roughed up, as if used as a punching bag, and he could barely stand. "You bitch!" I shouted.

Amira nodded, looking positively pleased. I studied her, recognizing her from the one time I had seen her at the grocery store. A young, pretty girl with dark hair and slightly narrowed eyes. "I told you I would bring him here," she said, shoving Beckett again, causing his chains to rattle as he slouched. "But I brought a backup just in case." She pointed at Yuri.

I turned back to Yuri. "So, to get back at the big bad wizard, you decided to attack a Regular, and then go into hiding. So brave..." I said with a sigh. "No wonder you're alpha material."

"Would you like to meet my second friend? The one who gave me this toy?" Amira asked, indicating Beckett. His chains quivered as he struggled to remain standing, swaying slightly. "Come on out!" Amira said, raising her voice, but not breaking our eye contact.

Nothing happened. And I burst out laughing. Her look turned wary. "Clever," she said.

I shrugged, arrogantly rubbing my fingernails on my coat. "I really don't need a roll call. Can we just get to the fighting already?" I asked, smiling at her. I had no idea who she had meant to surprise me with, but she didn't need to know my ignorance. My plan was kind of chaotic like that. Even I didn't know exactly what was going to happen.

All that mattered was that *something* had happened not according to her plan.

Amira snapped her fingers angrily, and *another* person was suddenly strolling into the ring from where Amira had entered. A woman in a hoodie. She stepped up a few paces away from Amira and tugged back the hood, revealing a familiar face. But not the one I had expected.

Brigitte.

CHAPTER 46

*N*ow, I had expected *someone* from the church to show, but
definitely not *her*. I had even harbored the thought that it might
have somehow been Benjamin all along. It was why I had asked Father
David to make a call – to check if Benjamin was still at the church or if he
had left for some reason. But he had been up, working away in the office,
despite the hour.

"I definitely didn't see you coming. Good job," I said, clapping softly.

Brigitte just stared back at me, eyes full of hatred. But… not just with
me. With everyone but Amira. "When God calls, we all must answer," she
said in a furious voice.

I blinked. What craziness was she on? "Um, God?"

"You're all *monsters*," she spat, ignoring my question. "Disgusting, vile
beasts. Benjamin is right. The world is better off without you. Thanks to
Benjamin, we have been heard. Angels now own this city, and they won't
tolerate your theft and abuse of Heavenly gifts." She was staring at Amira
with a wistful look of adoration, as if seeking approval from a mentor.

"That's a whole lot of crazy you're spewing." I said. "You think Amira's
an *Angel*?" Amira, for her part, was doing a splendid job of looking pious
and offended by my presence, which only fueled Brigitte's passion.

"Oh, I know all your tricks, Callie," Brigitte snapped. "Working for the
church, but not being part of the church. Amira showed me the truth.

You're a stain on the house of God, and Amira will help me destroy you once and for all, clearing this city of a plague."

I shook my head, not believing this. Had Amira brainwashed her, or was this just her? "What would Benjamin say?" I asked her softly. "You teaming up with a stranger to help murder people in his city."

She scoffed. "I haven't murdered *anyone*. I've only grown Benjamin's church. You read his flyers. He's a true believer. It's not his fault he stands alone against the forces of Hell. But my actions have shown him the true depths of my faith. My devotion. My love. Not just to God, but to *him*," she enunciated, a wistful smile on her face. "After one of our own was tortured on the steps of our church by a monster, everything became so clear. I prayed that night..." her eyes drifted adoringly to Amira, then back to me. "And Heaven heard me," she said wonderingly. "Showed me how to profess my love to a true Man of God."

I stared at her. "You're telling me... that you love *Benjamin?*" It was ridiculous. Brigitte wasn't that young, but she wasn't that old, either. I would have thought she would go for Desmond. But to do all this as some misguided quest for romance?

"Don't you *dare* speak his name. You *struck* him!" Brigitte screamed, eyes wild.

I turned to Amira. "You're one sick puppy, you know that? Filling this stupid woman's head with delusions of grandeur that you're somehow holy?" I pointed at Beckett's chains. "Your Angel has a shackled man in front of her, in case you missed it," I said, glancing at Brigitte.

"A corrupt policeman who was removed from the case for his incompetence. Holding his fellow officers back from catching the monster that killed a child of God," she sniffed.

I shook my head, wondering if I was supposed to take any of this seriously. I guessed it was better than an angry mob, but at the same time, it was worse. Because this woman had been manipulated. Sure, she had some horrible conclusions and ideologies, but ultimately, she had been duped. And Amira had used that fear, and her love for Benjamin, to strike like a snake, turning a sorrowful follower of God into a sociopathic zealot. Part of me wanted to reach out and save her, but another part of me knew I couldn't. She was a Regular, and no matter who won here, I knew Amira wouldn't let her live. But she wasn't going to believe anything I said.

But I wondered why she was here. If Amira had used her to rile up anger at the church, sowing chaos, that had already been done. What was Brigitte expecting to do *here*?

Beckett's chains clinked again as his leg almost gave out. If he was that groggy, my plan would die in a puff of smoke. I needed him to pull it together.

I glanced back at Amira to see her staring back at me, a mock look of sadness on her face. Then she turned to Brigitte. "Go forth, child. I will protect thee from the forces of Hell."

I glanced over at Yuri. "You seeing this?" He flinched, not looking at me, but at Brigitte. I turned back, and saw that her eyes were entirely yellow, and that black, bone claws were extending from her fingertips, inches long each. I stepped back instinctively, eyes darting from Amira to Brigitte. Amira was grinning madly, but Brigitte had only one thing on her mind.

My expulsion from this world. My boots no longer pinched when facing Amira. I swiveled them to point at Brigitte, and groaned as everything clicked into place. Now I knew why Brigitte was here. As a meat sack to be possessed by Amira. A punching bag for me to waste some energy on before the real fight. That was Amira's sole reason for breaking this woman. Just to buy her loyalty for this exact moment. As cannon fodder.

"Kill them both," Amira commanded, "as a sacrifice to the One True God!"

"Wait a minute," I heard Yuri growl uncertainly. "That wasn't the plan."

"All have sinned and fallen short of the glory of God. Repent!" Amira shouted icily, ignoring Yuri's sudden growl. Her eyes danced with glee.

"Well, if I'm on the menu, I'm taking you out first," he snarled, rounding on me. Then he exploded into his bear form, followed by a roar that made my skin tingle, skipping back a few paces to keep them both in my line of sight.

His bear eyes turned to me, merciless. His thick, brown fur rippled as he shook his shoulders, snarling hungrily as his eyes narrowed.

Then he began loping my way, much faster than Brigitte, but the two kept their eyes on each other, since we were apparently all enemies at this party. I realized that my plan was running *wildly* off skew. I had hoped that whoever came from the church would keep Yuri busy for a few minutes, leaving me to focus on Amira. But it looked like Amira had a similar plan.

Yuri pounded closer, and I instantly Shadow Walked a dozen paces behind him, ready to unleash a barrage of fire at him, turning him into a hairless, roasted piglet so I could square off with Brigitte, or find a way to attack Amira, forcing her to abandon her possession of Brigitte.

Which left me staring at Yuri's back, preparing to unleash an unreasonable amount of pain at that fat, hairy ass. But I paused as I saw a trio of bears pounding into the parking lot on all fours.

And Claire was *riding* Starlight. Seeing Yuri, she leapt from his back, screaming in mid-air. Her eyes were fire, and the tiny blonde exploded, fabric raining down like confetti.

"Claire! NO!" I shouted, knowing I was already too late. Armor had told me that emotional trauma could bring on the first shift, and that the monster would be in full control. But... maybe that was what we needed tonight.

For the ladies to be less... ladylike.

My instinctive fear was squashed as I finally saw my best friend's form, and a dark, anticipatory smile crept over my cheeks.

A ten-foot-tall polar bear landed on the ground, black claws tearing at the concrete from the shaggy white fur of her massive paws. She roared with a maw easily big enough to bite my torso in half without any effort. Yuri climbed up on hind legs, walking laterally in an awkward shuffle.

Clairebear did the same, much taller than Yuri, and roared again, thick strands of saliva stretching from canine to canine, as if she was salivating in anticipation of the blood to come. Then they hammered down to the ground and sprinted at each other like two dump trucks.

Armor, Kona, and Starlight had remained at the edge of the parking lot, and I turned to see Amira glaring at them with hatred. Too late, I remembered Brigitte.

She hit me with her demonic claws, slamming into my side, and sending me cartwheeling into a parked car. I struck hard, and fell to the ground. I glanced down at my coat, thankful I had worn it. My ribs were definitely bruised, if not cracked, but without the coat, I might have glanced down to find my lower torso missing. I stared at my shirt. "Wu-Tang Style, bitch," I muttered, gathering my anger into a sharp blade.

I climbed to my feet, abandoning my rational mind, and embracing the monster within.

It was time for a girl fight.

Amira laughed joyfully. "How delightful! She either kills you, or if you win, I kill the policeman," she shouted.

She had a point, unfortunately.

CHAPTER 47

I locked eyes with Beckett, and saw a faint smile cross his cheeks. He had been… *faking?* With a subtle flick of his wrists, the chains fell free. Since he had been constantly jingling them, Amira didn't even seem to notice the sound of them hitting the ground. She was too busy glaring at the two fighting bears and the three spectator bears, eyes calculating, as if wondering how she could use them to her advantage.

I blinked, happy for this unexpected development. We hadn't been able to specifically plan for this, but he knew what his goal was and that he had to get it done. Somehow. But without chains? No real injury? That would be *easy.*

Beckett flicked his heel up, and struck Amira directly in the kneecap with a solid blow, then swung his head back, catching her jaw as she instinctively leaned forward at the blow to the knee. She screamed in pain, hands darting to her face, and he made a break for it. She cursed, shaking her head once, and her eyes flashed yellow before she bolted after him, sharing her attention between Brigitte and Beckett.

I turned to see a very confused Brigitte staring at me. One second full of hatred, and ready to kill me with her demonic powers, and the next, her claws suddenly gone, leaving a scared, middle-aged woman. This happened back-and-forth a few times in rapid succession as Amira finally kicked

Beckett's legs out from under him, sending him face-first into the brick wall.

I sprinted at Brigitte, not giving one flying fuck how I took her out. Either as a Regular, misguided woman, or as a demon-possessed idiot. I flung three crosses – blazing bars of crackling blue light – at her face ahead of me. She held up her claws, batting two away, but the third struck her in the hip, knocking her on her ass, the flesh sizzling.

I glanced over to see Amira forcefully yank Beckett to his feet, pressing a dark blade to his throat. I shot a panicked look at him, but only saw him smiling back at me through a bloody nose from his impact with the wall. His eyes flicked up, his head unmoving, and I held my breath.

A faint creaking sound echoed off the brick walls from up above.

Beckett closed his eyes, clenching his fists, still smiling.

Amira glanced up just as a wall of water crashed down over her, exploding into a cloud of steam and the most glorious screams of anguish I had ever heard. I saw Beckett roll away, but it wasn't a smooth motion, almost like a drunken cartwheel. I saw a few bricks fall down into the steam, and understood. A brick must have broken free from the aged building as the massive tub of Holy Water cascaded down from the roof above – just like we had planned – courtesy of Cain.

I scowled up at the roof, and saw a hazy blur shrug apologetically.

Fucking Cain.

But his participation in the actual fighting was now complete. Not because I didn't need him, but because he was technically doing two jobs, and with the sudden awareness that someone was up above, playing Holy Water tricks, his other job was going to be more difficult. I saw his form blur to a new location on an adjoining section of the Bread Factory for a better view of everything. Also, in case Amira wasn't entirely down, which she wasn't.

As the Holy Steam bath cleared, rising up into the sky, I marveled at the damage. Her scalded form rose from the asphalt with a yellow glow, and at the same time, Brigitte climbed to her feet, looking dazed in her Regular form again. I kicked her in her pious boobs, just to be sure.

Then I slapped a bar of power over her neck like a band of light. A giant cross flickered, slightly darker than the rest of the magic collar, standing out prominently. Then I gripped her shirt to pull her up, and punched her as hard as I could in the nose, knocking her unconscious.

Part of this was pleasure, but the other part was that I couldn't risk Amira using her as a stunt double again, breaking my focus. So, I knocked her out. And I tied off the magic around her throat so that possession wasn't an option. She was out of the fight. I let her go, not feeling an ounce of pity as her head thumped onto the concrete.

Then I turned to check on the bears, who were in the middle of a slap fight, their claws biting deep into the flesh of the other, blood flowing freely. Claire struck a particularly good blow, and Yuri bellowed in pain. Claire grabbed him by the crotch and chest like a professional wrestler, and then threw him into a car to my left, knocking it off the blocks. It crashed to the ground, windows shattering. Yuri climbed to his feet almost instantly, then roared as he bounded back to Claire who was still standing on two feet, paws spread wide as if taunting the little bitch bear.

I turned to Amira to see her glowing demonic form in full view now, just like I had seen her at Johnathan's mansion, in that other place. Half goat, half beautiful yellow-flamed woman. Her nether region was a black patch of wild hair that rivaled the bears' downstairs mix-up.

She flung her hands out, her glowing breasts heaving as her hair rippled out behind her, still looking like it was frozen underwater, hovering in position until she suddenly moved.

She stared at me as she kicked Beckett in the ribs while he tried to escape. I heard ribs crack as he flew into a car, and then fell to the pavement. He groaned as he struggled weakly.

I Shadow Walked directly before her, between her and Beckett.

"Now that you've had your bath, let's throw down," I shouted, staring at her horribly burned body, which was much more obvious up close. "You thought you could pit everyone against each other, blame it on me, and get away with it?"

"Bingo," she said, grinning. "It was worth a shot," she added. But something about her eyes troubled me. As if maybe her plan was still running smoothly. I was missing something…

The bears roared behind me, both those fighting, and the three royal bears who were remaining apart from the mayhem. They didn't sit in the bleachers out of fear, but out of respect. This wasn't their fight. They were honoring Claire and I by letting us handle our problems alone.

Still, I could have used a little less honor and a little more tag team.

But their decision played directly into my plan, thankfully. Enough had gone wrong so far to make me seriously consider that all was lost, but Beckett's successful escape to lead Amira to Cain's Holy Steam bath had kept me in the poker game.

I just had to make it to the last card in the stack, hoping my luck was with me.

"I'm going to enjoy this, Callie. More than you could possibly know..." Amira snarled, droplets of fire dripping from her reptilian fangs.

"Bring it, bitch."

She did.

CHAPTER 48

*W*e circled each other, me having to look up at her as the two bears roared in the background, the sound of crashing metal, shattering glass, and heavy *thumps* marking their dance.

Fiery wings of yellow flame flecked with chips of black stone formed over her shoulders, but they looked mottled and diseased. Despite the decay, the feathers looked like razor-sharp swords hanging from the arachnid-like appendages poking out from her shoulder blades.

"Dance for me, little Nephilim. Scream for me, like a good little warrior priestess," she purred, her metallic feathers rasping and rattling together, raining sparks down around her.

"I'm not a Nephilim, hell-twat. I'm something much darker than that…" I grinned, extending my fingers as I embraced that new side of me, knowing I would need every advantage. Her face changed, then, looking startled as she stared down at my hands. I casually did the same, masking my face so that it appeared I was very familiar with whatever the hell she was staring at.

Huge, weightless, silver gauntlets encased my fists, and the fingers were long, menacing claws, like hers. My back throbbed, but I kept the pain from my face, fearing any hesitation would be my doom.

"No Angel would have you…" she said, wings rattling.

"You're probably right. This is something different. Something new." I smiled, stepping closer. She stared at my forehead, as if trying to read something. Then, without any tip off, she was charging at me. At the last second, she skidded to a halt, pounding her cloven hooves into the pavement and twisting her torso parallel to the ground as if to shake something off her back.

Her wing shot out like a spear. Well, dozens of spears, the air smoking as her demonic feathers flew at me. I took one single step closer, pivoted my hips, and punched the hell feathers with my gauntlet. I felt them touch my hand, even though it didn't feel like I wore any protection, and they shattered like glass, washing my wrist in flames that somehow didn't burn. Sparks washed over me, and the smoke made it difficult to see, so I rushed her.

I made it two steps before unleashing my other fist in a full-body uppercut. Her jaw made a *cracking* sound as she flew into the air, her one good wing and one broken wing flaring out at the last second to catch the air in great big billows – although crooked. It slowed her down enough to land awkwardly.

Where she found me waiting. I stomped on her lead foot, pressing down with all my weight as I threw a right cross at her throat. The skin was hard as it crunched like porcelain under my gauntlet, but it only seemed to stun her, not truly injure her. Which was when I hit her with the claws of my other hand, slicing up from her hellish pubic region across to her left boob, slicing open the skin in a wash of flame.

Yellow blood spewed out from the wound, and she gasped, punching out with both hands to send me skidding back, but I pressed down on my back foot, and stopped almost instantly, my perfectly-fitted Darling and Dear boots preventing me from losing my balance.

Amira clutched her chest in fury. Then she spat a glob of yellow flame into her claws and wiped it down the wound, sealing it instantly, leaving behind a puckered, orange scar. Her face had dozens of cracks in it, like an almost-shattered egg. My shoulders began to ache again as I stalked after her, but it was more of a dull, buzzing feeling.

She dove to intercept me, claws out. I lifted my forearm to block her, and her claws screamed as they scraped down the chrome constructs, but then I realized she was spinning as I saw the tip of a dozen fiery blades coming at my face again, repeating her earlier tactic. I ducked my head, feeling intense heat as her bladed feathers scraped across the collar of my

Darling and Dear coat. I stumbled, and her hoof came out of nowhere as she used her wing like a shoulder in a roll.

Her hoof struck me in my unprotected stomach, sending me flying, doubled over.

The sound of bears fighting was abruptly much closer, but I heard a very solid impact, and a fierce breeze followed by the snapping of jaws right in front of my face as I flew by.

Just then, my shoulders lit with fire as if I had been shot twice in rapid succession, and then they tore open. I can't think of any other way to describe the pain. I screamed, and glass shattered at my cry, but I froze in midair as if striking a heavy mattress. I glanced down to see my boots were not touching the ground, because that was about three feet below me as I bobbed up and down fluidly.

The bears had actually stopped fighting to stare at me. I risked a glance to see smoking silver wings lightly flapping, almost like they were made of dry ice. The cold bit deep, as if felt within my soul, but it didn't hurt or ache. It just simply *was*. As the smoke shifted back and forth, I could almost make out feathers beneath, just like Amira, but white rather than blades of fire.

"Plot twist," I laughed loudly, turning to grin at Amira.

She screamed, revealing double rows of yellow fangs tipped in black. Then she was flying at me, slightly off course with each beat of her broken wing. Rather than consciously think about it, I let my body act as it would, pretending I was on solid ground and fighting in the training room. I didn't want to try to *make* my wings work – because I had no idea how to *do* so.

I simply focused on my mind. This was just another sparring match. All I needed to see were my opponent's motions, and allow my body to respond and react to the thousands of subtle shifts and changes that marked an attack, a block, a testing jab, or a full-blown assault.

I would fight with my mind, and let my body figure out how to make it work.

I flew to meet her, watching her shoulders, and ignoring her various sharp protrusions. The shoulders were key indicators in any fight.

We slammed into each other, our wings flapping wildly behind us as we clawed, punched, and kicked. She tried to bite my throat, but my fist was suddenly in the way. Her teeth clamped down, and several snapped off against the metal, making her body quiver in agony like I had placed tinfoil on a filling.

She snapped out her wings, shoving me as she flew back a few paces. She was smiling.

I flung out regular, old, wizard's magic in a bar of air that caught her completely off guard – latching onto her hoof and flinging her mightily into the crane looming over her. She screeched as she slammed into the metal arm with enough force to crack bone and knock the wrecking ball free. It fell, fast, crashing just to the right of the three spectator bears. They didn't even flinch.

Too late, I realized why Amira had been smiling.

I heard the clambering of great beasts beneath me, and something grabbed me by the ankle, yanking me out of the air. It squeezed my ankle and threw me. I slammed into the wall on the other side of the parking lot, brick crumbling as my wings flared out to absorb the impact.

I fell limply to the ground, because even though my wings had taken most of the impact, I had still struck my head hard against the wall. I fell to my knees, staring out at Claire lying a few paces away, struggling to climb to her feet as she whimpered. Blood covered her pristine white coat, and I felt my heart break, shattering my rage in an instant.

My magic flickered and died, my wings no longer helping to support my weight, and I instantly felt as if I was covered in a lead blanket.

Then I saw Yuri plodding closer in a lazy gait, almost looking playful. He stopped a pace away, staring down with dark eyes, and bloody gashes all over his face. His ear had been torn off, and he sported just as many wounds as Claire did, but it didn't show as well on his thick brown coat.

I tried to call up my magic sticks to fight Yuri, but he simply swatted at my wrist hard enough to stun me, and then grabbed me with his other claw. He panted eagerly, staring at me from inches away, and then slowly began to open his jaws, revealing a row of stained yellow fangs as big as my pinkie, and a long, pink tongue. I scrambled for my magic, for anything, but thoughts of Claire dying beside me – combined with my exhaustion – left me useless.

His neck suddenly darted forward, and I slammed my eyes shut, wincing.

Nothing happened.

I opened my eyes as I felt myself beginning to fall, and saw a bloody white paw protruding from out of Yuri's open mouth. Black claws glistened with crimson blood, and then finally jerked back into his mouth, leaving a hole I could see through. Yuri and I crashed to the ground. Not a second later, I heard another heavy thump as Claire collapsed behind Yuri, wheezing.

I slid myself over – my wrist tingling where Yuri had hit me – to check on my best friend. Deep, black eyes stared back, blinking as she let out a relieved-sounding whine. She licked my hand with a thick, black tongue, but that was about the extent of her strength.

I squeezed her, covering myself in blood in the process, and used her to climb back to my feet, wobbling unsteadily as I stared back at Amira, who was back on the ground and had a frustrated look on her face. Then, seeing my weakness, she began to limp closer, injured.

"Looks like you're all out of tricks, Callie. Might be time to break out the Spear, now. Or else you can watch her die. Either works for me, really."

CHAPTER 49

*T*he demon reached out with a clawed hand and grasped Claire by the rear paw, yanking her closer. Claire's front paw swiped up my ankle on the way by, tripping me. I crashed down onto my chest with a grunt, my arms too weak to fully absorb the fall. I tried to prop myself up, but my arms shook violently, my wrist still throbbing from Yuri's blow.

The demon crouched over Claire, and began punching her thick, heavily muscled chest. She seemed to enjoy the fact that the thick polar bear hide allowed her to punch harder than she normally would with a human, prolonging the agony.

Claire grunted and whined with each hit, and I struggled to crawl after her, to defend her.

Use the Spear… I thought to myself.

But I stubbornly shook my head. I had seen what happened when I tried bringing the Spear against Amira. This fight was personal, and I was pretty sure anyone upstairs would consider it bad form to use a holy weapon to settle a grudge. But my subconscious still considered it.

I stared down at the ground, spitting blood, and saw a strap dangling freely. I stared at it for a second, frowning. Hadn't the message with the coat said something about a buckle? What was so special about this coat? The boots could change and adapt to different styles, and detect demons. But the coat?

I frowned, trying to focus on it and change it into something else, but it felt like any other jacket. I knew it could take a beating, but that seemed the extent of its power. I managed to flop down on my rear, hissing in pain, and noticed an empty buckle as I checked the back of my head for blood with my functional hand. I hesitated, staring at the buckle. Then I looked at the strap. Then the buckle again. With an effort, I grasped the offending strap, and clumsily forced it into its buckle. A wash of cold instantly rolled over me, and I felt my pain fading away. I shivered in relief. I was still exhausted, but at least most of my pain was gone.

I looked back up at the grunting sound to find Amira staring at me with hatred, looking angry to see that I wasn't even paying attention. I blinked, clearing my eyes as she went back to work. "The Spear, Callie. It's the only hope you two have. Either use it or I will end this wretched beast."

I was pretty sure my dazed look had accurately shown her all was not well in Callie Land.

But it hadn't just been a dazed look. Between us, I saw two feathers hovering a few inches off the ground, about three feet apart – one as white as snow and the other a solid silver. They rotated slowly, but as I focused on one or the other, that rotation increased, and I heard different whispers filling my head.

I stared at the silver one, guessing it was that of an Angel, or at least symbolized an Angel. *Destiny. Salvation. Vanquisher...* the voices whispered, but I quickly turned to look at the other.

The white one that likely symbolized my training as a wizard. *Knight. Hope. Strength. Justice...* different voices cooed.

Was I hallucinating, or was this a choice? But... that was an impossible one. I had both within me, and felt a connection with both sets of whispers.

The cracked door inside me began to rattle. Very, very loudly. Until I wondered if anyone else could hear it, too.

I tried to ignore the rattling as I crawled closer, feeling like it was forcing me into a decision. I wasn't a fan of that. I deliberated fast, because as strong as Claire was, she wasn't immortal. The whispers increased as I moved, the door kept on rattling for my attention, and I struggled to place one hand in front of the other, just wanting to close my eyes for a minute. But I shook my head angrily. No. I stared from one feather to the other, hearing more words and enticing promises from each. But, judging from what I had experienced today and when I had fought Johnathan, I had a tie to heaven in my blood, thanks to the droplet of Angel's blood that had merged with me.

I had freaking wings for God's sake. Well, not anymore…

Had that simply been a taste? An appetizer? If I chose the silver feather, would that make those powers permanent? And… would that mean I was no longer a wizard? Abandoning the gift from my birth mother, Constance?

But if I chose the white feather, would that be a slap in the face to Heaven? To the Angels and the Nephilim? Abandoning the gifts from my birth father? From God?

I scrambled forward faster, now, knowing that I needed one of them to have a hope at saving Claire. Either that or I took up the Spear. Which I didn't know how to make appear, anyway. Feathers it was, by default. I shuffled closer, debating, clumsy with exhaustion.

"Crawl to me, my dear. Save your friend. Use the Spear to save her. Or, be a saint and watch her die out of ignorant respect for your God – like all those before you, have chosen." She glanced up at me and I was careful to avert my eyes from the feathers. "Chosen and failed, I might add. We're still here, if you haven't noticed. We haven't changed. The Crusaders haven't changed. That's called a hint. God wants you to do this. But you're scared of God," she said, punching Claire again.

Could she not see the feathers? Was I really hallucinating? How hard had I hit my head?

I was only a pace away from them now, and I closed my eyes. Did choosing the white one make me a bad person? Did choosing the silver one make me arrogant enough to declare I was equal to Angels or Nephilim?

I remembered my talk with the silver reflection of myself, and felt a small smile tugging at my cheeks. *Stay true to yourself… and know that you are not required to make a life change.*

With my eyes closed, my heart open and suddenly warm, I reached out a hand, sensing that heat spread across my chest and down my arm. The door in my mind rattled, creaking against unseen hinges as if a tornado was on the other side.

The air in the parking lot stilled in contrast to the storm in my mind. I opened my eyes to see my hand encased in silver, a line of silver liquid trailing from my heart down my arm, over the fabric of my clothes. My fingers wrapped around the white feather, and the parking lot flashed with white light.

In my mind, the cracked door suddenly bulged, and then in a burst of splinters that was instantly consumed by a wave of liquid, white fire and a bed of silver coals.

I snapped my eyes closed instinctively at the brightness, and heard Amira scream.

I opened them a moment later to see the white feather in my hand slowly turning to silver from the bottom up, looking exactly like someone was pouring molten chrome over the feather – just upside down – starting where my hand touched it and spreading up, reaching for Heaven.

Then the feather was entirely silver.

My hand flashed once more, not as bright, and the feather winked out of existence.

My eyes blazed, and I found I was somehow on my feet staring at Amira, still too far away.

She screamed, shaking her head in outrage, and lifted her claws high overhead. Then she was shrieking maniacally as she brought the claws down towards Claire's neck, thrusting them forward like a spear, as if intending to punch straight through to the pavement.

Faster than thought, I flung out my hand. *Need*, I begged to myself.

I *needed* Claire more than anything in the world. She was my lifeline. My bedrock. The first friend who had shown me love after seeing my use of magic. The most important part of a solid, dependable structure. My cornerstone.

A white line appeared directly over Claire's exposed neck, and then flared with a ring of silver sparks, a horizontal, silver Gateway the size of a melon.

Amira gasped as her claws slipped through the Gateway, and then she gurgled, grunted and choked, not having sensed the *second* Gateway that had appeared directly *behind* her – below her shoulder blade, where her heart would be.

Her claw sunk into the first Gateway above Claire's throat, and protruded out the second Gateway and through her own chest, clutching a slimy, greasy, black-veined heart – like amber illuminated from within. She stared down at it, confused and struggling for air, burning blades falling to the ground behind her with metallic *clanging* sounds as her wings shed their feathers.

I stepped up to her and shoved her with my boot, knocking her body a few paces away as I smiled down at my Darling and Dears. Those ass-kicking, magical, fetching, kinky boots.

Because the sensation of demonic presence was entirely gone.

"These shoes are so metal," I whispered, adoring them.

Clairebear opened her eyes weakly, seeing me staring down at my feet. She might have nodded her head in approval or appreciation, but then closed her eyes, passing out. Amira dissolved into a pile of smoldering coals – and I was suddenly thankful I had kicked her away from Claire.

Before I could crouch down, I felt a presence behind me. I spun to find Armor, Kona, and Starlight assessing me with very thoughtful, considering looks. Then they looked at Claire.

"We should take her from this place," Armor said in a low rumble. "See to her wounds. When she wakes, it will not be good."

I frowned. "What do you mean, *it will not be good*," I said the last in a deep, huffing voice.

"I do not sound like that," Armor grumbled.

Kona coughed oddly, sounding suspiciously like a hushed laugh.

"She killed," Starlight said. "The first shift is hard enough without learning that you killed. We must help her through that trauma, so that she doesn't associate murder with her beast. We must help her shift far from humanity, in the woods, to get to know herself without the savagery. To see that it is not a thing to fear."

I smiled down at Claire. "That makes sense. Hippie stuff. She'll like that."

As I watched, Claire slowly returned to her human form – a small, naked, young woman. Tiny, really. Especially after her bear form. My heart broke for her pain – her body was a mass of bruises. "A polar bear," I said absently, shaking my head. "What's up with that?"

Kona shook her head thoughtfully. "She must have bloodlines up there."

I nodded, still smiling down at her. She was alive. And she had been a total badass. I couldn't wait to talk to her about it. Well, after she... rediscovered herself. I smiled up at Armor. "Admit it. She totally kicked ass out there. Better watch yourself. You thought I was a handful?"

He smiled for the first time. "Oh, we've gotten a small taste of her spunk. I fear she will be incorrigible, now."

I grinned wider, then followed the glances of the other two bears to where Yuri lay. "I take it you have your proof?" I asked warily.

Starlight nodded, eyes narrowing. "We already believed it, but he deserved his... day in court." He met my eyes, pensive. "I don't think I want to be in your court. Ever."

I nodded in agreement.

Armor spoke up. "We must be off. We'll speak again. Soon. But we'll likely be away for a while. Maybe even up north," he said with a rueful grin.

Kona picked her up on two legs, and carried her away over a shoulder, stroking her hair.

I heard footsteps behind me, and turned to see Cain supporting Beckett. The world's first murderer was shaking his head, laughing heartily. Beckett smirked casually, playing it cool, eyes darting to me frequently as if checking I was okay. I risked a glance at Brigitte to find her still unconscious, but her necklace gone. I immediately panicked, and then remembered that Amira the demon was dead. Still, the woman was a first-class piece of shit. For her beliefs, and for her ignorance. Not an immediate threat, but she would definitely need to be watched. Since I had absolutely no sympathy for her, I decided that Roland could babysit her.

Cain finally stepped up to me, and Beckett met my eyes with a proud grin.

"Holy shit, Callie. Do you have any idea how hard it was to sit up there? I felt like I was watching a prize fight in Vegas!" Cain hooted.

I smiled, staring down at the phone in his hand. "How was it?" I asked hopefully.

He was silent, so I looked back at his face, my heart skipping a beat. "*Thousands* of Freaks watched this live..." he said in disbelief. "Keeping up with the comments was impossible. They were cheering you on! Dorian sure knows how to get the word out, and he was very thankful when I showed up and told him he didn't have to be the one filming, like you had told him."

I sighed in relief. "I'm glad Father David blessed that water for you, or this could have gone an entirely different way..."

Cain grinned. "You should have seen the look on his face when I asked him to do it!"

A very slow clap interrupted us, and I glared up at the newcomer. So that was who Amira had been expecting to show, and I thought I understood what had happened, but we would see. "You can kill him if you want, Cain," I said neutrally.

CHAPTER 50

*H*aven stood before us, surrounded by his goons. I hadn't gotten a good look at him during the fundraiser, but his goons were familiar. "That was quite impressive," the new Master Vampire of Kansas City said, grinning like a shark. "Using a live stream to broadcast this fight. Letting all the freaks know to watch. To witness how Amira had played us all against each other."

"Even you," I added with a mocking grin.

"Perhaps," he said. "Or perhaps not."

Cain sighed dramatically. "I followed you, halfwit. Did you really think I was that clumsy? I placed a tracker on you in the alley when you took my friend, here. Now I know where you're holing up."

Haven slowly turned to study him, frowning. He didn't look pleased to hear this part. Not at all. But he finally nodded. "Do you blame me? When two Masters have died here in the space of a few months. Master Simon was my friend, Callie."

I didn't say anything, merely watched him. He returned my look, reading me.

"But after tonight, I must agree with the other rumor… that Master Simon's death was a setup. A frame job. Quite devious of them, really. Regardless, I played along with her demands, but not because I had any notion of partnering with her. It was a power play to solidify my territory. I was hoping to do something such as this, only with me as the star of the show. Turn the nations against her by getting her to admit her crimes."

"But you didn't get anything out of this, and there's no way for me to verify your claim."

He shrugged. "Do some magic to verify my words, if you must. I'll let you."

He waited, but I didn't do anything. Not because I trusted him, but because I wasn't powerful enough to tie my boots with magic at the moment. I was exhausted, and barely standing.

"We'll address that later. For now, I think there's been enough death and destruction. But…" I said, meeting his eyes. "Tomorrow's a new day, and I'm kind of curious of the reaction of the Freaks to what they saw tonight. I'm sure many of them will have stories to tell. Or people to tell *on*." I enunciated the last word, but not a flicker of concern crossed his crocodile eyes.

"I swear it on my title that I had no intention of working with Amira. I – and many other factions in town – were forced to comply. I'm new in town, and the vampires are not what they once were, of which Amira was very aware. She offered me strength and support, but having heard what happened to Master Simon, I was skeptical. Still, I couldn't stand against her. Not directly." He drew a sudden claw over his wrist, letting the blood drip to the earth. Then he extended his hand politely for me to shake.

I stared at it warily. "Did you kill anyone for her?"

He nodded slowly. "The wolf. But one thing you should know, if your police had any skill whatsoever," he added with a dry look at Beckett, who stiffened angrily. "Each victim was actually quite a terrible person. Every. Single. One." He must have noticed my doubtful look. "I can send you a copy of their files."

I nodded appreciatively. "Send one to the police as well. Anonymously."

"Of course," he replied, bowing his head slightly. Then he cleared his throat. "Amira hoped to smother you with their records, hoping you wasted time learning the truth about each as you tried to find a connection between them. She repeatedly informed me that I must choose someone terrible, because if I chose an innocent, her game might be noticed too early. But the vampires weren't to be touched. That's when I realized I was just another cog. That twat bear killed one of mine," he said, shooting a hateful look at Yuri. "I took one of his in return. Ragmussen," he said, smirking. "Amira wasn't pleased with my deviation, and so, commanded me to get him." He pointed at Beckett. "No hard feelings? I didn't strike you. And I did give you the key to your shackles."

I blinked at him, then rounded on Beckett. He smiled. "He did."

"And why wasn't this the first thing that was said?" I shouted angrily. The men shared a look. One of the guards even scratched his head, as if I had spoken a different language.

Haven puffed up importantly. "I heard Dorian's broadcast, and realized I might have a hero to latch onto. So, I gave my brief prisoner the key to his freedom before I handed him over." He turned back to me. "If you failed, none would have ever been the wiser," he added honestly.

I nodded, still not shaking his hand.

He sighed dramatically. "Look at it this way. I didn't want to come here. Too much sun. London is much nicer. But when an opening comes up, a fledgling Master must abide by the Sanguine Council. And if I'm going to rule somewhere, I'm going to do a good job of it. Not make the same mistake of blindly dealing with demons, like Master Simon – buying her lies hook, line, and sinker, believing they were on the same side. I never trusted her, but being the new kid on the block has its disadvantages. In all honesty, I came here tonight to hopefully witness this. But worst case, to stab Amira in the back after you tired her out. Well, shoot her in the back," he amended, pointing a finger up to the roof of a third building.

I saw a sniper sitting there. His gun pointed straight up. Seeing our attention, he lifted his hand in a gesture of *hello*.

"If I wanted you dead, I would have simply let him shoot you, rather than come say *hello*." Haven extended his hand again, and I finally sighed, shaking it with a firm grip. "And I wouldn't have given your friend the keys to his cuffs."

"This doesn't make us friends, Haven," I warned. "I respect your blunt honesty, but I don't fully trust you. Not yet. I tried to talk with you at the fundraiser and was rebuffed. We could have been working beside each other this whole time."

The muscle-head guard behind him shifted uncomfortably, and Haven actually turned to glare at him. "I wasn't aware of that…" he said, sounding sincere. "Do you know why she needed you to be angry?" he asked, turning back to face me.

I frowned. "What?"

"She was quite adamant about it. She needed you confused and angry. *Very, very angry*. She said it repeatedly."

I thought about it. Maybe it was because of the Spear. She had wanted me to use it. Likely to weaken it, or break it completely. Maybe she had hoped my rage would make that choice easier.

I had come into this angry, even remained so for some time, but something in me had changed during the fight. A sense of responsibility rather than joy. A job that needed doing. A story that needed to be shared with our private, online live-stream that Dorian had set up.

I shrugged at Haven.

"Well, I'd like to wish you congratulations, and to let you know you are welcome to come see my territory. To see for yourself. Even speak to my people. It would go a long way in earning their trust, and overcoming their fears after this," he said waving a hand at the general area. "I still can't believe Dorian managed to contact so many people so quickly to let them know this event was being played live online."

I shrugged disinterestedly. "I put him in a corner, and he used the service he uses for his parties. A big messaging system. I bet his contacts spread word from there, and much as gossip always does, it spread like wildfire. He's a party animal. And if one suddenly found themselves receiving a message passed on from Dorian Gray, pretty much any of them would be interested. Just to brag about it later. And would share it to look favored."

Haven nodded. "Very sneaky. I approve."

"This conversation has been pleasant, but my blood is still a little hot. Let's meet later. I think I would very much like to see your territory," I said neutrally, sounding as if it was simply something I could cross off my list of things to do.

He nodded, and turned to leave. "Oh, one last thing," he called over his shoulder. "I injected the policeman with Holy Water. Nasty, vile stuff. But I didn't want Amira biting him. Granted, it's not as good as giving her a Holy Water shower, but it would have been enough for her to toss him away on reflex if she had tried, giving him a chance to run to safety, where I had men standing by to assist," he said.

Beckett slapped his neck instinctively, face pale. I saw a small dot on the side of his neck. Not two, like a vampire bite, but one single, almost indistinguishable dot.

261

When I turned back to Haven, he and his goons were already gone.

Cain nodded to himself, eyeing the space they had occupied. "I like him."

I rolled my eyes. "That's just because he beat you handily. Let's go home."

CHAPTER 51

I pressed *stop* on the laptop, cutting off the audio file. Silence filled
the room.

Pastor Benjamin was shaking his head in profound sorrow. We hadn't
played him everything, simply Brigitte's confession to helping with the
chaos, the mobs. And that she had done it for love. For Pastor Benjamin.

Roland watched him thoughtfully, but Father David simply stared down
at the desk respectfully.

"Where…" Benjamin cleared his throat. "Where is she now?"

Beckett answered, standing apart from us. "She fled. The police are
looking for her."

Desmond was sobbing openly, but Pastor Benjamin's shoulders sagged
further. He was likely hit twice by this. Once for her crimes, twice for her
admission of love.

"I think…" he said, slowly climbing to his feet, staring down at nothing.
"I think I'm done here." And then he was walking out of the room. Desmond
sniffed loudly, wiping his face, and followed him. Beckett followed them out
of the room, leaving us in privacy.

"Well," Roland began, "as happy as I am to see him leave, I wouldn't wish
that on anyone."

Father David nodded his agreement.

"What will the Vatican do with her?" I asked.

"Keep her locked up for now. She could be susceptible to further influence if another demon found her. But she'll also feel right at home surrounded by Cardinals and Sisters," he smiled sadly.

Roland had only just arrived at the church, and we hadn't had time to talk about anything. He moved slowly, still in pain from his injuries, but shot me a withering glare if he caught me openly noticing it. I met his eyes, and then glanced at Father David when he wasn't looking. Roland sighed, motioning for me to continue, and looking as if he was bracing for torture.

"What if the bomber learns about her?" I asked.

"I received an update on that. The bomber was wearing a vest, killing himself, and any evidence linking him to a crime. His entire workstation was obliterated. I was lucky to be a few tables down from him that day as I researched records to try and find out who he was. He must have known me on sight, and activated a failsafe. To kill himself and destroy the evidence." He sighed tiredly. "After later going through his online records, they found proof of what he was looking into, but most of the physical proof was missing."

I frowned angrily. Not that I wasn't happy Roland was safe, but that the evidence was gone. I wouldn't find out who my parents were.

When I looked up, Roland was staring at me. "I found a single paper that confirmed your story. That you had been left at the church, but nothing about your parents. No names. Basically, a review of Father David's report when he first found you," he said sadly.

I growled.

"But to be fair, I'm not sure there ever was much more evidence than that. Because, why would there be? Your parents didn't exactly contact the Vatican to let them know your life story before leaving you here with Father David and then disappearing. They wanted you safe. So they kept their names out of it. It was just enough information for Johnathan to connect the dots."

I nodded numbly. Thinking about it made sense, actually. If there had been anything more, I was sure Father David would have found it and passed it on. Unless my parents had later decided to contact the Vatican to tell them my story, why would the Vatican have any knowledge of me? Giving the Vatican my story would have directly contradicted the entire point of their actions.

To keep me safe.

"At least we got the mole," I said dejectedly.

Roland nodded. "The evidence proves it. He was the only one to search those particular files. Other than Father David a few decades ago. Literally."

Father David piped up. "Does it really change anything, Callie? Would learning their names suddenly make you a different person? You are quite an incredible woman already."

My eyes burned at the thought. How could I explain? "A girl should know her father."

"Well, not to belabor the obvious, but we all share the same father…" he said softly. I looked up, eyes murderous, and saw him smiling. "But I do understand, Callie."

Roland cleared his throat. "Terry is your father. And if you ever need another, I'm here."

"Hey! I knew her first," Father David chimed in, smiling at me.

I lowered my eyes, nodding. They were right. Nothing had changed. I had no reason to suddenly be sad. But… the hope had messed with me. To find a picture, or a name, or something. Anything. I knew my mother's name was Constance, but who was my father?

"Callie, will you finally let me know what really happened last night?" Roland asked tiredly. "I'm exhausted, and you look like you could sleep for a week, so I know there's a story."

Without speaking, I opened up a new tab on the computer, scrolled down, and clicked *play*.

A video replay popped up, starting with me walking into a parking lot. I climbed to my feet and walked towards the door, not wanting to talk. "That should give you the gist of it," I said as I opened the door and exited the room. I closed the door behind me.

I walked down the stairs, imagining a nice, long nap. Beckett was still swimming in the aftermath of it all, unable to participate in the investigation, and forced to sit on his hands. Haven had made good on his promise to deliver the files on the victims, which probably meant he hadn't been lying about them. I hoped that evidence would vindicate Beckett. He was a good detective.

I opened a door at the base of the stairs and walked into the sanctuary.

I heard Arthur arguing and looked up to find a tall black man with dreadlocks looking extremely patient as he let Arthur's tirade wash over him. I froze. My stalker.

"She is busy, and without a name, you won't step one foot—" The man looked over Arthur's shoulder very suddenly, and Arthur stopped, turning to see me.

"Callie Penrose. My name is Alyksandre, and I would like to speak with you," he said in a very deep voice, all bass.

"I tried telling him to come back later, but he wouldn't listen," Arthur growled. "And it was too difficult to give me a name to pass on," he added, glaring back at the younger man.

"The name would have meant nothing to her. We are strangers," he replied politely.

I walked closer, studying him acutely. My boots didn't tingle or give off any indication of anything dangerous, and my magic didn't tell me he was anything dangerous either.

"Why would you like to speak with me?" I asked, placing a comforting hand on Arthur's shoulder, which seemed to calm him somewhat, although he still looked on the verge of throwing Alyksandre out on his ear.

"I was a friend of Gabriel," he said softly. My heart began hammering in my chest. Gabriel... the Nephilim Johnathan had killed. I nodded slowly, realizing that this man may have answers for me. "Would it make sense to you if I said we only did as commanded? That you needed to decide your own path before aid could be offered. That a certain feather you found broke a ward placed on you from birth, but that the full gift couldn't be given until you reached a certain personal decision?" His eyes studied me, full of deeper meaning. I felt my heart pattering wildly. Alyksandre glanced down at Arthur curiously, then back to me.

"He stays."

Arthur puffed up at that, which almost made me burst out laughing.

Alyksandre nodded. "I, too, needed to make this personal decision, although our circumstances are quite... different. Yours is truly unique."

"Speak plainly. Arthur is a big boy."

A wisp of a smile flashed across the Nephilim's face. "Speaking carefully has become a habit. A few of my brothers have died getting too close to you Missouri Wizards..." he said sadly. I hid my astonishment. Was he speaking about Nate? Had he also had a run-in with Nephilim? Maybe that explained our attraction, our shared white magic...

But I also found myself growing considerably angry. This man, and his people, or boss, or whatever, had been following me. Watching me. Not helping me. While Amira and Johnathan had run amok.

"Watching me does not constitute help. In fact, it kind of tells me you are cowardly," I said, coolly.

"Angel forbid it. As much as it pained us. You had to prove yourself."

That comment right there lit a fire under my ass. "I don't prove myself to anyone, little Nephilim..." And I began to turn away. "Please take out the trash, Arthur."

"Angel wants to meet you, Callie!" Alyksandre pleaded.

I paused. Well, that was something, at least.

I turned, studying him up and down like my mother had done so often to me.

"Just curious, but which Angel are we talking about? What's his name?"

The Nephilim frowned. "Angel," he said, as if repeating the obvious.

I blinked at him, suddenly understanding. "No. You can't be serious. This Angel's name is... *Angel?*" I asked incredulously.

He nodded, lips thinning at my amusement. "Yes."

"Okay. You just moved to the bottom of my priority list. Tell... Angel Angel that I'm busy. But that I just took care of Demon Demon for him." I shook my head, chuckling as I turned around. This had to be a joke. There weren't any Angels named Angel. That was just ridiculous.

"You can't ignore a summons."

I snapped my fingers, the world flashing to chrome in a blink.

I spun, and flung out my hands. The door crashed open behind Alyksandre, leading to the street. He spun instinctively, hand flashing to his hip. I ran up behind him and kicked him in the ass with my Darling and Dear boots. He grunted, and flew out the door at the added force of my magic powering my kick. I slammed the doors behind him as he flew through, and then dusted off my hands, turning to Arthur.

"I'm cranky and need a nap. Mind watching over the place for me?"

He stared at me in awe, a smile slowly creeping over his face. "As you wish, my lady." He walked up to the doors, and stood facing them, shoulders straight. I smiled. Arthur was a keeper.

I wasn't sure what was in store for me for the next couple of days, but I definitely wasn't going to go crawling to an Angel named Angel the morning after I had kicked serious ass all night, without any backup from Heaven.

No matter how they might take it. We had managed this long as strangers. A few more days wouldn't hurt.

Even though I desperately wanted information from them, going to them at their beck and call would put them in a subconscious position of power. When I decided to grace them with my presence, they were going to be quivering in their goose-down capes.

Hell, maybe I would even show up with my way cooler smoke wings and silver gauntlets. Then burn their door down with a healthy display of white fire.

"Feathers and fire," I murmured to myself, nodding. "I'll sleep on it..."

And I Shadow Walked back home to my apartment.

A stuffed unicorn was just begging for some cuddle time in my bed, and I had a lot to think about... Especially since the aftermath of my video would probably be felt for quite some time.

Who knew what would happen next.

And I felt like going shopping tomorrow. At Darling and Dear...

A girl loved to accessorize when stressed out. It was therapeutic.

~

DON'T FORGET! VIP's get early access to all sorts of Temple-Verse goodies, including signed copies, private giveaways, and advance notice of future projects. AND A FREE NOVELLA! Click the image or join here:
www.shaynesilvers.com/l/219800

~

Callie Penrose returns in **WHISPERS**... *Turn the page for a sample! Or* **get the book ONLINE!**

SAMPLE: WHISPERS (FEATHERS AND FIRE #1)

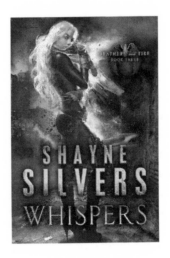

I stared down the big, hairy, mouth-breather. "Bring it on," I growled menacingly.

All one thousand pounds of Kenai, a shifter grizzly bear, barreled straight at me like a snowplow, ignoring petty laws like physics. The beast rose up on two tree-trunk thick legs, towering over me as he roared.

Starlight, the impish black bear, clapped excitedly from the sidelines, and Claire emitted a nervous gasp. I was still unsure where Starlight stood in the hierarchy of the bears. The Cave of shifters listened to his opinion even when it contradicted Armor, their Alpha, who was sitting beside Starlight in bear form, leaning forward as he watched. He was a ten-foot-tall brown bear, but his hair was longer and shaggier than a typical bear. More than a dozen other bears watched the bout from various places around the ring.

Claire was the referee for this particular matchup, one of many that would progress throughout the day. Their idea of a relaxing vacation. Kenai's jaws were alarmingly wide, and his long, ivory fangs were designed to rend flesh from bone. Standing against him in the ring was my fault. Too many drinks last night at the campfire had made this encounter inevitable. Drunken pride had brought me to this place.

A figurative cage-match in the middle of the snowy Alaskan tundra with a freaking grizzly bear. The upside was that shifters healed fast, and they had Claire in case I got too overzealous. On the other hand, I had no such protections. I hoped that wouldn't be my downfall.

He swiped at me, testing my fear.

Rather than staying back, I lunged within his swipe and scored a direct hit on his inner thigh with my blade. I wasn't using magic… yet. I wanted to push myself, and using magic seemed unfair – even though he was ten times my weight. Still, I wanted to wait as long as possible because Beckett was sparring next, and he had none of my special abilities since he was a Regular human. He wasn't a wizard, so no magic. He also didn't have ties to Heaven.

He only had those ancient abilities that had boosted mankind for thousands of years.

The instinct for self-preservation, improvisation, and sheer grit.

Kenai roared at the slash of pain, but I was already rolling away, using the hilt of my dagger to hammer into his hamstring on my way by. His stance faltered, and I ended up behind him. I immediately sliced and stabbed into his thick hide, knowing that the layers of fat would protect him from serious injury. Still, if I took it too easy on him I would look weak to the rest of the Cave – the term they used for a group of shifter bears – and he would likely beat me, making me look even more unfit to be the self-imposed protector of Kansas City.

Like all men seemed to think, I needed to finish this fast and hard.

Too distracted by my thoughts, I missed the backhanded swipe of his massive paw and he scored a solid blow to my chest, making the belts and buckles of my Darling and Dear coat clank together. I didn't know much about Darling and Dear, other than that they made magical gear with various types of leather. They had given me the coat and a pair of boots for doing them a favor, and that was good enough for me.

My boots were a thing of beauty. If I focused, I could change them into different shapes and styles, but right now they were calf-high riding boots, because I hadn't wanted to get snow inside them and soak my socks. Priorities.

The coat was like an armor of sorts, but Kenai's blow still hurt like a mother-lover. As I flew through the air, I immediately decided to forego my abstinence on magic in favor of survival, casting a blanket of air before me so that the approaching tree didn't break my face.

I bounced off, landing lightly in the snow, my Darling and Dear boots cushioning my fall. I lifted a smirk to Kenai – the big hairy lout. His eyes narrowed, noting my use of magic, but he didn't call me out on it. Bears were like that. Honorable, respectable, and not inclined to belittle someone for a mistake – unless there was a lesson to be learned. Still, we both knew I had resorted to magic. Not that it counted against me, but that it was some-thing we were both aware of. Just another fact on the table.

He settled his weight evenly across his four legs, debating whether to attack or wait.

I solved his moral dilemma and charged. Before he could react, I threw one of my blades at the ground near his lead foot, making him flinch in that direction to defend himself as I simultaneously ran up the nearby tree on his opposite side. He was so stunned by the fact that I had given up one of my weapons – and missed – that he didn't see what I had intended.

I took three steps up the tree trunk and catapulted myself off, flipping backwards to avoid the instinctive swipe of his inches long claws. He missed and I scored a direct hit across the back of the offending paw in the process, making him recoil instinctively.

Which gave me the perfect opportunity to stab him in the shoulder with the blade, using it as an anchor-point to swing my bodyweight directly behind his shoulders. With a quick flick of my wrists, my sneaky bracelet became a garrote, and I looped the metal wire around his thick throat in a tight choke, abandoning my dagger in his shoulder. I spun my wrists, crossing the wire for maximum control and then yanked back. Now I had reins for my pony-bear.

He tried to roar through his constricted windpipe, claws raking at his throat, but neither the thick pads of his paws nor his claws could find purchase as I choked him. I yanked back even harder, arching my back so that my weight pulled him off balance. I dug my feet into the fat of his back, arms straining as I tensed for the crash, anticipating he would try to use my body to break his fall.

He did try, but I danced across his back so that I wasn't in the way. He hit like a meteor, snow rippling around us in a wave. He scrabbled in the muddy snow, claws raking and digging for purchase, but he only managed to compact the snow into little barriers. He snarled and huffed desperately, but the lack of oxygen was affecting his muscles, weakening him.

I waited a few more seconds, letting him keep his honor for as long as he chose.

"Peace," he rasped like a whisper of wind, muscles going completely slack.

I let out a breath of relief and released one end of the wire. It whipped back into my bracelet with a hiss like a school janitor's key ring.

I hopped off him and took a few steps, shaking the soreness from my arms. Choking out a half-ton Grizzly was no walk in the park. The clearing was utterly silent.

Then a rasping wheeze emanated from the downed bear, which slowly turned into a rattling chuckle, his injuries repairing on the spot. After a few moments, his bellows of laughter thundered across the snow, echoing off the trees and nearby rocks.

Claire rushed over to him, studying his throat, thumbing back his eyes, and checking on the brief slashes from my blade. She shot me a look over his quivering form as she yanked my dagger out from his shoulder, not finding the situation as funny as Kenai did. Because as a veterinarian for the Kansas City Zoo, she was the person who healed wounds, not inflicted them. She ignored the smirk plastered on my face. It wasn't that she was offended by my win, but that Claire always considered consequences, and knowing my level of lethality, she always wanted me to use the lowest level of violence at my disposal. She didn't understand that her philosophy would get me killed in the real world.

Someday, it might get her killed, too. Because she wasn't just a veterinarian any longer. She was also a shifter-bear, and that was one of the reasons we were all out here. To help her get used to that, and to make peace with her first kill – a true son of a bitch named Yuri – the bear who had turned her against her will several months ago.

Kenai gently shoved her away, shifting back to his human form. A large, tanned naked man stood from the ground, his back easily four feet across and rippling with muscles. And back hair. A whole lot of back hair. His human form was even as hairy as a bear. No wonder he was never cold. He turned to face me, his dark beard extended down his neck and under his ears to connect with his jaw-length hair like a helmet. He dipped his head, his pale gray eyes twinkling through the curtains of his dark bangs. "Damn, girl," he finally chuckled, shaking his head.

"What does it feel like to have your ass kicked by a *hormonal little girl?*" I teased, using his statement from the night before.

He grinned. "Better than I imagined," he admitted with an easy shrug.

Then he bowed his head again, lowering his eyes this time. Part of me instinctively waited for a second attack, even though I knew better. Bears were ridiculously noble. To a fault, even. He lifted up his palms in surrender, walking away. "Callie wins."

I saw money change hands. The losers of the bet didn't look angry, just thoughtful. I had impressed them.

I made sure I didn't trip as I made my way over to Claire.

~

Get your copy of WHISPERS online today!

~

Turn the page to read a sample of **OBSIDIAN SON** *- Nate Temple Book 1 - or* **BUY ONLINE***. Nate Temple is a billionaire wizard from St. Louis. He rides a bloodthirsty unicorn and drinks with the Four Horsemen. He even cow-tipped the Minotaur. Once...*

(Note: Nate's books 1-6 happen prior to UNCHAINED, but crossover from then on,

the two series taking place in the same universe but also able to standalone if you prefer)

Full chronology of all books in the Temple Universe shown on the 'BOOKS IN THE TEMPLE VERSE' page.

TRY: OBSIDIAN SON (NATE TEMPLE #1)

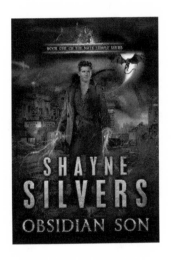

There was no room for emotion in a hate crime. I had to be cold. Heartless. This was just another victim. Nothing more. No face, no name.

Frosted blades of grass crunched under my feet, sounding to my ears alone like the symbolic glass that one shattered under a napkin at a Jewish wedding. The noise would have threatened to give away my stealthy advance as I stalked through the moonlit field, but I was no novice and had planned accordingly. Being a wizard, I was able to muffle all sensory evidence with a fine cloud of magic—no sounds, and no smells. Nifty. But if I made the spell much stronger, the anomaly would be too obvious to my prey.

I knew the consequences for my dark deed tonight. If caught, jail time or possibly even a gruesome, painful death. But if I succeeded, the look of fear and surprise in my victim's eyes before his world collapsed around him, was well worth the risk. I simply couldn't help myself; I had to take him down.

I knew the cops had been keeping tabs on my car, but I was confident that they hadn't followed me. I hadn't seen a tail on my way here, but seeing as how they frowned on this kind of thing I had taken a circuitous route just in case. I was safe. I hoped.

Then my phone chirped at me as I received a text.

My body's fight-or-flight syndrome instantly kicked in, my heart threatening to explode in one final act of pulmonary paroxysm. "Motherf—" I hissed instinctively, practically jumping out of my skin. I had forgotten to silence it. *Stupid, stupid, stupid!* My body remained tense as I swept my gaze over the field, sure that I had been made. My breathing finally began to slow, my pulse returning to normal, as I noticed no changes in my surroundings. Hopefully, my magic had silenced the sound and my resulting outburst. I glanced down at the phone to scan the text and then typed back a quick and angry response before I switched the cursed phone to vibrate.

Now, where were we...

I continued on, the lining of my coat constricting my breathing. Or maybe it was because I was leaning forward in anticipation. *Breathe*, I chided myself. *He doesn't know you're here.* All this risk for a book. It had better be worth it.

I'm taller than most, and not abnormally handsome, but I knew how to play the genetic cards I had been dealt. I had shaggy, dirty blonde hair, and my frame was thick with well-earned muscle, yet still lean. I had once been told that my eyes were like twin emeralds pitted against the golden-brown tufts of my hair—a face like a jewelry box. Of course, that was two bottles of wine into a date, so I could have been a little foggy on her quote. Still, I liked to imagine that was how everyone saw me.

But tonight, all that was masked by magic.

I grinned broadly as the outline of the hairy hulk finally came into view. He was blessedly alone—no nearby sentries to give me away. That was always a risk when performing this ancient right-of-passage. I tried to keep the grin on my face from dissolving into a maniacal cackle.

My skin danced with energy, both natural and unnatural, as I manipulated the threads of magic floating all around me. My victim stood just ahead, oblivious of the world of hurt that I was about to unleash. Even with his millennia of experience, he didn't stand a chance. I had done this so many times that the routine of it was my only enemy. I lost count of how many times I had been told not to do it again; those who knew declared it *cruel, evil, and sadistic*. But what fun wasn't? Regardless, that wasn't enough to stop me from doing it again. And again. Call it an addiction if you will, but it was too much of a rush to ignore.

The pungent smell of manure filled the air, latching onto my nostril hairs. I took another step, trying to calm my racing pulse. A glint of gold reflected in the silver moonlight, but the victim remained motionless, hopefully unaware or all was lost. I wouldn't make it out alive if he knew I was here. Timing was everything.

I carefully took the last two steps, a lifetime between each, watching the legendary monster's ears, anxious and terrified that I would catch even so much as a twitch in my direction. Seeing nothing, a fierce grin split my unshaven cheeks. My spell had worked! I raised my palms an inch away from their target, firmly planted my feet, and squared my shoulders. I took one silent, calming breath, and then heaved forward with every ounce of physical strength I could muster. As well as a teensy-weensy boost of magic. Enough to goose him good.

"*MOOO!!!*" The sound tore through the cool October night like an unstoppable freight train. *Thud-splat!* The beast collapsed sideways into the frosty grass; straight into a steaming patty of cow shit, cow dung, or, if you really want to church it up, a Meadow Muffin. But to me, shit is, and always will be, shit.

Cow tipping. It doesn't get any better than that in Missouri.

Especially when you're tipping the *Minotaur*. Capital M.

Razor-blade hooves tore at the frozen earth as the beast struggled to stand, grunts of rage vibrating the air. I raised my arms triumphantly. "Booyah! Temple 1, Minotaur 0!" I crowed. Then I very bravely prepared to protect myself. Some people just couldn't take a joke. *Cruel, evil,* and *sadistic* cow tipping may be, but by hell, it was a *rush*. The legendary beast turned his gaze on me after gaining his feet, eyes ablaze as he unfolded to his full height on two tree-trunk-thick legs, hooves magically transforming into heavily-booted feet. The thick, gold ring dangling from his snotty snout quivered as the Minotaur panted, and his dense, corded muscle contracted over his human-like chest. As I stared up into those brown eyes, I actually felt sorry...for, well, myself.

"I have killed greater men than you for less offense," he growled.

I swear to God his voice sounded like an angry James Earl Jones. Like Mufasa talking to Scar.

"You have shit on your shoulder, Asterion." I ignited a roiling ball of fire in my palm in order to see his eyes more clearly. By no means was it a defensive gesture on my part. It was just dark. But under the weight of his glare, even I couldn't buy my reassuring lie. I hoped using a form of his ancient name would give me brownie points. Or maybe just not-worthy-of-killing points.

The beast grunted, eyes tightening, and I sensed the barest hesitation. "Nate Temple...your name would look splendid on my already long list of slain idiots." Asterion took a threatening step forward, and I thrust out my palm in warning, my roiling flame blue now.

"You lost fair and square, Asterion. Yield or perish." The beast's shoulders sagged slightly. Then he finally nodded to himself in resignation, appraising me with the scrutiny of a worthy adversary. "Your time comes, Temple, but I will grant you this. You've got a pair of stones on you to rival Hercules."

I pointedly risked a glance down towards the myth's own crown jewels. "Well, I sure won't need a wheelbarrow any time soon, but I'm sure I'll manage."

The Minotaur blinked once, and then bellowed out a deep, contagious, snorting laughter. Realizing I wasn't about to become a murder statistic, I couldn't help but join in. It felt good. It had been a while since I had allowed myself to experience genuine laughter.

In the harsh moonlight, his bulk was even more intimidating as he towered head and shoulders above me. This was the beast that had fed upon human sacrifices for countless years while imprisoned in Daedalus' Labyrinth in Greece. And all of that protein had not gone to waste, forming a heavily woven musculature over the beast's body that made even Mr. Olympia look puny.

From the neck up he was entirely bull, but the rest of his body more resembled a thickly-furred man. But, as shown moments ago, he could adapt his form to his environment, never appearing fully human, but able to make his entire form appear as a bull when necessary. For instance, how he had looked just before I tipped him. Maybe he had been scouting the field for heifers before I had so efficiently killed the mood.

His bull face was also covered in thick, coarse hair—even sporting a long, wavy beard of sorts, and his eyes were the deepest brown I had ever seen. Cow shit brown. His snout jutted out, emphasizing the gold ring dangling from his glistening nostrils, catching a glint in the luminous glow of the moon. The metal was at least an inch thick, and etched with runes of a language long forgotten. Thick, aged ivory horns sprouted from each temple, long enough to skewer a wizard with little effort. He was nude except for a beaded necklace and a pair of distressed leather boots that were big enough to stomp a size twenty-five imprint in my face if he felt so inclined.

I hoped our blossoming friendship wouldn't end that way. I really did.

~

Get your copy of OBSIDIAN SON online today!

~

Turn the page to read a sample of **WHISKEY GINGER** *- Phantom Queen Diaries Book 1, or* **BUY ONLINE**. *Quinn MacKenna is a black magic arms dealer in Boston. She likes to fight monsters almost as much as she likes to drink.*

Full chronology of all books in the Temple Verse shown on the 'BOOKS IN THE TEMPLE VERSE' page.)

TRY: WHISKEY GINGER (PHANTOM QUEEN DIARIES BOOK 1)

The pasty guitarist hunched forward, thrust a rolled-up wad of paper deep into one nostril, and snorted a line of blood crystals—frozen hemoglobin that I'd smuggled over in a refrigerated canister—with the uncanny grace of a drug addict. He sat back, fangs gleaming, and pawed at his nose. "That's some bodacious shit. Hey, bros," he said, glancing at his fellow band members, "come hit this shit before it melts."

He fetched one of the backstage passes hanging nearby, pried the plastic badge from its lanyard, and used it to split up the crystals, murmuring something in an accent that reminded me of California. Not *the* California, but you know, Cali-foh-nia—the land of beaches, babes, and bros. I retrieved a toothpick from my pocket and punched it through its thin wrapper. "So," I asked no one in particular, "now that ye have the product, who's payin'?"

Another band member stepped out of the shadows to my left, and I don't mean that figuratively, either—the fucker literally stepped out of the shadows. I scowled at him, but hid my surprise, nonchalantly rolling the toothpick from one side of my mouth to the other.

The rest of the band gathered around the dressing room table, following the guitarist's lead by preparing their own snorting utensils—tattered magazine covers, mostly. Typically, you'd do this sort of thing with a dollar-bill, maybe even a Benjamin if you were flush. But fangers like this lot couldn't touch cash directly—in God We Trust and all that. Of course, I didn't really understand why sucking blood the old-fashioned way had suddenly gone out of style. More of a rush, maybe?

"It lasts longer," the vampire next to me explained, catching my mildly curious expression. "It's especially good for shows and stuff. Makes us look, like, less—"

"Creepy?" I offered, my Irish brogue lilting just enough to make it a question.

"Pale," he finished, frowning.

I shrugged. "Listen, I've got places to be," I said, holding out my hand.

"I'm sure you do," he replied, smiling. "Tell you what, why don't you, like, hang around for a bit? Once that wears off," he dipped his head toward the bloody powder smeared across the table's surface, "we may need a pick-me-up." He rested his hand on my arm and our gazes locked.

I blinked, realized what he was trying to pull, and rolled my eyes. His widened in surprise, then shock as I yanked out my toothpick and shoved it through his hand.

"Motherfuck—"

"I want what we agreed on," I declared. "Now. No tricks."

The rest of the band saw what happened and rose faster than I could blink. They circled me, their grins feral...they might have even seemed intimidating if it weren't for the fact that they each had a case of the sniffles

—I had to work extra hard not to think about what it felt like to have someone else's blood dripping down my nasal cavity.

I held up a hand.

"Can I ask ye gentlemen a question before we get started?" I asked. "Do ye even *have* what I asked for?"

Two of the band members exchanged looks and shrugged. The guitarist, however, glanced back towards the dressing room, where a brown paper bag sat next to a case full of makeup. He caught me looking and bared his teeth, his fangs stretching until it looked like it would be uncomfortable for him to close his mouth without piercing his own lip.

"Follow-up question," I said, eyeing the vampire I'd stabbed as he gingerly withdrew the toothpick from his hand and flung it across the room with a snarl. "Do ye do each other's make-up? Since, ye know, ye can't use mirrors?"

I was genuinely curious.

The guitarist grunted. "Mike, we have to go on soon."

"Wait a minute. Mike?" I turned to the snarling vampire with a frown. "What happened to *The Vampire Prospero*?" I glanced at the numerous fliers in the dressing room, most of which depicted the band members wading through blood, with Mike in the lead, each one titled *The Vampire Prospero* in *Rocky Horror Picture Show* font. Come to think of it…Mike did look a little like Tim Curry in all that leather and lace.

I was about to comment on the resemblance when Mike spoke up, "Alright, change of plans, bros. We're gonna drain this bitch before the show. We'll look totally—"

"Creepy?" I offered, again.

"Kill her."

∼

Get the full book ONLINE!

MAKE A DIFFERENCE

Reviews are the most powerful tools in my arsenal when it comes to getting attention for my books. Much as I'd like to, I don't have the financial muscle of a New York publisher.

But I do have something much more powerful and effective than that, and it's something that those publishers would kill to get their hands on.

A committed and loyal bunch of readers.

Honest reviews of my books help bring them to the attention of other readers.

If you've enjoyed this book, I would be very grateful if you could spend just five minutes leaving a review (it can be as short as you like) on my book's Amazon page.

Thank you very much in advance.

ACKNOWLEDGMENTS

First, I would like to thank my beta-readers, TEAM TEMPLE, those individuals who spent hours of their time to read, and re-re-read the Temple-Verse stories. Your dark, twisted, cunning sense of humor makes me feel right at home...

I would also like to thank you, the reader. I hope you enjoyed reading *RAGE* as much as I enjoyed writing it. Stay tuned...Callie Penrose returns in GODLESS with her book 7, Nate Temple returns in KNIGHTMARE with his book 12, and Quinn MacKenna returns in HURRICANE with her book 8—all in 2019!

And last, but definitely not least, I thank my wife, Lexy. Without your support, none of this would have been possible.

BOOKS IN THE TEMPLE VERSE

CHRONOLOGY: All stories in the Temple Verse are shown in chronological order on the following page

FEATHERS AND FIRE SERIES

(Set in the Temple Verse)

UNCHAINED

RAGE

WHISPERS

ANGEL'S ROAR

MOTHERLUCKER (Novella #4.5 in the 'LAST CALL' anthology)

SINNER

BLACK SHEEP

GODLESS (FEATHERS #7) — COMING SOON...

NATE TEMPLE SERIES

(Origin of the Temple Verse)

FAIRY TALE - FREE prequel novella #0 for my subscribers

OBSIDIAN SON

BLOOD DEBTS

GRIMM

SILVER TONGUE

BEAST MASTER

BEERLYMPIAN (Novella #5.5 in the 'LAST CALL' anthology)

TINY GODS

DADDY DUTY (Novella #6.5)

WILD SIDE

WAR HAMMER

NINE SOULS

HORSEMAN

LEGEND

KNIGHTMARE (TEMPLE #12) — COMING SOON...

PHANTOM QUEEN DIARIES

(Also set in the Temple Verse)

COLLINS (Prequel novella #0 in the 'LAST CALL' anthology)

WHISKEY GINGER

COSMOPOLITAN

OLD FASHIONED

MOTHERLUCKER (Novella #3.5 in the 'LAST CALL' anthology)

DARK AND STORMY

MOSCOW MULE

WITCHES BREW

SALTY DOG

CHRONOLOGICAL ORDER: TEMPLE UNIVERSE

FAIRY TALE (TEMPLE PREQUEL)

OBSIDIAN SON (TEMPLE 1)

BLOOD DEBTS (TEMPLE 2)

GRIMM (TEMPLE 3)

SILVER TONGUE (TEMPLE 4)

BEAST MASTER (TEMPLE 5)

BEERLYMPIAN (TEMPLE 5.5)

TINY GODS (TEMPLE 6)

DADDY DUTY (TEMPLE NOVELLA 6.5)

UNCHAINED (FEATHERS... 1)

RAGE (FEATHERS... 2)

WILD SIDE (TEMPLE 7)

WAR HAMMER (TEMPLE 8)

WHISPERS (FEATHERS... 3)

ABOUT THE AUTHOR

Shayne is a man of mystery and power, whose power is exceeded only by his mystery...

He currently writes the Amazon Bestselling **Feathers and Fire Series** about a rookie spell-slinger named Callie Penrose who works for the Vatican in Kansas City. Her problem? Hell seems to know more about her past than she does.

He also writes the Amazon Bestselling **Nate Temple Series**, which features a foul-mouthed wizard from St. Louis. He rides a bloodthirsty unicorn, drinks with Achilles, and is pals with the Four Horsemen.

He also co-authors the Amazon Bestselling **Phantom Queen Diaries** with Cameron O'Connell, about Quinn MacKenna, a mouthy black magic arms dealer trading favors in Boston. All she wants? A round-trip ticket to the Fae realm...and maybe a drink on the house.

Shayne holds two high-ranking black belts, and can be found writing in a coffee shop, cackling madly into his computer screen while pounding shots of espresso. He's hard at work on more Temple Verse novels as well as a few entirely new stories outside of the Temple Verse. **Follow him online for all sorts of groovy goodies, giveaways, and new release updates:**

Get Down with Shayne Online
www.shaynesilvers.com
info@shaynesilvers.com

facebook.com/shaynesilversfanpage

amazon.com/author/shaynesilvers

bookbub.com/profile/shayne-silvers

instagram.com/shaynesilversofficial

twitter.com/shaynesilvers

goodreads.com/ShayneSilvers

BRENTWOOD MUSIC LIBRARY

3 0615 00620 8309

Made in the USA
Middletown, DE
12 November 2019

78392821R10177